Deciding not to believe him, she looked past his shoulder to the door. "How did you get into my office without Pauline announcing you?"

He shrugged. "I told her she didn't have to bother. I like announcing myself. Besides, she was packing up to leave, and she told me to tell you that she would see you Monday morning."

Hunter glanced at her watch. She hadn't realized it was so late. That meant they were alone, and that wasn't a good thing with her present state of mind. The best thing was to send him packing. Picking up the manila folder off her desk, she offered it to him. "Here's what you came for."

Tyson moved toward her with calm, deliberate strides, and when he came to a stop directly in front of her, she tried ignoring the sparks going off inside of her. Instead of accepting the folder, he reached out and brushed the tips of his fingers across her cheek. "That's not what I came for, Hunter. This is."

And before she could draw her next breath, he leaned in and captured her mouth with his.

HIS FAVORITE TEMPTATION

NEW YORK TIMES BESTSELLING AUTHOR

Brenda Jackson

AND

Reese Ryan

Previously published as *Possessed by Passion*
and *Playing with Temptation*

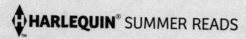 HARLEQUIN® SUMMER READS

Recycling programs for this product may not exist in your area.

ISBN-13: 978-1-335-00827-5

His Favorite Temptation
Copyright © 2019 by Harlequin Books S.A.

First published as Possessed by Passion by Harlequin Books in 2016 and Playing with Temptation by Harlequin Books in 2017.

The publisher acknowledges the copyright holders of the individual works as follows:

Possessed by Passion
Copyright © 2016 by Brenda Streater Jackson

Playing with Temptation
Copyright © 2017 by Roxanne Ravenel

For questions and comments about the quality of this book, please contact us at CustomerService@Harlequin.com.

® and TM are trademarks of Harlequin Enterprises Limited or its corporate affiliates. Trademarks indicated with ® are registered in the United States Patent and Trademark Office, the Canadian Intellectual Property Office and in other countries.

Printed in U.S.A.

CONTENTS

Possessed by Passion by Brenda Jackson   7

Playing with Temptation by Reese Ryan   207

Brenda Jackson is a *New York Times* bestselling author of more than one hundred romance titles. Brenda married her childhood sweetheart, Gerald, and has two sons. She lives in Jacksonville, Florida. She divides her time between family, writing and traveling. Email Brenda at authorbrendajackson@gmail.com or visit her on her website at brendajackson.net.

Books by Brenda Jackson

Harlequin Kimani Romance

Steele Family

Hidden Pleasures
Possessed by Passion
A Steele for Christmas
Private Arrangements

Bachelors in Demand

Bachelor Untamed
Bachelor Unleashed
Bachelor Undone
Bachelor Unclaimed
Bachelor Unforgiving
Bachelor Unbound

Visit the Author Profile page at
Harlequin.com for more titles.

POSSESSED BY PASSION

Brenda Jackson

To the man who will always and forever be the love of my life, Gerald Jackson, Sr.

To all my readers who waited patiently on another novel about those "Bad News" Steeles, this one is especially for you.

And to my readers who gave me their love, support and understanding as I endured a difficult time in my life. I appreciate you from the bottom of my heart.

Though thy beginning was small, yet thy latter end should greatly increase. —*Job 8:7*

Chapter 1

"I understand you became an uncle last night, Tyson. Congratulations."

Tyson Steele glanced over at the man who'd slid onto the bar stool beside him. Miles Wright was a colleague at the hospital where they both worked as surgeons. "Thanks. How did you know?"

"It was in this morning's paper. Quite the article."

Tyson shook his head as he took a sip of his drink. Leave it to his mother, Eden Tyson Steele, to make sure the entire city knew about the birth of her first grandchildren. Twins. A boy and a girl that represented a new generation of Steeles in Phoenix. Everyone was happy for his brother Galen and his wife, Brittany, but his mother was ecstatic beyond reason. Within the past three years, not only had three of her six die-hard bachelor sons gotten married, but as of last night she also had a grandson and granddaughter to boast about.

He wondered if Galen was aware of the article in this morning's paper since he hadn't mentioned it when Tyson had spoken to him earlier. Knowing their mother, Tyson wouldn't be surprised if the announcement appeared in the *New York Times* next. A former international model whose face had graced the covers of such magazines as *Vogue*, *Cosmo* and *Elle*, his mother still had connections in a lot of places and had no shame in using them.

Miles's beeper went off and with an anxious sigh he said, "Need to run. I got an emergency at the hospital."

"Take care," Tyson told his colleague, who moved quickly toward the exit door. He then glanced around. Notorious was a popular nightclub in Phoenix, but not too many people were here tonight due to the March Madness championship basketball game being held in town. Usually, on any given night, Tyson could have his pick of single women crowding the place, but not tonight.

His brothers had tried talking him into attending the game with them, but he'd declined after his team had been eliminated in the previous round. It didn't matter one bit when they'd laughed and called him a sore loser. So what if he was.

Tyson took another sip of his drink and checked his watch. It was still early, but he might as well call it a night since it seemed he would be going home alone, which wasn't how he'd envisioned spending his evening. Taking some woman to bed had been at the top of his agenda. Scoring was the name of the game. Women hit on him and he hit on women. No big deal. It was the lay of the land. His land anyway.

He stood to leave at the same time the nightclub's

door swung open and three women walked in. Three good-looking women. He sat back down, thinking that maybe the night wouldn't be wasted after all.

Not to be caught staring, he turned around on the bar stool. The huge mirror on the wall afforded him the opportunity to check out the women without being so obvious. Good, he noted. No rings. That was the first thing he looked for since he didn't believe in encroaching on another man's territory. Tyson figured it must be his lucky night when they were shown to a table within the mirror's view. The women were so busy chatting that they didn't realize he was checking them out.

For some reason his gaze kept returning to one of the women in particular. She looked familiar and it took a second or two before it hit him just who she was.

Hunter McKay.

Damn. It had been years. Eighteen, to be exact. She had been two years behind him in high school, and of all the girls he'd dated during that time, she was the only one with whom he hadn't been able to score. She'd had the gall to ask for a commitment before giving up the goods, and unlike some guys, who would have lied just to get inside her panties, he'd told her the very same thing then that he was telling women now. He didn't do commitments. His refusal to make her his steady girl had prompted her to end things between them after the first week. It had been the first time a Steele had ever been shot down. For months his brothers had teased him, calling Hunter "the one who got away." He frowned, wondering why that memory still annoyed him.

When he'd returned to Phoenix after medical school he'd heard she attended Yale to fulfill her dream of being an architect. After college she had made her home in Boston and returned to town only occasionally to visit her parents. Their paths had never crossed until tonight.

He'd also heard she had gotten married to some guy she'd met while living in Boston. So where was her ring? She could be getting it cleaned, resized or...maybe she was no longer married. He couldn't help wondering which of those possibilities applied.

Hunter had been a striking beauty back then and she still was. It had been that beauty that had captured his interest back in the day and was doing so now. It didn't appear as if she'd aged much at all. She still had that young-girl look, and those dimples in both cheeks were still pretty damn pleasing to the eyes.

The shoulder-length curly hair had been replaced with a short natural cut that looked good on her, and he couldn't help it when his gaze lingered on her lips. He could still remember the one and only time he'd kissed her. It has been way too short, yet oh so sweet.

He felt an ache in his groin and didn't find it surprising since it was a familiar reaction whenever he saw a beautiful woman. But it was Hunter who was affecting him, not the other two women. He remembered them from high school as well, but had forgotten their names. What he did recall was that they had been Hunter's best friends even back then.

"Ready for another drink, Doc?"

He glanced up at Tipper, who'd been the bartender at Notorious for years. "Not yet, but do me a favor."

Tipper grinned. "As long as it's legal."

"It is. Whatever drinks those three ladies are having, I want them put on my tab."

Tipper glanced over at the table where the women sat and nodded. "No problem. I'll let their waiter know."

"Thanks."

Tipper walked off and Tyson's gaze returned to the mirror. At that moment Hunter threw her head back and laughed at something one of the women said. He'd always thought she had a sensuously shaped neck, flawless and graceful. He'd looked forward to placing a hickey right there on the side of it. It was the place he would brand all the girls in high school who'd gone all the way with him. It had been known as the Mark of Tyson. But Hunter had never gotten that mark. What a pity.

His cell phone pinged with a text message and he pulled his phone out of his jacket to read his brother Mercury's message. My team is up four. Be ready to celebrate later tonight.

Tyson clicked off the phone and rolled his eyes. *When hell freezes over*, he thought. If his brothers thought he was a sore loser, then Mercury could be an obnoxious winner, and Tyson wanted no part of it tonight. After returning the phone to his jacket, he let his gaze return to the mirror and to Hunter. He couldn't help but smile when he made up his mind about something. Her name might be Hunter but tonight he was determined to make her his prey.

Hunter McKay appreciated sharing this time with her two best friends from high school—Maureen Santana, whom everyone fondly called Mo, and Kathryn Elliott, whose nickname was Kat. Both had been bridesmaids in her wedding and because they'd kept in touch over the years, they'd known about her rocky marriage and subsequent divorce from Carter Robinson. Mo, a divorcée herself, thought Hunter had given Carter far too many chances to get his act together, and Kat, who was still holding out for Mr. Right, had remained neutral until Carter had begun showing his true colors.

"Here you are, ladies," the waiter said, placing their drinks in front of them. "Compliments of the gentleman sitting at the bar."

Their gazes moved past the waiter to the man in question. As if on cue, he swiveled around in his seat and flashed them a smile. Hunter immediately felt a flutter in the pit of her stomach, a flutter that should have been forgotten long ago. But just that quickly, after all these years, it had resurfaced the moment she stared into the pair of green eyes that could only belong to a Steele.

"Well now, isn't that nice of Tyson Steele," Mo said with mock sweetness. "I wonder which one of us he wants to take home tonight."

"Take home?" Hunter asked, while her eyes remained on Tyson. For some reason she couldn't break her gaze. It was as if she was caught in the depths of those gorgeous green eyes.

"Yes, take home. He doesn't really date. He just has a history of one-night stands," Mo replied.

"Do we have to guess which one of us he's interested in?" Kat asked, chuckling, and then took a quick sip of her drink. "If you recall, Mo, that particular Steele was hot and heavy for Hunter back in the day."

"That's right. I remember." Mo turned to Hunter. "And if I recall, you dumped him. Probably the only female in this town with sense enough to do so."

With that reminder, Hunter tore her gaze from Tyson's to take a sip of her drink. In high school, Tyson, along with his five brothers, were known as the "Bad News" Steeles. Handsome as sin with green eyes they'd inherited from their mother, the six had a reputation as heartbreakers. It was widely known that their only interest in a girl was getting under her dress.

Galen Steele, the oldest of the bunch, had been a senior in high school when she'd been a freshman. Tyson was the second oldest. After Tyson came Eli, Jonas, Mercury and Gannon. Each brother was separated the closest in age by no more than eleven months, which meant their mother had practically been pregnant for six straight years.

"Tyson gave me no choice," Hunter said, finally replying to Mo's comment. "I liked him and for some reason I figured he would treat me differently since his family had been members of my grandfather's church. Boy, was I naive."

Kat chuckled. "But like Mo said, when you found out that you'd be just another notch on his bedpost, at least you had the sense to dump him."

"I didn't dump him," Hunter said, sitting back in her chair. She didn't have to glance over at Tyson to know he was still staring at her. "When he told me what he wanted, I merely told him I saw no reason for us to continue to date, because he wasn't getting it."

"That's a dump," Mo said, grinning. "And be forewarned, nothing about the Steeles has changed. Those brothers are still bad news. Hard-core womanizers. Getting laid is still their favorite pastime."

"At least three had the sense to get married," Kat added, taking another sip of her drink.

"Oh? Which ones?" Hunter inquired.

"Galen, Eli and Jonas."

Hunter vaguely remembered Eli but she did remember Jonas since they'd graduated in the same class. And she couldn't help but recall Galen Steele. He had gotten expelled from school after the principal found him under the gymnasium bleachers making out with the man's daughter. His reputation around school was legendary. "So, Galen got married?"

"Yes, a few years ago, and his wife just gave birth to twins," Mo explained. "Last night, in fact. The announcement was in the papers this morning. It was a huge write-up in the society section."

Hunter nodded as she tried ignoring the fact Tyson still had his eyes on her. "What does Tyson do for a living?"

"He's a heart surgeon at Phoenix Baptist Hospital," Mo responded.

"Good for him. He always wanted to be a doctor." She recalled their long talks, not knowing at the time their conversations were just part of his plan to reel her in. Unfortunately for him, she hadn't been biting.

"Don't look now, ladies, but Tyson has gotten up off the bar stool and is headed this way."

Although Kat had told them not to look, Hunter couldn't help doing so. She wished she hadn't when Tyson's gaze captured hers. He'd been eye candy in his teens and now eighteen years later he was doubly so. She couldn't miss that air of arrogance that seemed to surround him as he walked toward them. He appeared so powerfully male that every step he took conveyed primitive animal sexuality. There was no doubt in her mind that over the years Tyson had sharpened his game and was now an ace at getting whatever he wanted.

He was wearing a pair of dark slacks and a caramel-colored pullover sweater. She was convinced that on any other man the attire would look just so-so. But on Tyson, the sweater emphasized his wide shoulders, and the pants definitely did something to his masculine build.

"I understand whenever a Steele sees a woman he wants, he goes after her. It appears Tyson's targeted you, Hunter," Mo said as she leaned over. "Maybe he thinks there's unfinished business between the two of you. Eighteen years' worth."

Hunter waved off her friend's words. "Don't be silly. He probably doesn't even remember me, it's been so long."

It took less than a minute for Tyson to reach their table. He glanced around and smiled at everyone. "Evening, ladies." And then his gaze returned to hers and he said, "Hello, Hunter. It's been a while."

Hunter inhaled deeply, surprised that he *had* remembered her after all. But what really captured her attention were his features. He was still sinfully handsome, with skin the color of creamy butternut and a mouth that was shaped too darn beautifully to belong to any man. And his voice was richer and a lot deeper than she'd remembered.

Before she could respond to what he'd said, Mo and Kat thanked him for the drinks as they stood. Hunter looked at them. "Where are you two going?" she asked, not missing the smirk on Mo's face.

"Kat and I thought we'd move closer to that big-screen television to catch the last part of the basketball game. I think my team is winning."

Hunter came close to calling Mo out by saying she didn't have a team. She knew for a fact that neither Mo nor Kat was into sports. Why were they deliberately leaving her alone with Tyson?

As soon as they grabbed their drinks off the table and walked away, Tyson didn't waste time claiming one of the vacated seats. Hunter glanced over and met his gaze while thinking that the only thing worse than being deserted was being deserted and left with a Steele.

She took a sip of her drink and then said, "I want to thank you for my drink, as well. That was nice of you."

"I'm a nice person."

The jury is still out on that, she thought. "I'm surprised you remember me, Tyson."

He chuckled, and the sound was so stimulating it seemed to graze her skin. "Trust me. I remember you. And do you know what I remember most of all?"

"No, what?"

He leaned over the table as if to make sure his next words were for her ears only. "The fact that we never slept together."

Chapter 2

Tyson thought the shocked look on Hunter's face was priceless. He also thought it was a total turn-on. Up close she was even more beautiful. There had been something about her dark, almond-shaped eyes and long lashes that he'd always found alluring. But what was really getting to him was her lips, especially the bottom one. The curvy shape would entice any man to want to taste it. Nibble on it. Greedily devour it.

She interrupted his thoughts when she finally said, "And if you recall that, then I'm sure you remember why."

"Yes, I remember," he said, holding tight to her gaze. "You weren't one of those high school girls who slept around. You wanted me to make you my steady girl-friend and I had no intention of doing that."

"You just wanted me in the backseat of your car," she said.

He smiled. "The front seat would have worked just fine, trust me. I wanted you and my goal was to get you. For me it was all about sex then."

"Just like it's all about sex for you now?" she asked smoothly.

"Yes." He had no problem being up front with her or any woman, letting them know what he wanted, what he didn't want and, in her particular case, what he'd missed out on getting. She was the lone person in the "tried but failed" column. He intended to remedy that.

"I heard a while back that you'd gotten married, Hunter."

She took another sip of her drink and he remembered the one and only time he'd sampled the beautiful lips that kissed her glass. "Yes, I got married."

He looked down at her ringless hand before glancing back up at her. "Still married?"

"No."

Her response was quick and biting, which only led him to believe the divorce had been unpleasant. That might be bad news for her, but he saw it as good news for him since he was known to inject new life into divorcées. Over the years he'd taken plenty to bed, not necessarily to mend their broken hearts, but mainly to prove there was life after a shitty marriage.

"How long ago?"

Her eyebrows lifted. "Why do you want to know?"

"Just curious."

For a second, she didn't respond, and then she said, "Two years."

He nodded as he leaned back in his chair. "Sorry to hear about your divorce," he said, although he was anything but. Although his parents had a great marriage and it seemed his three brothers' marriages were off to a good start, he was of the opinion that marriage wasn't for everybody. It definitely wasn't for him and evidently hadn't been for her.

"No need to be sorry, Tyson. I regret the day I ever married the bastard."

He'd heard that line before. And as far as he was concerned there was no need for her to expound. It really didn't matter to him what she thought of her ex. What mattered was that divorcées were his specialty. He would gladly shift her from his "tried and failed" column to his "achieved" category. Every one of his senses was focused on getting her into his bed.

"So what brings you back to Phoenix, Hunter?" he asked with a smile.

Hunter was glad a waiter appeared at that moment to place a drink in front of Tyson. Evidently he was a regular, since the man had known just what to give him. It took only a minute but that had been enough time to get herself together and recover from Tyson's charismatic personality. It was quite obvious that he was a man on the prowl tonight and had set his sights on her. Mo and Kat had said as much, but at the time she hadn't believed them. The man had been a player in high school and eighteen years later he was still at it. She couldn't help wondering why he hadn't gotten past that mentality.

"Now, where were we? Oh, yes. I asked what brings you back to Phoenix."

She took another sip of her drink. There was no way she would tell him how after their divorce and the dissolution of their partnership, her architect husband had underhandedly taken all their clients. Starting over in Boston would not have been so bad if he hadn't deliberately tried to sabotage her reputation as an architect. Tyson didn't have to know that because of her husband's actions she'd decided to start over here. Instead of telling him all of that, she decided to tell him the other reason she'd come back home.

"My parents."

He lifted a brow. "Are they ill?"

She shook her head. "No, they aren't ill. My brother thinks they're having too much fun."

Hunter realized just how ridiculous that sounded and added, "A few months ago they purchased 'his and hers' Harleys, and before that they signed up to take skydiving lessons. Lately, they've been hinting at selling the house and buying a boat to sail around the world."

Tyson appeared amused. "Sounds to me like they're enjoying life. Maybe your brother needs to take a chill pill."

"Possibly, but his hands are full right now with his teenage sons and he feels Mom and Dad are driving him as crazy as they claim he's driving them. I decided it was best I came home to keep peace." Hunter had no idea how she would manage to do that. Her parents were intent on having fun and her brother was intent on getting them to act their age.

"You're an architect, right?" he asked her.

"Yes. How did you know?"

"Someone mentioned it at one of the class reunions that you never attended."

He was right, she hadn't attended any. At first it had been school keeping her away, and later trying to build her career and finally trying to save her marriage. Although Carter had made sure they attended all of his high school reunions, he had been dead set against attending any of hers, and as usual she'd given in to him.

"I understand you're a doctor."

He nodded. "Yes. A heart surgeon."

She smiled. "And I bet you're a good one."

"I owe it to my patients to do my very best."

And there was no doubt in Hunter's mind that he did. She remembered he was devoted to whatever he did, even if he was chasing girls.

"I'm glad you're back in Phoenix, Hunter."

"Why?" She really couldn't understand why he would be.

He leaned in closer. "Because we have history."

She couldn't keep the smile from tugging at her lips. "History?"

"Yes."

"What kind of history?"

"I think of you as the one who got away."

She had to keep from laughing out loud at that. "You mean the one who never made it to the backseat of your car?"

"Pretty much."

"It's been eighteen years. I would think you'd have gotten over it by now."

He shook his head and chuckled. "I had. However, seeing you again brought it back home to me, so I've come up with a plan."

She lifted a brow. "What kind of plan?"

"A plan to seduce you."

Hunter's breath caught in her lungs. His audacity was almost as great as his arrogance. What man told a woman he planned to seduce her? "Seriously? Do you think it will be that easy?"

The smile that appeared on his face almost made her heart miss a beat. Although all the Steele brothers had those killer green eyes, she recalled that Tyson and Mercury were the only ones with dimples. Why was it that whenever he flashed those dimples, her pulse rate went haywire?

"I didn't say it would be easy," he said smoothly. "What I said was that I had a plan. I see no reason that we can't rekindle what we had years ago."

"There's nothing to rekindle. Need I remind you that we didn't have anything mainly because you were only interested in one thing?"

His smile widened as he lifted his drink to his lips. Without saying a word, he was letting her know that nothing about him had changed and that he was still only interested in one thing.

"I suggest you go find someone else to seduce."

He shook his head. "I can't do that. I want you."

"You can't always have what you want. That's life."

Whatever he was about to say was lost when Mo and Kat appeared. "My team lost," Mo said, grinning. She glanced at her watch. "Tomorrow is a workday so we figured it's time to go."

Great timing, Hunter thought, and she stood.

Tyson stood as well and shoved his hands into his pockets. "I'll take you home, Hunter, if you aren't ready to leave just yet."

If he thought for one minute she would go with him, especially after admitting his plan to seduce her, he wasn't thinking straight. "Thanks, but I am ready. It was good seeing you again, Tyson."

"Same here, Hunter," he said, and she thought she saw something akin to amusement in his eyes. "I have a feeling we'll be running into each other again."

Hunter hoped not. She had enough to worry about with her parents, without being concerned about Tyson Steele trying to get her into bed. "Good night." She walked toward the door with Mo and Kat, feeling the heat of Tyson's gaze on her backside.

As soon as they were out the door she turned to her friends. "Why on earth did the two of you leave me alone with Tyson?"

Kat grinned. "Because we knew you could handle him."

"Besides, it was quite obvious you were the one on his radar and not us," Mo added. "So how did it go?"

Hunter shook her head. "You guys were right. Nothing has changed with Tyson. He's still looking for a pair of legs to get between."

"And you didn't make yours available to him again?" Kat asked, grinning. "What a shame."

"For him I'm sure it was, especially since he told me of his plan to seduce me."

Mo's eyes widened. "He actually told you that?"

"Without cracking a smile or blinking an eye."

Both Mo and Kat stopped walking to stare at her. "You don't sound worried."

Hunter stopped and glanced at her friends, lifting a brow. "Why would I be?"

"We're talking about Tyson Steele, Hunter. The man who's known to get what he wants. I heard from women that he's so smooth you won't miss your panties until they're gone. And for him to already have a plan of seduction for you sounds serious."

"Only in his book, not mine."

Kat tilted her head. "And this from a woman who's gone without sex for two years now."

"Actually four. If you recall, Carter and I slept in separate bedrooms for two years before our divorce. You can't miss what you never got on a regular basis anyway. I haven't had an orgasm in so long I've honestly forgotten how it feels."

"Then you're in luck," Mo said with a huge smile on her face. "There are quite a few women around town who claim the orgasms those Bad News Steeles give a girl can blow her mind to smithereens and have her begging for more. Rumor has it that you haven't truly been made love to unless it's been by a Steele. They're supposed to be just that good in the bedroom."

Hunter rolled her eyes. "I'm sure it's nothing more than a lot of hype."

"But what if it's not?" Kat asked seriously. "And just think. One of those Bad News Steeles has plans to seduce you. If Tyson succeeds then you'll never forget how an orgasm feels again."

"Whatever," Hunter said as they resumed walking. By the time they reached the car, Hunter decided whatever plan Tyson thought he had for her was no big deal, since she doubted their paths would cross again anyway. And even if they did, she was certain it was just like she'd told Mo and Kat. All those rumors about the Steeles were probably nothing more than a lot of hype.

"Is there a reason you're visiting me this time of night, Tyson?" Eli Steele asked gruffly, moving aside for his brother to enter his home. "And why aren't you at the basketball game with Mercury and Gannon?"

"I had better things to do."

Eli rolled his eyes. "In other words, your team didn't make it to the finals. Everyone knows what a sore loser you are."

Tyson frowned. "I'm not a sore loser." He then glanced around. "Where's Stacey?"

His once die-hard bachelor brother had defected and married, just like his brothers Galen and Jonas. The only thing redeeming about that was he'd married Stacey Carlson. She was the sister of a good friend and former colleague of Tyson's by the name of Cohen.

"Stacey's in bed, where most people with good sense are by now," Eli said, dropping down on the sofa. "I hear Brittany and the babies might be going home tomorrow."

Tyson nodded. "So I heard."

"Word also has it that Mom has volunteered to help out for a few days. I hope she doesn't get on Galen's nerves."

Tyson chuckled. "I doubt that she will. He's been in her good graces ever since he was the first to get married. Besides, helping out with the babies will keep her busy."

"And the busier she is the less chance she has to get into your business—and Mercury's and Gannon's—right?"

"Right," Tyson said, knowing Eli understood. Before he married, he'd gotten the Eden Tyson Steele's "sticking her nose where it doesn't belong" treatment, just like the rest of them. Now, with three sons married, she was relentless on the other three, prodding them along to get them to the altar. Tyson vowed it wouldn't work on him. "So who do you think the babies look like?"

Eli chuckled. "With those green eyes, forehead and lips, they favor Galen all the way. I haven't heard their decisions on names, have you?"

"Nope, but rumor has it they're allowing Mom to do the honors."

Eli shook his head. "No wonder she's blowing up the newspapers. She's up there on cloud nine."

"Fine. She can stay there for a while," Tyson said. "Just as long as she's not into my business while she's up there."

"You and Mercury and Gannon will get a slight reprieve, but don't think she'll let you guys off the hook for good." Eli didn't say anything for a minute as he stared across the room at his brother and then he said, "Okay, get it out. There's a reason you dropped by so late."

Tyson sat down in the wingback chair across from the sofa. "There is. Hunter McKay's back in town."

Eli's forehead bunched. "Who's Hunter McKay?"

Tyson rolled his eyes. "I can't believe you don't remember Hunter. But I shouldn't be surprised. Back in the day, the old Eli remembered bodies and not names."

A smile curved Eli's lips. "True. So was she one of those bodies?"

"Hell, no! She was my girl."

"You never had a girl, Tyson."

His brother was right and for the life of him Tyson wasn't sure why he'd said what he had just now. "Sorry, saying that was a huge mistake."

"I hope there's not a reason why you made it. And lower your voice or you'll wake up my wife and she needs her rest."

Tyson didn't need to ask why. It seemed that all his

married brothers had wedded women they enjoyed spending time with in and out of the bedroom. "There's not a reason."

Eli stared at him for a long moment and then asked, "So what's the big deal about this Hunter McKay being back in town?"

"It just is."

"Hey, wait a minute," Eli said, sitting straight up on the sofa. "That name is coming back to me. Isn't Hunter McKay the girl who dumped you in your senior year of high school?"

"She didn't dump me."

"That's not the way I remember it. And why are you interested in Hunter McKay? Didn't I hear something about her getting married some years back?"

"She's a divorcée now. I saw her tonight at Notorious and got that much out of her. And it was a nasty divorce."

"How do you know?"

Tyson stretched his long legs out in front of him. "She called her ex a bastard."

"Okay, her ex was a bastard. That doesn't explain why you're here at midnight."

Without hesitation Tyson said, "I want you to find out information on her."

Eli rolled his eyes. "Do I look like a friggin' detective?"

"No, but she's an architect and as president of Phoenix's business council, you would know if she's set up her own business in town or was hired by an established firm."

"And you want to know that for what reason?"

Tyson's lips curved into a smile. "Because I plan to

seduce her. And before you conveniently forget your own reputation before marrying Stacey and start acting holier-than-thou, just for your information, I gave Hunter McKay fair warning of my intentions tonight."

"You actually told her that you plan to seduce her?"

"Yes. You know how I operate, Eli. I don't play games and divorcées are my specialty. I'll be doing her a favor, especially if her ex was the bastard she claims he was."

Eli frowned. "You claim you gave her fair warning, so now I'm going to give you the same, Tyson. I had a plan for Stacey, although my plan was different from yours. My plan backfired. In my case it was for the best. My advice to you is to tread lightly and with caution, or you're liable to get possessed by passion. Once that happens, it will be all over for you."

Tyson frowned. "Possessed by passion? What the hell are you talking about?"

"You're cocky enough to think that once you get Hunter McKay in your bed, you're going to blow her mind."

Tyson smiled confidently. "Of course."

"Have you given any thought to the possibility that she'll end up blowing yours?"

Tyson stared hard at his brother. "No, I haven't given it any thought because *that* won't be happening."

Chapter 3

Hunter studied the older woman sitting across her desk. Pauline Martin had come to her highly recommended by Hunter's brother, Bernie, who was a good friend of the woman's son. Ms. Martin's husband had died last year and she wanted to do something other than stay in the house and stare at the walls. The administrative assistant position seemed perfect for her. From the interview, Hunter had known she was just what McKay Architecture Firm needed. Now if she could only get some clients.

She was scheduled to meet with an advertising firm later that day to discuss ideas on how she could promote her business. There were a number of architectural companies in Phoenix and the key to succeeding was to make sure hers stood out.

Hunter stood. "I'm looking forward to us working together, Pauline, and I'll see you in the morning."

"Thanks, Hunter."

An hour or so later Hunter had snapped her briefcase closed to leave for the day. Starting over in a business wasn't easy but, as her parents had reminded her that morning when she'd stopped by their house for breakfast, she was a fighter. What Carter had done was wrong, but instead of getting bitter, she had to do better. She had to look ahead and not look back. No matter what, she couldn't let him break her.

And more than anything, she couldn't believe all men were like Carter Robinson. Had he really expected her to remain his wife while he engaged in all those affairs? And when she had confronted him about it, he'd only laughed and told her to get over it. He'd said she wouldn't leave him because she had too much to lose, and that no matter what she accused him of, his family would stick by his side.

And they had.

Even his mother, who'd said she sympathized with Hunter over her son's wretched behavior, had stuck by him in the end. For Hunter, that had hurt more than anything because she'd assumed she and Nadine Robinson had had a good and close relationship. At least they had until the day Hunter had decided to bring her eight-year marriage to Carter to an end. Then Nadine had proven Carter right. Blood had been thicker than water.

Even with Carter's high-priced divorce lawyer, at least the judge who'd handled the divorce had sided with her and ordered Carter to give her fifty percent equity out of the company. He hadn't even wanted to do that. And the judge had been more than fair in making sure he did the same with their home, as well as all the other assets Carter had acquired over the years. Some she hadn't known about until the day the private investigator she'd hired had uncovered them.

So now she was back in Phoenix. In a way she felt like a stranger in her own hometown, since she'd made Boston her home ever since enrolling in MIT for her graduate degree. She'd been working a few years when she'd met Carter at a fund-raiser her architecture firm had given. He was a member of the Boston Robinsons, a family that took pride in their old-money status and the rich history that came with it.

They'd been married three years when she'd first found about Carter's affairs. He swore they meant nothing and begged her to forgive him, and she had. He became attentive for a year or two, and they'd even tried having a family, but with no success. Hunter wasn't exactly sure when his affairs had picked back up again, but she'd begun noticing the usual—lipstick on the collar, the scent of another woman's perfume and suspicious text messages. That's when she hired a private investigator. The PI's report had been the last straw. There was no way she could remain married to Carter after that, regardless of what her in-laws thought. In the end, they had sided with Carter in his campaign to destroy her.

She drew in a deep breath, refusing to give in to her sorrows. Somewhere out there were women in far worse situations than she. Her grandmother used to repeat that adage about making lemons into lemonade and Hunter intended to do just that.

At that moment the image of Tyson Steele came into her mind. Not that it had actually ever left since they'd run into each other last night. In fact she had dreamed about him. Of all things, in her dream she had let him do what she had refused to let him do eighteen years ago, and that was to take her in the backseat of a car.

Hunter shook her head. She couldn't believe how scandalous that dream had been and it was even worse that she had totally and thoroughly enjoyed it. Luckily it had been just a dream and not the real thing. But the dream had been enough. She had awakened panting, with heated lust rushing through every part of her. It had taken a long cold shower to calm down her body.

During the four years of her sexless life, the last thing she had thought about was having an affair. So why now? And why Tyson Steele? He was arrogant, confident and too cocky to suit her. They hadn't held a conversation for more than a few minutes before he was telling her of his plans to seduce her.

She shook her head as she headed for the door. Some men's attitudes simply amazed her. But then again, he was a Steele. Hearing three of his brothers had married meant there could be hope for him, but she wouldn't be crazy enough to put any money on that assumption.

But what really should be hilarious was that Tyson Steele thought he could seduce her. She figured he'd been all talk and that his words had been meant to get her sexually riled up, and they had…to a point. After her shower this morning her common sense was firmly back in place. All it had taken was a look around her apartment to remember all she'd lost because of a man. The last thing she needed was to get involved with another man for any reason.

But what about just for sex?

She almost missed her step when the idea popped in her head. Where had such a thought come from? She was a good girl. The granddaughter of a retired minister. A woman who'd always worked hard, played fair and been a good wife to her husband. And as Nadine had often claimed, the best daughter-in-law anyone could ask for.

Yet, regardless of all those things, she'd gotten royally screwed. And because of all those things Carter had figured she would never leave him. That she would stay married to him regardless. What he'd failed to take into consideration was that everyone had a breaking point. When she had taken as much as she could, she had walked away without looking back. She only wished she'd been strong enough to do it sooner.

As she locked up her office she figured she might as well dream about Tyson Steele again tonight. Dreams were safe. Besides, she had no reason to think their paths would cross again. For one, she didn't intend to return to that nightclub where he apparently hung out.

His parents attended the same church as hers, the one where her grandfather had been pastor before he'd passed away years ago. During breakfast this morning she'd deliberately asked her mother to bring her up-to-date on church members, former and present. It seemed the Steeles were still members of their church, and her mother said that although she would see Eden and Drew Steele on most Sundays, she rarely saw their sons and couldn't recall the last time one of them attended church.

Deciding she didn't want to think about Tyson Steele, she stepped inside the elevator to leave the office.

Tyson had stepped out of the shower and was toweling off when his cell phone rang. He recognized the ring tone. It was Eli. With three surgeries today back to back, he hadn't time to think about much of anything but his patients. The surgeries had gone well and he'd delivered good news to the families. Before leaving the hospital, he had made his rounds, completed his reports and given final instructions to the nurses caring for his patients. Now he was at home, on full alert and eager for any information his brother had for him.

He grabbed the phone off the vanity. "Eli, did you find out anything?"

"This is going to cost you."

Tyson rolled his eyes. "Who do you think I am? Galen?"

It was a running joke in the family that Galen worked the least but made the most. While attending college Galen and his two roommates had decided to do something to make money and since all three were computer-savvy, they created video games. After their games became a hit on campus, they formed a business and by the time they graduated from college they were millionaires. The three were still partners today and usually released one game a year around the holiday season. Galen enjoyed flaunting the fact that he was able to work less than twenty hours a week and still make millions.

Eli chuckled. "With twins Galen won't have as much free time on his hands."

Tyson smiled at the thought. "You think?"

"We can hope."

Tyson tossed the towel aside to slide into a pair of briefs. "So what did you find out about Hunter McKay? Did she establish a company here?"

"Yes. She opened an architect office in the Double-Row building a week ago." Eli paused a minute and then said, "And you were right. Her divorce from her husband was pretty nasty."

"How do you know?"

"The one good thing about being president of the business council of a major city is getting to meet other such individuals. The one from Boston, John Wrigley, and I have become pretty good friends. I gave John a call today. According to him, Hunter divorced her husband on grounds of adultery and had the goods from a PI to prove it. Her ex hired this high-priced attorney to fight to keep Hunter from getting a fifty-fifty split of the architectural firm they owned together, but the judge sided with Hunter. In the end Hunter's ex retaliated by making sure she didn't get any of their clients."

The man was a bastard just like Hunter McKay said, Tyson thought, easing a T-shirt over his head. "I think I'll pay her a visit tomorrow."

"That doesn't surprise me."

"As a client," Tyson added.

"A client? That *does* surprise me. I didn't know you were interested in getting a house designed."

Tyson smiled. "I wasn't before now."

"Hell, Tyson, you don't even own any land."

Tyson's smile widened. "Shouldn't be that hard to buy some." Even through the phone line Tyson could imagine Eli rolling his eyes.

"And you would go to all that trouble just for a woman?"

Tyson thought about his brother's question. "But she's not just any woman. She's the one who got away. And now she's back."

The next morning Hunter walked into her office and stopped dead in her tracks. Her eyes did a double take.

Was Tyson Steele actually sitting in her reception area, chatting so amiably with Pauline that neither noticed her entry?

"Good morning," she said, breaking into their conversation.

Pauline and Tyson both glanced up, and Pauline smiled brightly. Tyson stood as he gave her a slow perusal, his gaze moving over her from head to toe. His eyes returned to meet hers and she tried ignoring the acceleration of her heart, a result of the intensity of his stare.

What were the odds that the same man she had been dreaming about for the past two nights would be in her office this morning? And they were the kind of dreams that heated her just by remembering them.

An excited Pauline interrupted her thoughts. "Good morning, Hunter. I think we might have our first client."

"Do we?" Hunter asked, her gaze switching from Tyson to Pauline.

"Yes. Dr. Tyson Steele is here to see you about designing his home."

Hunter found that hard to believe, especially after what he'd told her two nights ago. He was more interested in seducing her than anything else. "Is he?"

"Yes, I am," Tyson said.

She tried ignoring the slow, languorous heat that flowed through her body at the sound of Tyson's deep, husky voice. She looked back over at him and wished she hadn't. She'd thought he was sinfully handsome when she'd seen him at the nightclub, but as he stood in the sunlight streaming through her office window he looked triply so. The man was totally gorgeous, one hundred percent male perfection. He looked like scrumptious eye candy in his jeans and dark gray hooded sweatshirt. For her, there was just something about a nice male body in a pair of jeans and it was almost too much for her this early in the morning.

"In that case, Dr. Steele, you and I definitely need to talk," she said, moving toward her office.

She heard Tyson close her office door behind him the moment she set her briefcase on her desk. She turned around and fought back the urge to moan. The way he was leaning back against the closed door, he was sexiness personified. And his razor-sharp green eyes were on her. Why, today of all days, had she worn a dress, one shorter than she would normally wear? Shorter but still appropriate for conducting business. Yet from the way Tyson was staring at her, one would think otherwise. In fact, one would think she didn't have on any clothes at all. Sexual vibes were pouring off him in droves and she could feel desire flowing through her veins.

Clearing her throat as she tried getting control of the situation, she said, "Please have a seat, Tyson, and tell me just what it is that you want."

Realizing that wasn't a good question to ask him, she rephrased it. "Tell me what design of home you're interested in."

Tyson thought she had asked the right question the first time. He certainly had no problem telling her exactly what he wanted. But first he had to get his libido back in check. It had begun smoldering big-time when he'd glanced up from his conversation with her administrative assistant to see her standing there. She was what sexual fantasies were made of, and when it came to her he had plenty.

She was a constant visitor to his nightly dreams. If that wasn't bad enough she'd also crept into his daytime thoughts. All this from a woman he hadn't seen in years. Usually he didn't waste time fantasizing about any one woman before moving quickly to another. But it seemed he was focused on Hunter McKay and no one else, and he couldn't figure out why.

Eli thought he was obsessed with her and Tyson was beginning to wonder if that was true. He had never been obsessed with a woman before and was convinced he only wanted her in his bed, nothing more. Every time he thought about them having sex his pulse went crazy. He couldn't help wondering if there was more to his desire for Hunter than her being the one who got away. Why was he turned on by almost everything about her? Like her dress, for instance.

He knew it was just a dress, but on her it looked simply fantastic. He especially liked the way it complemented her legs. The other night she'd been wearing slacks so today was the first time he'd seen them. Now it came back to him that in high school, she had been a majorette, and the one thing he had liked was that she had a gorgeous pair of legs. She still did. And in that dress and a pair of three-inch pumps, she was definitely presenting challenges to his peace of mind. She looked neat, professional and way too appealing.

"Tyson?"

Hunter's voice brought his focus back to their conversation. He stepped away from the door and slid into a chair across from her desk. Doing so put him in close proximity to her and he enjoyed inhaling her scent. She was wearing the same perfume she had the other night and he thought the fragrance was definitely her signature. He met her eyes and said, "I have no problem telling you what I want." He let that statement hang in the air between them for a moment before adding, "As far as a design for a house, of course."

"Of course," Hunter said, moving around her desk to sit down behind it. "Before I can help you there are a few things I would need to know," she said, picking up a notepad and pen.

"Like what?"

"Like the location of the property the house will be built on. I need to verify there aren't any restrictions in the area that might prevent you from building the type of home you want. And I need to make sure your lot is large enough to fit whatever design you have in mind."

He nodded. "I find your inquiries interesting. Why don't we have dinner tonight and talk about them?"

She leaned back in her chair and stared at him. "We need to discuss it now, Tyson, because I have no intentions of having dinner with you."

"Why?"

"Because after work is my time. A business dinner means extending my work time into my pleasure time."

"We can make it both."

Her mouth flattened into a hard line. "No, we can't, and I don't have time to play games. If the only reason for your visit is to—"

"Try my hand at seducing you?"

She held his stare. "You warned me the other night that would be your main objective."

A soft chuckle escaped his lips. "It still is. Trust me. I haven't changed my mind about it. But I do want to talk about a house design, as well."

Tyson was serious about that. Although he would

admit he'd initially had an ulterior motive for seeking her out today, all it had taken was for him to wake up to the noise outside his window to know he had put off moving long enough. Currently, he leased a condo in a very prestigious area of Phoenix not far from the hospital. It was large and spacious and had a great view of the mountains. But unfortunately it came with some drawbacks. Like the close proximity of his neighbors. Over the years he had gotten used to car doors slamming, horns honking and the early morning ruckus of parents hustling their kids off to school. Maybe it was time to pursue his dream of living in the countryside.

She was still staring at him, as if she was trying to figure out if he really was serious about getting a house designed. He decided to put her mind at ease. "What you might see as a problem is the fact that I haven't purchased the property yet. It doesn't matter, Hunter. You design my house and when I get ready to build it I'll buy enough land for it to sit on."

She was still staring and he had no problem with her doing so because he knew she was also thinking about him. Sizing him up. Trying to figure him out. He wished he could tell her not to bother because he was too complex for her to try.

"I need to ask you something, Tyson," she finally said after a few moments had passed.

"Yes?"

"When did you decide you wanted a house designed, and why did you come to me?"

He could tell her about his conversation with Eli yesterday, but decided to omit that part. "To be honest with you, I hadn't given much thought of designing a house. I live in a condo and that suited me just fine. However,

I knew you were an architect and I knew my plans for you, so I decided I wanted to see your work."

"Let me get this straight," she said, sitting up in her chair. "You planned to seduce me so you came up with the idea to have me design a home for you. A home you never thought about owning until after you saw me the other night. You would go to all that trouble to get a woman in your bed?"

He couldn't help the smile that curved his lips. "No. I wouldn't go to all that trouble to get a woman in my bed, Hunter. But I would go to all that trouble to get you there."

She frowned. "Don't waste your time."

"It won't be. I know women, Hunter. I can read them as well as any book that's ever been published. You gave me the same looks I was giving you at Notorious. The 'I want to sleep with you' looks."

"I was not!"

"Yes, you were. Maybe you didn't realize you were doing so, but you were. The sexual chemistry between us was strong that night. I felt it and I saw no need to play games. That's why I told you my intentions up front. Did you honestly expect me not to explore all those heated vibes you and I were giving off that night?"

"But to invent this—"

"I didn't invent anything. What I've done is take another look at my living situation. Of my brothers I'm the only one who doesn't own a home. Never gave much thought to doing so. My condo is not far from the hospital and pretty convenient to everything I want. But this morning I noticed things I had chosen to ignore. Like the closeness of my neighbors. The noise and such. And the more I thought about it, the more that house in the country, the one I had thought about building years ago when I first got out of med school, suddenly appealed to me again. So I thought—"

"That since I was an architect and you had plans to seduce me anyway, that you would kill two birds with one stone?"

"I guess that's one way to look at it."

Hunter shook her head. After a minute she said, "That night after I left the club I thought about you a lot."

"You did?"

She heard the delight in his voice. "Yes, I did. I tried convincing myself that I imagined it. There was no way that at after eighteen years you were as arrogant and conceited as you were back in high school. But, Tyson, I was wrong. You are. You assume all you have to do is say what you want and you'll get it. You love women, although you'll never fall *in* love with one. You enjoy sharing your bed with them but that's about all you'll ever share. You—"

"Don't blame me," he interrupted. "Blame my father."

She lifted a brow. "Your father? What does your father have to do with it?"

Tyson smiled. "I'm Drew Steele's son. My brothers and I inherited his genes. We got some from Mom, of course, but the womanizing ones came from my dad. He used to be a player of the worst kind in his day, and even got run out of Charlotte because of his scandalous ways."

"And you're actually using your father's past behavior as an excuse for yours?"

"Like I said, it's in the genes. But since my father is happily married to my mother and has been for over thirty years, I figure there's hope for me and my brothers. At least my mother is convinced there is and she might be right. Three have gotten married within a three-year period. Not that I have any interest in getting married, now or ever."

"I don't blame you," she said, not able to stop herself. "I tried it once and once was enough." He would never know just how much she meant those words.

"Are you going through the 'I hate all men' stage?"

She tried not to notice the breadth of his shoulders when he leaned back in his chair. Or the way his jeans stretched tight over his muscular thighs. "I have no reason to hate all men, Tyson. In truth, I don't hate my ex. I pity him."

He held her gaze. "So the reason you won't share my bed has nothing to do with him."

"No. It's mainly because of your attitude."

"My attitude?"

"Yes."

"What's wrong with my attitude?"

"You act entitled."

"Do I?"

"Yes. I guess it's from women always letting you have your way. Giving you whatever you want. They make it too easy for you."

"And you intend to make things difficult, Hunter?"

A smile touched her lips. "I intend to make things impossible, Tyson."

"Nothing is impossible."

He stood and she couldn't help but admire how sexily his body eased out of the chair. "And since you won't have dinner with me, how about lunch tomorrow?"

"Give me one good reason why I should."

"Because I'm a potential client who merely wants to discuss ideas about the kind of country home I want you to design for me."

Hunter stared at him. Was he really serious about wanting her to design his home? There was only one way to find out. "Lunch tomorrow will be fine. Make an appointment with Pauline on your way out."

"No, I'm making one with you now. Put me on your calendar for tomorrow. Noon. At Gabriel's. I'll meet you there."

He headed for the door. When he reached it, he turned around and smiled. "And you look good today, by the way. Good enough to eat."

And then he opened the door and left.

Chapter 4

Hunter was convinced she should have her head examined when she arrived at Gabriel's the next day at noon. Meeting Tyson for lunch wasn't a smart move. So why was she here? Even if Tyson wanted her to design his country home there were ulterior motives behind it. He had been up front about his plans for her. It was all about seduction. Plain and simple. But he would discover there wasn't anything plain or simple about it.

The last thing she needed was to get mixed up with Tyson, or any man for that matter. She had put her divorce behind her, moved to be closer to her family and start over in her business. Hard work lay ahead of her and she had very little time to indulge in an affair. Besides, hadn't a failed eight-year marriage proved she was lousy at relationships?

"May I help you, madam?"

"Yes," she said, glancing around. "I'm meeting Tyson Steele for lunch."

The maître d' smiled. "Yes. Dr. Steele arrived a few moments ago and requested one of our private rooms in the back. I'll lead the way."

"Thanks," she said, following behind the man. A private room? In the back? She didn't like the sound of that and had a mind to turn around and walk out. But Tyson was a client. And so far, he was the only one she had. She kept telling herself that once the advertisements she'd approved finally ran, business would pick up. She certainly hoped so.

The maître d' opened the door then stepped aside for her to enter. She looked around and saw Tyson. He stood and she could feel the air between them sizzle. She knew he felt it as well when she saw heat smoldering in the depths of his green eyes.

He must have come straight from the hospital since he was still wearing his physician jacket. Tightening her hand on her briefcase, she moved forward and tried to fight the attraction she felt toward him. "Tyson."

"Hunter. Glad you could join me." As if only realizing his attire, he took off his white coat. "Sorry, an emergency detained me."

No need to say she hoped it wasn't anything serious, because he was a heart surgeon, so anything he did was serious. "No problem. I know your time is valuable so we can go ahead and—"

"You look good again today."

"Thanks." Knowing they would be meeting for lunch, she had worn a pantsuit. The way he had checked out her legs yesterday had been too unnerving. "As I said yesterday, usually a client has purchased property, but since—"

"We'll discuss business later. Let's order first. I'm starving. I've been in surgery all morning and missed breakfast."

"Oh. Of course." She glanced down at the menu and tried ignoring the tingles of awareness going through her. It wasn't easy sitting across the table from such a sexy man. So far he seemed all business and hadn't said anything she considered inappropriate. She wouldn't hold that compliment on how she looked against him. In fact she appreciated him making the observation. Carter had stopped telling her how good she looked even when she'd gone out of her way to please him.

"I already know what I want."

She glanced up and swallowed deeply at the look she saw in his eyes. She wasn't imagining the sizzling undercurrents flowing between them. "Do you?"

"Yes."

She held his gaze and the sexual tension surrounding them began mounting. He had been referring to what he wanted off the menu, hadn't he? With Tyson, one could never be sure. She'd discovered that often his words had a double meaning. "That was fast," she said, breaking his gaze to look back down at her menu.

"I've never been accused of being slow, Hunter."

She glanced back up at him again. "And what did you decide to get?"

"The pork chops. That's what I usually get whenever I come here."

She nodded. He had been talking about what was on the menu, after all. "The pork chops sound good."

"They are and that's what I want for now. What I really want I'll put on the back burner until…"

She glanced up to find his focus totally on her, making the undercurrents between them sizzle even more. "Until what?"

"I can bring you around to my way of thinking."

Hunter couldn't help but chuckle.

"And what do you find amusing, Hunter?"

She leaned forward in her chair. "For a minute there I thought this would be one of those rare times that you would be good."

"I am good. Always."

His words flowed through her and with supreme effort she tried not to imagine just how good he would be. "I was referring to your behavior."

"Now, *that*, not always. According to my mother I can push the envelope at times."

She bet. Hunter was glad the waiter returned and with the amount of food Tyson ordered it was apparent he hadn't lied about being hungry. She wondered where he would put it all.

As if reading her thoughts, he said, "I plan to work it off later."

"I don't doubt that you will."

He reached across the table and his fingers caressed her hand. "I don't mean with another woman, Hunter. I have a membership at the gym."

She wondered what had given away her thoughts and figured it must have been her tone. Why had the thought of him sleeping with a woman bothered her? And why did him caressing her hand send shivers of desire through her? "You don't owe me an explanation. What you do and with whom is your business, Tyson. And need I remind you," she said, pulling her hand back, "that this is a business meeting?"

"Duly reminded," he said, smiling. "Temptation got the best of me."

Although she wouldn't admit to it, temptation had almost gotten the best of her, as well. She had loved the feel of his touch and could still feel the imprint of his hand on her skin. It was becoming pretty clear that this attraction between her and Tyson could lead to big trouble if she wasn't careful. Deciding to break up the sexual tension flowing between them, she steered the conversation to an innocuous topic. "So how are your niece and nephew?"

He lifted a brow. "I take it you read that article in the paper, as well."

She shook her head. "No, Mo did and mentioned it the other night."

He took a sip of his water before answering. "Brittany and the twins are home now. I got a chance to see them before they left the hospital yesterday and they're doing fine. Galen is doing okay, too. In fact, he's on cloud nine."

"I can't picture him married."

"I couldn't, either, but it happened. And I'll admit there's something pretty special between him and Brittany."

"She's not from here, right?"

"No. She's from Florida. She was in town on business when they met."

"Have they named the twins yet?"

"They gave my mother the honor and she came up with Ethan and Elyse."

A smile spread across Hunter's lips. "Oh, I like that."

"My brothers and I figured she couldn't help but seize the opportunity to give the twins names starting with the letter E to match hers."

Then he smiled and Hunter was amazed he could be even more handsome. But he was.

As they ate, Tyson tried not to glance over at Hunter. Conversation between them had stopped, and he couldn't help wondering what she was thinking. Although whatever thoughts going through her head were a mystery to him, those going through his own head were not. Simply put, he wanted her. How could a woman he hadn't seen in eighteen years hold his interest like she was doing? It didn't make sense. No woman had ever gotten to him this way and without any effort on her part. At least not any conscious effort. He doubted she was aware of just how alluring she was without even trying.

Even wearing a pantsuit he didn't miss her small waist and sexy curves. And on more than one occasion when he'd glanced at her while they were eating, he hadn't missed the hardened tips of her nipples beneath her blue silk shirt. That meant she wasn't as immune to him as she pretended to be. And when he had reached out to stroke her hand, he'd felt the sparks and knew she had, as well.

Somehow Hunter had managed to eradicate thoughts of other women from his mind. He hadn't even bothered dropping by Notorious last night. Instead, he had gone to his brother Jonas's house and stayed for dinner. Jonas's wife, Nikki, was an excellent cook and spoiled Jonas with all her delicious meals. Luckily neither Jonas nor Nikki seemed to mind his drop-in dinner visits.

He glanced over at Hunter again and liked the way she worked her mouth while chewing her food. He felt a tightening in his gut at the thought of her working that same mouth on him. And although his pork chop tasted good, as usual, he had a feeling she would taste even better. He closed his eyes and in his mind he could taste her. As sweet as honey.

"It's *that* good?"

He popped his eyes back open. "What?"

"Your pork chop. You had your eyes closed as if savoring the taste."

He wondered what her reaction would be if he confessed that he'd been thinking about her and not the pork chop. "Yes, it is good. Moist. Tender. Just the way I like it. What about your meal?"

"The baked chicken is delicious, as well. I'm glad you suggested this place. It's pretty new, right?"

"Gabriel's? It wasn't here eighteen years ago if that's what you're asking. Actually, it opened a few years after I returned home from medical school. The owner is a good friend of my brother Gannon so I tend to drop in occasionally."

"What made you decide to come back to Phoenix after medical school?"

And what made you stay away? As much as he wanted to ask that question, he answered hers. "I couldn't imagine living anywhere else. I missed home. I missed my family. I figured this was where I belonged. Phoenix is a beautiful city."

"Yes, it is."

"Yet you stayed away," he pointed out.

Regret darkened her eyes. "After living here all my life I figured it was time to see the world and going to school on the east coast helped. In Phoenix I was Reverend Hugh McKay's granddaughter and everyone expected me to act a certain way. In Connecticut, where no one knew me, I could be myself."

"I can't imagine you getting buck wild."

She chuckled. "I didn't go that far but I had my fun. I figured I deserved it because I studied hard. I was lucky to get a job with a top architectural firm after college in Boston. I felt my life was set."

"Then you met your ex."

He saw the regret in her gaze deepen. "Yes, then I met Carter Robinson. He worked at another firm. We met at a party and dated a year and then got married."

Tyson didn't say anything, but his mind was filled with thoughts of how different things might have been had she returned to Phoenix after college. Then maybe their paths would have crossed. *And then what?* he silently asked himself. *You aren't a serious kind of guy, never was. All you could have offered her was a romp between the sheets.* He took a sip of his water knowing that was true.

Hunter tipped her head to the side and stared at Tyson. When he wasn't trying to get a girl on her back, he was surprisingly easy to talk to. But then he very well might be so engaging just to reel her in like he'd tried doing in high school.

When the waiter came to remove the dishes she placed her briefcase on the table, opened it and pulled out her notepad. "Now for business."

"All right."

He was agreeable. She was surprised and had expected him to make some attempt to delay things. "So tell me what you would like in your house."

"Besides you in my bed?"

Now the Tyson Steele she knew had returned. "Won't happen, Tyson, so get over it."

"Doubt if I can, Hunter."

Whenever he said her name she felt a tingling sensation in the lower part of her belly. "Try real hard." With her notebook and pen in hand she forced herself back into business mode. "How many bedrooms would you like in your home?"

"At least six."

When she lifted her brow, he said, "A room for each of my brothers in case their wives ever put them out."

"At the same time?"

He shrugged. "You never know. And they're smart enough to not to move back home. Mom would drive them to drink."

She fought back a smile. "Not your mom. I remember her from church. I was always in awe of her. She was beautiful."

"She still is beautiful. However, she does have one major flaw."

"What?" Hunter asked, taking a sip of her water.

"She likes getting into her sons' business too much to suit us. If she had her way we would all be married."

"And, of course, that's a bad thing."

"For me it is. I can't speak for my brothers since she got to three of them already."

Hunter shook her head. "I'm sure it wasn't your mom that 'got to them.' I would think it was their wives. From what I hear they fell in love."

He gave her a smile. "You're right. They're pretty damn smitten. Now they're looking at me, Mercury and Gannon like they expect us to follow suit."

"But you won't."

"I won't. I like being single."

"I bet you do. Now, to get back to your design. You

want six bedrooms, one of them the master. Any specifics there?"

"Umm, I want it big and spacious. Huge windows. Large walk-in closet and the regular stuff that goes in a bedroom. Nothing far-out like what Galen has. He built a house in the mountains and his bedroom has glass walls and a glass ceiling. He likes lying in bed and looking up at the stars."

"Sounds beautiful."

"It is if that's your taste. Not mine. I want regular walls and when I lay in bed and look up the only thing I want to see is a ceiling fan."

"What about the kitchen?"

"I want a large kitchen."

She raised a brow. "You cook?"

"No. But for some reason women are impressed by the size of a man's kitchen."

She fought the urge to laugh. "Are they?"

"Yes. Some think if they get in your kitchen and cook you a good meal then you'll sweep them off their feet."

"Hasn't worked yet, I gather."

"When I sweep them off their feet I head for the bedroom and not the wedding chapel as they would like."

For some crazy reason the thought of him heading for the bedroom with any woman annoyed her. "What's the range of square footage you want?"

"Minimum of thirty-five hundred and max of fifty-five."

"That's a lot of house for a single person."

He smiled. "I figure I'll eventually have plenty of nieces and nephews and would want a big enough place for them to enjoy themselves when they come visit their uncle Tyson."

Over the next half hour Tyson continued to add on

to his wish list. And there were a few things she suggested that he hadn't thought about. With additional land, a home in the country would be different from one built in the city. Already ideas were forming in her head and she couldn't wait to get started on this project.

"I think that will be enough information for now," she said finally, putting her notepad away. "I should have some preliminary sketches for you within a week to ten days. You can call Pauline and make an—"

"I prefer calling you directly."

"Why?"

"I just do."

"I hired Pauline for a reason."

"Tell that to your other clients."

She glared over at him. What she should do is get up, thank him for lunch and leave. But he was her client and at the moment he was the only one she had. She pulled her business card out of her purse and scribbled her mobile number on the back of it. "Don't call unless it's about business."

He took the card and slid it into his pocket while smiling at her. "I'm beginning to think you don't like me."

He didn't know how close to the truth that was. Just when she thought he might have some redeeming qualities, he proved her wrong. "Time for me to get back to the office. Thanks for lunch."

"We need to do this again. Maybe dinner the next time."

Deciding not to address Tyson's suggestion, she stood. "Goodbye, Tyson." And then she walked off. Try as she might she couldn't ignore the heat of his gaze on her back...and especially on her backside.

Chapter 5

A week and a half later, with his heart heavily weighing him down, Tyson entered his condo. Losing a patient was never easy. Although Morris Beaumont and his family had known the risks, the married father of two—and grandfather of four—had chosen to have the surgery anyway. And he hadn't survived. Delivering the news to the Beaumont family hadn't been easy. They had been hoping to beat the odds and had taken the news hard.

Tyson clenched his jaw, trying to keep his emotions at bay. Sure, he was a doctor, saw people dying every day, and accepted death as part of life. But still, doctors were human. Caring and experiencing grief didn't make one weak, as some people thought. Staying detached, as one of his professors had stressed in medical school, wasn't always easy.

Needing a beer, Tyson headed toward his kitchen to

grab one out of his refrigerator. This had been a rough week with a full load of scheduled surgeries and a few unscheduled ones as well. One such emergency had been a newborn with a hole in her heart. She was doing great and if her condition continued to improve, she would be leaving the hospital and going home in another week.

Because of his workload, he hadn't followed up with Hunter, nor had she followed up with him, which probably meant she hadn't completed the initial sketches she'd talked about. Over the next number of days, which he had off, he'd get in touch with her.

The first thing on his agenda was getting laid. He needed sex like he needed this beer, he thought, popping the tab and taking a long, pleasurable gulp. He licked his lips afterward. He was beginning to feel restless and edgy. At least twenty-four hours of sleep would alleviate the former problem, but the latter would only be relieved between the legs of a woman. But not any woman. Hunter.

He took another swig of his beer. That thought filled him with concern. When had he begun lusting after just one woman? Even worse, when did his dreams just center on one woman? At night, whenever his head hit the pillow, he deliberately shut out unpleasant thoughts and only allowed his mind to conjure up pleasant ones. Hunter always headed the list.

Why was he focused on getting her to the one place she'd made it clear she didn't want to be, which was his bed? And why did he think that once he got her there the real thing would be far better than any dream?

Tyson's cell phone rang and the ringtone indicated which brother it was. He pulled the phone off his belt. "What's up, Mercury?"

"Just checking on you. Mom told us why you didn't make last Thursday night. You okay?"

Over the years his mother had deemed Thursdays as family dinner night at their parents' home. Eden Tyson Steele expected all six of her sons to be present and accounted for, grudgingly or otherwise, unless one had a good excuse. Tyson and his brothers knew their mother used the Thursday night dinners as a way to show her sons that although their father had once been a die-hard womanizer, after meeting her all that had come to an end. She wanted them to see with their own eyes that a man like Drew Steele, who'd been known for his wild ways, could fall in love one day, marry and be true to one woman for the rest of his days. Galen, Eli and Jonas had gotten the intended message. The jury was still out for him, Mercury and Gannon. As far as Tyson was concerned, the jury could stay out for him because he wasn't changing his mind about marriage.

He was having way too much fun being single and sharing his bed with any woman he wanted.

Except for one by the name of Hunter McKay. The one he wanted with a passion.

"Tyson?"

He'd almost forgotten his brother was on the phone. "Yes, sorry. Rough stretch at work. I plan to sleep it off."

"Good idea. I'm leaving town later today for Dallas. Might have a new client with the Cowboys."

"That's good." Mercury was a former NFL player turned sports agent. He enjoyed what he did and traveled a lot.

"I thought I'd check on you before I left. By the way, I visited with the twins yesterday. They're so tiny."

Tyson figured there was no need to mention to Mercury that most newborns were. "Yes, they are. But they'll grow up fast and be walking before you know it. Getting into all kinds of stuff."

"I can't see laid-back Galen trying to keep up with them."

Neither could he, but then he hadn't figured his oldest brother would ever marry, either. "What's Gannon up to?" His youngest brother had taken over the day-to-day operations of their father's trucking company when the old man had retired a few years ago. Gannon even enjoyed getting behind a rig himself every once in a while.

"Gannon is planning to drive one of his rigs for a pickup in Florida later this week."

"That's a long ride."

"Yes, but knowing Gannon, he'll have fun along the way."

Tyson frowned. That was what worried him. While growing up, since he and Galen had been the oldest two Steeles, his parents—especially his mother—had expected them to look out for Gannon, who was the baby in the family. Although Gannon was now thirty-two, Tyson was discovering that old habits were hard to break. "I'll talk to him before he hits the road."

"It might be a good idea for you to do that. I'll talk with you later, Tyson."

"Okay and have a safe trip." Tyson clicked off the phone and returned it to his belt.

After he finished off the last of his beer, he released a throaty, testosterone-filled growl. It was a testament to how long he'd gone without a woman, which was so unlike him. He needed to step up his game, be the conqueror he knew he could be. Turn up the heat and do what he had warned Hunter he planned to do and seduce the hell out of her.

A smile touched his lips as he headed for his bedroom. First he would get the sleep he needed and then he would make it his business to seek out the object of his passion. Hunter McKay thought she'd given the last word, but he had news for her.

"Yes, and thanks for calling, Mrs. Davis. I'm looking forward to meeting you as well."

Hunter hung up the phone as a huge smile touched her lips. That would be the third new client she'd gotten in a week. It didn't even bother her that all three referrals had come from Tyson. The first, Don Jamison, was a colleague of Tyson's at the hospital. Dr. Jamison and his wife were new to town and currently living in an apartment. They had recently purchased land on the outskirts of town and were anxious to build their home.

Tessa Motley's mother was a patient of Tyson's. When she had mentioned that she and her husband planned to build a house on property that Tessa had inherited from a grandmother, Tyson had recommended Hunter.

Then there were the Davises, an older couple with dreams of building a house on beachfront property they had recently purchased in Savannah.

Hunter rose to her feet and walked over to the coffeepot to pour herself a cup. Her thoughts couldn't help but dwell on the man who'd helped to give her business a kick start. It has been two weeks since she'd seen or talked to him. She had called and left a message with him two days ago that the preliminary sketches for his house were ready. However, he hadn't bothered to call her back.

In a way she should be glad he'd given up on pursuing her, but for some reason she wasn't. Mainly because if he wasn't chasing her that meant some other woman was holding his interest now. Why did that bother her? Probably because he still managed to creep into her nightly dreams, which were getting steamier and more erotic. Going without sex for four years had finally caught up with her. Even now the thought of being seduced by Tyson Steele wasn't as unappealing as it had been originally. She took a sip of her coffee, not believing she was actually thinking that way.

She turned when she heard the knock on her door. "Come in."

The door opened and the very subject of her thoughts walked in. Tyson strode in with the casual arrogance that was so much a part of him. She was forced to admit the man was the most sensuous piece of artwork she'd ever seen. So much so it was mind-boggling. He was the last person she'd expected to see today and his surprise visit had her breathless.

He gave her a sexy smile that made her knees weaken. She could actually feel the sexual chemistry sizzling between them. "Hunter."

The sound of his voice actually made her skin tingle. What were the odds that the very man she'd been thinking about suddenly appeared? How strange was that? Somehow she found her voice to ask. "Tyson? What are you doing here?"

"I got the message you left on my phone."

"That was two days ago." She hoped he hadn't heard the testiness in her voice.

"I know. I slept for almost two days."

Hunter fought back the temptation to ask the question that burned in her mind. *With whom?* Instead she put her coffee cup down and moved to stand in front of her desk. She felt the heat of his gaze with every step she took. Every other time, the fact that he closely watched her every move had annoyed her, but not now. It thrilled her.

When she reached her desk she turned and looked over at him to find his piercing green eyes staring her up and down. She fought back a heated shiver and asked, "Is anything wrong?"

"What makes you think something is wrong, Hunter?"

She wished it didn't do things to her whenever he said her name. "You're staring." She'd worn a dress today and his gaze continued to roam up and down her legs.

"I am, aren't I? My only excuse is that you're good to look at."

Carter had rarely given her compliments, so hearing them from Tyson definitely boosted her feminine confidence. He might be checking her out but she was doing the same with him. She couldn't help but appreciate how good he looked in his jeans and the way his shirt fit over his well-toned muscles. She forced her eyes away. "I'm sure that's a line you've used on a number of women."

"No. It's not."

Deciding not to believe him, she looked past his shoulder to the door. "How did you get into my office without Pauline announcing you?"

He shrugged. "I told her she didn't have to bother. I like announcing myself. Besides, she was packing up to leave, and she told me to tell you that she would see you Monday morning."

Hunter glanced at her watch. She hadn't realized it was so late. That meant they were alone and that wasn't a good thing right now with her present frame of mind. The best thing was to send him packing. Picking up the manila folder off her desk, she offered it to him. "Here's what you came for."

Tyson moved toward her with calm, deliberate strides, and when he came to a stop directly in front of her, she tried ignoring the sparks going off inside her. Instead of accepting the folder, he reached out and brushed the tips of his fingers across her cheek. "That's not what I came for, Hunter. This is."

And before she could draw her next breath, he leaned in and captured her mouth with his.

Tyson hadn't lied when he'd told Hunter that this was what he'd come for. He refused to suffer through another dream where he'd kissed her madly without getting a taste of the real thing. And now he was discovering that no dream could compare. It didn't come close.

He'd known when he took her mouth that he risked getting his tongue bitten off. Evidently she needed this kiss as much as he did if the way her tongue was mating with his was anything to go by. He could taste her hunger in this kiss, and he could feel the passion and the desire engulfing them. He was greedily lapping up her mouth.

He'd kissed her once before, years ago behind the lockers at school. It had been way too short and at the time he hadn't known how to use his tongue like he did now. He hadn't known how much kissing could thoroughly arouse a man when done the right way and with the right woman.

Tyson wrapped his arms around Hunter's waist to bring her closer. Never had any woman's mouth tasted so delicious, so hot that it was heating the blood rushing through his veins. In seconds he had her purring and himself moaning.

He heard the folder she'd been holding fall to the floor seconds before she wrapped her arms around his neck as he continued to feast on her mouth. He moaned again when he felt her hardened nipples press into his chest. And if that wasn't bad enough, her scent was all around him, seducing him in a way no other woman had ever been capable of doing.

He knew this kiss was the beginning and was determined for it not to be the end. He had succeeded in breaking through her shell, but it was imperative not to push too hard and too soon. So he did what he really didn't want to do—pull back from the kiss.

Before she could say anything—he was certain it would be something he didn't want to hear right then— he leaned close and whispered against her moist lips. "Have dinner with me, Hunter."

Hunter could only stand there, feeling weak in the knees, while she gazed into the green eyes staring back at her. One minute Tyson had been standing in front of her and the next he had his tongue in her mouth. And the minute she tasted it she was powerless to resist him.

His kiss had been possessive. It had sent her emotions in a tailspin, accelerating out of control. At the time, something had convinced her that she desperately needed the urgent mating of his tongue with hers and she'd given in to it. Now that the kiss was over, common sense had returned and she was thinking more rationally. At least she hoped so.

"Hunter?"

She drew in a deep breath. He had asked her to have

dinner with him and there was no way she could do that, especially after that kiss. He had shown her what could happen if she lowered her guard with him just for one moment. "I can't have dinner with you."

He frowned down at her. "You can't or you won't?"

It was basically the same thing in her book. "Does it matter?"

"Yes."

"Not to me, Tyson."

"What are you afraid of?"

That question irked her. "I'm not afraid of anything."

He crossed his arms over his chest. "Do you know what I think?"

"Not really."

"I'm going to tell you anyway. I think you're afraid that I have the capability to make you feel like a woman again."

Hunter swallowed deeply, knowing what he said was true, but she'd never admit to him. "Sorry to disappointment you but—"

"You could never disappoint me, Hunter. Only please-sure me."

If his words were meant to take the wind from her sails, they succeeded. She wished he wouldn't say things like that. Words that could slice through her common sense and make her want things she shouldn't have. "Doesn't matter."

"It does to me. Let's have dinner and talk about it."

That was the last thing she wanted to do—discuss how she'd come unglued in his arms. "I'd rather not."

"I wish you would. What I told you earlier was true. I've been sleeping for almost forty-eight hours."

"Why?"

"A lot of surgeries at the hospital." He paused a moment and then added, "And I lost one of my patients during surgery last week."

His words sliced through her irritation. "Oh, Tyson, I'm so sorry to hear that." Without realizing she was doing so, she reached out and touched his arm.

He drew in a deep breath. "Doctors aren't superheroes and we can only do so much but…"

"But you did your best."

"Yes," he agreed somberly. "I did my best. Unfortunately for Mr. Beaumont, my best wasn't good enough."

A part of Hunter understood how Tyson was feeling. All she had to do was to recall that time when her grandfather had first taken ill. She had been at the hospital with him when a commotion out in the hall had drawn her attention. She'd stepped out in time to hear some family member of a person who'd just died accuse the doctor of not doing enough. The doctor had tried to calm the person down, saying he'd done all he could. Hunter had known the accusations hurled at the doctor had hurt. For a quick second she'd seen the agonized look in the doctor's eyes. And then she'd understood. The man was a doctor but he was also a human being. Just like family members grieved for their lost loved ones, doctors grieved for the patients they lost.

Tyson leaned down to pick up the folder she had dropped earlier. When he handed it to her, he said, "Look, I didn't mean to mention that. I asked you to dinner, not to attend a pity party."

"I'm glad because a pity party isn't what you're going to get. If the offer for dinner still stands, then I'll take it."

He eyed her curiously. "Why did you change your mind?"

"Because although you have the ability to irritate me, I do need to go over these with you," she said, handing the folder back to him. "And I really should be nice to you."

At the sensual gleam that suddenly appeared in his eyes, she quickly said, "Not *that* nice."

He chuckled. "And why do you think you should be nice to me?"

"Thanks to you, I have three new clients. I appreciate the referrals."

Tyson shrugged. "No big deal."

"It's my business we're talking about, so to me it is a big deal. Thank you."

"You're welcome. But there's one thing I forgot to mention about dinner."

She looked up at him. "What?"

"It's at my place."

She frowned, not liking how he'd easily maneuvered that one. There was no way he could have forgotten to mention that earlier. "I thought you couldn't cook."

"I can't," he said, heading for the door. "But I know how to pick up takeout. I hope you like Thai food."

Hunter did, but she wasn't sure having dinner at his place was a smart idea. She was about to tell him so when he added over his shoulder, "I'll text you my address. See you in an hour."

And then he opened the door and walked out, closing it behind him.

Chapter 6

Hunter stared at the closed door and a part of her wished there was more going on between her and Tyson than physical attraction. The sexual vibes they emitted whenever they were together were so strong she bet a person walking across the street could pick up on it.

And that kiss…

Just thinking about it made her weak in the knees so she moved around her desk and sat down. The kiss had started off gentle and when she began participating, mingling her tongue with his, it had gotten downright passionate to a degree she'd never experienced before. Who kissed like that? Evidently Tyson Steele did. She didn't recall the one time they'd kissed back in high school having this type of effect on her. He had definitely gotten experience over the years. The man knew how to use his tongue in a way that could be destructive to a woman's mind. It had definitely obliterated her common sense. For a minute there she hadn't wanted him to stop and had been disappointed when he'd done so.

The kiss had evidently affected him, too. She had been able to feel the heat radiating from his body as he kissed her. And when she had wrapped her arms around his neck and pressed her body closer to his, she had felt evidence of his desire. His huge erection had pressed into her middle and all she could think about was how it would feel inside her.

Like in her dreams.

Hunter drew in a deep breath. That kiss had gotten out of hand, and on top of that, she had agreed to have dinner with him at his place. What could she have been thinking? Tyson had told her what he wanted from her and now he probably thought it was within his reach. That was the last thing she wanted him to think.

Hunter was about to pull her cell phone out of her purse to call Tyson and cancel dinner when it rang. She frowned when she recognized the ringtone. Why would Nadine Robinson be calling her? She hadn't talked to her mother-in-law in over two years. Not since Hunter had filed for a divorce. Carter's father, Lewis Robinson, had forbidden the family from having anything to do with Hunter for divorcing his son.

Curiosity got the best of her so she clicked on the phone. "Yes, Nadine?"

"Hunter? Glad I was able to reach you. I was afraid you had changed your number."

It was on the tip of Hunter's tongue to say although she hadn't changed her phone number, she had blocked certain callers from getting through, like Nadine's son.

She would have blocked Nadine's number as well, but figured the older woman had no reason to ever call her.

"This is a surprise, Nadine. What can I do for you?" Hunter decided to get straight to the point. There was no reason for her and the woman to engage in friendly chitchat.

"I called to warn you. About Carter."

Hunter lifted a brow. "Why would you want to warn me about Carter?"

"His world is falling apart. He's losing clients right and left and several employees have quit."

That didn't surprise Hunter. Although Carter had underhandedly taken her clients away, she figured it was only a matter of time before he lost them. As for the employees, although Carter was a pretty good architect, he lacked people skills, so that wasn't a shocker.

"That's not my problem, Nadine."

"I know, but he intends to make it your problem."

Hunter drew in a breath. "And how does he think he can do that?"

"I overheard him and Lewis talking. They've come up with a plan for you to return to Boston and get back with Carter."

When hell freezes over. Hunter sat up straight in her chair. "What plan?"

"Carter will be in Phoenix on business in a few weeks and he plans to look you up when he gets there. He told Lewis he will apologize to you for all he's done, tell you how much he regrets losing you and that he can't live without you. The plan is to tug on your heartstrings."

"My heartstrings?"

"Yes."

Hunter raised a brow. "What does my heart have to do with it?"

"Because you're still in love with him."

Hunter shook her head. Now she had heard everything. "Nadine, why would anyone think I'm still in love with Carter?"

"Because you haven't been seriously involved with anyone since your divorce. You didn't date when you were here in Boston and from what Carter is hearing, you haven't dated anyone since you've moved back to Phoenix."

Hunter frowned. "And how can he know that?"

There was a pause on the line before Nadine said, "Carter has friends in Phoenix and they occasionally report back to him on your activities. You're not involved with anyone so it seems you're still carrying a torch for him."

"Well, whoever thinks that is dead wrong."

"I'm glad. I was getting worried. You did the right thing by ending your marriage to my son."

Hunter frowned. "That's not what you told me, Nadine."

"I know. But trust me, I did you a favor. I saw what was happening and refused to let you become a mini-me. Carter had begun treating you like Lewis treated me. You had started believing the lies and accepting his behavior. I knew you deserved better. The best thing you did was divorce my son. He's out of your life and I hope you won't let him back in."

Hunter hated admitting it, but Nadine was right. She had started letting Carter get away with murder and he knew it. Instead of divorcing him, for two years she had bought into his crap that her life would be nothing without him. She'd opted to stay married to him but moved into the guest bedroom.

It had been goodbye and good riddance to Carter Robinson. And that's the way she would keep it.

"Trust me, Nadine, there's no way I will ever get back with Carter. And if he has this bizarre delusion that I'm still in love with him then he is dead wrong."

"Good. I'm glad you moved back to Phoenix. But you need to get involved with someone. You need a life. As long as you don't have one, Carter is going to think he has a chance with you again."

As far as Hunter was concerned, Nadine had no right to tell her what she needed. And Carter could think whatever he wanted. "Let me assure you, Nadine, I do have a life."

"So you're seeing someone?"

Tyson's image suddenly came into her mind. "Yes, I am seeing someone. In fact I'll be meeting him for dinner in a couple of hours." What she'd just said hadn't been a total lie.

"I'm glad. I know you probably won't ever forgive me for siding against you during the divorce, but I did what I felt I had to do for your own good. Goodbye, Hunter. I wish you the best and hope your young man makes you happy."

"Goodbye, Nadine."

Hunter clicked off the phone, shaking her head. Carter actually thought he could show up in Phoenix with a plan to get her back? Did he really think she was pining away for him just because she hadn't gotten seriously involved with anyone since their divorce?

At that moment her phone rang and she recognized

Mo's ringtone. She was glad it wasn't Nadine calling her back. "Yes, Mo?"

"Kat called earlier. She has a date and Eric decided to come to town this weekend. Just wanted to make sure you'd be okay."

She shook her head. "You guys don't have to keep me company like I don't have a life, you know." At that moment Hunter realized she had lied to Nadine because in all honesty, she really didn't have a life.

"Mo, can I ask you something?"

"Sure."

"Do you think I'm still in love with Carter?"

There was a pause. "To be honest with you, the thought had crossed my mind a time or two. Where did that question come from?"

Hunter let out a deep sigh and told Mo about her conversation with Carter's mother. "How can you or anyone think I still care for him, Mo?"

"Well, it has been two years, Hunter, and you haven't as much as dated another man."

"The first year after my divorce I swore off men," she said, unable to keep the bitterness out of her voice.

"That's understandable."

Hunter knew that the reason Mo had divorced her ex hadn't been about another woman but about Larry's gambling addiction. When he had refused help and had sold every single item in their home to feed his habit, Mo had had enough.

"What about now since you've moved back to Phoenix?" Mo asked, interrupting Hunter's thoughts.

"I'm busy trying to start my business here."

"Then you need to learn how to multitask. And to be honest, it sounds to me like you're making excuses.

Being in a relationship with someone won't consume that much of your time, Hunter. You've even got one of those Bad News Steeles hot on your tail. Do you know how many women in town would love to be in your shoes?"

"Then let them. I prefer not to do casual relationships."

"After what Carter put you through do you honestly prefer a serious one? All you'll get is nothing but heartache...unless you're entertaining the thought of marrying again."

"Never!"

"Then what's wrong with casual? I'm not saying you should start hopping from bed to bed or that you should get involved with Tyson Steele but..." Mo trailed off.

"But what?"

"If I was going to do casual after going without sex for as long as you have, Tyson would be my man. One night with him would probably make you realize what you're missing. You claim you haven't had an orgasm in so long that you've forgotten how it feels. That's sad for any single woman to admit to...unless you're doing the celibate thing."

"No, that's not it."

"Then what is it? I can see why Carter thinks you're still carrying a torch for him. What you need to do is declare your sexual independence."

"My sexual independence?"

"Yes, and I think the ideal person to start with is Tyson. The word *serious* is not in his vocabulary so you're safe there. And if the rumors about him are true, he'll make you remember just how explosive an orgasm can be and have you screaming all over the place. He told you that he had plans to seduce you, so let him."

"If I were to do that, then I become just another notch on his belt. I didn't want that when we were in high school and I don't want that now."

"Then what do you want?"

Hunter should be woman enough to admit she wanted Tyson. She couldn't help but want him after all those erotic dreams she'd been having of him lately. But she didn't want him on his terms and told Mo how she felt.

"In that case then why not take the initiative and seduce *him*? That way you'll maintain control."

Hunter gazed out her window and stared at the mountains in the distance. The sun was going down and cast a purple glow on the skyline. "Seducing a man might be easy for you, Mo, but it wouldn't be for me." She just could not see herself using her feminine wiles to get a man in bed.

Mo intruded on her thoughts. "For once will you accept that you're a woman who has needs like the rest of us? A woman who's capable of planning her own seduction and doesn't need Tyson Steele to plan it for her?" She blew out an exasperated breath. "There's no manual detailing how to go about it. You do what comes natural."

"What comes natural?"

"Yes, and it's easier than you think. There's physical attraction between you and Tyson, as well as strong sexual chemistry. Kat and I felt it that night at the club. All you have to do is let that chemistry be your guide."

Mo's words echoed in Hunter's mind long after they ended the phone call. They haunted her as she began closing her office for the weekend, knowing she had little time to decide just how she would handle Tyson. Her conversations with Nadine and Mo had made her realize it was past time to take control of her life. For a change, she needed to do whatever pleased her.

An image of Tyson suddenly appeared in her head. The thought of sharing a bed with him sent heated shivers through her body. And if he was really a master in the bedroom, as those rumors went, then he was just what she needed. In fact, he was long overdue. However, like she'd told Mo, she had one big issue with Tyson. He'd already planned how he intended for things between them to end—with his seduction of her. He probably had a spot in his bed with her name on it— right along with all those other women he'd had sex with in that same bed.

What man targets a woman for seduction and, worse, is arrogant enough to tell her, as if it's a gift she should appreciate? Only a man with the mind-set of Tyson Steele.

She would just love to best him at his own game and still get something out of it. It was about time some woman knocked him off his high horse. It would serve him right for being so darn egotistical. Could that woman be her? It would mean her stepping into a role she'd never played before, but it would be well worth it if she got the results she wanted and on her terms.

Moments later she left her office, deciding that tonight she would not allow Tyson to seduce her. She would be seducing him.

Tyson smiled as he gazed around his kitchen and dining-room areas. His sister-in-law Brittany would be proud of him. The table was set perfectly. Brittany owned Etiquette Matters, a school that taught etiquette and manners. Tyson's mother was into all that etiquette stuff and although she'd made sure they had impeccable manners while growing up, she felt her sons needed to take a refresher course. When Brittany opened a school in Phoenix after marrying Galen, Eden Tyson Steele strongly suggested that her sons enroll in one of Brittany's classes. To pacify their mother, they had.

Tyson checked his watch and drew in a deep breath, not wanting to think about this being a first for him. He didn't prepare dinner for women. They prepared dinner for him. Although he hadn't actually prepared this one, he had invited her to his place and would be feeding her. He had crossed plenty of boundaries with Hunter and wasn't sure what he should do about it.

Hell, he wasn't even sure he wanted to do anything about it. And that in itself was crazy. Why was there such strong sexual chemistry between them? What exactly had brought it on and when would it end? He had tried to recall the exact moment he'd lost his head. Had it been the moment he'd seen her when she had walked into Notorious? Or had it been when he'd conversed with her while sitting at her table? Or had it been when he'd dropped in on her unexpectedly that first time at her office? Or had it been when he'd kissed her? All he knew was that if he wasn't careful, she could easily get under his skin and he refused to let that happen.

Why was she making his plan of seduction so damn difficult? She wanted him as much as he wanted her, he was sure of it. But she continued to deny what they both wanted—one night in his bed. Was that too much to ask? He didn't think so, but evidently she did.

His phone rang, nearly startling him out of his reverie. He recognized the ringtone. It was Gannon. He picked up his cell phone from the kitchen counter. "It took you long enough to call me back, Gannon."

He could hear his youngest brother's chuckle. "Now that Galen's married, am I supposed to report in with you now?"

Gannon was becoming such a smart-ass. "Wouldn't hurt."

"Don't hold your breath, Tyson. What's up?"

"I hear you're driving one of your rigs to Florida."

"That's right. Do you want to go along for the ride?"

He'd done it before and had to admit he had fun. The women they'd met along the way had been worth it. "Wish I could but I can't."

For some reason he didn't want to leave Phoenix right now. He refused to believe Hunter McKay had anything to do with it. Hadn't he gone two weeks without seeing her? He forced the thought to the back of his mind just how miserable those days had been.

"Too much is going on at the hospital, Gannon," he added. "I was lucky to get this time off." And he was spending it with a woman who wasn't sharing his bed. How crazy was that?

"I dropped by and saw Brittany and the twins today."

"How are they?"

"Everybody's fine. Galen was changing Ethan's diaper. Can you imagine that?"

"No, but he's a father now and with it comes responsibilities. Keep that in mind if you get it into your head to invite some woman into your rig for the night."

Gannon chuckled. "Please don't cover the birds and bees with me again, Tyson. I got it the last time."

"Just make sure you remember it. And stay condom safe."

"Whatever. I'm headed out in the morning. I just left the folks' place and they're still beaming over the twins. Mom has taken over a thousand pictures already."

"Doesn't surprise me."

At that moment Tyson's doorbell sounded. "My dinner guest has arrived. I'll talk to you later."

"Dinner guest? You can't cook."

"Not trying to cook," he said, moving around the breakfast bar to head for the door.

"I can't believe you invited a woman to your place."

Tyson rolled his eyes. "Women have been to my place before, Gannon. Numerous times."

"As a bedmate. Not a dinner guest."

He didn't need his brother reminding him of his strange behavior. "Be safe on the road."

"Okay. See you in a week."

"Will do," Tyson said, clicking off the phone and sliding it into the back pocket of his jeans. He stopped in the middle of his living room and inhaled deeply, convinced he could pick up Hunter's scent through the door. He shook his head. He had to be imagining things.

He glanced around his condo again. Although he appreciated his cleaning lady, she never had a lot to do because he spent most of his time at the hospital. But still, he was glad he wasn't a slob and kept a pretty tidy place. Hunter ought to be impressed.

Tyson shuddered at where his thoughts had gone again. Who cared if she was impressed or not? A completely physical, emotion-free involvement was what he wanted with Hunter. Inviting her to dinner was a means to an end, and the end was getting her into his bed.

He walked to the door, opened it and faltered at the same time he was certain his jaw dropped. He could only stand there and stare wide-eyed. What in the world...?

"I hope I'm not late, Tyson."

He inhaled sharply as deep-seated hunger nearly took control of his senses. Hunter had changed clothes. The coral dress she was wearing now fitted her body like another layer of skin, showing every single curve. The neckline dipped low at just the right angle to show enough of her breasts, while at the same time enticing him to want to see more. She always looked totally feminine in whatever outfit she wore, but in this particular dress she looked like sex on two legs. And speaking of legs... They looked even more gorgeous in this short dress with a pair of killer heels on her feet. The entire ensemble was meant to push a man's buttons and it was pushing his in a big way. Somehow she'd transformed her image from a good girl to a totally naughty one.

For a moment he couldn't say anything. His mind filled with thoughts of just how he would take this dress off her later. He fought the urge to do it now. He was tempted to reach out and touch her all over to see if the material of her dress felt as sensuous as it looked. Instead he stood there, leaning against the doorjamb while his gaze roamed up and down her body, appreciating every stitch, inch and curve he saw.

"Tyson, I hope I'm not late."

She repeated herself so he figured it was time to rein in his desire and respond. "You're right on time."

And with the feel of his erection pressing hard against the zipper of his jeans, he meant every single word. "Come in," he invited, moving aside.

She entered, walking past him. He appreciated the sway of her hips and how her every step placed emphasis on her delectable-looking backside, as well as those killer heels on her feet. And if that wasn't mind-boggling enough, her delicious scent almost made him moan.

"Thanks for inviting me to dinner," she said, turning around in the middle of his foyer.

Hell, he would invite her to dinner every single night if she showed up looking like this. If she bent over even just a little he was certain he would be able to see her panties. That thought made his erection even harder.

Lust began taking over his mind, drugging him, gripping him, and he hoped he could make it through dinner. After that the night would belong to him and he intended to make good use of his time. She had to have known wearing this outfit would increase his desire for her. He wanted her so badly his entire body ached.

"No need to thank me," he said, leading her to the living room. He wished they could skip dinner altogether and head straight to the bedroom.

"We're having Thai, right?"

He turned and his gaze automatically went to her legs. He could envision her doing a lot with those legs and all of them included him between them. He forced his gaze from her legs up to her face. Why did her lips look like they needed to be kissed? "Sorry. What did you ask?"

Hunter smiled at him. "I asked if we're still having Thai."

She might be having Thai but he was having her. "Yes. The table is all set and the food is ready."

"Good. I'm starving."

So was he. So were his hands. His fingers. His mouth. His shaft. All were anxious to touch her. Taste her. Get inside her.

Tyson drew in a deep breath, trying to get back the control he was quickly losing. She had a lot of guts wearing this outfit to his place tonight. Had she thought he would focus on dinner and not on her? Especially when he'd warned her of his plans to seduce her?

Wait a minute… Warning bells began going off in his head. This whole thing was too good to be true. Why did he smell a setup? Tyson crossed his arms over his chest. "Okay, Hunter. What's going on? Why are you dressed like this?"

She lifted a brow. "Dressed like what?"

"Like you'll be my dessert once we finish dinner."

Chapter 7

Hunter took a deep breath, trying to ignore the intense nervousness floating around in her stomach. What had Mo said about just doing what came naturally? If that was the case then why was she suddenly feeling like a fish out of water? Now she was wondering if she'd overdone things, especially with this outfit. She had dropped by Phase One, a boutique she'd passed several times on her way home. A twentysomething salesgirl had been more than happy to help her shop for the perfect seduction outfit.

"So, do you intend on being my dessert, Hunter?"

She licked her lips and saw his gaze follow the movement of her tongue. "Your dessert?"

"Yes." Dropping his hands, he closed the distance separating them. "Do I need to go into details? What about a demonstration?"

She wished his eyes didn't captivate her, or that huge erection she couldn't help but notice didn't hold such promise. When he'd covered the distance separating them, he did so with the ease of a hunter stalking his prey. She had a mind to take a step back, but decided to stand her ground. "Neither is necessary, Tyson. Do you have a problem with what I'm wearing?"

A smile curved the corner of his lips. "No, I don't have a problem with it, as long as you know what it means."

"And what does it mean?"

A serious smile touched his lips. "A woman wears a dress like this to give a man a sign as to how the evening will end."

"I suggest you don't jump to conclusions. I merely decided to change into something more comfortable. But if my dress makes you uncomfortable then…"

"Doesn't bother me as long as you know I'll be trying like hell to get you out of it later."

"Do you always say whatever you want?"

"No need to play games when it comes to us. I told you my plans for you that first night. Now, let's enjoy dinner."

Hunter drew in a deep breath. Tyson Steele might think he had his own plan, but he would find out soon enough she also had hers.

As he led her over to the dining room table and pulled out a chair for her, she looked around. "You have a nice home, Tyson. It's pretty spacious for a condo. The architect in me likes the layout. I have a fondness for the open floor plan. Great for entertaining."

He shrugged. "I don't consider it as home. Since I

spend a lot of time at the hospital, I think of this as the place where I eat and sleep."

Hunter figured he could have said that this was the place where he ate, slept and had sex. She figured he had a revolving door to his bedroom.

She couldn't help noticing how nice he'd set the table. Fine china and silverware, cloth napkins and crystal glasses. "Pretty fancy for takeout."

He leaned close and stared into her eyes as he poured wine into her glass. "Thought I'd impress you."

"You have."

"Good. I'll be back with everything in a second."

Hunter didn't release the breath she'd been holding until he left to go into the kitchen.

Tyson decided not to question his luck tonight. Hunter could pretend indifference all she wanted, but there had to be a reason she'd worn that dress. She was a very sensual woman and tonight he was very much aware of her body, more so than ever in that outfit.

Gathering all the dishes, he left the kitchen to reenter the dining room and she glanced in his direction. "Need help?"

"No, I got this," he said, placing several platters and serving utensils in the middle of the table. He quickly returned to the kitchen to grab the bowl of tossed salad, the only thing he could actually claim he'd made. "I love Thai, and Latti's makes it just the way I like. Red roast duck on rice is my favorite. I think you'll enjoy it."

"I'm sure I will. It looks delicious."

"Then let's dig in," he said, taking the chair across from her.

"Umm, why don't you serve me?"

He glanced over at her. "Serve you?"

"Yes," she said, holding up her plate expectantly.

He held her gaze for a moment before picking up the serving spoon and proceeded to place several spoonfuls into her plate. What the hell was going on here? When did he serve women? He forced back his irritation and figured he would get his just reward later that night.

She took a forkful and moaned. Then she licked her lips.

Tyson felt a tightening in his groin as he watched her. He would serve her food again if she licked her lips like that one more time. It had him remembering the kisses they'd shared. Made him anticipate the ones he intended to share later.

"This is delicious, Tyson."

Why did her compliment make his chest expand? It's not like he'd cooked it himself. "Glad you think so."

For the next few minutes they ate in silence. Instead of using the quiet to his advantage to regroup and make sure he was back in control of his senses, he found himself becoming even more aware of her. Like that cute tiny mole just below her right ear. Why hadn't he noticed that before?

"I guess I really was starving."

Her words made him look at her plate. It was clean. Mercury swore that a woman who had a healthy appetite when it came to food also had a healthy appetite in the bedroom. Tyson never noticed a correlation, but tonight he was hoping there was one. "I guess you were. Want seconds?"

"Don't tempt me."

He didn't see why he shouldn't when she was definitely tempting him. It wouldn't take much to clear this table and proceed to spread her across it. "I won't tempt you. Would you like more wine?"

"Yes."

He could have poured the wine from where he sat but decided now was the time to make his move. He walked around the table to stand beside her and poured the wine into her glass. "I hope you left room for dessert."

She looked up at him and held his gaze. He could feel her need even if she was trying to downplay it. She wanted him as much as he wanted her. He knew the signs. He could see it in her eyes. Desire was lining her pupils, drenching her irises. The nipples of her breasts had formed into tight buds and were pressing against her dress. But the telltale sign was her feminine scent. The aroma was getting to him and he didn't want to play games if playing those games would delay things. He was ready to take things from the dining room straight into the bedroom.

He watched her tongue when she nervously licked her top lip. "I guess this is where we need to talk, Tyson."

Talk? The only talking they needed to do was pillow talk and that would come later. "What do we need to talk about?"

Instead of answering him, she picked up her glass and took a sip of her wine. She placed the glass back down and held his gaze once again. "About your misconception that if I sleep with you tonight it will because you seduced me into doing so."

He didn't see it as a misconception, but as a fact. "Do you have a problem with me seducing you, Hunter?"

She nodded. "Yes, I have a problem with it. I refuse to be just another one of your conquests."

Tyson hoped history wasn't repeating itself. If he

recalled, she'd said something similar eighteen years ago. Back then she wanted to be his one and only girl. Surely she wasn't asking for some sort of commitment from him, because if she was she wouldn't be getting it.

He hated to ask but really needed to know. "And just what do you want to be?"

"The one doing the seducing."

"Why?"

Hunter had expected Tyson's question. "I told you. Because I refuse to be another one of your conquests. That night at Notorious you stated you plan to seduce me. If we sleep together tonight, I don't want you to think you've succeeded. I want to set the record straight that if we share a bed it will be because it was my choice and not because you've done or said anything to persuade or entice me."

"So you want to play a mind game?" Tyson asked.

"No. I don't want to play any games. I just don't want you thinking that like all those other women, I fell under your spell. I can get up and walk out the door right now if that's what I choose to do. There's no way you can touch me, kiss me or talk to me that will make me change my mind unless it's something I want to do."

An arrogant smile touched his lips. "You think not?"

"I know not."

"You wouldn't be the first woman who thought so. But fine," he said, taking a step back. "If you want to seduce me, go right ahead. Don't expect me to resist. It will be a first."

Hunter lifted a brow. "No woman has ever seduced you before?"

"No. If a woman wants me and I'm not interested

in her, no amount of seduction on her part will make me change my mind. And if it's a woman I want, they usually fit into two categories. Those who are willing and those who aren't."

He paused a minute as if to make sure she was keeping up with his logic. "Now, if it's a willing woman then there's no need for seduction because getting together will be mutual."

"And if she's unwilling?" she asked.

An egotistical smile touched his lips. "Those are few, but any woman who resists my interest just needs a little coaxing. That's when my seduction comes into play. And just so you know, I'm an expert at it."

He was conceited enough to believe that, Hunter thought. She figured he classified her in the latter group, which was why he'd put his plan of seduction in place. "And you thought I needed coaxing?"

"Yes. But I can always move you to the willing category if it makes you feel better."

Hunter frowned. He just didn't get it. She wanted sleeping with him to be her choice and not his. She didn't want to be just another woman seduced by Tyson Steele. She stood and said, "I think I need to go. Dinner was great and—"

"Wait." He stared at her while he shoved his hands into the pockets of his jeans. "What's going on, Hunter? What is this about?"

"Nothing is going on. I've simply changed my mind about seducing you. I suggest you do the same."

"What are you afraid of, Hunter?"

She lifted her chin. "What makes you think I'm afraid of anything?"

"Because you're running."

He was right. She was running. "You want to seduce
me and I won't let you. I want to seduce you, but you
don't think I can. So what's the point?"

"I didn't say I didn't think you could seduce me. I
merely stated no woman ever felt the need to try because I've always picked the women I wanted." He
looked back at her, stared at her as if she was a puzzle
he was trying to figure out. Then he added, "I want you,
so it doesn't matter to me who seduces whom."

"It does to me."

"I see that and I'm trying to understand why."

She forced her gaze away from him and knew there
was no way she could explain it to him. All this was a
game to Tyson, a game he intended to win, and if he
seduced her then he would be winning. It was just like
with Carter. He'd played games with her for eight years.
She'd been a contestant with no chance of winning, not
even his heart. And God knows she'd tried. Well, those
days were over and now she flat-out refused to let any
man best her ever again.

But she couldn't possibly get Tyson to understand
her past. "It's too complicated to explain."

"Try me," he said, reaching out and touching her
arm.

She drew in a sharp breath at his touch. And held
it when he slowly caressed her skin, making tingles of
desire spread through her.

"And try this," he added, leaning forward and using
the tip of his tongue to lick her lips. "And I would just
love for you to try this," he whispered, deliberately
pressing his body closer to hers so that she could feel
his hard erection against the juncture of her thighs.

"You're trying to seduce me," she accused in a

breathless whisper and could feel herself getting weak in the knees. Resisting him in his domain would be harder than she thought.

"I'm showing you that we want each other, Hunter. The desire is mutual. You can arouse me just as much as I can arouse you. So why does it matter who's seducing whom?"

A part of Hunter knew it shouldn't but for her it did. "It matters to me, Tyson. I refuse to be seduced by you."

He paused a moment before releasing her and taking a step back. "Fine. Since it matters so much to you, then go ahead. Seduce the hell out of me."

Tyson wasn't sure what was going on with Hunter, but he figured it had something to do with her ex. She wouldn't be the first woman who'd brought baggage into his bedroom. And on more than one occasion he'd allowed them to do so knowing that after his first thrust into their body, whatever issues they were dealing with would take a backseat to the pleasures they would experience in his bed.

Hunter was being difficult and he didn't need a difficult woman. So why was he even putting up with it? And why, even now, did he want her more than he'd ever wanted any woman? He shook his head. Because she was the "one who got away." All it would take was one night of tumbling between the sheets with her to get her out of his system. Hell, he probably didn't need the entire night. A few hours should work just fine.

As he watched her gaze sweep him up and down, he knew she was aware of his arousal. He refused to waste this opportunity to get her into his bed. "Do it, Hunter," he whispered hoarsely. "Seduce me."

For the longest time they stared at each other and then she took a tentative step closer, reducing the distance between them. Standing on tiptoes, she slanted her mouth across his.

Holy hell, Tyson thought the moment she slid her tongue inside his mouth. At that moment he wasn't sure what was getting to him more—the way her tongue was overpowering his mouth, or the feel of her hardened nipples pressed against his chest. He thought he could just stand there and let her use his mouth to work out whatever issue she was dealing with. But he soon discovered his desire for Hunter went deeper than that.

There was no way he could ignore the erratic pounding of his heart or the insistent way his erection pressed against his zipper. He fought back a moan and then another, and when she shifted her body to meld it even closer to his, he wrapped his arms around her waist. She continued to take his mouth in a way that rocked him to his core. He'd kissed, and been kissed, by scores of women, but it wasn't just Hunter's kiss that had him weak in the knees. It was her taste. Her personal flavor had blood rushing fast and furious through his veins even as he shivered on the inside.

Then suddenly she broke off the kiss. "I want to finish this," she said in a raspy tone, licking her lips.

His gut clenched. He wanted to finish this, as well. Tyson was about to suggest they go into his bedroom when she began moving toward his living room. "Hey, my bedroom is this way," he said.

She looked over her shoulder. "Yours may be but mine is not."

He frowned, wondering what the hell she was talking about. He got even more confused when she grabbed her purse off his sofa. She turned around and said, "I can't share a bed with you here."

"What?" he asked, mystified.

She placed the strap of her purse on her shoulder. "I can't share the bed that others have shared with you."

He stared at her and saw the seriousness in the dark eyes staring back at him. "Why?"

"This is my plan of seduction and I want to finish it at my place. In my own bed. Not one you've shared with a zillion others."

No other woman had ever made such a bold request. He would not have allowed it. So why was he allowing it now? And why was she concerned with how many women had slept in his bed? It was *his* bed and he claimed all rights to it. And for her information, not all his conquests had been brought back here. He'd taken a few to a hotel. But, he admitted only to himself, he rarely went to a woman's home. Very rarely.

Tyson knew men handled things differently when it came to having sex with women. Some didn't invite women to their home, saying it felt like the woman was invading their personal space. Galen and his cousin Donovan Steele from Charlotte had both had the same mind-set in their bachelor days. Tyson never had a problem with it because any woman that he had sex with here knew not to return without an invitation.

"I'm leaving." Hunter turned and headed for the door.

He stared as she walked away, not missing that backside he'd made plans to ride and those gorgeous legs he'd intended to slide between. What in the hell had gone wrong? One part of him wanted to think her leaving was for the best because she certainly thought a lot of herself if she assumed she could call the shots. But another part, the one determined to have sex with her regardless of whose bed he did it in, overruled his common sense, and so he asked, "What's your address?"

She rattled it off over her shoulder. When she reached his door she turned around. "I'll be waiting, Tyson."

"You won't be waiting long." He barely got the words out before she opened the door and closed it shut behind her.

Without even thinking about the craziness of what he was doing, Tyson rushed into his bedroom, grabbed an overnight bag and quickly began throwing items into it. She hadn't said anything about him being an overnight guest, but she would soon find out that he had a few conditions of his own.

Before zipping up the overnight bag he opened the drawer to his nightstand, reached inside and grabbed a handful of condoms. He was about to close the drawer, but then stopped and grabbed some more. Hell, for this little inconvenience, he intended to make tonight worth his while.

Chapter 8

Hunter glanced around her bedroom. Several candles were lit and the fragrance of vanilla floated in the air. She had changed the linens and sprayed vanilla mist over the sheets and pillows for an extra touch.

How many times had she envisioned setting up a bedroom room like this for Carter only to have him make fun of her attempt? That was after he'd accused her of trying to burn the house down with the candles and spraying stuff that he was probably allergic to. Her ex hadn't had a romantic bone in his body. Even during those times when they were trying to have a baby, he refused to let her turn their drab-looking bedroom into a romantic hot spot.

Now she had her hot spot. It was an important component in her plan of seduction. She didn't intend to start bed-hopping with men, by any means, but hopefully after this one time with Tyson, she would have the courage to at least date other men and see where it led.

She had no desire to ever get married again, nor was she interested in engaging in a serious relationship. Occasional dating would suit her just fine. If she liked the man well enough, she saw no reason why they couldn't share an intimate night once in a while. Granted, she had to feel the man was worthy of sharing her bed.

Then what was up with Tyson Steele? Was he worthy?

She wasn't sure about that, but he did know the right buttons to push to arouse her. And there was that element of sexual chemistry between them. So he might as well be her first test. Mo was right. If she was going to declare her sexual independence then it might as well be with Tyson.

At that moment the doorbell sounded. If that was Tyson, he'd arrived sooner than she'd anticipated. She figured he would at least take some time to mull over her offer. Since it appeared that he hadn't, she took it as a strong indication of just how eager he was to have sex with her.

They would have this one night together. In the end she would declare her sexual independence as well as get him out of her system. And if what everyone claimed was true, she would experience her first orgasm in years. Hopefully the dreams would stop coming and she could get a good night's sleep without waking up the next day with an ache between her legs.

Leaving her bedroom, she headed for the door. Halfway there she paused to draw in a deep breath. There was no need to get cold feet now, she told herself. Although she and Tyson might have different ideas regarding how to go about getting what they wanted, she was certain they wanted the same thing. This was not the time to question her decision to seduce him. It would be a win-win situation for the both of them, she reminded herself. Tyson could then move on to the next woman and she could concentrate on building her company.

Hunter opened her front door and he stood there. She could only stare at him, taking in all six feet and more of him. Tyson had a way of making any woman's body snap to salacious attention whenever she saw him. Already the tips of her breasts were responding to his masculine form. Sexual hunger, the likes of which she experienced only in his company, was taking a greedy hold on her.

She saw his overnight bag. Did he honestly assume she would invite him to stay the night? If so, he would be sorely disappointed later when showed him the door. She moved aside. "It didn't take you long to get—"

That was as far as she got. Once inside, he shut the door, dropped the overnight bag to the floor and pulled her into his arms, slanting his mouth across hers.

Tyson hadn't meant to kiss her. This was her show and he'd intended to let her play it out however she chose. He had every intention of just being a willing participant. But when she'd opened that door and he'd gotten a glimpse of that dress again, he couldn't resist pulling her into his arms and kissing her like he'd wanted to do at his place but hadn't gotten the chance. Now he was getting his fill of her taste.

At least she hadn't tried breaking free of his kiss. In fact she was kissing him back with a hunger that nearly matched his own. He loved the way their tongues

mated, how hers mingled with his. His heart was racing. He tried to recall the last time a woman did that to
him, but couldn't.

Tyson was fully aware that being here with her was
overriding common sense and overlooking good sound
judgment. He knew better, yet he was refusing to heed
those warnings that went off in his head on the drive
over here. He had called himself all kinds of fool for
chasing after a woman for a one-night stand.

He would deal with the craziness of that later, once
he'd gotten her out of his system. But for now all he
could do was accept that there was something about
Hunter McKay that had him wanting sex, sex and more
sex. But only with her.

Moments later, just like he'd been the one to initi-
ate the kiss, he was the one to end it, drawing in a deep
delicious breath that included a whiff of her scent. But
he was in no hurry to release her. Instead he held her in
his arms while he pressed a series of kisses around the
curve of her mouth and the tip of her nose. Knowing if
he didn't stop touching her now that he never would,
he released her and took a step back. The separation
almost killed him.

He looked over at her and saw her looking at him.
A part of him wanted to read her thoughts, but he figured it was probably best if he didn't know them. She
didn't seem upset or annoyed, just somewhat pensive.
He'd learned a woman absorbed in her own thoughts
was the worst kind because he had no idea what they
were thinking...or planning.

Finally, she spoke. "Now that you've gotten that out
of your system, will you let me be in charge from here
on out?"

Was her assumption true? Had he gotten anything out of his system? He seriously doubted it. Instead of sharing that doubt with her, he shoved his hands into the pockets of his jeans. It was either that or pull her back into his arms.

Forcing that thought from his mind, he dwelled on what she'd asked him. She wanted him to relinquish his control to a woman. To her. Under normal circumstances he would never agree to something like that. But he'd reached the conclusion while racing from his condo to here that nothing about any of this was normal.

"So, Tyson, are you going to let me handle things or not?" she asked again when he evidently hadn't responded quickly enough.

She'd asked him to let her handle *things*. As far as he was concerned, *things* didn't necessarily include him, but he wouldn't tell her that just yet. He was curious to see what she had up her sleeves. If truth be told, sleeves be damned. What he was really interested in was what was up under her dress.

"I suppose I can let you handle things," he finally said.

She raised a brow. "You 'suppose'? Need I remind you that the moment you walked through that door you entered my territory? You came to me."

He frowned. Did she have to rub it in? "And we both know why," he said. "So why are we still talking?"

She smiled calmly. "You're trying my patience."

He chuckled. "And you've been trying mine since that night we ran into each other at Notorious."

"Would you like to sit and talk a while?"

"No. I have nothing to say and that's not why I'm here."

"I know why you're here, but first I think we need to understand each other," she said.

"Meaning?"

"For starters, I don't know what's up with that bag. Since you aren't a doctor who makes house calls, I can only assume you think you're spending the night. Well, you aren't. You will leave when we're done."

When they were done? Did she assume they would only go one round? He intended to stay the night and take her again and again, well into the morning hours.

"We can discuss that later, Hunter." He figured after he had her once, she'd beg him for more.

"No, I think we need to discuss it now."

He simply stared at her for a moment and then nodded. "Fine. I'll go along with whatever you want," he said, telling her what she wanted to hear. Evidently he'd said the magic words, if the smile that spread across her lips was anything to go by. "I guess I just made your day," he said drily.

"Yes, and I plan to make your night, Tyson Steele."

Hunter felt in control and she intended to use it to her advantage. She'd never done anything like this before, but she was ready to set the stage for what she had in store for Tyson.

"Go sit on the sofa, Tyson, and get comfortable. Make yourself at home."

A smile touched the corners of his mouth. "At home I tend to walk around in the nude. Can I do it here?"

"No." The thought of him doing such a thing made her nipples harden even more. "Would you like something to drink?"

He shook his head as he moved toward her sofa. "I had wine at dinner. I'm good."

Hunter watched how he eased his body down on her sofa, and how the denim jeans stretched across his muscled thighs. She couldn't wait to actually see those thighs in the flesh. In her dreams she had kneeled between them and—

"Nice place."

She hoped he hadn't noticed the splash of color that had appeared on her cheeks, a result of where her thoughts had been. "Thanks. Not as roomy as yours but it suits me just fine."

He stretched his arms across the back of her sofa as he leaned back in a comfortable position. Doing so brought emphasis to his chest. She looked forward to removing his shirt and was itching to rub her hand against his hard chest and flat stomach. Then she would ease her hands lower to cup him, to feel the part of him that had played a vital role in her dreams.

She could feel more heat in her cheeks. For a woman who hadn't been sexually active in four years, and who hadn't even thought much about it, her mind was having a field day.

Deciding to set the mood, she flicked off the ceiling lights so the living room could be bathed in the soft glow of the two floor lamps. She glanced over and saw him watching her, and desire rippled down her spine. She joined him on the sofa, sitting beside him but not too close. She found the distance really didn't matter. Nothing could eliminate the manly heat emanating from him. Because of it, her skin felt noticeably warm through her dress.

"So, Tyson, how was your day?" She decided a neutral topic was a perfect way to break the ice. But with all the heat surrounding them she knew anything cool didn't have much chance of survival.

A slow, sexy smile spread across his lips. "I don't recall most of it. I slept for the past forty-eight hours, remember."

"Yes. You did mention that."

"Now I'm wide-awake, full of energy and horny as hell."

The man knew just the right words to say to make every hormone in her body sizzle. "Are you?"

"Yes."

"Sleep makes you horny?" She glanced down at his thighs and saw the huge erection bulging between them, pressing against his zipper.

"Only when you occupy my dreams."

His words surprised her and she glanced up and stared into his face. Had he been dreaming about her like she'd been doing of him? "And what were we doing in your dreams?" she asked, as if she really didn't know. It made sense that when a man like Tyson had dreams they would be nothing but erotic.

"We were making love."

She arched a brow. "For forty-eight hours?"

He chuckled softly, as if remembering. "Yes. We had a lot of ground to cover. A lot of years to make up for. A lot of positions to try."

Imagining a few of those positions had her pulse pounding. "Did we?"

He gave her a sensuous grin. "Yes, we did."

Hunter released a heated breath as his words painted an erotic picture in her mind, making shivers rush up her spine. She held his gaze, felt the stimulating attraction between them. Her face lowered again to the area between his thighs. Was she imagining it or had his erection gotten larger? Thicker? Harder?

She glanced back up at him and saw his smile had widened, as if he'd read her thoughts. But there was no way he could have, she assured herself. He was holding her gaze and sensations began pricking her skin. She didn't have to wonder what the look in his eyes meant.

"Now I know your secret weapon for seduction, Tyson," she said.

"I didn't know I had one."

"You do."

"Then tell me what it is," he said and she didn't miss how he'd spread his legs so his thigh brushed her thigh, which wasn't covered by her short dress. The contact was stimulating and she was tempted to close her eyes and moan.

"It's your eyes," she said, staring into them. "You can literally seduce a woman without opening your mouth. All you have to do is level those green eyes on her."

"You think so?"

"Aren't you trying to seduce me?"

"No. We agreed that you would seduce me. The look you see in my eyes is nothing more than an indication of just how much I want you."

If he thought his words were getting to her, then he was right. Maybe it was time she let a few of hers get next to him.

"I've turned my bedroom into a romantic hot spot just for tonight," she said softly.

She saw the desire in his eyes deepen. "Did you?"

"Yes. I think you'll like it."

"A long as you're in there with me, there's no doubt that I will."

Hunter drew in a deep breath. "It's the first time I've ever done that." She wondered why she felt the need to mention that.

"Lucky me."

Yes, lucky you, she thought. The husky tone of his voice had her easing a little closer to him. It felt like the natural thing to do. And then she reached out and placed her hand on his thigh. Doing that felt natural, as well. The muscles in his thigh tightened beneath her fingers and she heard his sharp intake of breath. She couldn't help but be pleased with his response.

"What if I told you that I've dreamed of you, as well, Tyson?" she whispered close to his ear. He smelled good. He smelled like a man.

"Would you like to compare notes?"

His question made hot and sharp desire claw at her. Comparing notes with him *would* be interesting. "That's not necessary. I have a few good ideas of my own."

"I was hoping you did."

Considering that this was Tyson Steele, who went through women quicker than he changed his socks, Hunter wondered if what she had planned would suffice. She was a novice and he was so damn experienced. But he had agreed to let her handle things and she would, in her own way.

She felt in control. Bold. Daring. And she intended to play out her fantasies. Who said only men were allowed to have them? There were a few she hadn't shared with anyone, not even Mo or Kat. She had tried sharing them with Carter, only to get laughed at. She had a feeling Tyson wouldn't find any of them amusing. Her heart skipped a beat at the thought that with this bad boy of Phoenix she could be a bad girl. Besides, it was only for one night.

Hunter slid her hand closer to his crotch, and as she slowly stroked him there, she heard his breath hitch.

When her nerve endings began feeling somewhat edgy and the area between her legs began tingling, she decided there was no reason to waste any more time. She stood up. "Umm, it's hot in here. I think I'm wearing too many clothes."

And then, while he watched, she began removing them.

Chapter 9

Tyson leaned forward in his seat, resting his forearms on his thighs and not taking his eyes off Hunter. If a strip show was part of her seduction then she could seduce him anytime or anyplace…including here, the place she called home. His objection to spending the night in her bed instead of his own lost some of its punch. The main thing on his mind right now was seeing her naked body. The body he had dreamed about every single night since their paths had crossed.

She had kicked off those killer heels and the first thing he noticed was that her toenails were painted a fiery red. He thought she had pretty feet. Sexy feet. Tyson had never been a toe kisser, but had to admit that seeing hers was giving him some new ideas.

And then she went for her dress, that very short dress, and began easing it down those gorgeous legs.

Slowly she exposed a black lace bra and then matching panties. Seeing Hunter stand before him in just her bra and panties, he felt a slow, sensuous stirring in the pit of his stomach that made his erection even harder.

And when she reached up and released the front clasp to her bra, he almost tumbled off the sofa. Her breasts weren't just beautiful. They were absolutely, positively perfect. The nipples were dark and already hard. His tongue moved around in his mouth, in anticipation of licking them. Just staring at the twin globes made him eager for the feel of them in his hands and pressed against his bare chest.

She had a small waist and a flat stomach, and her thighs were a lover's dream. So perfect, he could imagine his body being cradled inside them.

His gaze was drawn to her fingers as she placed them beneath the waistband of her panties. From their slight tremor, it appeared she was getting somewhat nervous as a result of his intense gaze. But it couldn't be helped. He didn't intend on missing a thing. His brothers were either breast or leg men, and although he appreciated both, he was a vagina man all the way. As far as he was concerned there was no part of a woman's body that he found more fascinating than her V. So, he couldn't help it when his gaze lowered to her center in anticipation.

"I see I have your attention, Tyson," she said in a husky breath.

"You had my attention the moment you stood up, Hunter."

"Did I?"

"I wouldn't lie to you."

He wondered if the pose she was standing in—her legs braced apart and her fingers tucked into the flimsy lace material—was deliberate on her part to make him crave her even more. "After I remove my panties it will be your turn to take everything off," she declared huskily.

"It will be my pleasure."

"No, Tyson. I'm going to make sure it's *my* pleasure."

He didn't have a problem with that because he knew any pleasures that came under this roof tonight would be shared by the both of them. Tyson shifted his body somewhat to ease some of the hardness behind the zipper of his jeans, as well as to get a closer eye view of the part of her she was about to unveil. She paused a minute and held his gaze. She had to know what she was doing. All this stalling was nothing short of pure torture for him.

"You're panting, Tyson."

Was he? It wouldn't surprise him if he was.

"I'm certain you've seen this part of a woman many times," she said in a sultry tone. "And I'm also sure if you've seen one you've seen them all."

Hardly, Tyson thought, trying to retain his sanity. He had seen this part of a woman many times, but it would be his first time seeing hers and for some reason the thought had him aching. What in the hell was this woman doing to him? Never in his life had he been this desperate to see a woman totally naked.

"Since you seem to have such a high degree of interest in this, would you like to finish undressing me?" she asked him.

He swallowed a deep lump in his throat. "You trust me to do that?" he asked.

She chuckled. "It's just a pair of panties, Tyson. All you have to do is take them off me. Besides, you're here on my turf, so no matter what happens from here on out, it's still my seduction and not yours."

Why she had a problem with getting seduced, he still wasn't sure. But at the moment, he didn't care. He had a feeling that tonight would be a night that he wouldn't forget in a long time. He intended to make it so.

"Well?"

"I'd love to." Tyson eased from the sofa to stand in front of her for a second, before kneeling down on his knees. He was now on eye level with the one part of her that he wanted most. His erection throbbed, begging for release. She was sexy as hell and the man in him appreciated everything about her…especially this.

Tyson leaned forward and pressed his face against the lace. He couldn't resist nuzzling her while drawing in deep breaths, needing to absorb her intimate fragrance through his nostrils.

"What are you doing?" she asked him in a choppy voice.

"Inhaling your scent." He figured that Hunter could pretend indifference all she wanted, but this intimate act had to be doing something to her. "I love your personal fragrance, Hunter." *Maybe too much*, he thought, but pushed that reflection to the back of his mind.

"Do you?"

"Can't you tell?" Leaning back on his haunches he slowly began easing the lace panties down her legs, exposing what had to be the most beautiful V any woman could possess. She was wrong. When you saw one you hadn't seen them all. He was convinced that just like a fingerprint, a woman's feminine mound, the very essence of her being, was an exclusive part of her.

And this was hers. It belonged to Hunter McKay and

it was beautiful in all its natural setting. Some men were big on the shaved or waxed look, but he wasn't one of them. This was his preference.

When she stepped out of her panties and kicked them aside, he reached up and began caressing her thighs, loving the feel of her soft skin beneath his fingertips. Then he began stroking her stomach, thinking that even her belly button was beautiful. His tongue itched to lick her, but instead he used his index finger to draw circles around her V a few times before running his fingers through the beautiful curls covering it.

"Tyson…"

His name was spoken from her lips in a sensuous whisper. He lifted his head and met her gaze. He saw all the heat flaring in the dark depths staring back at him and understood the feeling. He was there, close to the edge, right along with her. "Yes?" he answered huskily, while his fingers continued to stroke between her legs. She was wet…just the way he liked.

"I—I need f-for you to take off your clothes," she said, barely getting the words out.

He figured that might be her need, but his tongue had a different need right now. "Can I get a lick first?"

The heat he saw in her eyes flared and his fingers could feel her get wetter. "Just one?" she asked, holding tight to his gaze.

"Possibly two. Maybe three. I'll admit that I'm one greedy ass."

Color had come into her cheeks so he could only assume her ex either hadn't gone down on her too often, or not at all. What a damn shame. Well, he intended to make up for it.

"In that case," she finally said, "help yourself."

Filled with a need he didn't understand but one he was driven to accept, Tyson spread her thighs apart and used his fingers to open her before dipping his head. The moment his tongue captured her clit he moaned deep in his throat the same time she did. He licked once, twice, three times. And when he couldn't get enough her of delicious taste, he locked his mouth to her, held tight to her thighs and drove his tongue inside her as far as it could go. She'd told him to help himself, and he intended to do just that.

The Tyson Steele way.

Hunter felt her world spinning. Weak from the feel of Tyson's tongue thrusting deep inside her, she reached out to grab hold of his shoulders for support. Nothing, and she meant nothing, could have prepared her for what she was feeling. She had no idea that something like this could bring her so much pleasure. Oral sex was something Carter had frowned upon. More than once he'd said that a man's mouth was not meant to go between a woman's legs, and he claimed most men felt that way.

Evidently Tyson had a totally different opinion about that, judging by the way he was working his tongue inside her. The man was a master at this, an undisputed pro. She arched her back to give him further access as every nerve ending in her body threatened to explode. She'd told Mo and Kat that she hadn't had an orgasm in so long she'd forgotten how it felt to have one. Tyson was rekindling her memory in one salacious way. If he didn't release her soon, she'd climax right in his mouth.

She tightened her grip on his shoulders and in a ragged voice said, "You got to stop, Tyson. I'm about to—"

Too late. She screamed at the same time spasms

speared her body, detonating in an explosive orgasm and nearly shattering her to pieces. Instead of removing his mouth, Tyson drove his tongue even deeper inside her. The lusty sounds he made pushed her over the edge again. And he still wouldn't release her.

When the last of the spasms had left her body, he freed his mouth from her and eased back on his haunches to look up at her. She moaned at the sight of him licking his lips.

He eased to his feet and said, "Now I get to take off my clothes."

Tyson couldn't resist licking his lips again. Hunter's taste was simply incredible. He was convinced it was the most delicious flavor he'd ever tasted. He figured her taste was imprinted on his tongue and would remain there forever.

Forever. He went still. Surely he didn't think that. Forever was something he could never equate with any woman. All he was feeling at the moment was some exceptional brand of passion, one so remarkable it had temporarily affected his brain cells.

The only other excuse he could come up with to explain such crazy thoughts was that he'd relinquished control to her just by showing up here. He had allowed her to seduce him and wasn't sure doing so had been the right thing. It had been seduction this time, but what if she tried making him beg for it the next? Tyson inwardly cringed at the thought and knew giving her any type of empowerment again wouldn't be happening. He had a mind to leave right now. Walk out the door and not look back.

But there was no way he could do that. He wanted

her way too much and didn't plan to go anywhere. So much for taking the upper hand and putting things in perspective, he thought. But then he looked at it in another way. It was about getting Hunter out of his system and getting from her what she had refused him eighteen years ago. After tonight she would be out of sight and out of mind.

He glanced over at her, saw her studying his mouth as if she couldn't believe what he'd just used it for. *Believe it*, he wanted to say. *In fact, I plan on using it again the same way before the night is over.*

Moments later her gaze shifted from his mouth to his eyes. She looked at him with an intensity that he felt in every part of his body. She'd accused him of using his eyes to seduce her, but whether she knew it or not, at that moment she was using hers to render him totally helpless. He felt a degree of passion he'd never felt before.

The chemistry surrounding them had heightened. He was aroused to a level that at any other time—and with any other woman—he would have considered unnerving. The fact that she was standing a few feet away from him completely naked, and that he'd just gotten a damn good taste of her, had to be the reason his erection was throbbing mercilessly behind his zipper.

Breaking eye contact, Tyson eased down on the sofa to remove his shoes and socks. He then stood and his hand went to the waistband of his pants—he knew she was watching his every move.

He unsnapped his jeans, began lowering the zipper and slowly slid the jeans down his legs before stepping out of them. He had stripped down to his briefs and

could feel her gaze roaming over him. His body became more heated.

Tyson was tempted to return the favor and asked
if she wanted to remove his last stitch of clothing, but
couldn't. If she was to touch him, he would tumble her
to the floor and take her then and there. So he slowly
eased his briefs down his legs, noting how her eyes
widened.

"You're huge," she gasped with wonder in her voice.

His lips curved in what he knew was an arrogant
smile. "You're handling things and you can handle this,"
he assured her. "Trust me."

Hunter stared at Tyson, finding it difficult to breathe.
He was standing barely three feet away, naked as the
day he was born and proudly displaying an erection so
huge she figured it would put every other man to shame.
Her stomach began quivering just from looking at it.
The thought of it inside her filled her with a need she'd
never felt before.

But that wasn't the only part of him she found impressive. Tyson Steele was beautiful from the top of his
head to the soles of his feet. The man was built. Perfectly. All muscle and not an ounce of fat anywhere. He
was a true work of art with firm thighs, strong masculine legs, a muscular chest and broad shoulders. At
some point before the night was over, she intended to
make it her business to lick every inch of him.

The very thought of doing that caused a slow stirring to erupt in the pit of her stomach. When had she
become this sensuous being who suddenly needed sex
like she need to take another breath? And why had it
taken Tyson to make her feel this way?

Her gaze met his and she was captured by the intensity of his green eyes. He moved to retrieve something from his overnight bag and she saw it was a condom packet. As he walked back to her, his stride was slow, masculine and sexy as hell. Just watching his approach made her weak in the knees. When he came to a stop directly in front of her, he shifted his gaze from her eyes to her chest. Specifically her breasts. Her nipples automatically hardened to tight buds.

Without saying a word he lowered his mouth and took a nipple between his lips. She couldn't do anything but moan at the sensations that suddenly rammed through her. The sounds he was making while feasting on her conveyed his enjoyment, and she reached out and placed her hands on both sides of his head to hold him there. Yes, right there.

A while later he released one nipple and immediately sought out the other, and she let out another deep moan. He'd already made her come twice from his mouth between her legs and now he threatened to make her explode a third time just from having her breast in his mouth.

"Tyson, w-we need to get t-to the bedroom," she said in a heated breath, while fighting to hold back yet another moan.

Before she could take her next breath, he swept her off her feet and into his arms. "Tell me where, so I can take you there."

Chapter 10

Tyson placed Hunter on the bed then took a step back, letting his gaze roam over her from head to toe. He doubted he'd ever seen a more perfect woman. Every inch of her was flawless. He'd taken a good look at her while she'd been standing naked in her living room. But there was just something about a woman stretched out in bed, waiting to be taken, that did something to him every time.

Especially with this woman.

His gaze moved around the room. She had referred to it as a romantic hot spot and he could see why. There were candles and throw pillows situated around the room, wineglasses, a bottle of wine chilling in an ice bucket and a tray of different cheeses on a small table near the bed. Soft music was playing and the bedcovers were turned back. The ambiance was one of romance and at that moment he was looking forward to a night of passion with her.

"This room looks wonderful, Hunter. You did a great job setting the mood."

"Did I?"

He heard the surprise in her tone and glanced at her. That's when he saw the brilliance of her smile and knew his compliment had pleased her greatly. That made him wonder. Had she done a similar setup for that ass she'd been married to and the man hadn't appreciated her effort?

"Yes, you did," he assured her. "You know how to take seduction to one hell of an amazing level. Hunter McKay, you can seduce me anytime." And at that moment, he truly meant it.

He appreciated that she still lay on top of the covers, where he'd placed her, and hadn't gotten beneath them. His gaze roamed all over every inch of her body. He would enjoy making love to her, touching her, licking her all over, tasting her again, and was driven by a desire to savor every minute of doing so. Just looking at her, thinking of everything he intended to do to her and how he would do it, made his erection harder.

But first he needed to prepare himself for her. While she watched, he sheathed himself with a condom. "You just brought one?" she asked him.

He glanced up at her and smiled. "No. I brought a few." He figured it was best not to admit to having an overnight bag full. He didn't want to scare her.

Then he moved forward. He kneeled on the bed and slowly crawled toward her. He remembered that first night at Notorious, when he'd decided he would be the hunter and she his prey. Now he wasn't sure which one of them had truly been captured.

He went straight for her mouth, needing to kiss her.

The kiss was meant to arouse her, but when she began responding, he was the one getting even more aroused. Their tongues mingled, tangled madly, mated hotly, and his hands began to move, cupping those same breasts he'd sucked on earlier, loving how they fit in his hands.

Moments later he released her mouth and his lips trailed a path down to her breasts, needing to taste them again. The nipples were hard and ready for his mouth and he devoured them with a greed he only had for her.

Not able to hold off any longer, he tore his mouth away from her breasts to move up over her body. He glanced down at her. She looked beautiful, the glow from the candles dancing across her features.

He braced himself on his elbows as he continued to stare down at her. And then he sucked in a deep breath when she deliberately pushed up her breasts to rub them against his chest, as if doing so had been her fantasy. The feel of her hard nipples brushing against his chest did something to him. From the look on her face it was doing something to her as well.

"You like that?" he asked her.

"Yes. What about you?"

He didn't have to think about his answer. The feel of her nipples teasing the hair on his chest felt damn good. "Yes, I like it. Umm, what do you think of this?"

He reached down and widened her legs before lowering his body to settle his chest between them. And then he began deliberately moving his body to stroke his chest hair against the curls covering her V. He could tell from the look in her eyes that she found what he was doing stimulating.

"I like this," she said in a breathless tone.

"So do I," he said, feeling her dampen his chest.

"Now for the main attraction." He eased his body back up until his erection touched the entrance to her body.

He glanced down at her and smiled. "You seduced the hell out of me tonight, Hunter. I liked it."

And with that, he thrust into her.

Hunter moaned at the feel of Tyson filling her so completely. She could actually feel his erection get harder while sliding deep inside her. He began moving, going in and then withdrawing, establishing a sensuous rhythm that had her alternating between clawing his back and gripping the bedspread. His hips and thighs jackhammered with lightning speed and when she let out one moan, she was already working on the other.

Had four years of abstinence done this to her? Make her body hungry? Greedy? Needy? She knew deep down that the length of time she'd gone without sex had nothing to do with it. It was Tyson and what he was doing to her. How he was making her feel. Whoever started the rumor that a woman hadn't truly been made love to unless it was by a Steele knew exactly what she was talking about.

Being here with Tyson was what true lovemaking was all about. The giving and sharing of pleasure was so profound she could feel it in her bones. Neither was dominant over the other; rather, they were equals. She couldn't help but let herself go and was caught up in the pounding of his body into hers.

When he threw his head back and let out a voracious growl it seemed the cords in his neck would pop. As if on cue her body detonated with his and sparks of passion began flying everywhere, igniting inside her a maelstrom of need that only Tyson could satisfy.

He bucked and then plunged downward at the same time her hips automatically lifted to receive him. He went deeper than before and she could feel every inch of him inside her.

She screamed at the same time he shouted her name while thrusting into her several more times as if he couldn't get enough. She held him tight and continued to move her body with his when she felt another delicious shiver race down her spine. And then she was screaming again, and from the way he was thrusting into her body she knew he'd had another orgasm, as well.

"Hunter..."

He said her name moments before collapsing onto her. A short while later he held up his head, eased up toward her lips and without saying anything, he kissed her again, this time with a tenderness that had a thick lump forming in her throat.

When he released her mouth she smiled up at him and he smiled back. Her heart began fluttering deep in her chest at the realization that she was the one responsible for his smile.

Hours later, Tyson eased his body off Hunter to lie beside her, flat on his back. Seeing that she had dozed off to sleep, he let out a whoosh of heated breath. How many rounds had this been so far? Five?

The two of them were mating like damn rabbits, and he still hadn't gotten enough of her. Every part of his body was sizzling for more. In the bedroom Hunter had been one of the most giving and one of the most passionate of any women he'd ever slept with, and considering his history with women that said a lot. She had totally overwhelmed him and no woman should have the ability to do that.

He would have frowned at the thought, but he couldn't help but smile as he recalled the look on her face when, after their first time, he'd dumped a handful of condoms on the table by the bed. He'd told her there was plenty more where those came from, and her eyes had gotten as big as saucers and her mouth had dropped open. "Do you really expect to use all of them?" she'd asked. Well, it was a moot point now, he thought as he looked at the handful of empty packages.

They had worked up an appetite after round three and sat naked in bed while drinking wine and eating an assortment of cheeses. They used that time to talk. He brought her up-to-date on former classmates and what they were doing now. He told her about his brother Jonas and his marriage to Nikki, Eli's marriage to Stacey and how his parents had stepped into the role of grandparents to Galen's twins with ease.

In turn, she told him about this house she'd designed a few years ago for a well-known NBA player, and how she'd taken a Mediterranean cruise last year with some college friends. He'd noted she hadn't brought up anything about her ex and he was glad she hadn't.

Afterward, they had made love a couple more times and each had been just as intense and passionate as the other times had been. He discovered there was more passion in Hunter's pinky finger than some women had in their entire bodies. He loved the way she responded to his kisses, his touch and even the naughty, explicit words he would whisper in her ear to let her know just what he intended to do to her and how.

Jeez. When had he wanted a woman so badly, that

even now he felt a surge of hot energy consume his groin? Just thinking about her, he was hard and longed to slide his erection back inside her to start round six. But he refused to wake her up. She needed her rest.

And, dammit, he needed to think.

Now was the time for logic to set in. Instead of waiting for her to wake up so he could make love to her again, he should be putting on his clothes and hauling ass, not caring if their paths ever crossed again. But logic wasn't working in his favor tonight. He didn't want to put on his clothes, and leaving was the last thing on his mind.

Why?

The question echoed in his head in the quiet room. He had gotten what she'd refused to give him eighteen years ago and he should be feeling like a score had been settled. The one who'd gotten away was now had. So why wasn't he pounding his chest with his fist, proud of himself, pleased with the way the night had turned out? Oh, he was pleased with the way the night had turned out, but it had nothing to do with him settling an old score. Far from it.

For the first time in his life he had truly enjoyed making love to a woman—every single aspect of it. The touching, tasting and thrusting had been off the charts. Mind-boggling. Super awesome. And the Mark of Tyson wasn't just on her neck, but was probably on every single part of her body. But he didn't see the mark as a sign of conquest. In his mind it had become a sign of possession.

Possession? Tyson rubbed his hand down his face as he tried to figure out how in the hell he could fix his mind to even think that way. He was a die-hard bachelor who enjoyed too many women to get hung up on just one. So there had to be a reason why he was having these possessive feelings toward Hunter.

One reason could be that for the first time in his life a woman had been a challenge. That had to be it. Other women made things easy for him, and the novelty of Hunter giving him a hard time had him thinking crazy thoughts. All it would take to clear his mind would be a few more rounds of sex with her to be assured that she was out of his system. A good night's sleep in her bed wouldn't hurt, either. When he woke up in the morning there was no doubt in his mind he would be thinking straight. When he left here it would be business as usual.

But still…

For some reason he was driven to mentally replay every single thing that had happened to him since running into Hunter more than two weeks ago. One thing stood out: he hadn't slept with another woman since then. Given his track record, that was odd. No, it was downright strange. He'd gotten plenty of calls, even one from that cute little ER nurse who was helping out temporarily in Cardio. Her name was Macy Phillips and she was on his "to do" list. So why hadn't he done her? What was he waiting for? She was definitely willing. And what about Kristen Fulbright, Nancy Heartwood and Candace Lane? Why had he begun thinking of them as history?

Hunter stirred beside him in bed and he glanced over at her just as her eyes flitted open. At that moment he thought the same thing that he had when he'd seen her that night in Notorious. She was beautiful. She stared back at him with a sleepy look in her eyes. For a minute it was as if she was trying to recall why he was in her bed.

"Do I need to remind you?" he asked, seeing her dilemma and leaning over to kiss her on the lips.

She drew in a deep breath and shook her head. "No, I remember now. What time is it?" she asked as she yawned and pulled herself up in bed. The sheet covering her breast slid down and she quickly jerked it back up. *Seriously, Hunter, don't get all modest on me now when last night those nipples had seemed like a permanent fixture in my mouth.*

Instead of calling her out on it, he glanced over at the digital clock on her nightstand. "It's three in the morning."

She yawned again. "Sorry, I passed out on you."

"That's fine. You definitely needed your rest." He saw the color that flashed across her cheeks. "You're embarrassed?"

She shrugged. "Shouldn't I be? I screamed around ten times tonight. I can just imagine what my neighbors think."

"It was twelve."

She lifted a brow. "Excuse me?"

"You screamed twelve times. Not ten. And your neighbors probably thought you were having a hell of a good time and wished it was them."

The color in her cheeks deepened. "Yes, well, I was having a good time. But all good things must come to an end, including your visit to my bed."

Tyson frowned. "You're kicking me out?"

"I told you that you weren't spending the night."

Yes, she had. "But that was before the twelve screams."

She actually had the gall to look confused. "What does that have to do with anything?"

Tyson figured if she had to ask then maybe he needed

to make sure she screamed twelve more times. She had seduced him earlier, so maybe it was his time to seduce her. Instead of answering her question, he asked one of his own. "Do I get a kiss for the road, since this will be our last time together like this?"

She seemed to ponder his question for a second and then nodded. "Sure. Why not? Kiss me and then I'll walk you to the door."

Tyson smiled, thinking that by the time he finished kissing her she wouldn't be walking him anywhere.

She leaned toward him, evidently expecting a peck on the lips. He leaned in as well and started off with just a light peck, but then he slid his tongue into her mouth at the same time his hand slid under the covers to settle beneath her legs.

Tyson was prepared for her reaction and deepened the kiss. He began dueling with her tongue, deliberately inflicting all kinds of sensual torment, while at the same time his fingers did the same. He loved touching her this way. She was such a passionate woman and so damn hot.

He heard the groan in her throat but she didn't pull back from his kiss. Nor did she resist moments later when he eased her down on her back and continued to kiss her, thoroughly, deeply and possessively.

Possessively…

There was that word again. Why was it determined to invade his mind when it came to Hunter? Dismissing the question since he didn't have an answer, he turned his full concentration on the seduction of Hunter McKay. His desire revved up a notch when she returned his kiss as provocatively as he was giving it. When he felt his fingers get damp from the wetness between her legs, he knew what was next.

Round six.

He pulled back from the kiss to stare down at her and saw deep-seated desire etched in her eyes. She was aroused and so was he. He leaned in and whispered against her moist lips. "I want you. Say you want me again, too, Hunter."

Chapter 11

Tyson saw the battle taking place in the eyes staring back at him. Common sense versus intense desire. He recognized it because of a similar encounter with his own emotions earlier. He still hadn't figured out what was going on with him. The only thing he knew for certain was what he'd just told Hunter. He wanted her again.

"Say it," he whispered, brushing a kiss across her forehead. "Say you want me again, too." He tried to keep the urgency out of his voice, the hunger and need. But it couldn't be helped. The bottom line was that he needed to make love to her again as much as he needed to breathe.

She hesitated a minute longer, then said, "I want you again, too, Tyson."

Tyson released the breath he'd been holding and moved

aside and made quick work of putting on another condom. In no time he was back, easing in place between her legs. He leaned in and captured her mouth at the same time he slid his hard erection inside her.

Once he was deeply embedded in her, he began moving, gently at first, one long stroke after another. But when he felt her nails dig deep into his back at the same time she rolled her hips beneath him, he picked up the pace and began pounding into her, hard and fast. He broke off the kiss and continued to thrust hard, over and over again. Grazing his jaw against her ear, he growled low in his throat. "Come for me, baby."

No sooner had he made the request than her body bucked in a bow beneath him and she screamed his name. "Tyson!"

But she didn't slow down. The spasms kept coming and she continued moving frantically beneath him, keeping up with the sensuous rhythm he'd established. Tyson decided that if she wanted a multiple orgasm this round then that's what he would give her. He sank deeper and deeper inside her while thrusting harder and harder.

His stomach clenched with need every time it touched hers and the hairs on his chest stirred to life whenever they came in contact with the hard nipples of her breasts. She tightened her legs around him and screamed his name at the same time he growled hers.

Fireworks seemed to go off inside Tyson's head. His entire body ignited into one hell of a gigantic explosion. He drew in a deep breath, thinking never had an orgasm felt so good. So perfect. The impact had his entire body quivering. Leaning down, he captured Hunter's mouth in a long, drugging kiss before easing off her to lie on his side.

Tyson pulled Hunter into his arms, entwining his legs with hers, still needing the connection. From the sound of her even breathing, he knew she had drifted back to sleep and he held her closer. Glancing down, he studied her features. She was a woman who didn't go out of her way to be sexy, yet she was sexy anyway. A woman who claimed she'd never seduced a man, but she had seduced the hell out of him. A woman who'd turned her bedroom into a romantic hot spot to set the mood for seduction. And a woman who had refused his advances until she'd gotten ready to accept them.

His brain felt as if it had short-circuited and he still didn't know why. So instead of getting more confused than he already was, he followed Hunter's lead and closed his eyes to join her in sleep.

As sunlight filtered through the window in her bedroom, Hunter slowly came awake. The even breathing close to her ear let her know she wasn't alone. She hadn't meant for Tyson to spend the night and had been pretty adamant that he didn't. All it had taken was a kiss, followed by another and topped with the best lovemaking she had ever experienced in her life to make her change her mind. Although she hadn't given Tyson the okay to stay, he had known. Why wouldn't he, when all he'd had to do was slide his hands between her legs or his tongue in her mouth and she became putty in his hands?

Probably just like all those other women.

She closed her eyes, not wanting to dwell on that thought now. But she knew she had to. She had no regrets about last night. Far from it. Tyson had opened her eyes to a lot of things, such as just how much of an ass Carter had been to deny her the very things she needed, not only as a wife but also as a woman.

She thought how she hadn't experienced an orgasm in four years, even longer if she was to count the times she'd shared Carter's bed and hadn't been fulfilled. Thanks to Tyson, she'd gotten more in one night than she'd had in all her years of marriage. She didn't want to think how many times she had screamed and wouldn't be surprised if her throat was sore this morning. So regardless of anything else, she appreciated Tyson for reminding her what it felt like to be a woman again. And what it felt like to have needs and have those needs satisfied to the fullest.

Not only had he given her a chance to seduce him, but he'd also agreed that she could to do it the way she wanted. Even after she'd told him she had never seduced a man before. Yet he had allowed her to take control, to "handle things," even when he hadn't fully understood her need to do so. He had no idea that last night restored her confidence in herself as a woman. It was the confidence Carter had painstakingly stripped from her.

However, upon waking up this morning she was faced with the realization that all good things must come to an end. After today, Tyson would go his way and she would go hers. In a day or two she would only be a fleeting memory to him, if that. At least she could say she never shared Tyson Steele's bed. He'd shared hers.

"You're awake."

Before she could react to his words, Tyson surprised her by drawing her even closer into the curve of his warm body. It had been a while since she'd awakened with a man in her bed, especially one who liked to snuggle and hold her through the night. Even when she and Carter had slept together, he had stayed in his corner of the bed and she'd stayed in hers. And those times when they did have sex, afterward they returned to those corners. It had never bothered her before because she'd gotten used to it. But spending one single night with Tyson was a stark reminder of what she'd put up with in her marriage.

Hunter tilted her head to look at Tyson and wished she hadn't. He had that early morning look—sleepy eyes with dark stubble along his chin and jaw—that begged for her touch. She was tempted to reach out and run her fingers along his chin to feel it for herself. She was convinced no man should look this sexy in the morning.

Finally, she responded to him. "Yes, I'm awake."

"Good. Take a shower with me before I leave."

Why did she get the feeling he seemed rather anxious to leave? And he wanted them to shower together? She honestly didn't think that was a good idea and was about to tell him so when he added, "Just one last thing we can do together."

He'd practically said the same thing about that kiss last night. Only problem was one thing had led to another and then another. She could see taking a shower with him that lasted for hours. She'd discovered Tyson could be very creative when it came to sex and could just imagine some of his artistic ideas for her in the bathroom.

When she hesitated he nudged her. "Are you going to deny me the chance for you to wash my back?"

She couldn't help but chuckle. "Or deny you the chance to wash mine?" she countered.

"Umm, I have no problem washing your back...or any other part of you that you'd like me to give attention to."

Yes, she bet he wouldn't have a problem with it. "I think you gave enough attention to my body parts last night. I'll be surprised if I'm able to walk today."

"Sorry about that."

She waved off his words. "Don't apologize. I needed last night. Screams and all. Trust me."

He shifted to stare into her eyes. "Why?"

He didn't need to know, she thought. The less he knew about her needs, the better. "Doesn't matter. And I'll pass on sharing that shower with you. I'm not ready to get up yet."

"You sure?"

"Positive."

He stared at her for a second and then without saying anything else, he eased away from her, got out of the bed and headed out of the bedroom. "The bathroom is that way," she said to him, trying not to notice his nakedness. He had no shame walking around naked and she had no shame getting an eyeful. He had a beautiful body, one any woman would appreciate.

"I know. I need to grab my overnight bag from the living room."

She nodded, remembering the infamous bag. The one containing all those condoms they'd nearly gone through last night.

It took him only a minute to get the bag and she watched when he walked back through the bedroom and headed for the bathroom. He stopped and glanced over at her. "You're sure you don't want to join me?"

No, she wasn't sure, but she knew it would be for the best. Too much of Tyson could become addictive. "Yes, I'm sure."

Flashing a sexy smile, one that caused her pulse to race, he entered the bathroom and closed the door behind him.

Hunter shifted in the bed when she heard the sound of the shower. She glanced around the room. The candles had burned down but the fragrance of vanilla lingered in the air, along with that of sex. She felt a tingling sensation in her stomach at the memories of their lovemaking.

Hunter felt sore between her legs but the soreness would be a reminder of all the pleasure Tyson had given her. He had made back-to-back love to her, allowing her the chance to take naps in between. He had licked her all over and she didn't have to look down at herself to know he'd probably left passion marks all over her body. Hopefully by Monday they would have faded away. At least she wouldn't have to see anyone over the weekend. Her parents had gone to a motorcycle race, and her brother and his family had taken off to Disneyland.

She would lie around and recover from Tyson's lovemaking, although she knew it would take more than a weekend for her to do that. He had awakened desires in her that she hadn't known existed. No wonder he was in such high demand with women.

Deciding to cover her nakedness, she reached out and pulled open the drawer to the nightstand, where she kept her oversized T-shirts. Sliding one over her head, she didn't miss the passion marks on her chest, stomach and thighs. She figured she'd find the majority of them between her legs. His mouth seemed to particularly like that area of her body.

Hunter glanced over at the closed bathroom door, tempted to go join Tyson in the shower. She knew she wasn't thinking with her head, but with overactive hormones. The only good thing was that he was now out of her system, and she was sure she was out of his.

"I'm ready to leave."

She twisted around in bed. She hadn't heard Tyson come out of the bathroom, but there he was, standing in the middle of the room, fully dressed in a pair of khakis and a polo shirt. He'd shaved but she much preferred the rugged look on him. Still, he looked good.

"I'll walk you to the door." She eased out of bed and winced, feeling a definite soreness between her legs. She grabbed her bathrobe off the chair and put it on.

"You okay?" he asked, quickly crossing the room to her with a concerned look on his face.

"Yes, I'm fine. I just need to soak in a bath today for a while."

"Do you want me to run your bathwater before I go?"

She thought it was kind for him to offer. "No, that's not necessary, Tyson. I can manage."

He searched her face. "You sure?"

"Yes, I'm sure. Don't worry about me. I'll be fine." But even as Hunter said the words, a part of her wondered if she truly would be. Unknowingly, Tyson had given her something last night that no other man had given her. A chance to be herself. To live out her fantasies. To be the sensuous and passionate woman she'd always suspected she was.

Tyson nodded and for a long moment he stood there

not saying anything and just looking at her, and she could feel his stare as if it was a heated caress. Then when she was about to ask him if there was something wrong, he finally said in a deep husky voice, "I don't want you to walk me to the door, Hunter."

She arched a brow. "Why?"

"Because I want you to get back in bed. That's the memory I want to leave here with. You in that bed. Your bed. Where we spent most of the night."

She didn't understand his request. "Why?"

A seriousness she'd never seen before touched his features. "I just do. Last night was special for me." He paused a moment and then said, "And about those house plans. When I get a chance to look over them I will. After I do, I'll get back to you."

She shrugged. "You don't really have to do that. We both know the real reason you hired me to draw up those plans."

He didn't deny it. In fact he didn't say anything for a long moment and then he leaned down and brushed his lips across hers. She figured the kiss was supposed to be short and sweet. However, the moment their lips touched, he pulled her into his arm and went after her mouth with the greed she'd grown accustomed to.

Resisting never entered her mind. Instead she returned the kiss in the same way she figured he was accustomed to her doing as well. The intensity of his tongue mating with hers nearly brought her to her knees. She moaned in pleasure not only from the kiss, but also from the feel of his masculine strength. And although she should have preferred otherwise, she liked the feel of his hard, engorged erection cradled intimately at the juncture of her thighs. It wouldn't take much to tumble back in bed and take him with her. There was no doubt in her mind if that was to happen she would eventually let out more screams.

But Tyson suddenly broke off the kiss.

He straightened and then gently brushed his knuckles across her cheek. "Go ahead and get back in the bed, Hunter."

She nodded and removed her robe. For a quick second she was tempted to remove her T-shirt as well. However, she refused to give in to temptation. The last thing she wanted was to tempt him to stay and make love to her again. They were doing the right thing by parting this way. He was who he was and she was who she was. Besides, last night had only been about sex, so there was no need to get all emotional.

She tossed her robe on the chair and slid beneath the covers. Stretching out in bed she gazed up at him. "Goodbye, Tyson."

He stared at her for a long moment before finally speaking. "Goodbye, Hunter." And with his overnight bag clutched in his hand he walked out of the bedroom.

Hunter didn't release her breath until she heard her front door open and then close behind him.

Chapter 12

"So, what's been going on with you, Tyson?"

Tyson glanced over at his brother Galen. He had stopped by to see how Brittany and the twins were doing, as well as to see how his laid-back older brother was faring. It seemed Galen had everything under control and had accepted his role as father to twins pretty easily. Almost as easily as he'd stepped into his role as husband.

To this day it still confused the hell out of Tyson. Of the six of them, Galen had been the most notorious womanizer. His reputation had extended from Phoenix all the way to the Carolinas, specifically Charlotte, North Carolina, where their Steele cousins lived. Galen was the last person Tyson thought would settle down with one woman. Yet now he was a husband and a father. Tyson shook his head. And had he heard Brittany right at dinner tonight when she mentioned them buying a van? Galen was known for his love of sports cars and as a collector of muscle cars. A van was the last vehicle Tyson would have thought his brother would be caught driving.

Deciding to answer Galen's question, he said, "Nothing's been going on with me but the usual. I've been pretty busy at the hospital." But not too busy to think about Hunter McKay, Tyson thought.

This time last week he'd been inside her. It was hard to believe a full week had passed. He thought of her often. Too damn much, in fact. The days weren't so bad, since like he told Galen he was pretty busy at the hospital. But it was at night, mainly when he went to bed, when he mostly thought about her. Not making love to her in his bed had turned out to be a good thing, otherwise he would never get any sleep.

But still…he had made love to her and that was the crux of his problem. They had shared passion, passion and more passion. And now he couldn't get all that passion out of his mind. He would get an erection just remembering their times together. And what was even worse, it seemed his desire for other women had abandoned him. Women called but he didn't call them back. How crazy was that?

"It's Friday night and you're off work," Galen pointed out. "Why aren't you hanging out at Notorious? That's usually your mode of entertainment on the weekends."

He didn't need his brother to remind him of that. "Would you believe me if I told you I'm getting bored with the place?"

Galen stretched his legs out in front of him. "Not

unless there's a reason. Scoping out the women there used to be your favorite pastime."

Tyson was tempted to remind Galen that Notorious used to be Galen's favorite hangout for that same reason before his Brittany days.

"Is there a reason, Tyson?"

Tyson shrugged. "No reason."

It got quiet and that didn't bode well for Tyson. He knew Galen. He was trying to figure out things that weren't his business. Just because he was the oldest, Galen thought he had a right to know everything about what his five brothers were doing. That assumption might have had some merit when they were kids, but now he, Eli, Jonas, Mercury and Gannon were adults and didn't need their big brother looking over their shoulders.

"What's her name?"

Tyson frowned. "Whose name?"

"The woman who left her mark on you."

Tyson almost chuckled at that. Especially when he recalled all the marks he'd left on Hunter. "No woman left her mark on me, Galen. You're imagining things."

"Am I?"

To be honest, Tyson wasn't sure. He still dreamed of Hunter and thought about her all the time. It was quite evident to him that their tumble between the sheets hadn't worked her out of his system. That annoyed the hell out of him.

"Did I tell you how I met Brittany?"

"Yes," Tyson answered, taking a sip of his wine. "The two of you met for a brief while in New York when we were there for Donovan's wedding." Donovan Steele was their cousin who'd gotten married several years ago. If everyone thought Galen falling in love was a shocker, then Donovan doing so was an even bigger one.

"True, that's when we first met. We ran into each other again six months later here in Phoenix at the auction house. To make a long story short, she had something I wanted and I had something she wanted."

Tyson nodded. "And what did you have that she wanted?"

"The title to the house she's now turned into a school."

"And what did she have that you wanted?"

"Sex."

Tyson nearly choked on his drink. And then he quickly glanced around for his sister-in-law, hoping she hadn't heard what his brother just said.

Galen smiled. "Relax. Brittany went upstairs to put Ethan and Elyse to bed. But even had she heard me, she would have backed up my story, because it's the truth."

Tyson stared at his brother. "And you're telling me this why?"

"Because I know you, Tyson. I might not know all the particulars about what's going on with you—especially why you dropped by here tonight instead of going to Notorious, where there're a slew of women just waiting for you to make an appearance. For you to deny yourself a chance to take a woman home to warm your bed can only mean one thing."

"What?"

"There's some woman you've fallen for."

Tyson frowned. "I haven't fallen for her. Not exactly. Let's just say she left a lasting impression on me."

Galen chuckled. "In other words, she was good in bed. Almost too good to be true. And you're wondering if it was great sex or something else."

Tyson's frown deepened. Was that what he was really wondering? No, he assured himself. It wasn't anything other than great sex. His problem was that he wanted more of that great sex, which meant he wanted more of Hunter. One night hadn't been enough. "You're getting carried away, Galen. It's not that serious."

"Isn't it?"

"No."

"You sure?"

He hesitated a minute, then said, "Yes. I'm sure."

"I hope you're right. Take it from a man who thought there couldn't possibly be a woman out there I'd want forever. If there's that possibility, then you owe it to yourself to find out."

"So how was your night with Tyson?" Kat asked.

"Did he remind you just how great having an orgasm can be?" Mo queried.

Hunter figured the questions would come sooner or later. In a way she was surprised they hadn't come earlier. After all, it had been a week. She couldn't believe it was Friday already. This time last week she and Tyson were engaging in what had turned into a sex marathon. She no longer had dreams to contend with. Now she had full-fledged memories, which she discovered was even worse. Now she knew how it felt to be touched by a man, tasted by a man, and all she had to do was close her eyes to remember those hard thrusts into her body.

"Well, if you're not going to tell us, then…"

Hunter rolled her eyes. "I have no problem telling you what you want to know, since it was one and done. Yes, Kat, I went out with Tyson. We had dinner at his place and later we went to mine."

Kat arched a brow. "Why?"

Hunter took a sip of her tea before continuing. "Because I knew how the night would end, and I refused to be seduced by him and share a bed that a zillion other women had shared. I told him I would be the one doing the seducing and it had to be done at my place. In my bed."

Both women stared at her with something akin to amazement on their faces. "And he actually went along with it?" Mo asked.

"Yes."

Kat and Mo stared at each other for a minute, and then they stared back at her. Kat shook her head. "I can't imagine a Steele running behind a woman."

"He didn't run behind me, Kat. He merely came to my house to be seduced."

"Okay, forget the seduction part for now," Mo said. "Did you get the big *O* at least once?"

Hunter thought it would serve no purpose confessing just how many times she had gotten it. Whenever she thought about it, she found the entire experience almost too overwhelming. Tyson had the ability to make her come with his mouth on her breasts, licking around her navel, between her legs... She shifted in her seat just thinking about it. But all she said was "Yes."

"And was it worth all the trouble?" Mo asked.

Hunter couldn't help but smile at the memory. "Definitely. I can't speak for the other Steeles, but I can say the rumors about Tyson are true."

"Hot damn," Kat said, grinning.

"This calls for a toast," Mo added. "Your dry days are over and we have Tyson Steele to thank."

"Whatever," she said, deciding it was time to change

the subject. Especially since talking about Tyson was making her think of him, wonder what he was doing, who he was with.

"Do you think the two of you will get together again?"

"No," Hunter said, responding quickly to Kat's question. "There was a lot of sexual chemistry between us and we needed to work it out of our system."

"Did you?" Kat asked.

"Did I what?"

"Get Tyson Steele out of your system?"

"Yes."

Mo didn't look convinced. "Are you saying that you haven't thought of Tyson Steele—not once—since that night? That you don't dream of the two of you reliving memories of last Friday night?"

Hunter glanced around the restaurant, hoping Mo's voice hadn't carried. "I'm not saying anything."

"Umm," both Mo and Kat said simultaneously.

Hunter frowned. "And what do you guys mean by *umm*?"

Mo smiled sweetly. "Trust me. You'll find out soon enough."

Tyson entered his home and glanced around. This was a Friday night and he was away from the hospital, yet he would be going to bed alone. It was so unlike him. And he'd been acting strangely in other ways, as well. In fact, lately he had begun finding Macy Phillips's phone calls so annoying that he had removed her from his "to do" list.

Had he somehow been turned off from beautiful, sexy women? He sucked in a deep breath, knowing that wasn't true. If given the chance, he would do Hunter

McKay again in a heartbeat. Even more times than he'd done her last Friday night.

He threw his car keys on the table as he thought about what Galen had said. Sometimes his older brother talked pure nonsense, but tonight Tyson couldn't help wondering if perhaps he should heed his brother's words. Should he find out if the reason he couldn't get Hunter out of his mind was because of the great sex or something else?

He pulled his phone out of his back pocket and searched his contact list for her phone number. He was a second from calling her when he regained his senses. He repocketed the phone and went into his bedroom. He would get a good night's sleep, convinced that when he woke up in the morning, his outlook on things would be different. He forced a smile. He'd even give one of the women still on his "to do" list a call.

Chapter 13

"Honestly, Mom, skateboarding?"

Hunter had rushed to the hospital after getting a call from the ER nurse that her mother had been brought to the emergency room by ambulance due to an accident on a skateboard. She hadn't known what to expect and gave a sigh of relief upon discovering there were no broken bones, just scrapes and bruises.

"I wore a helmet and knee pads, Hunter," her mother said, seemingly somewhat aggravated over all the fuss being made over her.

"And it was a good thing you did, Mrs. McKay," the ER doctor said, shaking his head. "Your injuries could have been a lot worse. You'll be sore for a couple of days, but the X-rays don't show anything broken."

"Oh, I could have told you that," Ingrid McKay said matter-of-factly. "In fact I tried to tell you, but you wouldn't listen," she said, scolding the doctor.

"Just following procedures," the doctor said, writing information in the chart he held in his hand. "You took a nasty fall. I'm writing a prescription for any pain you might start to feel later. And I suggest you stay off the skateboard for a while."

"Whatever," her mother grumbled under her breath.

Hunter rolled her eyes, hoping her mother took the doctor's advice. "Where's Dad?"

"Today was his golf day, so I had that nice nurse call you instead of Bernie. I didn't want to upset him. And I sure wasn't going to call Bernie Junior."

Of course you wouldn't, Hunter thought. Her brother would have read their mother the riot act. Now she understood his concerns about their parents' risky playtime activities. "Can you walk out to my car or do you want me to have the nurse get you a wheelchair?" she asked.

"Why would I need a wheelchair? I can walk."

"Just asking, Mom."

She was leading her mother toward the exit door when a deep, husky voice stopped her. "Hunter?"

Hunter didn't have to turn to know who the voice belonged to. The stirrings that suddenly went off in the pit of her stomach were a dead giveaway.

She turned around and before she could regain her composure enough to answer, her mother exclaimed, "Hey, aren't you one of those Steele boys?"

Hunter fought back a smile. The male standing before them was definitely no boy. She knew for a fact he was all man. Her pulse rate escalated when she recalled just how she knew that. It had been twelve days since she'd seen Tyson last. Twelve days. Not that she was counting. He looked good, even wearing scrubs.

She studied his features, the ones that still domi-
nated her dreams every night. Her gaze latched on to his
mouth, a mouth that had sent her over the edge so many
times. And as she looked at him she saw the corners of
his mouth hitch up in a smile at her mother's question.

"Yes, ma'am, I am," he said respectfully, extending
his hand out to her mother. "I'm Tyson Steele."

Ingrid accepted Tyson's hand. "Those green eyes
gave you away." She peered over her glasses to study
the name tag on his jacket. "So you're a doctor?"

"Yes, I'm a heart surgeon. Someone came through
ER needing my services." Tyson's gaze left Ingrid to
return to Hunter. "Is everything okay?"

She nodded, not sure she could speak at that moment. Then she found her voice. "Yes, everything is
okay. Mom took a fall on a skateboard. It could have
been worse."

Tyson lifted an amused brow. "A skateboard?"

"Yes. Hopefully it was her first and last time trying one out."

"Don't count on it," Ingrid muttered under her breath.
Before Hunter could give her mother a scolding retort,
Ingrid spoke up. "I recall when the two of you attended
the same high school."

"Yes, we did," Tyson said, nodding.

Hunter hoped that was all her mother remembered.
The last thing she needed was her mother bringing up
the short time she and Tyson had dated. "Well, we better get going," she said. "I want to get by the pharmacy
to pick up Mom's prescription."

"All right," Tyson said, but he didn't move away. He
held her gaze.

The sexual chemistry. The physical attraction. The desire. They were still there. She felt it and from the look in his eyes she knew that he felt it, too. Hadn't they worked all that out of their systems that night at her place?

Evidently they weren't the only ones feeling it, because at that moment Ingrid cleared her throat. When they both glanced over at her, Ingrid asked Tyson, "Are you the one who got expelled from high school for being caught under the bleachers with the principal's daughter?"

"Mom!"

Ingrid shrugged. "Just asking."

Tyson chuckled. "No, that was my brother Galen."

Hunter figured she needed to get her mother out of there before she remembered something else that was best forgotten.

She wasn't quick enough and Ingrid asked, "What about church?"

Tyson lifted a brow. "What about it?"

Ingrid had no problem telling him. "I see your parents on Sundays but I don't recall seeing you and your brothers."

Tyson grinned at her mother's observation. "I haven't been to church in a while. Usually I work on Sundays."

"Every Sunday?"

"Mom!" Hunter shook her head. "Sorry about that, Tyson."

A smile spread across his lips. "No need to apologize. And to answer your question Mrs. McKay, no, I don't work every Sunday. In fact I'm off this weekend, so you can look for me on Sunday."

"Don't think that I won't," Ingrid said in a serious tone.

Hunter thought it would be best to get her mother out

to the car quickly before Ingrid invited Tyson to Sunday dinner or something. "Well, I'll be seeing you, Tyson."

"Same here."

Taking her mother's arm, Hunter led her over to the exit door. She couldn't resist looking over her shoulder. The attractive nurse who had taken care of her mother—the one whose name was Macy Phillips—had approached Tyson and was all in his face. She was touching his arm while chatting away with a huge smile on her face.

Hunter felt a pain stab her heart when she saw that Tyson was smiling back at the woman.

"Well, at least he's not the one who got caught with that girl under the bleachers."

Ingrid's words reclaimed Hunter's attention. She was still holding tight to her mother's arm as they exited the building. "Mom, that was over eighteen years ago. Galen Steele is now married with twins."

"Umm, I guess that means there's hope for those Steele boys yet. I recall they used to have quite a reputation."

Hunter was close to saying that they still did. At least the single ones. However, she decided to keep her mouth shut.

"So what's going on with you and Dr. Steele?"

Hunter almost missed her step and glanced over at her mother. "What makes you think something is going on?"

Ingrid rolled her eyes. "I wasn't born yesterday, Hunter. I saw the way he was looking at you and the way you were looking at him."

"You're imagining things. Tyson is nothing more than a client."

"If you want me to think so."

Hunter didn't say anything to that. So what if she and Tyson were looking at each other in a way that raised eyebrows? No big deal.

As Hunter opened her car door for her mother, she truly hoped that it wasn't a big deal.

Tyson tossed and turned in the bed, finding it difficult to sleep. Each time he closed his eyes, images of Hunter and that night they spent together flooded his mind. The images were so vivid and powerful that he could lick his lips and taste her there.

Feeling frustration in every part of his body, he slid out of bed and headed for the living room. It seemed that sleep would evade him tonight, so he might as well see what was on television.

Moments later he felt even more frustrated. How could someone have over one hundred channels and not find a single thing of interest on television? He tossed the remote on the table and walked out of the living room into the kitchen, where he opened the refrigerator, needing a beer.

Something had to give, he thought, pulling a beer from the six-pack and popping the tab. Today, answering a page to the ER he had rounded the corner and seen Hunter standing there. Desire the likes of which he'd never felt before had consumed him. And when she'd turned and looked at him, their gazes had met and locked in a way that gave him sensuous shivers just thinking about it.

It didn't make sense. After all he and Hunter had done that night, how in the world could she still be in his system? Or he in hers? He knew the feelings were mutual. He had felt the chemistry, known she had felt it as well. They'd been standing there and he'd been able to actually feel her heat seep into him. It had penetrated every single pore in his body. Neither of them had said a word but their gazes had told it all.

He took a long gulp of his beer but it couldn't wash away the memories. Why was he remembering the way she would whisper his name right before she came, and the way she would scream when caught in the throes of passion? Why was he reliving in his mind all the times his body had straddled hers? Thrust into hers?

And why, considering all of that, was he beginning to believe it wasn't all just about sex? If not sex, then what? Could there be any credence to what Galen had said? That's what Tyson needed to find out before he endured any more sleepless nights.

Leaving the kitchen, he went back into his bedroom and retrieved his cell phone from his nightstand. He glanced over at the clock and saw it was after midnight. Hell, if he couldn't sleep, neither would she. He punched in Hunter's number.

A sleepy voice answered. "Hello?"

"We need to talk, Hunter."

"Tyson?"

He loved hearing her say his name. Even when it was in a lethargic voice it sounded sexy. "What other man would be calling you this time of night?"

"Why are you?"

He couldn't help but smile at her comeback. "I told you. We need to talk."

"Now?"

"No, not now. Tomorrow. I need to drop by your office."

"Fine. Call and make an appointment with Pauline."

"No. I make appointments with you personally. Expect me tomorrow. Good night."

Hunter frowned when she heard the click in her ear. *Expect me tomorrow.* Who did Tyson Steele think he was? Did she even remotely look like that young nurse who'd been all in his face today, flirting and grinning all over the place? Touching his hand? The same one he'd flirted back with? He should be making an appointment with Macy Phillips instead of with her.

And maybe you need to tone down that green streak, Hunter McKay. Jealousy doesn't become you.

She hung up her phone and then slid out of bed to glance over at the clock. Tyson had a lot of nerve calling her at this hour. But then, if there was anything she knew Tyson possessed it was nerve. Right along with an abundance of arrogance.

And what did he want to talk to her about anyway? She preferred continuing on this trend of them not having anything to do with each other. But then that hadn't stopped her from thinking of him. From remembering. From dreaming.

Sliding into her slippers, she went into the kitchen for a cup of tea. Hopefully that would help her sort out a few things in her mind. Her mother's questions hadn't ended at the hospital. Once they'd gotten on the road Ingrid McKay had been determined to uncover all the details she could. The last thing her mother needed to know was that two weekends ago she had turned her bedroom into a real live hot spot. And that Tyson had taught her sexual positions that should be outlawed.

Not only that, but all those packs of condoms were also just where he'd left them on the table in her bedroom.

A short while later, as she sat down at her kitchen table sipping her tea, Hunter couldn't stop the shivers that raced through her body at the thought of seeing Tyson again.

Although she had no idea what was on his mind, she had to remember that he only wanted to talk.

Chapter 14

Hunter paced her office, calling herself all kinds of fool for being nervous about Tyson's visit. And she also tried convincing herself the dress she'd chosen to wear to work that morning had nothing to do with knowing he would be dropping by. So what if it was a tad shorter than the ones she normally wore to the office? Tyson telling her how much he liked seeing her legs had nothing to do with it. Nor was that the reason she'd replaced her comfortable pumps with a pair of high heels.

She glanced at her watch. Pauline would be leaving for the day in less than five minutes. Had Tyson deliberately timed his arrival when he figured they would be alone? She shook her head, telling herself she was jumping to conclusions. Tyson's visit to her office might just be strictly business. There was a possibility he had questions about those preliminary house plans. Yes, those same house plans she'd already dismissed as inconsequential. She knew he had no more intention of building a house in the country than she did. But she had put her time, concentration and energy into them. That was why she had billed him for them anyway. And she hadn't been cheap. He could be questioning the size of his bill, but a personal visit wasn't needed for that.

The buzzer on her desk sounded and she inhaled deeply before crossing the room to push the button. "Yes, Pauline?"

"I'm about to leave, Hunter. Do you need me to do anything before I—"

When she heard a voice in the background she knew her conversation with Pauline was being interrupted by someone. "Excuse me, Hunter. But Dr. Steele is here. He said you are expecting him."

There was no need to tell Pauline to send him in because at that moment, her office door opened and Tyson walked in. She glared at him, a little put out that he assumed he could just walk into her office whenever he felt like it. But then that thought faded from her mind when her eyes roamed over him. No man could wear a pair of jeans better.

Nor could a man remove them better, either.

She tried not to remember that night in her apartment when he had stripped out of his jeans for her. Remembering also made her recall just what he was packing behind the zipper of those jeans.

"If there's nothing else you need for me to do then I'll see you tomorrow, Hunter."

At that moment she realized she still had Pauline on the line. "That's fine, Pauline. Enjoy your evening and I'll see you tomorrow."

She clicked off the line and lifted her chin at Tyson, but before she could give him a piece of her mind, he asked, "How's your mother?"

"Mom's fine. Thanks for asking." So, okay, it was nice of him to inquire…but still. "It would have been nice if you'd given me a time as to when to expect you, Tyson."

He actually looked remorseful. "Sorry about that. It was late last night when I called you and—"

"Trust me. I know how late it was."

A small smile touched his lips as he leaned back against the closed door. "I couldn't sleep and figured if I couldn't sleep you shouldn't be able to sleep, either. Sounds pretty juvenile, doesn't it?"

"Yes, especially since I wasn't responsible for your inability to sleep."

He straightened and took a few steps into the middle of the room. Hunter's stomach immediately knotted and her breathing suddenly seemed forced. The man was testosterone personified. And why did those thighs, those hard muscular thighs that had ridden her so many times, look perfect in his jeans?

"But you are responsible, Hunter," he said, interrupting her intense appraisal of him. "That's why I'm here."

Hunter frowned. What he was saying didn't make much sense. "Okay, so you can't sleep at night and for some reason you think I'm to blame. If that's the case, what do you expect me to do about it?"

"Give me a week. I want a week in your bed since a mere night didn't do a damn thing to eradicate you from my system."

Tyson looked at the beautiful woman with the shocked look on her face. At some point he needed to stop astonishing her this way. He'd gotten the same reaction from her that night at Notorious after stating his plans to seduce her.

He shoved his hands into his pockets, readying himself for what was to come. She could get mad or glad. Either way he intended to get his week. Hell, he needed that week. When time ticked by and she didn't say anything, just sat behind her desk and gazed at him like he was stone crazy, he finally asked, "Well?"

Tyson knew he'd pushed too hard when a furious expression finally overtook her expression. She eased out of her chair to come around her desk and stand in front of him with her hands planted firmly on her hips. He could actually see fire in those gorgeous brown eyes of hers and should have had enough sense to step back, but he didn't. The way he saw it, he didn't have anything to lose at this point and he intended to stand his ground.

"You sex-crazed womanizing ass!" she said in a loud, angry voice. "What's wrong, Dr. Steele? That little nurse didn't work out for you so you thought you could just show up here demanding more sex from me because you need it? Let me tell you just where you can—"

"I don't just need sex, Hunter," he interrupted her in a voice that matched her volume. "I need *you*. And what little nurse are you talking about?"

"I'm talking about that ER nurse who was flirting with you yesterday. And I saw you flirting back."

A fierce frown covered Tyson's face when she brought up Macy Phillips. "For your information, Macy Phillips was on my 'to do' list, along with several other women," he snapped.

"Then by all means do them. What's stopping you?" she snapped back, getting in his face.

"You're stopping me, dammit, and I don't know why," he retorted, hating he had to admit such a thing. "Ever since that night I saw you at Notorious, I haven't wanted another woman. I haven't thought of anyone else. I figured that once I made love to you my life would return to normal. But things have gotten worse for me. For some reason you aren't out my system. I dream about you at night. I think about you during the day. My cleaning lady has been to my place twice since that night you were there for dinner, but I swear I can still smell your scent."

To Tyson's surprise Hunter took a step back. It was as if his words had finally gotten to her, were now sinking in. So he decided to plunge forward. "So I came up with a plan."

"Another one?" she asked flippantly.

"Yes, another one," he said, more than a little agitated. "There has to be a reason I can't get enough of you, and whether you want to admit it or not, I'm not out of your system, either. I can tell. Anyone who's within ten feet of us can pick up on the strong sexual chemistry between us. I think your mother even picked up on something."

"She did," Hunter said in a somewhat calmer tone. "I told her there was nothing going on between us but I don't think she believes me."

Then, as if she realized she'd gone soft, her spine straightened and her voice became firm. "And don't you dare stand there and tell me what I don't have out of my system. You have no way of knowing that."

He lifted his chin. "Don't I?"

She crossed her arms over her chest. "No, you don't."

"Are you saying that you don't still want me? That

you don't go to bed with thoughts of me inside of you? Kissing you? Tasting you? Riding you hard?"

He saw heat flare in her eyes at his words. He also saw blatant desire that fanned the flames of what he was feeling. "Well, are you?"

She squared her shoulders and glared at him. "I'm not saying anything."

"Then it's admission by omission."

"I am *not* admitting to anything. If I'm not out of your system then that's your problem, one you need to deal with on your own. Contrary to what you seem to think, you're out of my system, Tyson. Nothing you say or do will prove otherwise," she said haughtily.

A slow smile spread across his features. "You think not?"

Hunter didn't like his tone, nor the "let me prove differently" look in Tyson's eyes. For once she felt she might have said too much, tossed out a dare she hadn't intended to make. And now he had that predatory look on his face. The one that meant he intended to prove her wrong. She took a few more steps back and came to a stop when her backside hit against her desk.

"Isn't tonight Thursday? You're having dinner with your folks, right?" she asked.

"What about it?"

During their talk over wine and cheese in her bedroom, he mentioned that over the years his mother had insisted on Thursday dinners as a way to show her six sons that married life would be wonderful. Tyson had stated that as far as he was concerned, the only thing his mother was showing him was what a great cook she continued to be. For him it was the delicious meals that were the draw.

"I wouldn't want you to be late for dinner," she told him.

A smiled curved his lips. "Are you trying to get rid of me, Hunter?"

She leaned back against her desk. "What do you think?"

"I think it's time I show you that you want me as much as I want you."

A slow stirring erupted in the pit of her stomach when Tyson began walking toward her. His expression was serious, his eyes dark and honed in on hers. Her heart pounded in her chest with every step he took. She was tempted to run, but her feet felt cemented in place. Besides, from the look on Tyson's face she knew that he wouldn't think twice about chasing after her.

Did she even want to run?

She frowned at the doubt that clouded her mind. Of course she wanted to run, to escape, to get the hell out of here. *Umm, maybe not*, she thought when Tyson stopped and kicked off his shoes and then took the time to remove his socks.

Hunter had a pretty good idea where this was going, and a part of her wanted it more than anything. She hadn't been completely honest by claiming he was out of her system. But a week-long affair wasn't necessarily the answer. It might work for him, but she ran the risk that he'd get even more under her skin.

As she continued to look at Tyson, he straightened and went for his shirt, undoing the buttons and easing it from his chest and broad muscular shoulders. Hunter tried not to remember the feel of that chest rubbing against her hardened nipples, but she failed. She heard herself moan.

"You said something, Hunter?" he asked, staring at her with a predatory look.

She swallowed and shook her head, unable to speak for a moment. When she could, she said, "No, I didn't say anything." But she knew she should. She should speak up and put an end to this madness. But a part of her was curious to see just how far he would go before she sent him packing.

And speaking of packing... He eased his jeans down his legs to reveal a pair of sexy briefs and it was obvious just what he was packing between those massive thighs.

"Is there a reason you're removing your clothes in my office?" she asked, deciding she needed to say something before he went any further.

He smiled over at her as he inserted his fingers in the waistband of his briefs. "Yes, there's a reason."

And then, without saying another word, he lowered his briefs and showed her the reason. In all its arousing and throbbing glory.

As far as Tyson was concerned, the worst thing Hunter could do at that moment was lick her lips. Major bad timing on her part. Especially when he saw the sexual hunger in her eyes.

Then she lifted her chin. "I won't be removing my clothes, Tyson."

He stood in front of her totally naked and he couldn't help noticing she had a hard time zeroing in on his face. Instead her gaze kept straying to his groin. "I don't recall asking you to take your clothes off, Hunter, mainly because I intend to take them off for you."

She narrowed her eyes at him. "You wouldn't dare."

He chuckled. "I would. And I will." He took a step toward her.

"If you come any closer, I'll scream," she threatened.

His mouth curved into a smile. "Baby, you're going to be screaming anyway, so one more scream is a moot point." He trailed a finger down her thigh. "You want to convince me you didn't wear this short dress just for me?"

"Think whatever you want."

"In that case, I think you did wear it just for me," he said, loving the feel of his fingers on her bare skin. "And I want to thank you properly for doing so." Then Tyson lowered his mouth to hers.

Hunter knew the moment Tyson's tongue touched hers there would be nothing proper about this kiss. She was proven right when he began devouring her mouth with an intensity that had her fighting back moans. Pushing him away was not even a consideration. Instead, she eased up on tiptoe and wrapped her arms around his neck to deepen the kiss.

When his hand began easing up her dress, instinctively, her legs spread apart. Just like the last time, his touch was like an aphrodisiac, making her crave things she shouldn't have but wanted anyway. And topping the list was Tyson. She wanted him doing all those naughty and sinful yet delicious things to her.

Her thoughts were suddenly snatched from her mind when Tyson's fingers settled between her legs. Oh, yes, she remembered these fingers and just what they could do to her, how they could make her feel. He knew how to work them with a skill she found astounding. The man had an uncanny ability to take her breath away.

He broke off the kiss and stared down at her, deliberately holding her gaze while his fingers worked their magic inside her, making her moan, gasp and then moan again. "You sure you want this?" he asked in a deep, husky voice. "After all, you claim I'm the only one with the problem. That I am out of your system."

Hunter knew he was toying with her, trying to make her admit something she had adamantly refuted. "You're wet, Hunter," he said, moving his fingers in slow, circular motions inside her. "I like stirring you up this way, and do you know why?"

She fought the urge to ask but failed. "No, why?"

"Because doing so escalates your scent. There is something about your scent that's powerful and intoxicating. It arouses me whenever I'm around you. Makes me want to taste you here," he said, inserting an additional finger inside her. "I miss tasting you that way."

She didn't want to admit it but that particular part of her body missed being tasted that way, too. His fingers and tongue should be considered weapons of mass seduction. He held tight to her gaze, daring her to look away, while his fingers slowly and provocatively began pushing her over the edge. "Am I out of your system, Hunter?"

Did he really need for her to answer that? Especially when her nipples had hardened and her hips moved with the rhythm of his fingers. She drew in a deep breath and shook her head.

"Not good enough. I want to hear you say it," Tyson said as he leaned down close to her lips just seconds before his tongue swiped across them. "Say it, Hunter."

There was no way she could refuse him. Not now when he'd whipped her body into a need she could not deny. "No, you're not out of my system."

Her words made an arrogant smile touch his lips. "Glad we're in agreement about that." He pulled his fingers from inside her and instantly she felt bereft. And then he was pulling her dress over her head, skillfully removing her bra in the process. His hands were there to cup her breasts the moment they were free. "Beautiful," he whispered huskily. "I missed these girls. They spoiled me."

No, in all honesty, he had spoiled them, Hunter thought. And they had definitely missed him. When he sucked a nipple into his mouth, she knew he was about to spoil them some more. She drew in a deep breath and struggled to hold herself up when she was about to slither to the floor. Tyson came to her rescue then, grabbing her by the hips to hoist her onto her desk.

"Now to get to what we both want," he said, using the tips of his fingers to trace a path toward her inner thighs. Hunter felt her heart pick up a beat when his hand closed possessively over her feminine mound through her lace panties.

"You like lace, I notice," he said throatily.

"Yes, I like lace," she responded, barely able to get the words out.

"That's good to know."

Hunter was about to ask why he thought so when he tugged on her panties and automatically she lifted her hips so he could ease them down her legs. Once that was done he captured her gaze as he gripped her hips and moved forward, leading the head of his engorged erection toward her womanly entrance.

He was almost there when common sense invaded her mind. "Stop!"

He loosened his hold on her. "Stop?" he repeated with an incredulous look on his face.

She nodded. "Condom."

The shocked look in his eyes let her know he couldn't believe he'd been less than an inch from entering her without having given any thought to protection. "Condom. Right," he said, slowly backing away to retrieve a packet from the jeans he'd tossed on the floor. "Thanks for the reminder. This has never happened to me before."

Hunter believed him and unashamedly watched as he expertly sheathed his erection. Looking back over at her, he said, "Ready to pick up where we left off?"

"Yes." She was more than ready. Shivers raced through her body at the intense desire she saw in the depths of his green eyes as he headed back toward her. And to show him just how ready she was, she boldly spread her legs. She'd never been taken on a desk before and was curious to see how they would pull it off.

When he returned, he said, "Grab my shoulders and hold on tight."

He lifted her hips, guiding his erection unerringly inside her. She threw her head back and moaned at the impact. Her inner muscles clenched, tightening around him. Tyson being back inside her felt good. Like he belonged there.

She swallowed, wondering how she could allow her mind to think that when it came to Tyson. A man whose favorite pastime was bedding women. All thoughts fled her mind when he began thrusting into her in long, hard strokes. The intensity of them shook her to the core. She understood why he told her to grab his shoulders when he began pounding into her at the same time he eased her back on the desk, nearly covering her body with his. Luckily, she had a big desk because they needed the space.

Suddenly Hunter's body jerked from what seemed like an electrical shock that traveled through her body straight to her nerve endings. It was all she needed to push her over the edge. And Tyson joined her. She released a guttural scream mere seconds before he leaned in and took her mouth with a greedy kiss that swallowed up her cry. Just when she came down to earth, he moved against her again and she was hurled into yet another orgasm. Why had she ever claimed to be over this man?

"Glad we're in agreement about that week."

Hunter glanced over at Tyson as she slid back into her dress. He had gotten dressed and was leaning against her desk watching her do the same. No, they weren't in agreement since she hadn't agreed to anything. "We had tonight, Tyson. That's the best I can do."

"I want a week."

"You got tonight."

"I want a week, Hunter."

He was persistent. After smoothing her dress down her body she stared at him. "Why, Tyson? What will a week do for you?"

"I'm convinced I'm a man possessed."

Hunter raised a brow. "Possessed?"

"Yes, possessed by passion. Yours."

Now she'd heard everything. She barely knew all the things to do in the bedroom so how could an experienced man like him get obsessed with her? It didn't make much sense. She opened her mouth to ask the question but his words stopped her.

"Please don't ask me to explain it, Hunter, because I can't. All I know is that you're the only woman I want and I need to know what we just did won't be the last time. I need that week. I'll even let you call the shots and set the grounds rules during that week if that's what it takes. But I've got to get you out of my system for good."

She hated to ask but she had to. "But what if that one week doesn't work?"

He stared at her without saying anything, and she realized that in his mind it was simply not an option. "We'll think positive. It has to work."

She didn't say anything for a minute as she remembered what they'd just done on her desk. A week of Tyson wouldn't kill her. Besides, if she was honest with herself, she would admit that a part of her wanted him just as badly. She had craved his touch, had dreamed of him inside her. However, she wouldn't go so far as to say she was possessed. She just hoped the week gave him what he wanted. Freedom from her once and for all.

"Fine. You'll get your week, Tyson, but I'm setting the ground rules. If you think you're going to keep me on my back 24/7 then you're wrong. We will do other things."

He arched his brow. "Other things like what?"

"I'll think of something."

"Yes, you do that, Hunter. In the meantime…"

He crossed the room to her, leaned forward and captured her lips with his.

Chapter 15

There had to be a reason he couldn't get enough of Hunter, Tyson thought, recalling how after making love to her on her desk, they had gotten dressed only to end up making love a second time on the sofa in her office.

And how could he have almost forgotten to use a condom that first time? That was something he'd never done before with any woman. He had truly acted like a man possessed and he needed to get his life back on track. If he didn't know better he would think Hunter was a witch. A beautiful, delicious and sensuous witch who was wreaking havoc on his brain cells to the point where he couldn't think straight. Hell, he wasn't thinking at all. When had he ever wanted to go a full week with any woman? But with him it hadn't been an option. It had been about survival. And that's what bothered him more than anything. When had he ever admitted to a woman that she was in his system like he was some kind of sex addict or something? Why hadn't he been able to let go and walk away like he'd done with all the others? For the umpteenth time he had to ask himself, what made Hunter so different?

"You're quiet tonight, Tyson."

He glanced down the dinner table. Of course it had to be Mercury who noticed. "Don't have anything to say."

He had arrived late at his parents' house for dinner. He knew his mother assumed he'd gotten detained at the hospital, but that was far from the truth. He had arrived in time to see the photos Galen and Brittany had been passing around of the twins, which had, luckily, deflected any questions about why he'd been late.

He noted these Thursday dinners were getting rather large with three of his brothers now married. And for the first time the grandkids were present, which had to be the reason his mother was smiling all over the place. Not to mention the growing family had given her an excuse to buy a new dining room table, one that seated fourteen people. Tyson could do the math. It was quite apparent that Eden Tyson Steele was counting on her three bachelor sons producing wives to fill the vacant seats at the table one day.

"Oh, you're in one of those moods," Gannon said, grinning. "That's what happens when you prepare dinner for a woman."

That got everyone's attention. "You prepared dinner?" Galen asked, surprised. Anyone who knew him knew he didn't cook for himself, much less for anyone else.

"I ordered take-out. No big deal."

"You actually fed a woman?" Jonas asked, staring at him with disbelief.

He glared at his brother. "Like I said, Jonas, no big deal." Usually he didn't get agitated easily, especially with his siblings, but for some reason tonight he was. He should be overjoyed Hunter had granted him another week, but there was that risk that it wouldn't be enough. Then where would he be?

"I ran into Ingrid McKay today at the grocery store," his mother said, eyeing him speculatively. "You didn't mention that Hunter McKay had moved back to town."

He stared at his mother, wondering why she would bring that up...especially now. And as far as mentioning it to her, he hadn't known she even knew Hunter. Had she kept a log of every girl he'd hit on in high school? "I didn't mention it because I didn't think it was a big deal. I didn't even know you knew Hunter."

"Of course I know Hunter. She was Reverend McKay's granddaughter. She sang in the choir and had an awesome voice. I also recall she was a beautiful girl with impeccable manners. How could I not know her when we attended the same church?"

But so did four hundred other people, Tyson thought, taking a sip of his iced tea.

According to his mother Hunter had a nice voice. He'd heard Hunter scream a lot of times but never sing. Nor could he recall her singing whenever he attended church back in the day. Must have been those Sundays when he'd dozed off during the service.

"Hunter McKay," Jonas said, smiling. "I remember her from high school. We graduated together. Isn't she the one who dumped you, Tyson?"

Tyson glared at Jonas for the second time that night. "She didn't dump me."

"That's not the way I heard it," Galen said, grinning.

"Well, you heard wrong."

Brittany, who seemed to have acquired the role of peacemaker since marrying Galen, spoke up and changed the subject. "I forgot to mention that Jonas wants to use the twins in his next marketing campaign. Isn't that wonderful?"

Tyson gave Brittany an appreciative smile. Everyone at the table got so caught up with her announcement that any further conversation about Tyson and Hunter was abruptly forgotten.

He took a sip of his tea and glanced across the table at Eli, who was looking at him with a grin on his face. Eli was the only one who'd known of his plan to pursue Hunter. He was grateful Eli was the brother who knew how to keep his mouth shut, although he liked giving his opinion much too often to suit Tyson. He couldn't help wondering what Eli found amusing since he still had that silly-looking grin on his face. Then Tyson remembered. Eli had warned him about getting possessed by passion. Damn. For once he wished he'd taken his brother's warning to heart. Now he had a feeling he was way over his head where Hunter was concerned.

Hunter began drying off her body with the huge towel. She much preferred taking showers, but tonight a good hot soak had done wonders for her body, a body that had gone through intense lovemaking with Tyson Steele.

She hadn't counted on him taking her on her desk and her sofa, all in the same afternoon. In all honesty, she hadn't counted on being taken at all.

And now she had agreed to spend a week with him. Because of that decision she could see herself taking even more baths. But like she'd told him, their week would be filled with more than just lovemaking. One sure way to get her out of his system, if she was as deeply embedded into it as he claimed, was to come up with activities he didn't do with women. The thought made her smile. In the end he would thank her.

His admission still baffled her. Personally, if she felt possessed by any man he would certainly be the last one to know it. But Tyson had pretty much placed his cards on the table without any care as to how she played them. Just as long as he got his week with her. That was the craziest thing she'd ever heard.

Still, she couldn't discount the changes making love with Tyson had done to her and for her. Thanks to him she now knew firsthand just what an ass Carter had been, especially in the bedroom. And thanks to Tyson she had discovered a lot about her own sexuality. He'd opened a door to sensual exploration and adventure for her. With Tyson nothing was taboo, nothing was off-limits or forbidden. He wouldn't be the only one using this week to his advantage. She would, too, but for different reasons. For her it would be a week of sexual journeys and sensuous excursions. But the big question for her was how to keep her emotions out of the equation. For Tyson this was about sex and nothing more and she had to remember that. More than once she'd felt a pull at her heart whenever they made love. She had to fight hard not to get lust mixed up with love.

Hunter had slid into her nightgown and was about to grab a magazine off her coffee table to read in bed when the sound of her doorbell startled her. She could think of only one person showing up at her place tonight. Hadn't they made love twice already today? He'd warned her that he was a greedy ass. Now she was beginning to believe him.

Dismissing the rush of desire moving up her spine, she put down the magazine and went to her door. A quick look out the peephole confirmed her suspicions. It was Tyson.

She fought back the sensations she felt just knowing he was on the other side of that door. The thought that she was beginning to be just as insatiable as he didn't sit well with her. Releasing a deep sigh mixed with frustration and desire, she opened the door.

He stood there and held her gaze. Although she didn't want to, her body felt heated from his deep, penetrating stare. Blood was rushing to every part of her body and she knew there was no way to stop it. Instead of saying anything, she moved aside for him to enter. And when he walked past her she inhaled his rich, masculine scent. The same one she'd washed off her skin less than an hour ago.

He paused in the middle of her living room. Hunter was surprised he hadn't just headed straight for the bedroom. Tyson was arrogant enough to do so. He turned and she felt the heat of his gaze as it moved up and down her baby-doll nightgown.

"Believe it or not, Hunter, this isn't a booty call," he finally said, breaking the silence.

She leaned back against her closed door. "Is there a new name for it now?" She wouldn't be surprised if he'd coined his own term.

"I didn't come here to make love to you…although I have no qualms about doing so if you want."

She crossed her arms over her chest and ignored

how his gaze moved to her breasts. She felt her nipples harden. "Then why are you here?"

A smile touched the corners of his lips, so adorable she had to blink to make sure it was real. "I decided to drop by tonight, Hunter, because I want to hear you sing."

Tyson loved Hunter's facial expressions whenever he caught her off guard. He'd shocked her again. Without waiting for an invitation he took a seat on her sofa.

"Sing?" she asked. "What makes you think I can sing?"

"My mother. She mentioned it over dinner." At another shocked look, he smiled. They just kept on coming.

"Why would your mother bring up my name at dinner?" she asked, leaving her place at the door to sit down in the wingback chair in the living room.

"She ran into your mother at the grocery store and found out you'd moved back to town. She wanted to know why I hadn't mentioned it to her. I told her I didn't even know she knew you. That's when she said you used to be in the choir at church and had a nice voice."

Hunter smiled. "That was kind of her to think so. I'm surprised she remembered. That was years ago."

Tyson chuckled. "My mother rarely forgets anything, trust me. So are you going to sing for me?"

"No."

"Why not?"

"Other than humming occasionally when I take a shower, I haven't sung in years."

"So? I'd like to hear you sing."

"Why?"

Tyson wasn't sure. All he knew was that when he left his parents' home he had wanted to come straight here and get her to sing for him. "I just want to hear you, that's all."

She stared at him for a minute and he knew she was trying to figure him out. He wanted to tell her not to waste her time, when lately even he hadn't been able to figure out his actions, at least not when it came to her.

"Fine," she finally said. "Is there a particular song you want to hear?"

"Anything by Whitney Houston."

He saw the smile that spread across her lips and it stirred his insides. "Throw me a real challenge, will you? But okay, I got this. Lucky for you I happen to love all her songs." Easing from her chair, she grinned. "I really feel silly doing this, but you asked for it. Here goes."

And then while he watched she threw her head back, closed her eyes and began belting out "The Greatest Love of All."

Tyson sat there spellbound, mesmerized and totally captivated. His mother was right. Hunter had an awesome voice and listening to her sing touched him deeply. There were so many facets of Hunter McKay and he wondered if her husband had appreciated every single one. Apparently not.

He couldn't take his eyes off her, standing there in the middle of her living room, singing for him and him alone. She appeared shrouded in sensuality and his pulse throbbed at the effect she was having on him. It was crazy. It didn't make much sense. Yet it was happening. Hunter McKay was drawing everything out of him and without very much effort.

Moments later when she finished and opened her

eyes, she stared across the room at him, a tentative smile touching her lips. "Okay. I'm done."

Tyson knew in all honesty, so was he. Hunter had done him in. He felt his heart pounding in his chest. She looked beautiful standing there in her short lacy nightgown that showed off a pair of beautiful legs. It sounded crazy but he was beginning to think this entire thing with Hunter was more than her being deeply embedded in his system. It was more than him being possessed by her passion. And he needed this week to figure it out.

Standing, he clapped his hands. "Bravo. You were excellent. Superb. If you ever quit your day job you can—"

"Become a backup singer for Prince? That was my childhood dream for the longest time."

He chuckled. "Was it?"

"Yes."

"If you didn't make it, then it was his loss." He crossed the room to her. "Thanks for singing for me. Mom was right. I had no idea. You have a beautiful voice."

She shrugged. "Carter never thought so. He claimed I always sang off-key."

Tyson shook his head. "The more I hear about your ex-husband, the more I believe you were right."

She raised a brow. "About what?"

"About him being a bastard." He then leaned down and placed a light kiss on her lips. "Walk me to the door."

Another shocked look appeared on her face. "You're leaving?"

"Yes." He took her hand as he headed toward the door. "I have surgeries in the morning, but call me tomorrow afternoon to let me know of your plans for our weekend. I have the entire weekend off."

"All right."

Before he opened the door he couldn't resist taking her into his arms and devouring her mouth. He knew leaving her alone tonight would be hard but it was something he had to do. Hunter was a puzzle he had to piece together for his peace of mind.

When he released her mouth, he whispered against her moist lips. "Good night."

"Good night, Tyson."

And then he opened the door and walked out.

Chapter 16

"This is Dr. Steele. May I help you?"

Hunter loved the sexy sound of Tyson's voice. "Yes, Dr. Steele, this is Hunter and you can definitely help me."

She heard the richness of his chuckle and wished it didn't make her pulse rate increase. "And what can I do for you, Ms. McKay?"

"I thought we'd take in a movie tonight. Anything you prefer seeing?"

There was silence on his end and Hunter knew why. Rumor had it that if Tyson Steele took a woman out, his bedroom was as far as they got. This week wouldn't be status quo for him. He'd said she could set the ground rules and she had.

"Doesn't matter," he finally said. "Anything you want to see will be fine with me. I'll pick you up at seven. Is that a good time for dinner and a movie?"

She was surprised at his suggestion of dinner. "Yes, seven is fine. I'll see you then."

"And, Hunter?"

"Yes?"

"Bring your dancing shoes. I want to take you dancing after the movie."

He wanted to take her dancing? "Okay." After ending her call with Tyson, Hunter leaned back in her office chair as she remembered his visit to her apartment last night. No booty call, he'd just wanted to hear her sing. How strange was that? Had he asked to spend the night she probably would have let him. But he hadn't asked.

She hated admitting it, but Tyson Steele was beginning to confuse her. Like his suggestion of dinner, dancing and him picking her up. She'd honestly assumed that he would ask what time the movie started and say he would meet her there. Anything else would constitute a real date, and Tyson Steele didn't do real dates. He'd told her that himself during their little bedroom talk that night over wine and cheese. He claimed dating would encourage women to get the wrong ideas regarding the nature of his intent.

So why this sudden change of behavior? She could only assume that he figured she knew the score so she wasn't anyone he had to worry about. He was trying to work her out of his system and nothing more.

She looked at her watch. If Tyson was going to take her to dinner, a movie and dancing, she needed to make a few shopping stops before going home. Her goal was to make this a week neither of them would forget. And tonight was the kickoff.

"You dance as well as you sing," Tyson whispered to Hunter hours later when he led her to the center of the floor for another dance. This one was a slow number. About time, he thought, as he pulled her into his arms. He was beginning to think line dancing was all they'd be doing tonight.

"Thanks. I love to dance."

Tyson could tell. Even when they'd sat out a few she had moved from side to side in her chair, keeping time with the music.

He had picked her up promptly at seven and when she opened the door he had to stand there for a moment to get his bearings. From head to toe, she looked fabulous. And he had told her so many more times than he probably should have tonight. He totally liked her short, tight-fitting dress and killer heels.

They had dined at Toni's, an Italian restaurant located in the heart of the city. Over dinner she had told him about the additional clients she had acquired and again thanked him for the three he had referred. He was glad everything seemed to be working out for her.

Tyson wrapped his arms around her, loving the feel of holding her as they moved slowly around the dance floor. Tonight had been great and he had enjoyed her company. He'd even enjoyed the movie she'd chosen for them to see. He was surprised to discover that, like him, she liked Westerns. This one had been one of the good ones and had held his attention most of the time. Hunter held it all the other times. He had to admit he'd enjoyed sitting beside her in the theater, sharing popcorn with her. Holding her hand.

She pressed her cheek against his chest as they slowly swayed to the music. Their movements were so slow that at times it appeared neither of them was moving. And their bodies were so close he could feel her every curve. He was getting sexually charged just thinking about tonight and how it would end. Again, she'd made it clear that she would not spend a single night this week in his bed, and he had no problem wearing out the mattress at her place if that's what she preferred.

Resting his cheek against the top of her head, he couldn't help but think there was more to his relationship with Hunter than just great sex. Dinner and the movie had proven that and he looked forward to spending more time with her outside the bedroom this week.

When he felt her stiffen in his arms, he glanced down at her. "You all right?"

She glanced up and met his gaze. "My ex is here."

Tyson lifted a brow. "Your ex? Here?"

"Yes. I heard he might be coming to Phoenix on business, and I can only assume that's why he's here. He just walked in with a group of men."

Tyson nodded. "If his presence makes you uncomfortable, we can leave."

She shook her head. "No. He's seen us and maybe that's good thing."

"Why?"

"My mother-in-law overheard Carter's plan to contact me while he's here and play on my heartstrings."

"Your heartstrings?"

"Yes. He has this crazy notion that since I hadn't dated since our divorce that I'm still in love with him and would take him back, even after all he's done."

Tyson didn't know what all the man had done, but just from the time he had spent with Hunter he knew she felt only loathing for her ex. "You say he's seen us?"

"Yes. In fact he's sitting at the table, staring at us now."

"Good."

Tyson pulled Hunter closer into his arms, leaned down and covered her mouth with his.

Hunter suddenly sat straight up in bed. When she saw a naked Tyson sleeping beside her, she realized it hadn't been a dream at all. They'd gone to dinner, a movie and dancing. The evening had gone great. Not even seeing Carter had put a damper on things, because Tyson had refused to let it.

Although it had been pretense, he had gone out of his way to give the impression that the two of them were a hot item. In addition to kissing her in the middle of the dance floor, when they had returned to their table Tyson had taken her in his lap and hand-fed her the chips and dip they'd ordered. She couldn't help but enjoy Tyson's attentiveness, even if it was playacting. He had lavished her with attention and affection. Tonight Tyson had made her feel significant, appreciated and desired right before Carter's eyes.

From the angry look she'd seen on her ex's face, he'd gotten the message Tyson had intended. The message that she belonged to Tyson. And in a way she did... even if it was for just a week. They had left the nightclub only after Carter had done so, satisfied their mission had been accomplished.

The moment they had entered her apartment Tyson had swept her off her feet and carried her into the bedroom. There he had undressed her and his skilled body had taken her over the edge. Not once. Or twice. Three times before they'd finally drifted off to sleep.

Smiling now, she settled back down in bed and snuggled her body deeper into his. Why was she allowing herself to get wrapped up in the moment?

And why tonight, when she had seen Carter again after all this time, had she felt nothing...absolutely nothing? It seemed her mind, body and soul refused to waste any more emotions—loathing or otherwise—on the man she'd spent eight years trying and failing to satisfy. But now, thanks to Tyson, she knew the failures weren't her fault, but were Carter's.

She drew in a deep breath. In Tyson's mind, he had wanted another week with her because he believed he was possessed by passion. And she would admit the two of them could generate a lot of that. But now she could finally admit to herself the reason she'd agreed to a week with him. She had fallen in love with him.

It really didn't matter how it happened or when but she knew it had. She wanted to believe it happened the first time they'd made love. He had treated her like a woman who deserved to be treated with dignity and respect. But he'd gone even further by treating her like a woman who deserved to be appreciated. Each and every time they made love he'd made her feel special, like a woman worth having, even in the bedroom.

It didn't bother her that he didn't return her love or that he would never know her true feelings for him. Loving him was her secret. After this week was over and he returned to his world—the one filled with all those other women—she would always have these precious memories.

"You okay?"

She glanced over at Tyson. She hadn't meant to awaken him. "Yes, I'm fine."

"Baby, I know you're fine. That dress you wore tonight showed just how fine you are."

She chuckled. "You liked my dress?"

"I told you I did. A number of times. I like every out-fit you put on your body. And I like your body, as well."

"Do you?"

"Yes, I do."

She eased out of his arms to straddle him. "Your erection is rock-hard. I definitely want to put something like that to good use."

"And your girls wants my attention," he said, reaching upward to cup the twin mounds in his hands. "I plan to put them to good use, as well."

"Not before I give you a little attention, Mr. Steele."

And then she eased down in bed and took his shaft into her mouth. He grabbed hold of her shoulders to pull her back up, but she figured the feel of her lips and tongue pleasuring him enticed him to change his mind. Instead he let his fingers tunnel through the curls on her head as he began groaning deep in his throat.

"Hunter! You got to stop. I'm about to come."

She recalled giving him a similar warning one night that he'd ignored just like she intended to do. Instead of stopping, she took him deeper and suckled him right into an orgasm.

"Hunter!"

A short while later she lifted her head and looked up at him and smiled. In her heart she knew she loved him but he would never know.

"You, Hunter McKay, are a naughty girl," he said throatily.

"And you, Tyson Steele," she said, licking her lips, "are one delicious man."

"Tell me about your ex-husband," Tyson said, holding Hunter in his arms. It had taken him a minute to recover from the orgasm she'd given him. It had been explosive and left his entire body reeling.

Hunter lifted her head and he could see the surprise in her eyes. If she found his request odd, then she wasn't alone. He'd never asked a woman about her ex. Usually her past didn't matter. It certainly didn't have any bearing on the present. But with Hunter it mattered. He'd seen Carter Robinson tonight and other than what Eli had told him, Tyson didn't know everything the man had done.

She didn't say anything for a long moment, and then she finally spoke. "I guess after tonight I owe you an explanation."

"No explanation needed. You told me why you needed him to see us together. The heartstrings thing. But I want to know about him. I'm having a hard time understanding what man in his right mind would let such a passionate woman like you get away."

She snuggled deeper in his arms, as if she needed his closeness to tell him what he wanted to know. "That's just it. Carter never thought of me as passionate." She paused a moment. "We met at a party a couple of years after I finished grad school. We dated for a year and he asked me to marry him. I thought we were perfect together. We shared the same profession and the same dreams and goals. Three years after we were married I discovered he was having an affair with a former client. He asked for my forgiveness, said it wouldn't happen again. But it did. By then he didn't care that I knew and said if I left him I would have more to lose than he did. I believed him, so I stayed, although we didn't share a bed. I moved into the guest room."

She drew in a deep breath. "Things continued that

way for two years until I hired a private investigator who uncovered a number of things, including the fact that while I slept in the guest room upstairs, Carter would on occasion sneak his mistress into the house to spend the night with her in our bed."

Anger flared through Tyson at the thought of any man disrespecting his wife that way. No wonder she had a problem with sharing a bed with him where she'd known other women had been before her. "Did you confront him about it?"

"Yes, and I told him I was divorcing him. He laughed, and said I didn't have the backbone to do such a thing. He saw how wrong he was the day he was served the divorce papers. Everyone turned against me for divorcing him. His family. People I thought were our friends. And then on top of all that, he set out to hurt me by taking my clients and making things difficult for me in Boston." She drew in a deep breath. "In a way my brother's request that I come home to help with our parents gave me the perfect excuse to return to Phoenix to start over."

While he listened, Hunter also told him how during her marriage her ex had tried eroding what little self-confidence she had. How he had tried making it seem that his involvement with other women was her fault and how he'd tried controlling her. "And to think Carter actually believed I could still love him and he could get me back after all he did." He could hear the sadness in her voice as she spoke.

Tyson didn't say anything as he continued to hold her in his arms. He felt a huge sense of protectiveness swell inside him where Hunter was concerned, and knew at that moment he would never give any man the chance to hurt her ever again.

Chapter 17

"What's this I hear about you making a fool of yourself with a woman, Tyson? You've been seen around town on several occasions, taking her to dinner, movies, dancing and concerts. I even heard you attended church with her one Sunday."

Tyson had known when he'd opened the door to find Mercury standing there that there had to be a reason for his visit. "And what of it?"

"Acting all infatuated with a woman is not like you."

Yes, Tyson agreed. Mercury was right, it wasn't like him. But he had discovered his interest in Hunter had gone beyond just the physical. It was a lot more than being possessed by the passion they could generate, as he'd assumed. What was supposed to last only one week was now going into its third week. Neither he nor Hunter had brought up the fact that the one-week time limit had expired. They both seemed to be intentionally overlooking it.

Because of the ground rules she'd established, all their time together hadn't been in the bedroom. They were doing other things, activities he would not have bothered doing with a woman. In addition to movies, dinner and dancing, they'd taken walks in the park, gone to the zoo, tried mountain climbing...and he'd even made an appearance at church. During the course of that time he had gotten to know Hunter in ways he hadn't thought possible. He knew her likes, her dislikes, things she tolerated and things she considered not up for negotiation. Likewise, he'd opened himself up to her as well. He felt comfortable telling her about his days at the hospital, and he even let her in on the Steele brothers' early plans for their parents' fortieth wedding anniversary.

This morning before leaving her bed he had been able to put the final piece of the puzzle in place. Now he knew why she had gotten under his skin, why he'd let her stay there and why he hadn't been able to get her out of his system. And why with her he felt possessed by passion. Bottom line was that he had fallen in love with her.

He'd tried convincing himself it was only lust, but he knew that wasn't the case each and every time they made love. Now he fully understood how Galen, Eli and Jonas felt about the women they'd fallen in love with and married. And as hard as it was to believe, he had no problem being included in that group, mainly because he couldn't consider his life without Hunter as a part of it.

"Tyson, are you listening to me?"

He really hadn't been. "Sorry, what did you say?"

"I asked who she is."

Tyson had no problem giving his brother a name. "Hunter McKay."

Mercury lifted a brow. Tyson could tell from his brother's expression he was recalling the time Hunter's name had come up during one of their parents' Thursday night dinners.

"Well, I hope you have a good reason for what you're doing."

He met his brother's stare. "Trust me. I do."

After Mercury left, Tyson knew exactly what he needed to do. He pulled out his cell phone to place a call. "Hi, Mom. Would it be a problem to set out an extra place setting for dinner tonight? You will be happy to know I've found the woman who will be permanently filling one of those three empty spots at the table."

"The flowers are beautiful."

Hunter had to agree with Pauline. The huge bouquet of red roses that had been delivered to her that morning was simply beautiful. She didn't have to read the card to know that Tyson had sent them. They had gone over their one-week agreement and were now into a third. She figured their time together had come to an end and the flowers were his parting gift to her.

Before leaving her apartment this morning he'd asked if he could decide where they would go tonight. She didn't have a problem with his request. He hadn't said where they would be going. All he'd said was to dress casual and be ready at six.

Then she had arrived at work to see the flowers sitting on her desk. It had been years since she'd received flowers and like she told Pauline they were simply beautiful, although their suspected meaning caused a pain in her heart.

After Pauline left Hunter's office she sat behind her desk and drew in a deep breath. She'd been hoping…

What? That like her, Tyson would continue to ignore that they'd gone beyond the week they were to spend together? That he would claim she still wasn't out of his system, that he still felt possessed by passion and wanted more time together? Maybe that's what she was hoping, but unfortunately, the flowers were a clear indication that he had gotten over her and was now ready to move on.

Once again she had fallen in love with a man who would never truly love her in return. Story of her life, it seemed. But she would get over it because whether Tyson realized it or not, these past three weeks had meant everything to her. They had reinforced her belief in herself and she owed that to him.

He had made every single day with him special. Instead of protesting about anything she'd had on their list for them to do, he had readily embraced every activity. Whether it was going out to dinner, movies, concerts or dancing, he didn't seem to have a problem being seen with her. He'd even kept his word to her mother and gone to church with her. And because they had sat together, more than one pair of curious eyes had been on them.

The buzzer on her desk sounded. "Yes, Pauline?"

"Dr. Steele is on the line."

"Thanks." Was he calling to cancel tonight? Had he figured there was no need to wait until later to end things between them?

"Yes, Tyson?"

"Have you had lunch yet?"

"No."

"Good. I'll pick you up in a few minutes. There's something I want you to see."

He sounded rather mysterious but she went along with him. "Okay."

She hung up her phone, wondering what Tyson wanted her to see.

"Where are we going?"

Tyson smiled over at Hunter. He figured she would be curious since he hadn't given her much information. They had left the Phoenix city limits and were now headed toward the outskirts of town. "I think I've mentioned my cousin Morgan Steele to you before."

"He's the one who's the mayor of Charlotte, right?"

"Yes. His wife, Lena, owns a real estate company that has expanded into several states, including this one. I hired her to find some property in the country for me."

Hunter raised a brow. "Why?"

"To build that house you designed for me."

She frowned. "Tyson, we both know why you had me draw up those plans."

"Do we?" He knew Hunter thought she had things figured out.

"Of course. That was just a part of your plan to seduce me."

"Was it?"

Her frown deepened. "Okay, Tyson. What kind of game are you playing?"

A smile touched his lips. "No game. What if I told you I was dead serious about those house plans?"

"That would be news to me. Until today you haven't mentioned those plans since I gave them to you over a month ago."

Tyson brought his car to a stop in front of a wooded piece of property. He looked over at her. "I guess you can say I was waiting for a good time to do so."

The male in him appreciated her outfit. Today she was wearing another dress and although it wasn't as short as he'd like, it still showed off her gorgeous legs.

He glanced out the car window. "This is the property Lena found for me. What do you think?"

Hunter glanced around. She thought the land was pretty nice and told him so. Even from the car she could see a view of the mountains. The drive hadn't been too far from town, which wouldn't make his commute to the hospital too much of a hassle. Once he got on the interstate it would be a straight shot and he could get to work probably within twenty minutes.

"It's twenty-five acres on a private road," he said, intruding into her thoughts. "Not another house around for at least ten miles, and I think I'll like the seclusion. There's a huge lake on the property and plenty of trees."

"I think you'll like the seclusion, too," she said, not missing the excitement in his voice.

He pushed the button to extend his seat back to stretch out his legs. "Any ideas how the house will fit on it?"

Hunter shrugged as she glanced out the window again. "It shouldn't be a problem if you face the front of your house to the east. That way your bedrooms can take advantage of the view of the lake and mountains from any window."

He nodded. "I'm thinking of increasing the square footage to add a few more bedrooms. When I marry and have children I want to make sure they have plenty of space."

Personally, Hunter thought the house she'd designed had more than enough space already. However, if he thought he needed more than that, it was his business. She tried dismissing from her mind that this was the first time he'd ever mentioned a wife and children. He'd claimed he had no interest in ever getting married. Even when he'd given her specifics for what he wanted in a home, the subject of a wife and children had never entered the equation. "You're the client," she said. "I can modify the plans any way you want."

"I hope I'm more than just a client to you, Hunter."

Hunter nibbled on her bottom lip, not sure how to address that comment. She couldn't help but remember the roses sitting on her desk and what they probably meant.

"Thanks for the roses, by the way."

"You're welcome. Glad you liked them."

She drew in a deep breath. Even now while sitting in a parked car in a secluded area she could feel the chemistry between them. It seemed over the past few weeks, instead of diminishing, their physical attraction had gotten stronger. That would probably account for why their lovemaking was even more intense every night.

Tyson claimed he wasn't playing games, but for some reason she felt that he was. She was about to tell him so when he said, "You didn't respond to what I said about me being more than a client to you."

She studied him and then decided to turn the tables on him. "My response depends on whether I'm more than an architect to you."

* * *

Tyson knew he could put her mind to rest about that and intended to do so. He wasn't sure how she felt about him, but he figured any woman who'd given him as much of herself as she had during the time they'd spent together had to feel something for him.

He reached out and took her hand. "Hunter, there's something I need to say."

She pulled her hand away from him. "You don't have to say anything. I got the message with the roses."

He raised a brow. "And just what message did you get?"

"That you want us to end things."

He didn't say anything for a minute, and then he asked, "And you got that message from me sending you roses?"

"I had an employee back in Boston years ago. When her boyfriend broke up with her, instead of sending her a 'Dear Jane' letter, he sent her a dozen 'Dear Jane' roses."

"And you figured that's what I did?"

"Isn't it?"

"No. You're right about me wanting us to end things…at least, wanting to end this phase of our relationship. But only for a new beginning."

She nodded. "I get it. You want another week."

He chuckled. "No, Hunter. I want forever." Tyson watched her face and wasn't surprised when shock spread across her features. He was tempted to lean over and kiss it right off her face.

"Forever?"

He nodded, watching her closely. "Yes, forever."

She evidently wasn't sure they were on the same

page, because she asked, "You mean forever as in till death do us part?"

He chuckled. "Yes, that pretty much sums it up."

She stared at him like he had suddenly developed some kind of mental problem. "Why?"

"That's easy to answer. Because I've fallen in love with you."

She continued to stare at him for a long moment and then she shook her head. "That's impossible."

"And why is it impossible?"

"B-because you're Tyson Steele."

"I know who I am."

She glared at him. "Need I remind you that you're a man who goes through women quicker than you change your socks?"

"Last time I looked you're the only woman I've been with in well over a month now. I told you that I hadn't desired another woman since that night I ran into you at Notorious."

"But our relationship has been only physical."

"I beg to differ. Think about what we've been doing for the past few weeks. What we've shared. I've enjoyed spending time with you and doing things that had nothing to do with the bedroom."

When she didn't say anything he added, "I appreciate the time that we've gotten to know each other. Now more than ever I know you're the woman I want in my life."

When she didn't say anything but continued to stare at him, he pressed on. "I know I've laid a lot on the table and you need time to take it all in. I also know you probably don't reciprocate my feelings but I feel strongly that one day you will."

* * *

Hunter could not believe the words Tyson had spoken. He loved her? Really loved her as much as she loved him? She tried hard to fight back tears. "But I already do," she said, swiping the tears that were determined to fall anyway.

"You do what?"

"Reciprocate your feelings. I love you, too, Tyson. I think I fell in love with you the first time we made love. You made me feel so special. Like a woman who was truly appreciated. But not in a million years did I think you would, or could, love me back. You have… shall we say, a history with women."

"Yes, I do. But you effectively destroyed that history. You're the only woman I want. The only woman I could and will ever love."

More than anything she wanted to believe him, but hadn't Carter told her that same thing? But then, hadn't she discovered that Tyson wasn't anything like Carter?

"Hunter, will you marry me?"

She blinked. "Marry you?"

He nodded. "Yes."

"But how can you be sure that I'm the woman you want to spend your life with?"

He smiled. "I'm sure. Trust me, I fought it. Marrying anyone was the last thing on my mind, but my dad was right."

"About what?"

"Jonas said Dad once told him that a smart man knows there's nothing wrong with falling in love if it's a woman you can't live your life without. And I can't live my life without you, Hunter."

She wanted so much to believe him. "But what about those other women?"

"They don't matter. Not one of them had me possessed by passion. But you do, Hunter. I believe a man knows he's run his course with other women when they no longer interest him and none of them is more important to him than the one he wants to wake up with every morning and make memories with forever. And that's you."

He paused a moment to clear his throat. "So, I'm asking again. Hunter McKay, will you marry me? Will you be the only woman in my life? The one to share this house I'm building for us here on this property? The only one I want to be the mother of my children? The only one I want to wear the name of Mrs. Tyson Steele?"

At that moment, numerous emotions ran through Hunter and she knew what her answer to him would be. He was the only man she wanted in her life as well. "Yes, Tyson. I will marry you."

A huge smile curved Tyson's lips and he leaned over and captured her mouth with his. Shivers raced all through her body from the way his mouth was devouring hers. He was building passion neither of them could contain. And when he slid his arms around her waist to pull her over the console and into his lap, she followed his lead and returned the kiss with the same sexual hunger. Their tongues mated hotly, greedily. The degree of her desire for Tyson always astounded her, made her appreciate that she was a woman who wanted this man. And just to know he loved her as much as she loved him sent her soaring to the moon.

Moments later when the need to breathe overrode everything else, she pulled back from the kiss. He reached up and traced his finger across her moist lips. "I can sit here and kiss you all day," he said huskily.

"Umm, I prefer we do something else," she said leaning in to trail feathery kisses along the corners of his lips and chin.

"Something like what?"

"This," she said, climbing over his seat into the back and grabbing his hand to entice him to follow. He did. And then she shoved him on his back and straddled him. "We can start here. We never got around to doing it in the backseat of your car eighteen years ago."

He chuckled softly as his hands grabbed hold of her thighs, easing her dress up nearly to her waist. "Back then you were a good girl."

"Now I'm bad," she said, pulling his zipper down. "Tyson's naughty girl."

"Soon to be his naughty wife," he said and then sucked in a deep breath when she reached inside his pants and took the solid thickness of his erection in her hand. When she began stroking him he released a guttural moan.

"You did say this is a private road, right?" she asked.

"Yes, it's very private."

"Good."

She opened her legs to cradle him and then remembered something. "Condom."

"Here," he said after working a packet out of his back pocket.

She took her time to sheathe him the way she'd seen him do many times. When he eased her panties aside she slid down, releasing a deep moan when the head of his erection touched her center just seconds before he tightened his hold on her hips and slowly entered her.

It was as if he was savoring the moment, though for her it was pure torture. She needed all of him now. She leaned in and bit him gently on the lips. In retaliation he thrust hard into her, melding their bodies.

"I thought that would get you going," she said, licking the mark her teeth had made on his lips.

Instead of responding he began moving, stroking her insides, thrusting in and out, over and over again. Never had she felt so thoroughly made love to except for with Tyson. He had the ability to make her purr, yearn and become obsessed with everything he was doing to her.

"Hunter!"

When he screamed her name, she knew his world had tipped over the edge and hers would soon follow. He continued to stroke her while groaning out his pleasure. And she moaned, saying his name on a breathless groan, as the two of them were tossed into waves of pure ecstasy.

When Hunter found the energy to lift her head from his chest, she met his gaze. Their bodies were still intimately connected, and sexual chemistry, as explosive as it could get, still flowed between them the way it always did. A flirty smile touched her lips. "Let's do it again, Tyson," she said, leaning in close to lick the underside of his neck.

He smiled at her. "Yes, let's do it again. And then we'll go to the jewelry store for your engagement ring."

Epilogue

A beautiful day in August

Hunter couldn't stop looking down at the wedding ring Tyson had slid on her finger. It was beautiful. And then she glanced up at him. He was beautiful, as well.

"Tyson, will you repeat after me," the pastor said, reclaiming her attention. "With this ring, I thee wed."

Tyson held her gaze as he repeated the pastor's words loud and clear. She couldn't stop the tears from rolling down her cheeks. Mo and Kat would kill her for messing up a perfectly made-up face, but she couldn't help it. It was her wedding day and she could cry if she wanted to.

"By the power vested in me by this great state of Arizona, I now pronounce you husband and wife. Tyson, you may kiss your bride."

She smiled as he pulled her into his arms, sealing their vows with a kiss. When he released her he swept her off her feet as the pastor introduced them. "Dr. and Mrs. Tyson Steele."

As he carried her out the church while holding her in his arms, somewhere in the audience Hunter heard a voice say, "Another Bad News Steele bites the dust."

She tightened her arm around Tyson's neck, grateful that this particular Steele was hers.

Tyson tried to keep the smile off his face as he spoke with his brothers. "We're happy for you, man," Gannon said. "Hunter is wonderful."

"I think she's wonderful, too." He glanced over at Mercury. "Sorry, but the heat is going to be on you two guys. Maybe it won't be so bad since Eli and Stacey announced they are having a baby. That might keep Mom occupied for a while."

Mercury chuckled. "We can only hope. And I agree with Gannon. Hunter is great for you. She makes you happy and we can see it."

"Yes, I'm a very happy man." Tyson took a sip of his wine while glancing around Hunter's parents' beautifully decorated backyard. He and Hunter had decided on an outdoor wedding with only family and close friends. He saw his wife of one hour standing in a group talking to the wives of his cousins from Charlotte.

It was time for their first dance together as husband and wife. "Excuse me, guys."

He headed across the patio and as if she sensed his approach, Hunter glanced up and met his gaze. She smiled, excused herself from the group and met him halfway.

"Dr. Steele."

"Mrs. Steele. Ready for our first dance together?" he asked, taking her hand in his.

"Yes, I am ready."

"The sooner we can start our honeymoon the better," he said. They would be flying to Aruba, where they would spend the next two weeks.

"You sound rather anxious."

"I'll show you how anxious I am once I strip you naked," he said, leading her to the area designated for the dance floor.

Hunter lifted her head from Tyson's chest as they shared their first dance as husband and wife. "I never wanted to marry again, Tyson, but you made me change my mind about that."

He smiled down at her. "And I didn't want to ever marry but I was a man possessed and I couldn't do anything about it, sweetheart. You stole my heart before I knew what was happening."

She couldn't help but be filled with love for this man, who continued to show her what true love was about. He was the one who went out of his way to make her feel that she was everything a woman should be. Worthy of his love. Hunter couldn't help but remember that day they'd made love in the backseat of his car. Afterward, he had taken her to Lola's, one of the most exclusive jewelers in Phoenix. Together they had selected her engagement ring—a beautiful four-carat cushion diamond with a halo setting—as well as their diamond band wedding rings.

That evening he had surprised her by taking her to his parents' home to take part in the family's Thursday night dinner. Tyson's parents and the rest of the family had congratulated them, and of course the women had fallen in love with her engagement ring. Dinner had been special and since that night she'd been included in the Steeles' Thursday night dinners. She loved his parents and loved getting to know all of Tyson's brothers, as well as their wives.

"What are you thinking about, sweetheart?" Tyson asked, leaning down to whisper close to her ear.

"I was thinking just what a lucky woman I am."

"I feel lucky as well. You are everything I could ever want, Hunter."

He pulled her closer into his arms. He couldn't wait to be in their new home, dancing in their own backyard. Already the property had been cleared and construction had begun. According to the builder, they should be ready to move into their dream home in about six months.

"There are only two single Steeles now," Hunter observed, seeing Mercury and Gannon standing in a group talking with their cousins from Charlotte.

"I know, and I can't wait to meet the women who make them believe in a forever kind of love," Tyson said. "They're going to find out the same thing I did. You can't run from love."

Then he leaned down and captured her mouth with his, ignoring the claps and catcalls from their audience. When he released her mouth, she pulled in a deep breath. "What was that for?"

He chuckled. "Don't you know, baby? I am a man possessed. Not only am I possessed by your passion, I'm also possessed by your love."

Hunter sank closer into her husband's embrace and smiled up at him. "And I'm possessed by yours."

* * * * *

Reese Ryan writes sexy, deeply emotional romances full of family drama, surprising secrets and unexpected twists.

Born and raised in the Midwest, Reese has deep Tennessee roots. Every summer, she endured long, hot car trips to family reunions in Memphis via a tiny clown car loaded with cousins.

Connect with Reese at ReeseRyanWrites on Instagram, Twitter and Facebook, or at reeseryan.com/desirereaders.

Books by Reese Ryan

Harlequin Desire

The Bourbon Brothers
Savannah's Secret
The Billionaire's Legacy

Texas Cattleman's Club: Bachelor Auction
His Until Midnight

Harlequin Kimani Romance
Playing with Desire
Playing with Temptation
Playing with Seduction

Visit the Author Profile page at
Harlequin.com.

PLAYING WITH TEMPTATION

Reese Ryan

Dedicated to self-sacrificing single mothers like my mother and paternal grandmother. And to devoted fathers like my husband.

Acknowledgments

Thank you to author Michele Summers for driving out to the boonies for an into-the-wee-hours brainstorming session for this story.

Thank you to my good friend and beta reader Lani Bennett for allowing me to bounce ideas off you for this story and others.

To Shannon Criss, Keyla Hernandez and the rest of the Kimani editorial team. Thank you for providing insight and feedback that made the story stronger while also allowing me to remain true to my vision.

Chapter 1

Nate Johnston entered the private dining room at his favorite seafood restaurant and froze, his expensive Italian loafers rooted to the floor.

The ghost of relationships past.

Kendra didn't need to turn around for him to recognize the woman he'd once shared his bed with; the mother of his six-year-old son. He sensed her presence—like something warm wiggling beneath his skin—the instant he stepped into the room.

Nate was in the midst of the biggest crisis of his eight-year-long professional football career. Why would his brother invite him to dinner with the woman who shattered his heart seven years ago?

"Glad you're here, Nate. Have a seat." His brother Marcus indicated the seat next to Kendra.

Nate narrowed his gaze at his brother and took the

seat beside him instead. "You asked me to meet you for dinner to discuss the *situation*."

As if Kendra and every other sports network viewer hadn't seen the grainy cell phone footage of him in a club, after a few drinks, ripping his teammates to shreds following the ass-whipping they'd endured at the hands of their division rivals. A devastating loss that put the brakes on the Memphis Marauders play-off run for the third year in a row.

The video had been edited to make him look like the villain. It didn't include him detailing how his own mistakes—a dropped pass and a costly fumble—had contributed to the loss.

"That's why she's here." Marcus's response was terse. As Nate's sports agent, Marcus's job had become ten times harder since the tape hit the airwaves that morning.

"Hello, Nate." Kendra's apologetic smile indicated she knew something he didn't.

Nate's attention was drawn to her expressive face. How did she manage to get more beautiful every time he saw her?

Head full of short, dark curls. Sheen on high blast. Style on point. Body-hugging knit dress in his favorite color on her—Marauders blue. The color perfectly contrasted the expanse of smooth brown skin exposed by the neckline of her dress.

An uneasy feeling crawled up his spine. Nate turned to his brother. "What do you mean *that's why she's here*?"

"It means we've got a ton of damage control to do, in addition to negotiating your new contract with the Marauders and trying to renew your two biggest endorsement deals. I can't handle everything alone. I've asked for Kendra's assistance."

Marcus had every right to be pissed, and Nate expected a little brotherly payback. But Marcus was a few cans short of a six-pack if he expected him to work with the woman who left him on one knee, ring in hand.

"What's wrong with the PR firm we've been using?"

"They're great when things are good, but we're in crisis mode. We need someone tough who'll get ahead of this thing and change the narrative out there about you."

"And out of all the possibilities in the free world, you believe the woman who rejected my proposal is the best person for the job?" He slid his gaze to Kendra. Her cheeks glowed beneath her warm, dark skin.

A twinge of guilt settled in his gut. It was a low blow, but so was walking out on him when he asked her to marry him seven years ago. He'd convinced himself he was over it and her. Yet the rejection still stung, especially being relegated to a part-time father.

Nate's father had tucked him and his six siblings into bed every night. Read them stories, taught them how to fish, fix their bikes and change the brakes on a car. He was still very much part of their lives. Nate had looked forward to being the kind of father who was present in his kids' lives every day.

Kendra had destroyed his chance of being that kind of dad to Kai.

When she'd responded to his marriage proposal by walking out, she'd left a hole in his chest where his heart had once been. Discovering the pregnancy a few weeks later, then announcing she fully intended to raise the baby on her own, had ripped out his soul and left him in a tailspin.

He still couldn't forgive her for reducing him to a baby daddy. For being the reason he didn't get to tuck Kai into bed most nights. Now Marcus wanted to put his future in her hands?

Oh, hell naw.

"I *know* she's the best person for the job." Marcus's expression was unwavering.

"I understand why you're still upset." Kendra's eyes conveyed the apology he'd already heard too many times. "But this isn't about our past. It's about ensuring your future on your terms. I can help you do that because I'm damn good at what I do. But I don't want to be here if you don't want me here."

"Good, then it's settled. What's for dinner?" Nate picked up his menu.

Marcus pushed the menu down. "Don't be a smart-ass, Nate. More importantly, don't let your ego get in the way of what's best for your career and your bank account. You've dug a king-size hole for yourself, little brother. It's my job to get you back on solid ground. I can do that, but I need Dray's help."

Nate narrowed his gaze at Marcus. *Dray? Really?* They were suddenly cozy enough that his brother was using the nickname he'd called her when they were together?

He turned his attention to Kendra. Her arms were folded, inadvertently pressing her breasts higher. His heartbeat quickened and his throat suddenly felt dry.

Focus, buddy, and not on those.

He gulped water from his glass, then cleared his throat. "I don't doubt your ability, Kendra, but given our history, working together is ill-advised. Am I the only one who gets that?"

"It's an awkward situation," Kendra acknowledged with a soft sigh, "but you're Kai's father. We'll always have a connection. Whether you believe it or not, Nate, I want what's best for you. That hasn't changed."

Nate swallowed the lump in his throat. "Let's not pretend this is a charitable arrangement. It's your chance to make a name for yourself."

Kendra pursed her lips painted a rich, velvety red reminiscent of a full-bodied glass of vintage port. As proud and stubborn as her mother, the woman was allergic to accepting help. It had taken him nearly a year to convince her to accept child support for Kai.

"This *is* an opportunity for me, which means I'm invested in your success. When we worked together, informally, you were a media darling."

Nate tapped his finger on the table. Kendra wasn't wrong. She'd been a huge help back then. He'd even asked her to help a couple of his college buddies who'd run into trouble.

He sucked in a deep breath. "You're good, but that isn't the point."

"Then what is the point?" She leaned forward, her arms folded, elbows on the table, providing an excellent view of her cleavage.

Nate was beginning to think she was doing it on purpose. Distracting him and trying to get him off his game. He swallowed hard, ignoring the blood emptying from his brain and rushing below his belt.

He glanced over at his smirking brother, who seemed to enjoy watching Kendra take him to task.

"You're going to make me say it? Fine." Nate leaned

forward, palms pressed to the table. "I prefer to work with someone I know has my back. Someone who'll ride this out instead of hitting the door the second the road gets hard. I want to work with someone who'll stand their ground and fight for me."

Kendra grimaced, as if he'd knocked the wind out of her.

Part of him relished the pain evident in her eyes. It didn't begin to rival the pain she'd inflicted on him. Yet another part of him couldn't bear to see the hurt in her chocolate-brown eyes.

"Your feelings are valid." Marcus spoke after what felt like a full minute of silence. His tone was apologetic, though Nate wasn't sure if the apology was meant for him or Kendra. "That's why you two need to hash things out."

"You're not hearing me, Marcus. There is nothing for us to hash out."

Marcus placed a firm hand on his shoulder. "You're my brother. I'd take a bullet for you. But as your agent, I have to be the voice of reason. Tell you what you need to hear. You screwed up. Royally. At the worst possible time. This is mission-critical. We need Dray. She knows you better than anyone, and she's a master at crisis management. Besides, she has a vested interest in seeing you succeed. All of our futures are on the line here, Nate. I wouldn't bring Dray in if I didn't trust her implicitly."

Kendra gave Marcus a grateful smile. She sat taller and returned her attention to Nate. "I can do this, Nate. I won't let you down."

Nate ignored her plea. He turned to Marcus. "I think we're pushing the panic button here."

"Cards on the table, bro?" Marcus motioned for the

server to come over. "It was Bat-Signal time the second that video hit the airwaves. The building is on fire. Don't be too proud to accept the help of a friendly face wearing a cape and toting a fire hose."

Nate gritted his teeth as Kendra held back a grin, her eyes gleaming. He sat stewing as Marcus explained to the server that he'd be leaving, so she should deliver his meal and the bill to Nate.

He loved his family, but it was a universal truth that older brothers could be asses.

Marcus stood and slipped on his wool coat. He gripped Nate's shoulder. "You said you'd do whatever it took to make this right. I'm playing that card now. You're two adults with a common goal. Figure it out." He shifted his gaze to Kendra. "Walk me out?"

She grabbed her wrap and followed him out.

Damn.

Next time he'd be careful with the promises he made his brother. His only hope was to convince Kendra to walk away.

Again.

Chapter 2

"You seem pleased." Kendra pulled the wrap tightly around her shoulders to combat the biting winter wind rushing into the lobby as patrons entered and exited. It was an unusual cold spell for North Carolina. "I'm not sure we were in the same room, because Nate isn't buying this."

"Not yet, but then you were prepared to turn me down when you arrived. What changed your mind?"

Her cheeks warmed. She agreed to dinner because she'd been intrigued by Marcus's proposal. It was her chance to finally establish a boutique PR and media coaching firm that catered to high-end talent. But she'd decided to take Nate on as a client the moment she laid eyes on him. Six feet three inches of brown-skin Adonis. Handsome and fit as ever. There was no way she'd admit that to his brother or to anyone.

"Despite what Nate thinks, he needs my help. Besides, I owe him." She couldn't erase the pain she'd caused when she'd walked away seven years ago, but she could make things right for him. Allow him to end his career on his terms.

Marcus squeezed her arm. "You don't owe either of us anything, but I'm glad you're on board."

"This isn't a done deal. I meant what I said. I'm willing to work through Nate resenting my help, but I won't do this if he's resistant. If he won't listen to me, this doesn't work."

"Then you've got some convincing to do." Marcus winked, tipped the valet and drove off.

Great. Kendra drew in a deep breath, then strutted back into the restaurant, spine straight and tall. *You've got this, girl.*

Nate didn't bother standing when she returned. He stared as if he couldn't believe she had the nerve to sashay her tail back into the private dining room. As if he'd expected her to turn and run.

"You need convincing, so let's talk. Ask me anything you want. We can discuss the ideas I have so far or the crisis management work I've done for high-profile corporate clients."

The server set their meals on the table. When she left, Nate took a swig of his beer, then set the glass on the table with a *thud.* "Fine. Let's talk about what happened between us."

"Nate…" Her voice wavered for a moment. She cleared her throat and lengthened her spine, holding his gaze. "We've talked about this."

"'I'm so sorry, Nate, I just can't do this' isn't a discussion, Kendra." The veins in his neck corded as he repeated her words that night verbatim. "You've shut me down anytime I've tried to have a real conversation about that night. If you want me to trust you, start by being honest about what happened between us."

"This isn't productive." She shivered beneath his cold stare. "Discussing my proposed PR plan is."

"If Marcus says you can do the job, I trust his judgment. What I need is to know I can trust you. So for once, be honest with me about why you walked out. Why you waited until I asked you to marry me and you were pregnant with my son to decide I wasn't the right man for you."

Her heart clenched at the bitterness that laced his words. It took her back to that night. The night she'd made the biggest mistake of her life.

"I underestimated how difficult it was to be the wife of a pro athlete."

"I'd been with the Marauders for a year by then. How would your life have been any different?"

"There's a huge difference between being the live-in girlfriend and being the wife and mother of your children."

"A marriage license is just a piece of paper, Kendra. Other than having it and my last name, nothing would've changed."

She tipped her chin, determined to keep her emotions in check. "It isn't a meaningless piece of paper. It's a lifelong commitment. That means something to me."

Nate snorted. "If it means so much to you, why'd you turn it down when I offered it?"

"I couldn't be one of those football wives who doesn't have a life of her own and pretends not to know what happens on the road."

His expression morphed from anger to hurt again. "So it was about that girl who let herself into my room in Cleveland. I told you, I didn't know her, and nothing happened between us. When I discovered her in my room, I called security and they sent her ass packing. End of story. I called you right away and told you about it. I wasn't trying to hide anything."

"The sports channels picked up the story. I would've heard about it."

Nate ran a hand through his close-cropped curls and heaved a sigh. "So that's what you think of me? That the minute I'm out of sight I can't keep it in my pants? News flash, Kendra, if I'd wanted to be with someone else, I would've been. Football groupies have been throwing themselves at me since high school. I didn't want them. I wanted you. I loved you. You obviously didn't feel the same."

"That isn't true." The accusation hit her like a bullet to the chest, piercing her heart and severing arteries. Nate was the only man she'd ever loved. She loved him still, but their time was past, and it was all her fault. "I'm a realist. You're only human. A man can only take so much temptation."

"If you felt that way, you should've come to me. We could've worked things out."

"How, Nate? You weren't going to leave the team, and I'd never ask *you* to give up your dream." She hadn't meant to stress the word.

Nate shifted in his seat, lowering his gaze. He hadn't missed the implication. She'd supported his dream, but he hadn't supported hers. He took another sip of his beer. "I never gave you any reason to doubt me."

"It was my issue, not yours. I fully own that."

"Just to be clear, you blew up our relationship, our family, because you thought I *might* eventually cheat on you?"

"It isn't as simple as that." She poked at the flounder she no longer had an appetite for. "My fears are very real, and I have them for good reason. That's my problem, not yours."

Nate laughed bitterly. "It sure as hell felt like my problem when you turned down my proposal in a roomful of our family and friends."

She cringed, remembering the moment he dropped to one knee and presented her with a beautiful, custom diamond engagement ring. The memory of that moment was as vivid now as it was then. Euphoric joy immediately followed by debilitating fear and a panic attack that stole her breath.

Chest heaving and the room spinning, she had only one clear thought—she couldn't marry Nate.

Until that moment, she'd anticipated the day he'd propose and dreamed of an intimate wedding ceremony on the beach. Then Nate asked her to marry him and the room went black.

Visions of ruthless groupies who'd do anything to get with a ballplayer filled her head. Her own father hadn't been faithful to her mother. How could she expect Nate to do so with so much temptation?

She'd broken it off, packed her things and made the long drive back to Pleasure Cove. Weeks later, she discovered she was pregnant with Kai.

"You didn't deserve that. I should've told you how I'd been feeling, but—"

"You didn't trust me enough to have an honest discussion then. Give me one reason I should trust you now." The ache reflected in his dark eyes penetrated her skin more than the bone-chilling air outside had.

Kendra choked back the thickness in her throat. "Because I'm the same girl who cheered you on at every game from peewee to the pros. The one who wouldn't let you give up on your dream when you weren't drafted."

Nate's expression softened, but he didn't respond.

Encouraged, Kendra continued. "We were so young then, Nate. I handled my feelings poorly. But I've never been anything but supportive of your career, and I've proven that I'm willing to go to bat for you. Who was it that convinced those arena football teams to give you a shot? Who sent your arena highlight clips to pro teams until the Marauders invited you to try out?"

"You." He rubbed his chin. "I owe my entire career to you."

"Our relationship may have ended, but my support of your career hasn't. No consultant will fight for your career harder than I will. Deep down, I think you know that."

Nate kneaded the back of his neck. "Okay, fine."

"Really?"

"Just until we secure my new contract."

Her buzz was quickly doused—like a too-short candlewick. The muscles of her face strained to maintain her smile. "Of course."

"We'll make it a six-month contract. You'll be well paid and Marcus will give you references, contacts... anything you need to rebrand your business. All right?"

"It's a generous offer, thank you. I accept."

"All right then." Nate inhaled Kendra's sweet scent: a gentle breeze wafting through a summer garden bursting with jasmine and gardenias. He pretended not to notice the disappointment on her face. It tugged at his heart and made him want to promise her the world just to see a genuine smile light those brown eyes. "I'll call Marcus tonight and have him draw up the contract."

"Great, I'll have my lawyer review it and we can go from there."

"How is your brother doing?" Nate sipped his beer, amused by how formally Kendra referred to her brother, Dashon, a contract law attorney.

Kendra shrugged. "He's still Dash. Being himself and doing his own thing."

"New York must be treating him well. I hear he rarely returns to Pleasure Cove." Nate carved into his prime rib covered with a creamy mushroom and lobster sauce—one of Nadine's specialties.

Kendra's mouth twisted. He'd obviously touched a nerve. He wouldn't pry further. They didn't need to be best friends. Just have a personable working relationship. "He comes home about as often as Quincy."

Touché. His globe-trotting younger brother was quickly making a name for himself as a photographer. His shadow rarely darkened the Johnston family's doorstep.

Nate contemplated the quiet look of concern that furrowed Kendra's brows. "Did I say something wrong?"

She stopped pushing the food around her plate and put down her fork. "No, but there's something we need to address, so I'm just going to say it."

He put down his utensils and sat back warily. "I'm listening."

"What happened between us in Memphis—"

"Which time?" Nate couldn't help the smirk that

tightened his mouth when he remembered how an argument between them had descended into hot, angry sex on two different occasions.

"Both." Kendra clearly wasn't amused. Nor did she seem to have the same fond memories of those occasions. "That can't happen again."

"I was hoping it would be one of the amenities you'd throw into the deal." He held back a grin as he drained the last of his beer.

She pointed one of her painted fingernails at him. "See, that's what I'm talking about. If this is going to work, you have to take me seriously."

"Oh, I took what we did very seriously." He raised an eyebrow and resumed eating his meal.

She let out a frustrated sigh and settled back in her seat. "This is your career we're talking about here, Nate. I need to maintain my focus, and I can't stay focused on cleaning up your rep if I'm thinking about…" Her words trailed off and there was a deep flush in her cheeks beneath her smooth brown skin. She shook her head, as if trying to shake off the memories. "Neither of us can afford the distraction."

"Agreed." He adjusted in his chair, his own body reacting to the memories. Her scent. Her taste. The sound of her soft pleas. "Though it worries me that my media consultant can't multitask."

They dissolved into laughter, and for a moment, it felt like old times. It was the first time either of them seemed relaxed since he'd arrived.

Nate smiled, relishing the sound of her laughter. One of the countless details about her he missed. "Okay, Ms. Media Consultant, where do we begin?"

Chapter 3

"This sounds like a great opportunity." Maya Alvarez, Kendra's half sister, sipped her mocha latte as they sat at the breakfast bar in the gorgeous penthouse Maya shared with her fiancé, hotelier Liam Westbrook. "So why aren't you excited about it?"

Kendra took a sip of the frothy peppermint mocha her sister made for her and let out an appreciative moan. "I am, but what if I'm jumping out of the frying pan and into the fire?"

"It's a tricky situation. I certainly couldn't work with the girls' dad. Not for all the money in the world." Maya placed a hand on Kendra's in response to her fallen expression. "But it's different with you and Nate."

"How? Carlos walked out on you, just like I walked out on Nate. The only difference was you and Carlos were married." Kendra drank more of her coffee. "He feels the same way you do. Honestly, I can't blame him."

"You've maintained an amicable relationship. Friendly enough that you two hooked up." Maya peered over her coffee cup, her dark eyes dancing with amusement.

"Shut. Up." Kendra pointed a finger at her giggling sister. "I shouldn't have told you that. I still can't believe it happened. Twice."

"Are we talking instances or the actual amount of times you guys—"

"Stop it, Maya!" Kendra's face and neck warmed. "Everyone knows you're not supposed to hold the things your sister says when she's drunk against her."

"All right, fine." Maya was still giggling. "I'm just saying, things can't be *that* bad between you. Besides, Nate's a terrific guy, and we both know you still have feelings for him."

"Of course I care about him. That doesn't mean we should be together." It was too quiet without the children around. Nothing to distract her from a conversation she'd rather not have. Liam had taken them to see the aquariums he'd just had installed at his family's luxury resort so she and Maya could talk. "Things between us are…complicated."

"Things were complicated for us, too. Every day I'm grateful Liam recognized that what we have was worth fighting for, despite the complications." Maya's face glowed when she spoke of Liam.

Kendra missed that feeling—the infinite joy of being in love with a man who adored her. She ignored the growing sense of envy that felt like a boulder tethered to her ankle, threatening to drown her in a sea of self-pity. She forced a smile. "I'm happy for you. You're perfect together, and Liam is so good with the kids."

"Sofie and Ella adore him."

"So does Kai. He talks about his Uncle Liam all the time. You'd think he was a superhero or something. He's making the Johnston men jealous."

"Liam has really taken to Kai, too." A warm smile lit Maya's eyes like a candle lighting a paper lantern from within.

No matter how many times Kendra saw that smile— and it was often in the weeks since Liam and Maya had gotten engaged—she couldn't stop her reaction to it. Intense joy for her sister, followed by deep sorrow for herself.

Maya seemed to recognize her pain. Her brows furrowed with concern. "I'm glad you accepted the offer, but I'm a little worried, too. Are you sure you're going to be okay with this? Six months is a long time."

"This is my shot to finally build the kind of clientele I've always wanted. I'm not going to blow it. Besides, Nate needs my help. I know it won't make up for how I hurt him, but at least it's something."

"When is your first meeting?"

"Tomorrow, so I'd better get it together."

Maya's smile was reassuring. "Everything will be fine, and who knows? Maybe you two will make up."

"Don't even go there, and please don't give Kai false hope about me and his dad getting back together. I don't think he could bear that. He misses him so much when he's away during the season. Now that the girls have Liam in their lives, Kai is more aware of his father's absence."

"I didn't realize—"

Kendra squeezed her sister's forearm. "I'm thankful

Liam's in his life. What he's feeling now…it would've come up eventually. We'll deal with it. He'll be fine."

"Either way, I know this is going to work out for the best. You have to believe that."

"It has to. If Nate ends up with a West Coast team, Kai will see him even less. He'd be heartbroken." Kendra's voice wavered. She sipped her coffee, hoping her sister didn't notice. "If I can prevent that from happening, I have to at least try."

Kendra avoided Maya's gaze and the pity she knew she'd see there. They both turned toward the front door in response to the jangling of keys that signaled Liam and the children's arrival.

Kai practically jumped into her arms. He was a sweet, affectionate boy. She kissed her son's forehead, dreading the days when he got older and would think it uncool to give her a big hug and a sloppy kiss.

She took in her handsome, smiling child. Wide, round eyes. Nate's nose—a narrow bridge with slightly flared nostrils. A wide smile stretched his Cupid's bow mouth—a near duplicate of hers. His thick ringlets were cut into a frohawk. He was only six, but his long arms and legs indicated he would be tall—like his father.

Kai was the perfect mélange of her and Nate's features, and he'd inherited an ideal mix of their personalities. He was truly the best of them.

Kendra smiled, warmth spreading through her chest as she choked back tears. Maybe she didn't get their relationship right, but she would always have the best part of Nate.

For that she was grateful.

Chapter 4

Nate fluffed the pillows on the sofa in his office for the third time, then readjusted the chain on his neck again.

This isn't a date. It's business. Be cool.

He eased onto the sofa and drummed his fingers on his knee. Kendra would arrive shortly for their first official meeting.

She and Marcus had met before the ink dried so she could lay out her ideas and they could come to consensus on a plan. Marcus had thought it was best for him to sit out that meeting.

Fine by him.

He recognized the necessity of jumping through PR hoops. Still, he resented wasting time and money defending himself about truthful comments made in private.

Not that there was any such thing as privacy anymore in the social media age.

A car door slammed. Nate glanced at his watch and smiled. On time, as always. Kendra was right; in many ways, she hadn't changed. Organized and efficient, she'd never been late for anything.

Nate opened the door before Kendra could ring the bell, startling her. She dropped her leather portfolio, her papers sailing across the porch.

He planned to help her recover them, but froze, mesmerized by the perfectly round shape of her curvy bottom in a narrow black pencil skirt as she bent to retrieve them. Finally shaken from his daze, he stooped to pick up a few sheets that had landed near his feet. He handed them to her, his fingertips grazing her soft skin.

Kendra withdrew her hand, as if she, too, felt the spark of electricity that charged his skin when they touched. She gave him an uneasy smile as she accepted the papers and stuffed them back into the portfolio. "Not the graceful entrance I hoped to make."

"Also not quite as entertaining as your entrance to the junior prom." He grinned.

"You did not just go there. You're never going to forget that, are you?"

He chuckled. "Don't think anyone in Pleasure Cove ever will. Principal Dansby nearly crapped himself when you came strolling up to the stage in your purple Prince tribute gown with your right butt cheek on display."

Kendra shuddered, shifting the portfolio to her other arm. Her cheeks glowed red beneath her dark brown skin. "You know the ass-baring feature was completely unintentional. I told my mother wearing panty hose was a bad idea. If I hadn't been wearing them, my dress couldn't have gotten tucked into the back of them. I still blame her for the entire fiasco."

"We managed to have a good time, despite getting tossed out—thanks to your indecent exposure." He smiled at the warm memory of the two of them strolling on the beach that night, hand in hand.

They'd crashed a sunset wedding on the beach. Kendra had been moved by the ceremony, her eyes brimming with tears. She said it was the most perfect thing she'd ever seen. He wiped the tears from her face and promised to marry her one day in a sunset ceremony right there on that beach.

He'd attempted to keep his promise, but look how that turned out. Nate shook his head, purging the memory from his brain. Jaw stiff, his hands clenched into fists.

Kendra seemed aware of the shift in his mood. She clutched her portfolio. "Is this still a good time?"

"As good as any." He opened the door wider and stepped aside to allow her to enter.

"This place looks incredible." Her eyes danced as she glanced around the open space. "I haven't been here since they first broke ground."

That had been by design. He'd bought the land and had this place constructed because he expected to build a life here with her. To one day watch their children surf the same beaches they'd surfed together as kids. When everything fell apart, he'd done his damnedest to keep her out of the space that was meant to be theirs.

"Thanks." He crammed his hands into the pockets of his jeans. "Can I take your coat or get you anything before we get started?"

She removed her wrap, unveiling a low-cut silk

blouse that complemented her curves nicely. "That coffee smells great. I'd love a cup."

"Coming up." He headed for the kitchen. "Is it okay if we work in here today?"

"Of course. I want to make this as convenient as possible. I'm willing to accommodate your schedule in any way necessary." Kendra set her portfolio and laptop on the black, poured concrete kitchen countertop.

He grabbed two mugs from the cabinet, filled her cup, added cream and handed it to her.

Kendra thanked him and settled onto her seat, then opened her laptop and pulled two copies of a thick, bound document from her leather bag. She handed him one and opened the other. "I'd like to give you the overview of the plan Marcus and I agreed on."

Nate thumbed through the document quickly. Neat, efficient, color-coded. *Very Kendra.* He dropped it onto the countertop with a *thud.* Leaning back in his seat, he sipped his coffee. "Shoot."

Nate was determined to make her turn and run, just as she had seven years ago. Well, they were beyond that. She'd signed her name to a contract and walked away from her most lucrative client.

No turning back.

She'd stayed up late the past few nights working on the proposal, and Nate wouldn't give it more than a cursory glance?

Fine.

She hadn't expected him to give in easily. But if he was already annoyed with her treatise on how to get his career back on track, he certainly wasn't going to like the steps she'd outlined.

Too bad.

This was what needed to happen if he wanted to get out of this predicament and land his new contract and endorsements.

Kendra met his defiant gaze. "Our campaign will focus on three strategies. First, you need to meet with each person you mentioned on that tape and apologize. Talk to them man-to-man and explain what happened—before we go public. Call anyone you can't get a sit-down with. Then we make the public apology."

Nate was growing more agitated by the minute. He folded his arms. "If I'm apologizing to each of them individually, what's the purpose of a public apology?"

"You said your tight end was more concerned with his individual stats than winning a championship. That your quarterback, and long-time friend, has been dialing it in all year. You slammed your defensive players for skating on their natural talents and having poor work ethics. And you claimed your running back is three years past his expiration date. All of that is public. So your apology needs to be, too."

"It's not like I didn't call myself out for my mistakes, too. Funny how they didn't include that part."

"I get it. That makes me believe that this Stephanie Weiss who broke the story is out to get you. This was calculated. Vindictive."

Nate bristled at the mention of Stephanie's name. "If they were going to leak the video, I just wish they'd shown everything."

"Fortunately, someone leaked the full video. Probably the person who actually recorded it. At the press conference, we'll play the missing part where you skewer your own mistakes, too. Then you'll make a statement. We'll go from the emotional angle of the disappointment you were feeling—with yourself and the rest of the team. Any sports fan can sympathize with that. Explain that while the critique was your honest assessment of what led to the loss, you regret the harsh words you used to express it."

Nate's lips puckered like he was sucking on a lemon. He nearly drained his coffee mug. "Fine. Anything else?"

"Be honest. Tell them your team is your family, and like most family disputes, this one will be resolved behind closed doors, not in the public arena."

"Won't they want to ask questions?"

"Doesn't mean you have to answer them." She shrugged. "We'll establish from the outset that you won't be entertaining questions."

"That's an idea I can get behind," he mumbled. "What's the second strategy?"

"We have to change the narrative out there about you on our terms. We'll cherry-pick media outlets that are trustworthy, but we'll lay the ground rules about which topics are off-limits."

"If I'm not talking about the tape—which is what they're all going to want to talk about—what am I there to discuss?"

"At this time of year, there are a million opportunities to discuss the play-off games—on radio, television, newspapers and blogs. You can offer your razor-sharp game analysis there. Plus, you'll set yourself up for a career as an analyst once you retire."

Nate shrugged. "I could do that, I guess."

"And you'll be phenomenal at it." Kendra smiled, encouraged that Nate had taken well to at least part of the plan. "You'll also need to talk about your philanthropy."

He frowned, his eyebrows forming angry slashes over his dark eyes. "The Johnston Family Foundation isn't some cheap publicity stunt. I'm not looking to blow my own horn."

"I know, which makes the work you do all the more admirable." She held up a hand, holding off the next wave of protest. "But just think how much more good you could do if you publicized the work you're doing with wounded veterans and high-risk children from low-income families."

Nate stood and paced the floor. "Our clients have been through enough. They need someone to give them a hand, not someone else who only sees them as a means to their own end. No." He shook his head. "I won't do it."

Kendra inhaled deeply, then took a different approach. One Nate might better understand.

"You don't want to take advantage of your clients. I admire that. But if we can't repair your reputation, you won't be in a position to help them as much as you'd like."

He didn't respond, but stopped pacing and rested his chin on his closed fist.

"Besides, if more companies—including your current sponsors—were aware of the programs your foundation offers and the difference you're making in people's lives, they'd want to contribute. That means you'll be able to help even more people. Isn't that what you want?"

"You know I do, but I won't betray their trust."

"I'd never ask you to do that." Kendra softened her

voice. "All I'm asking is that you give them the opportunity to help themselves and others. I'm sure a lot of the families your foundation has helped would be eager to participate in a goodwill campaign to spread the word and increase funding."

Nate dropped into his seat, as if he were exhausted from a fight. "Fine. I'll agree to *some* media coverage for the foundation programs, but I need final approval on anything we put out there."

"Absolutely." She hoped he didn't see how relieved she was. "Any other concerns?"

"Yeah. What if the interviewers aren't willing to stick to the script?"

She nodded solemnly. "Always a possibility. One we'll make sure you're prepared to handle in a way that won't aggravate the situation."

"You make it sound so easy."

"It will be." She smiled, hoping to reassure him.

"And the third strategy? Do I even want to know what it is?"

He knew her well enough to know she'd saved the option he'd like least for last.

"It's time for you to come out of the Stone Age and start using social media."

"C'mon, Kendra. I've got a crisis on my hands. You said so yourself. I don't have time to mess around on social media."

"The public is only seeing you through the filter of the news media and talking heads out there. Social media puts you in control of your own message, in real time. Your fans—and potential sponsors—will get a better sense of who you are."

He shook his head slowly, thoughtfully. A marked

improvement over the adamant refusal issued moments earlier. "The last thing I want is more people in my business."

"I understand your reluctance. Especially in light of what's happened. The reality is, they're already in your business. This way you become the gatekeeper. You let them in, but in a way you completely control."

Nate grunted. "Don't really have a choice, do I?"

Kendra tried to hold back her grin. "Not really, but I promise to make it as painless as possible. I'll actually be running the accounts for you, so it won't be as much work as you're imagining. Promise."

He nodded reluctantly. "If you really think this is the only way we win, okay. I'll do it. Anything else we need to discuss?" His posture was tense. As if he couldn't wait to get her out of his house.

She tried to pretend it didn't hurt that he wanted her as far away from him as possible. "Actually, there is something else we need to discuss. What's the story on Stephanie Weiss?"

Nate frowned. "Marcus didn't tell you?"

"He thought it would be better if you explained." She shifted in her chair. "I gather you two were together at some point, or Marcus wouldn't have been so cryptic about your connection."

"Not one of my best decisions." He tapped a finger on the countertop, staring beyond her. "Stephanie dragged me into the middle of a scandal back then that nearly ruined my relationship with my teammates. Now she's done it again."

"Exactly what happened with her?" She sighed when he narrowed his gaze at her. "If I'm going to help you, I need to understand what's going on, and not just what

I've read on the internet. I need the complete picture. We can't afford to get blindsided again."

An uncomfortable silence settled over them as he stared out the window onto the backyard. He didn't want to talk to one ex about another.

She got that. She'd probably feel the same. Still, she needed to know more about this Stephanie Weiss. Beyond what she learned from watching her reports online and reading her bio. And if she was being honest, it wasn't just her professional curiosity that needed to be satisfied. "Did you love her?"

He scowled, the corners of his mouth pinched. His resentment of the question rolled off him in waves. His answer was quiet, but emphatic. "No."

Kendra went to the coffee machine and refilled her cup. She held her hand out for his. "You don't have to worry about hurting my feelings. I'm a big girl. I can handle the truth."

"I told you the truth. I wasn't in love with her." He thrust his empty cup into her hand. "We were only together a few months. What difference does it make, anyway?"

"Helps me understand her frame of mind. If we're dealing with a woman scorned nursing a vendetta, we need to stay two steps ahead of her." She returned the mug to him, filled with black coffee.

"That's the only reason you want to know?" He peered at her over the rim of his mug as he took a sip of his coffee.

She returned to her seat and tapped a few keys on her computer, waking the screen up. "Of course."

He smirked, unconvinced. With good reason. She was lying through her teeth.

"So, what led to this scandal and why does she have it in for you?" Kendra put down her mug, prepared to type her notes.

"Do we really need to get into all of this? It's ancient history."

"Not to her, I'm guessing."

"Stephanie was listening to my phone calls. Checking my text messages. She discovered a teammate of mine was in serious trouble. She broke the story using the info she'd gathered, saying it was from an unnamed source. When I read the story, I recognized what she'd done. Since we were dating, my teammates and the public believed I'd been feeding Stephanie information. I broke it off with her, publicly denied I was the source and discredited her story." He frowned. "She was fired, and none of the top media outlets wanted anything to do with her."

"I'm sorry you ended up in the middle of it."

"Should've known better than to sleep with the enemy, right?"

"Real journalists aren't your enemy. They won't always give you the glowing praise you want, but the good ones are honest and fair. They're only interested in the truth. Those are the media personalities we need to make our allies."

"Good luck finding any of those." He finished his coffee and moved to the sink to rinse his cup.

"Got a few in mind. I think you'll be pleased."

He grunted, his biceps bulging as he folded his arms over his chest. The gray quick-dry athletic material stretched to accommodate his firm pecs. He flipped his wrist and checked his watch. "Anything else?"

Kendra swallowed, her throat suddenly dry. Nate

seemed fully aware of her reaction to him and utterly pleased with himself for evoking it. She shook her head. "No, I think we're good. For now. I'll keep you updated. Marcus's assistant, Kara, gave me access to your calendar. I'll add any interviews and appearances as I book them."

"All right." He pinned her with his gaze. "Is that all?"

"Kara will make the flight arrangements for your apology tour once you request meetings with each of the guys. I'd begin with Marauders' owner Bud Flynn and then the head coach."

The smug expression crumbled. "Why? I didn't say anything about either of them."

"This media circus is disruptive to the entire team. Besides, Bud has been like a second father to you. He gave you your big break. Don't you think you owe him an apology?"

Nate sighed. "I'll call him as soon as I'm done."

"Good."

"Don't mean to rush you." He checked his watch again. "But I have another appointment."

"Right. Sorry. I know you're busy." Kendra put on her wrap and packed up her things. She slipped her bag on her shoulder, tucked the portfolio under her arm and turned around, nearly running into Nate.

"Look, I know I'm not the easiest guy to work with, but I do appreciate the work you've put into this." He leaned in closer, his warm breath whispering against her skin. "And I just want you to know…"

The doorbell rang. Nate sighed and cursed under his breath before turning toward the door.

"Nate, what were you going to say?" Kendra followed him, her heart beating hard. Something in her desperately needed to know what Nate was going to say before they'd been interrupted by the bell.

"Doesn't matter." He shook his head then turned to open the door.

"I came a few minutes early so we could work on those positions you had so much trouble with the other day." A tall, gorgeous blonde wearing a short skirt, a cropped top and thigh-high boots floated inside carrying a large duffel that looked like it weighed twice as much as she did. The woman finally noticed Kendra. "Oh, I'm sorry, I didn't realize you had company."

"I was just leaving." Kendra forced a polite smile.

Nate placed his hand low on the woman's back and introduced them. "Layne, this is Kendra—Kai's mom. She'll be handling my PR. Kendra, this is my friend Layne."

Layne gave Nate an odd smile before offering Kendra a limp handshake. "Pleased to meet you. I've heard so much about you." She turned to Nate without waiting for a response. "I'll go ahead and get everything set up."

"Great. Thanks, Layne."

The woman sauntered off, obviously familiar with the house.

"She's pretty." The words came out before Kendra could reel them back in. "She's built like a dancer."

Nate smirked, holding the door open a bit wider. "She takes great care of her body. And mine."

"I certainly don't want to get in the way of that." Kendra forced a smile despite the deep ache in her chest at the thought of Nate and Ms. Ballerina Body doing God knows what. "I'll follow up tomorrow to see how the phone calls went, and if I need to run interference with anyone."

"Don't think that'll be necessary, but thank you. Kiss li'l man for me. Tell him Dad's got a surprise for him this weekend."

Before she could respond, he'd closed the door behind her. The sound echoed in her head like the closing of a vault.

Maybe she was still nursing feelings for Nate, but he'd obviously gotten over her.

Chapter 5

Nate sank into the whirlpool after his hot yoga session with Layne and made his calls.

He'd tucked his tail and done a good bit of explaining. First to Bud Flynn, then to Coach Emerson. Bud was out of the country. He tentatively accepted Nate's apology by phone, but insisted they meet in person once he returned. He scheduled a meeting with Coach Emerson.

Nate left a message for two of his teammates and had incredibly awkward conversations with a few others.

Except for the team's quarterback, Wade Willis, who agreed his performance had been subpar, none of the guys went easy on him. Eating a king-size slice of humble pie was exactly what he deserved for running his big mouth.

Tomorrow he'd board a plane to meet with Wade

at his ranch in Montana. Then he'd head to Memphis for meetings with Coach Emerson and Lee Davis, the head of team personnel. He dreaded the meeting with Lee—the only member of the Marauders' front office he'd never really seen eye-to-eye with. Lee had been itching to trade him, and the video scandal was just the ammunition he needed.

Nate slipped deeper into the water, allowing the warmth to wash over his aching muscles. The heat eased the tension in his shoulders and worked out the kinks in his back.

After eight years in the league, he was nursing his fair share of injuries. Each season it became more difficult to rebound from the beating his body took on any given Sunday.

If he were smart, he'd forget about a new contract and retire. Accept that he was a great player in his own right, but would never know the pride of hoisting a championship trophy. He'd be in good company. A host of athletes in every major sport were on that list.

Still, he wasn't ready to give up. The Marauders were a few pieces shy of being a contender with a legitimate shot at the championship. He shifted to get the knot in his back closer to the jet.

His recent actions certainly hadn't made the task of getting the Marauders championship-ready any easier.

Closing his eyes, he tried to relax—something he'd never been very good at. His brain seemed to go a mile a minute—even when he slept.

Nate massaged the knot that formed in his neck as he recalled the hurt and anger in each man's voice. The tension he'd created between them. Then there was the meeting with Kendra.

His body reacted to the vivid vision of her that crept over his senses. Kendra was sexy as ever in that fitted skirt and a low-cut blouse. He'd had to shove his hands in his pockets, not trusting that he'd keep his hands to himself.

When she spoke, he'd been mesmerized by her lips, overwhelmed with the desire to taste her mouth and slide his fingers in her dark curls.

Get it together, man.

He shook his head and stood, the chilly air assaulting his wet skin. Nate stepped out of the tub and slipped on a thick terry cloth robe. He slid on his sport sandals and went inside.

Nate uncapped a beer from the fridge and took a long pull. Kendra's words echoed in his head.

Neither of us can afford the distraction.

There was too much at stake. His career, the foundation and most of all...his heart. If he let her in, she'd shatter it again.

Twice, he thought he could have her body without getting caught up in the feelings they once shared.

He'd been wrong.

Kendra had walked away unscathed, while he was left brooding like a wounded animal, lashing out at everyone around him.

Nate finished his beer and tossed the bottle in the recycle bin before hopping into the shower.

This time he'd keep his hands and his heart to himself.

Kendra settled in behind the rickety old secondhand desk in her office, which doubled as the spare bedroom.

Marcus had already arranged for Nate to be a guest

on a few of the smaller sports commentary shows on the major sports network.

She reviewed the list of media personalities she'd compiled. Kendra was confident that half of the people on the list would agree to their stipulations about topics Nate wouldn't discuss. The other half were iffy, but the riskiest options offered the biggest return. She needed to see what Marcus thought of those. She dialed his cell.

Marcus answered immediately. "I was just about to ask Kara to call you."

"Why, what's up?" Kendra stopped scrolling through the list. Something in his tone told her she wouldn't like what he was about to say.

"Nate called everyone on the list."

"Great. Will he be meeting with all of them?"

"Bud Flynn's out of town. They'll meet when he gets back, but he accepted his apology, for whatever that's worth."

"And the rest of the team?"

"Wade was cool. Everyone else was pretty pissed, as we expected. Two of the guys haven't returned his calls."

"Let me guess, Tyree Thomason and Dade Hendricks." According to Nate, his relationships with the tight end and running back were strained even before the video was leaked.

"You've got it. Nate also arranged a sit-down with Lee Davis, the team's personnel manager. The guy is definitely not a fan. He's been trying to get the team to trade Nate since the upheaval Stephanie caused three years ago, but Bud Flynn won't go for it."

"Nate needs to be smart about what he says when he talks to these guys. It's one thing to be contrite during a phone call. It's another to keep it together in person. I hope he remembers everything we talked about."

"He won't have a choice. I'm sending you with him." Marcus said the words so fast she nearly missed his meaning.

"Wait…what? We didn't discuss me going."

"I know, and I'm sorry. I don't mean to spring this on you at the last minute, but I've been thinking about it all day. It's too risky to send Nate alone."

"Then why don't you go with him?"

"I would, but I have meetings scheduled with the networks and one of the team execs. I can't miss them."

Kendra groaned. "Fine. When is he leaving?"

"Tomorrow morning."

"Are you kidding me?"

"No, and again I'm sorry about this. I realize how inconvenient this is, and I wouldn't ask if it wasn't so critical. Will your mom or Maya be able to watch Kai for a few days? If not, my mom or Alison would be happy to."

"I'll make arrangements. Just have Kara email me everything I need to know."

"Great. Oh, and Kendra?"

"Yes?"

"Pack for a week. Just in case."

Kendra ended the call and gritted her teeth. There was an empty feeling in the pit of her stomach. She curled her fingers to her palms in response to the visceral memory of the electricity she felt when Nate's fingers brushed her skin.

Sitting across the table from Nate during their first two meetings had been tough, but she'd found strength in the knowledge that their meetings would be brief. She could retreat, lick her wounds and summon her courage before it was time to do it again. Being confined on a small plane with Nate for hours would be difficult for both of them.

Kendra drew in a deep breath and picked up the phone. First, she called her mother to make arrangements for Kai. Anna Williams didn't bother to hide how ecstatic she was that Kendra would be spending the next few days on the road alone with Nate. She gladly agreed to care for Kai.

After messaging her sister to let her know about her trip, she dragged her luggage out of the closet and packed.

Kendra closed the book she was reading to Kai. He'd been asleep for at least ten minutes. She finished reading the story anyway, needing an excuse to hold him a bit longer.

She slipped her arm from beneath Kai, tucked the covers under his chin and kissed his forehead.

Her cell phone rang. She followed the sound to the kitchen, where she'd left it.

"Hey, Maya. What's up?"

"Got your message. I wanted to check on you. You sure you'll be okay on the road with Nate for an entire week?"

Kendra collapsed onto the sofa, physically drained from preparing for the trip, mentally exhausted from wrestling with the same question. "Don't really have a choice, do I?"

"We always have a choice," Maya said. "But sometimes fate pushes us in the right direction."

"You're not going to tell me you think this is the

stars aligning again—like they did for you and Liam—
are you?"

"Are you going to try to tell me again that you don't
still have feelings for Nate?" There was a smirk in her
sister's voice.

"He's my son's father, so we'll always have some
sort of—"

"Connection." Maya finished her sentence. "I know,
I know. That's not what I asked. I'm asking if you're
still in love with him."

"We've been through this before."

"And you've never given me a straight answer." The
pitch of Maya's voice rose.

"Seems like a clear hint I don't want to talk about
it." Kendra paced the floor, then rearranged photos on
the mantel. "So leave it alone."

"So it's all right for you to be all up in my business,
but when it's your turn, suddenly you're invoking the
Fifth?"

Kendra pressed a palm to her forehead. Maya usually
dropped the topic once her agitation became apparent.
Suddenly her sister wasn't inclined to let the subject go.

"I'm not sure how I feel," Kendra admitted. It was
unsettling to hear the words spoken aloud where she
could no longer hide from them. "Being around him like
this…it's definitely making me feel some kind of way."

Maya's tone softened. "I know it's probably a little
overwhelming, but that doesn't mean it's a bad thing.
Just be open to wherever this takes you. Nate's a good
guy. He adores Kai, and I have a strong feeling he's still
very much in love with you."

"Don't know about that. It was kind of hard to read
with his arm draped around the skinny chick who

showed up at his place as he was rushing me out the door." Kendra hated the pouty tone with which she conveyed the news.

"Is he seeing her?"

"I guess so. She seemed to know her way around his place well enough. From the size of the bag she was toting, she planned to stay awhile."

"How did he introduce her?"

"As his friend."

"Well, there you go." There was a lilt in Maya's voice again. "She's his friend until we hear otherwise."

"Like you and Liam were just 'friends' over the summer?"

Maya huffed. "You're determined to ruin this, aren't you?"

"Maya, seriously, do I need to have the same talk with you I had with my mom? This is business—not a romantic getaway. Nate doesn't want me on this trip any more than I want to be on it."

"Wouldn't be so sure about that. We'll see."

"Enough with the matchmaking," Kendra said. "I still have a ton of things to do. Oh, and my mom has a doctor's appointment on Friday, so she won't be able to pick Kai up from school. Is it okay if he goes home with Sarah and the girls until my mom can pick him up?"

Liam's housekeeper, Sarah, had taken on the expanded role of part-time nanny since Maya and the girls had moved into his penthouse.

"I'm sure it won't be a problem. She loves Kai. That boy is a charmer, just like his dad."

Kendra thanked her sister and ended their call, hoping she'd be strong enough to resist Nate's charm this time around.

Chapter 6

Nate climbed the stairs to the small private plane they sometimes chartered for his travel. He got a whiff of a familiar scent. Jasmine with a hint of gardenias.

No, no way.

He removed his shades and stood, stunned, taking in his ex's apologetic expression.

"Guess that answers my question about whether you knew I was coming along." She brushed off her skirt and crossed her legs.

Nate tucked his shades in the inside pocket of his jacket. He stood trying to decide whether or not he'd sit across from Kendra.

He grunted and flopped into his usual seat adjacent to the couch. She seemed relieved he'd chosen to sit across from her.

"No." He held back a few choice names he had for

his brother right now. "Marcus failed to mention it. I realize I screwed up, but I don't appreciate the two of you treating me like a child. I'm a grown-ass man."

"Then start acting like one." Her expression was neutral, her tone unbothered. "Channel your passion for the game in a way that will help your team rather than hurt it. Tap into your desire to win in a way that will motivate your teammates instead of alienating them."

Nate turned to survey the calm waters of the Atlantic Ocean, visible from the window. "Damn. I see we're not pulling punches today."

Kendra smiled sweetly, one long leg crossed over the other and her hands folded in her lap. "You didn't hire me to soothe your ego. You hired me to get results, and that's what you'll get, as long as you stick to the plan."

Nate tried to hold on to the resentment he felt when he realized Marcus had sent Kendra to be his babysitter. That anger was quickly losing ground to the other feeling that grabbed hold of his chest the moment her eyes met his.

Longing.

He wanted her. In his arms. In his bed. In his life. A sentiment he'd fought for the past seven years. Being in such close proximity to the constant object of his affection wasn't helping him win that battle.

Kendra was smart as a whip, sexy as hell and confident in her abilities. Something about that combination made his heart beat faster. That and the expanse of smooth brown skin framed between the hem of her skirt and the top of her leather boots.

Nate raised his hands, his palms facing her. "Relax. I don't plan on going off script again. After all, that's why I'm headed to freaking Montana in the middle of winter, isn't it?" He pulled his jacket closer around him, just thinking of the thirty-degree temperature drop they'd experience once they landed.

She tilted her head, assessing him before responding. "Hopefully, you're also doing it because it's the right thing to do. Wade isn't just your quarterback, he's your friend."

They weren't playing touch football anymore. Kendra had delivered a full-contact, center-mass hit that had knocked him on his ass.

Deservedly so.

She wasn't tiptoeing around his ego. He admired that. Only Kendra Williams could piss him off and make him want her with a single utterance.

It was going to be a rough few days. For him, at least. Kendra seemed unaffected by him. That gave her the upper hand.

He needed to find a way to change that.

Kendra gave herself a mental high five. She stood her ground and told Nate the cold, hard truth while remaining calm, despite the anxiety raging beneath the surface.

Handling Nate with kid gloves wouldn't benefit either of them. Marcus hired her because she'd always been straight with Nate and told him what he needed to hear—whether he wanted to hear it or not. Their painful history aside, she would do just that.

She'd hoped her resolve to be tough with Nate would mitigate her feelings for him. It hadn't. Judging by the half frown that softened the edges of his mouth, a mischievous grin lay just beneath his show of displeasure. So it wasn't deterring him much, either.

Kendra held her poise, despite her increasingly shallow breaths as Nate's gaze raked over her. Heat curled its way up her spine like a black snake climbing a southern red cedar tree in search of prey.

"Of course Wade is my friend, but this is a business," Nate said finally, shifting his gaze out the window for a moment before returning it to her. "Wade understands that more than anyone."

The pilot announced they would take off soon. A growing sense of panic made her limbs feel heavy. She fumbled with her seat belt. It wouldn't catch. They were going to take off and she'd go sailing across the plane.

"Relax. I've got it." Nate knelt in front of her, his large hands covering hers, stilling their movement.

The warmth of his skin penetrated hers and trailed up her arms, her heart beating faster and her breath quickening. Her skin tingled, electricity zipping along her spine.

Even kneeling, Nate's large body loomed over hers. His broad chest and wide shoulders invaded her space as he leaned forward and buckled the seat belt effortlessly.

Nate's gaze met hers and one corner of his mouth curved, his eyes twinkling.

Kendra's hands shook as she inhaled his scent. Her body remembering when last he'd been this close to her on his knees. Her nipples pebbled and a small, inadvertent gasp escaped her mouth.

Nate grinned, then licked his lower lip.

Maybe he was remembering that night, too.

Kendra shut her eyes briefly and exhaled.

No, no, no. This is strictly business. Nothing more.

"Thank you." She settled back against the headrest. "But you'd better get back in your seat."

Nate gave her a knowing grin as he returned to his seat and fastened himself in.

Kendra released a small sigh, missing his nearness, yet thankful for the distance.

"This flight is nearly five hours, and these smaller commuter planes...well, the ride can be a little bumpier than on a commercial flight. You sure you want to do this?"

Kendra nodded in response as she focused on taking long, deep breaths. She wasn't terrified of flying, it just wasn't her preferred mode of travel.

Nothing a rum and Coke or two couldn't resolve.

Only this wasn't a pleasure trip. It was strictly business, and she needed to keep her head clear. That meant toughing it out.

Nate regarded her with apprehension. "Look, I appreciate your commitment, but you don't need to do this. I can handle this on my own, so just say the word and we'll get you off this flight. But I need to know now. *Before* we take off."

"No." Kendra shook her head vehemently. "I'm fine."

"All right." Nate settled back in his seat, his eyes glued to her, as if he expected her head to start spinning.

"I appreciate you looking out for me, despite the fact that you'd rather I not be here."

He shrugged, looking out the window again as the plane taxied down the runway. "Maybe I just didn't want you killing my vibe with your projectile vomiting."

Kendra couldn't help laughing. She dissolved into a fit of giggles that escalated to a laugh so hard it made her belly ache.

Nate laughed, too. He wiped tears from the corners of his eyes. "Better now?"

She stopped laughing long enough to realize that the tense muscles in her back and neck had relaxed. They were airborne and the plane was leveling off. She nodded. "Much. Thank you."

He winked at her. "Good. Now, I assume that in addition to being assigned babysitting duty, you tagged along so we could go over a few things."

She nodded, pulling her portfolio from her bag. "How far outside the box are you willing to go?"

Nate crooked a brow and shifted in his seat, folding his right ankle over his left knee. "What do you mean?"

"A popular home improvement show is looking for a few celebs who want to surprise a family member with a kitchen redo. Marcus suggested they do your mom's kitchen."

"That means my parents would have to be on the show." He ran a hand over his head. "Don't know if I like that. They don't like being in the spotlight."

"Marcus said your mom loves these shows and she's always wanted to be on one." She tapped her pen on her pad. "This is a great opportunity for you to do something fabulous for her, Nate. Something you've always wanted to do. The bonus is it would be great for your image, too."

Nate groaned as he pressed his head against the headrest. "If Marcus thinks Mama will go for it, fine. I'll do it. Anything else?"

"By the end of the day, your brother should have more info on those guest spots to discuss the play-offs and a finalized list of media personalities that we'll pitch additional guest spots to."

"Great. Make sure I get a copy of that list."

"Absolutely." Kendra made another note, then put her

pen and pad away. "Now, about these meetings with the team and your teammates."

"I don't need you standing next to me like some ventriloquist." Nate's tone was tinged with annoyance. "I know what to say to these guys."

"Great. Then you won't mind running it by me." Kendra gave Nate a warm smile, but he wasn't buying it. "I'm here to ensure you're prepared for these meetings and that we stay on message, but I won't be in any of them. These guys are like your family. It'll only make things weirder if I'm there."

"Good." He nodded, seemingly relieved.

"Let's just go over the basics of what you plan to say to Wade. I'll check out a restaurant in town and get some work done while you meet with him."

"Not going to work."

"Why?"

"There was a change of plans this morning. My meetings in Memphis were bumped back a couple of days, so Wade asked me to spend a couple of days with him and Greer. Thought you knew."

I'm going to kill Marcus if he has any more surprises up those expensive sleeves of his.

Unperturbed, Nate composed a text message on his phone.

Probably to the woman she'd encountered at his home the day before.

"There must be a hotel or something where I can stay in town. Shouldn't be terribly difficult to book a room at the last minute in Montana in the middle of winter."

He silently tapped away on his phone.

Good to know you're concerned. She smoothed her

skirt and tried not to pout about her ex's lack of interest in her dilemma.

He's your client, not your boyfriend. Get used to it.

"All set." Nate slipped the phone into his pocket.

"You booked me a hotel room?"

"Better. Wade and Greer want you to come to the
ranch with me. He and I will chat as soon as we get
there. Get all this nonsense out of the way. Then we'll
have dinner with them tonight. They also asked us to
spend the day with them tomorrow while the older kids
are at school."

"Are you sure they don't mind taking on another
person? I don't mind staying at a hotel."

Nate gave her a small smile, but sadness lingered in
his eyes. "Greer asks about you and Kai all the time.
She'll be thrilled to see you."

"It'll be good to see her and Wade again, too. I've
always liked them."

He settled back in his chair, his legs crossed again.
"Then it's settled."

"Won't your friend Layne be upset about this?"

"Why?" His expression was stoic. She couldn't read
him at all.

"So you're saying you two aren't together? Or is
your relationship casual and open?" Kendra couldn't
help herself. "I'm asking as your media consultant slash
publicist, of course."

He chuckled. "Okay, media consultant slash publicist, my relationship with Layne is casual, open and
very professional."

Kendra's eyes widened. "You mean she's a—"

"What? Of course not." He laughed. "She's my hot

yoga instructor. Sydney recommended her. Layne dated Nick for a while."

"Oh." Kendra pushed a curl back from her forehead. His sister Sydney and her best friend Nick had been roommates for the past few years. "Those two still pretending they're not in love?"

Nate frowned. "They're just friends and roommates. At least, they better be," he added, mumbling under his breath.

"Whatever helps you sleep at night." She couldn't help teasing him. "After all, we started out as best friends, too."

Nate unbuckled his seat belt and sprawled out on the couch. "Yeah, and just look how that turned out." He sighed and dragged a hand down his face. "Sorry, I shouldn't have—"

Kendra waved a hand and shook her head. "I get it. You've always been protective of your baby sister. Just like your twin sister has always been protective of you."

A half grin lit Nate's eyes as he chuckled. "Protective? She acts like she's my mama."

Kendra acknowledged his statement with a small nod. Navia had been furious with her when she broke up with Nate. The rest of the Johnston clan eventually made peace with the situation, but not Navia. She'd probably never forgive her for hurting her twin brother.

"How is Vi doing, anyway? Still calling for my head on a stake?"

Nate grinned. "Nah. She's softened up a little. Now she just wants to see you in stocks for a week or two."

Kendra laughed. "She's warming up to me again. Good to know. And what does she think about this little arrangement?"

He slipped off his expensive leather shoes and shrugged his broad shoulders. "Haven't talked to her about it yet. You know how worked up Vi gets about everything. Marcus and I thought it was best if we waited until we had some viable results to show her."

"Guess I'm not the only one who's afraid of your sister."

"I spent nine months sharing a very small space with Vi." He grinned as he spread a cream-colored cashmere throw over himself. "No one knows better what she's capable of. If I were you, I'd try to wow her."

Kendra pursed her lips. Nate was teasing her. Didn't mean she wouldn't check underneath her car seat for ticking devices—just in case.

Chapter 7

"Hello, Nate." Greer Willis gave him an awkward hug—unlike the dozens she'd given him before. "Wade'll be here shortly. He picked Jake and Mariah up from school."

Greer's demeanor was pleasant, but the narrowing of her blue eyes and the sharp pronunciation of his name—without any of the soft edges of her deep Southern accent—sufficiently conveyed her indignation.

She was sweet and cordial, but also fiercely protective of her family. An endearing quality when he wasn't on the wrong side of it.

Today, he clearly was.

"Kendra!" An authentic smile lit Greer's face, highlighting her natural beauty. She wrapped Kendra in a tight embrace. "Honey, it's so good to see you. Hasn't been the same without you."

"Good to see you, too, Greer. I can't wait to see the kids. How old are they?"

Greer threaded her arm through Kendra's, leading her to the living room. "Jake is ten and Mariah is eight. They've grown like weeds since you saw them last. Noah is three and baby Allie is thirteen months. The little ones are down for a nap. You'll see them soon enough. Can I get y'all something?"

"No, thank you. We're good." Kendra surveyed the impressive house. The architectural gem was made up mostly of local fieldstone, walls of glass and a symphony of light-colored woods. "My God, Greer, this place is gorgeous. The architecture…and those views. It's stunning."

Greer's grin widened and her cheeks colored. She was still a small-town Alabama girl who grew up on a working farm, never imagining a charmed life. It was one of the reasons Nate had always genuinely liked and respected her. Greer and Wade were good, down-to-earth folks. His friends.

He'd hurt them both.

"Still can't believe we get to wake up here every day." A strand of Greer's wavy honey-blond hair escaped her low ponytail. She tucked it behind her ear. "I'll show you around when the little ones wake. Meantime, have a seat. I'll ask Edison to fetch y'all's bags and take 'em to the guesthouse."

"There's a guesthouse?" Kendra eased onto the large gray sectional. It blended nicely with maple flooring stained the same shade of gray as the driftwood that washed ashore on the beach back home. Kendra laughed. "What am I thinking? Of course there's a guesthouse. How much land do you have here?"

"'Bout a hundred acres. We'll take you for a tour tomorrow, when there's plenty of daylight."

Chest burning and his mouth dry, Nate paced behind the sofa rather than taking a seat.

Until he saw the anguish that dulled Greer's blue eyes, he hadn't considered the collateral damage he'd caused.

"Greer, I'm sorry I got you caught up in this." The words blurted from his mouth.

"I know you are, Nate. But it's a bell you can't un-ring." She shrugged. "Who knows, maybe somethin' good'll come out of all of this after all. Now, have a seat, please. You're making me nervous as a long-tailed cat in a room full of rocking chairs, pacing like that."

Nate took a seat on the other side of Kendra and massaged the tension in his neck. He stayed quiet, responding only to direct questions from Greer and Kendra as they caught up.

The baby monitor alerted Greer that Noah and Allie were up from their naps. She excused herself and stepped away.

Nate released a long breath when Greer left the room.

"Harder facing them than you expected?" Kendra leaned closer, her tone compassionate and her expression thoughtful.

"I was so focused on how this whole thing impacted my life, my career..." Nate raked his fingers through his hair, trying to quell the guilt gnawing at his gut as he imagined how disappointed Jake and Mariah must have been at his remarks about their father. Wade was their hero. "I didn't think about how my words must have hurt Greer and the kids or Tyree's mom—Ms. Eleanor. People I know and respect."

"That's why you're here, to smooth things out." Kendra's voice was reassuring as she placed a hand on his knee to still it. "If they weren't interested in repairing the relationship, they wouldn't have invited you to stay overnight."

Nate found comfort in the warmth from Kendra's hand seeping into his skin through the layer of fabric between them. She'd always had a calming effect on him; the perfect balance to his fiery personality.

"Take a deep breath and relax. Be honest with Wade about why you said what you did, and about how you feel, knowing you've hurt him."

Nate heaved a sigh. He didn't come here to grovel. He hadn't asked for this situation, and nothing he said that night was news to anyone inside the Marauders organization.

He boarded that plane expecting it would all be so simple. He'd lay out the facts and apologize for talking publicly about team business—even if he hadn't intended to.

Experiencing Greer's anguish firsthand…suddenly it didn't feel so simple.

"Nate, good of you to come all this way."

Nate and Kendra turned toward Wade. He stood in the doorway, each arm draped around a child. His thin smile hovered at the surface, not reaching his wary brown eyes.

"Thanks for seeing me, Wade, and for inviting us to stay." Nate stood, his gut churning as he crossed the room to shake his quarterback's hand. He stooped so his towering frame was closer to the children's height. "Jake, Mariah, you've both gotten so big."

Neither child responded. They stared at him blankly. Mariah drew closer to her father like Nate was the Big

Bad Wolf, rather than her beloved "Uncle Nate." Her reaction hit him like a body slam on Astroturf.

"Say hello to Uncle Nate and Ms. Kendra." Wade squeezed their shoulders.

They mumbled their hellos. Mariah's eyes brimmed with heartache; Jake's glowed with animus.

Wade dispatched the kids to wash their hands and faces before their after-school snack. Then he crossed the room and pulled Kendra into a bear hug, inducing a fleeting moment of envy that heated Nate's face. Wade's Texas accent deepened. "Lemme borrow Nate for a bit."

"Of course." Kendra waved a hand.

Wade flashed his trademark smile. The one plastered on no. less than half a dozen glossy magazines each year. "Greer will be down with the kids in a sec. And don't worry, I promise to bring 'im back in one piece."

"Have a seat." Wade closed the doors to his office. The walls were covered with well-worn shiplap. Mounted antlers hung over the roaring fireplace and rainbow trout replicas flanked either side. Faux animal rugs accented the space.

"Beer?" Wade opened a large wooden console that concealed a drink cooler.

"Thanks." Nate sank into the metal-studded brown leather couch broken in over the years.

Wade pulled out two domestic beers, popped the tops and handed him one. He sank onto a large cushioned chair. "All right, Nate. You traveled twenty-four hundred miles so we could talk man-to-man. You got my undivided attention."

Nate took a long drag of his beer, then set the bottle on a coaster hewn from tree bark.

"I can't tell you how sorry I am about this. Not just to you, but to Greer and the kids. Didn't mean for any of this to happen. It's not my style. You know that."

Wade nodded thoughtfully. "'Preciate that, Nate, but the story's out there now. Nothing either of us can do about it."

"Believe me, I'd do anything to take that entire night back."

"Bet you would. Them pretty little things caused you a lot of trouble. Hope you got a helluva night out of it." Wade chuckled bitterly, referring to the two young women who'd cornered Nate in the VIP section, gotten him riled up again about the loss and recorded his rant.

"Didn't sleep with either of them. I was so amped and more than a little drunk." Nate's face grew hot, thinking of how the blonde and her friend manipulated him. How he stupidly played right into their hands. "About what I said—"

"You meant every word. Just didn't mean for it to go public." Wade took a healthy swig of his light beer and set the bottle down. He leaned forward, his elbows on his knees. "I know. You been telling me as much for a while now. If I'd listened earlier, maybe we'd still be in this thing with a shot at winning it all."

Nate stood, pacing in front of the fireplace. "We all had a hand in it." He jerked a thumb toward himself. "My screwups cost us big."

"Kind of you to own up to your part, Nate, but the truth is, those throws weren't crisp and my timing was off. You wouldn't have dropped them if I'd done my job right. I was scrambling, anticipating another hit."

So that was it. Wade's heart hadn't been in the game for the entire season. Nate thought Wade had resigned himself to never winning the big one. That he was just riding out the remainder of his contract. Instead, he was afraid of taking another hit like the one that leveled him near the end of the previous season. He'd suffered a concussion and two broken ribs.

Wade's performance dropped off considerably when he returned. Two years ago, he was one of the top quarterbacks in the league. He could be again.

"All those times I rode you for not being focused… why didn't you tell me the truth?"

"Who's gonna trust a QB who admits he's scared to take another hard hit? Besides, saying it out loud meant admitting it to myself. For me, that was worse than everyone else knowing."

Nate sank onto the sofa. What could he say?

He'd taken bad hits in his career. Suffered injuries that still nagged him, reminding him the sand was running out in the hourglass of his pro football career. The first few games back were always hard. He was unsure of the injured body part—an ankle and later a knee. Then there was the fear of getting reinjured. For him, it was mind over matter. He focused on his goal: winning a championship. He could spend his retirement resting and nursing his aching joints.

"Look, I know you probably don't want to hear this, but the Marauders work with a sports psychologist. Maybe—"

"Already tried that." Wade stood suddenly, agitated. He got two more beers from the fridge, opened them and placed one in front of Nate.

"You've already been to Dr. Mays?"

"Didn't want the team to know I was having panic attacks. My first game back, this big-ass defensive end came at me and I broke into a cold sweat. Heart beating a mile a minute. Happened again in the next game and the next. Went to an independent sports psychologist."

"Did it help?" Nate gripped his bottle, fully aware of the answer, based on the distressed look on his friend's face.

"I'm fighting my natural self-preservation instincts every time I step onto that field. Told myself time and again it's all in my head. That I can get past it." Wade shrugged again. "But short of taking antianxiety drugs, nothing seems to help. If I gotta drug up just to do my job…maybe it ain't the right job for me anymore."

"You're not thinking about retiring, are you?" It hurt that he was the reason Wade was considering walking away from the game they loved.

"Not like I need the money." Wade nodded toward the wall of glass at the far end of the room with its view of the mountains and a pristine lake. "We've been smart. Saved. Invested. I was trying to hold out and fulfill the final two years of my contract, but maybe it's time to pack it up and walk away." Wade was matter-of-fact about the prospect, as if he'd already resigned himself to it.

"There has to be another answer. We'll make adjustments. Work harder. I got a hand on those passes, so I should've been able to haul them in and hold on to them, simple as that."

Wade met Nate's gaze. "Or maybe you were right all along. Time for me to walk away."

"I *never* said that."

"Been in the league ten years, Nate. It's been a good ride, but that's a hell of a long time. I don't want to be one of those guys who can't enjoy his life by the time he walks away."

They sat in silence as Nate wrestled with what to say to shovel himself out of the six-foot-deep ditch he'd dug and dragged his team into.

"You talk to Greer about this?"

"She's thrilled that I'd be here year-round to help with the kids. She's put her life on hold so I could live my dream. Maybe it's time I support hers. She has a couple of business ideas. Stuff she's been talking about a long time. Maybe it's my turn to be her cheerleader."

Nate assessed his friend, who didn't seem enthused about the prospect. "I know Greer would love to have you home, but what did she say when you told her you were considering retiring?"

Wade chuckled softly. "She said Willises don't run scared. We stay and fight."

Nate laughed, too. "*That* sounds like the Greer Willis I know. I'm just thankful she didn't meet me at the door with a shotgun rather than one of those Hollywood hugs."

"Not gon' lie, she was madder than a hornet when she saw that video." Wade took another swig of his beer. "I hid her phone for two days to keep her from calling you and telling you off."

"I deserved it." Nate gripped his beer, raising his eyes to Wade's. "What about Jake and Mariah? Don't think I've ever felt like as much of an ass as I did seeing myself through their eyes today."

"You're their Uncle Nate. So yeah, they're pretty upset. Jake's angry. Mariah's feelings are hurt."

Nate drained the remainder of his first beer. He took a gulp of the second. "If it's okay with you and Greer,

I'd like to apologize to them. I won't push," he added quickly, in response to the concern in Wade's eyes. "But I want them to know how sorry I am."

Wade nodded solemnly. "I'll talk to Greer about it. If she doesn't have a problem with it, neither do I."

"Thanks," Nate said quietly. "And about you retiring… I know I have no right to ask, but I wish you'd reconsider."

"Oz will be just fine. The kid's good. Really good. Better than me," Wade said, referring to Osgood Wells—the Marauders' backup quarterback who'd been playing behind Wade for the past three seasons. "He went 3 and 1 when I got hurt last year. You said yourself the kid is star material."

"And I still say he's star material." Nate smirked. "But he ain't a star. Not yet. He could use a mentor in his ear helping him along."

"Been doing that the past three years."

"Yeah, but the past three years he was also your competition. Maybe now you'll teach him some of the tricks you've been holding back."

Wade sipped his beer thoughtfully, not denying that mentoring Oz had been the last thing on his mind these past three years. "I'll think about it. But as for us…this thing is over as far as I'm concerned. You're a good friend, Nate. Don't see the need to talk about this again."

Nate's shoulders relaxed as he reached across the table to shake his friend's hand.

Chapter 8

Kendra bounced little Allie on her lap. The infant cooed and giggled, blowing spit bubbles.

"She's adorable." Kendra kissed the girl's round cheek. Inhaled her irresistible, baby scent. "All the kids are, and they're so well-mannered."

"Told you I was lucky." Greer grinned, cutting three turkey sandwiches into triangles for the children.

"No, you're a good mom. Wade and the kids are lucky to have you."

"Thanks." Greer stacked the sandwich triangles on plates and set them on the table. She sighed. "God, I miss having you there whenever I'm in Memphis. You were the one person whose intentions I never doubted. I always felt like we would've been friends even if Wade and Nate weren't."

"Me, too." Kendra smiled, rearranging little Allie's headband. "You were my favorite, hands down."

Greer poured apple juice into acrylic tumblers. "I'm thrilled you and Nate are back together. Sure, I'm a little miffed with him now, but he's always been a good friend to me and Wade. Broke my heart to see how miserable he's been without you and Kai."

"We're not back together." A knot tightened in Kendra's throat. She shifted Allie on her lap, steering the infant away from the gold hoop she was trying to rip from her ear. "I'm his media consultant."

Greer put the juice away and set the cups and plates on the kitchen table. She turned to Kendra. "You do realize he's still in love with you?"

Without waiting for a response, Greer called the children down for their snack.

It was just as well. Greer's words left her head spinning.

The attraction was still there. That was evident from the way he'd scanned her figure on more than one occasion. But was it possible he still loved her?

The resentment on Nate's face when he first laid eyes on her at the restaurant and his aggravation with her when they met at the beach house suggested otherwise.

The one-night stands they'd had were products of their lingering chemistry, bottled-up frustrations and close proximity, not love.

Greer took Allie, who was reaching for her. She settled the girl on her lap, tied on her pink bib and fed her green baby food out of a chunky plastic spoon. "Thinking about what I said?"

Kendra watched Jake, Mariah and Noah nibbling their sandwiches and drinking apple juice. "No, I was wondering what you're feeding Allie. Looks like strained peas, but it smells better than any baby food I remember."

Greer grinned. "It's one of the baby food formulas I've been working on. Allie here is my personal guinea pig."

"She doesn't seem to mind. In fact, I've never seen a baby so enthusiastic about eating her vegetables." Kendra nodded toward the infant, who happily consumed the strained peas, some of which now dotted her chin. "Is this just for Allie or are you thinking of going commercial?"

Greer's eyes lit up. "Been thinking of starting my own baby food company. Everything will be fresh and organic—shipped right to your door. I want to start it as soon as Wade retires."

"What does Wade think?"

"He's been so supportive. He insists I don't need to wait for him to retire, but I'd like at least one of us to be focused on the kids."

"If Allie's enthusiasm is any indication, you've got a hit on your hands."

"Oh my gosh." Greer looked down at her daughter, who evidently wasn't satisfied with the speed at which her mother was feeding her. She dipped her chunky little fingers into the bowl and sucked strained peas from her fingers, getting it all over her face and in her nose. Greer grabbed a wipe and cleaned Allie's hands and face. "I'm excited about the possibility, but I'm scared to death by it, too. You must understand that."

"I do." Kendra took the dirty wipes from Greer and tossed them in the trash. "Never more than when I agreed to take Nate on as a client."

"Let me guess, it was Marcus's idea." Greer grinned as she resumed feeding Allie.

"How'd you know?"

"Had a feeling." Greer shrugged, her Alabama twang evident. "He's an old romantic soul like me and Wade. We been praying you two would figure out you were meant to be together."

"I hate to disappoint all of you, but this arrangement is strictly business."

"Got yourself convinced of that, don't you?" Greer shook her head. "You don't want to tell me? That's fine. But if you're lying to yourself…well, that's another matter altogether."

"What are you talking about?" Kendra tamped down the irritation rising in her chest.

"Isn't it obvious?" She smiled sweetly. "You're still in love with him, too."

Kendra glanced toward the sound of Nate's and Wade's voices approaching. She pointed a finger at Greer. "No more of this me-and-Nate-getting-back-together talk."

"Fine." Greer grinned, spooning more peas into Allie's mouth. "But it's gon' make y'all's sleeping arrangements mighty awkward."

"You mean to tell me this huge guesthouse only has one bedroom?" Kendra stood in the living room, her arms folded.

"There's another bedroom, but we're renovating it. The furniture's gone and there are ladders and paint buckets everywhere." Wade ran a hand through his longish brown hair, which dusted the collar of his suede jacket. "Honest."

Kendra propped a hand on her hip as she surveyed the space. "The sofa looks comfy enough. Got any extra blankets?"

"Sure thing." He gave Nate an apologetic stare. "I'll grab 'em for you."

"Look, it's my fault," Nate said. "I should've been clearer when I explained you were coming along. Didn't think about it because I knew the guesthouse has two bedrooms. I'll take the sofa."

"I'll be fine here." Kendra raised a hand before he could launch into his objection. "End of discussion."

Kendra sank into the bubbles threatening to spill over the side of the old claw-foot tub and sighed. She inhaled the yummy candles perched on the window ledge, which provided the only light in the room. The mingled scent of cranberry and orange wafted through the space, calming her frazzled nerves. She stared up through the skylight, admiring the stars dotting the sky.

Just a few more days. I can handle this.

She repeated the words in her head because the truth was, she didn't know if she could handle spending this much time with Nate. Especially after what Greer had said.

You do realize he's still in love with you? You're still in love with him, too.

Kendra dunked her head beneath the water, holding her breath a few seconds before emerging. Maybe that would disrupt the rogue thoughts of Nate Johnston roaming around the guesthouse barely dressed.

She wiped the water from her face and sat up, pressing her back to the still-cool cast-iron tub as she hugged her knees to her chest.

Concentrate on the job. Nate is just another client.

This was business. She was helping Nate and advancing her career. In fact, over dinner, Greer asked her to consider taking her on as a client once she got the baby food company up and running.

She'd planned to move her consultancy to exclusively serve athletes, but Greer was more than just a potential client. She was a friend. Besides, Kendra believed in what Greer was doing. Having tasted a few of the samples herself, she'd be crazy not to consider it.

There was a light tap at the door. Kendra froze, wrapping her arms tighter around her knees. "Yes?"

"Kai wants to say good-night."

"It's not even eight. I'll call him back as soon as I'm out of the tub."

"It's nearly ten there," Nate reminded her.

She sighed, making sure all of her essential parts were shielded by the bubbles. "The door isn't locked." Another apparent casualty of the remodeling. "Come in."

Light from the hall spilled into the room as Nate stepped inside wearing fitted jeans that hugged his bottom and a tight gray athletic shirt that outlined the hard-earned muscles of his chest and biceps. He handed Kendra his cell phone, then stood back against the door frame, his eyes roving anywhere in the room except on her.

"Kai Kai. How are you?"

"Good. When are you and Daddy coming home?"

"As soon as we can, sweetie. We're in Montana with Uncle Wade and Aunt Greer."

"You know them, too?" Kai had been with his dad whenever he visited with Wade and his family.

"Since before you were born." She smiled. "Auntie Greer's an old friend."

"Are Jake and Mariah there? Does Jake still have his train set?" Kai's voice rose with excitement.

"They're not here with me now. I'm...we're in the guesthouse. But yes, he still has his train. Are you being a good boy for Nana?"

"Yes."

"Did you brush your teeth before bed?"

"Yes, Mommy." He sighed. "I always brush my teeth before bed."

"Good. Now, no more stalling. Go to sleep."

She bid Kai a final good-night, blew a kiss through the phone, then handed it to Nate. "Thank you. I hate not tucking him in tonight. I would've been so disappointed if I'd forgotten to call him before bed."

Nate frowned, his mood suddenly surly. He shoved his phone into his back pocket. "I'll let you get back to your bath."

He left, closing the door behind him.

Kendra sank beneath the water, her eyes readjusting to the candlelit room.

What the hell was that about?

Chapter 9

Nate trudged back to the master bedroom, undressed and hopped in the large, rugged, stacked-stone-and-glass shower.

He lathered himself, gritting his teeth as he recalled Kendra's words. She was distraught over missing a single night tucking Kai in.

Welcome to my world, princess.

Most nights he had to settle for wishing Kai goodnight by phone, as he had tonight. Did she have any clue how much it tore at him that he seldom got to tuck his own son into bed at night?

Kai was growing up so fast. Already six years old, soon he'd be too old for bedtime stories and good-night kisses. And he was missing all of it. Moments he'd never get back.

He'd witnessed his son's first words and first steps

via a video recording. He didn't want to miss out on any more milestones in Kai's life, but Kendra hadn't given him much choice.

The steaming hot water sluiced over his skin, relaxing his tired muscles and aching joints.

Wade was right; the game had taken a toll on their bodies. He wasn't as fast as he'd been a few seasons ago when he was so explosive he could outrun every cornerback in the league in a footrace to the end zone.

He never imagined retiring without hoisting that trophy over his head at least once. The Marauders were close to reaching the next level. They just needed a few tweaks to the defense and a couple more offensive weapons. He couldn't throw in the towel when they were so damn close.

Nights like this, when he was missing the goofy grin and contagious laughter of his son, he gave fleeting consideration to the prospect of retiring sooner rather than later.

Nate shook off the thought. He had a plan. Two more years, then he was out. This wasn't just about him; it was about securing the future of his family and his foundation.

He toweled off and slipped on his underwear. After a few minutes of scanning channels, Nate turned off the television and dropped to the floor to do push-ups.

How the hell had he managed to be mad at, grateful to and turned on by one woman, all at the same time?

Kendra.

He groaned, gritting his teeth as he switched to one-armed push-ups, not caring that he'd need another shower if he kept this up.

All day he'd kept his attraction to her in check—despite the fact that she looked good enough to pour in a glass and serve on ice in that body-hugging gray pencil skirt and knee-high boots. In spite of the electricity humming along the surface of his skin when she'd placed her hand on his, comforting him. But seeing her in the tub with her slick brown skin and wet curls—that was more than any man could be expected to handle.

He'd tried to distract himself by counting the bathroom tiles and studying every feature of that damn bathroom like he'd have a pop quiz on it the next morning. Still, his eyes roamed back to her in that tub again and again. Fortunately, she'd been too busy talking to Kai to notice.

Nate slipped on his flannel pajama bottoms and slippers, then padded to the kitchen for a snack. He opened the fridge and smiled. Wade and Greer had stocked it with leftovers.

Nate cut a few slices of ham, then added some macaroni and cheese and green bean casserole to his plate before heating it in the microwave.

"What smells so good?"

Nate turned, startled by Kendra moving toward him in purple pajamas. Her damp curls were wrapped in a white turban.

"Leftovers." He turned back to the microwave to watch the timer count down.

She shoved a few items into her luggage, then inched closer. "I shouldn't be eating this late—but now I'm hungry again. Any more?"

Arms folded, he tipped his head toward the fridge. "Plenty."

Kendra cocked her head to the side, her brow furrowed. She opened the fridge. "Thanks."

She made her plate in silence as he waited for his to finish heating.

Nate removed his plate from the microwave, grabbed his utensils and headed back to his room. He needed to put space between them, get a good night's rest and let his annoyance subside.

"Wait." Kendra's plea halted him. "Have I done something to upset you? Everything seemed fine, then suddenly I'm getting grunts and one-word answers."

"Everything is fine, Kendra. I'm tired, and I'd like to go to bed, if that's all right."

She shrugged. "You don't want to talk about it? Fine. But if I've somehow pissed you off, you should at least be mature enough to tell me what I did wrong."

"Like you were when you packed your bags and took off seven years ago?" He swung around. "That the kind of maturity you're talking about?"

Kendra lowered her gaze. "I didn't know exactly how to handle what I was feeling."

"I was prepared to spend my life with you, and you gave me the 'it's not you, it's me' speech. You said the life you would've had with me wasn't the one you envisioned for yourself. Do you have any idea how that made me feel?" Nate put the plate on the table and clenched his fist.

"Shitty," he supplied when she didn't respond. "Everything I'd done up to then was so that I could give you the life you deserved."

Head tilted, her brow creased. "That's sweet, Nate, but I never asked you to take care of me. I'm fully capable of caring for myself."

"I know, but..." Nate ran a hand through his hair and huffed. "All those years I watched your mom struggle to support you and Dash, working long hours and still managing to be a good mother. Most days she was tired to the bone. Apologizing because she couldn't be at your brother's track meets or your school plays. I didn't want that for you. For us. I wanted to give you everything. Anything you wanted."

"What I wanted was to have a relationship *and* a career. I wanted to do what I loved during the day and go home to the person I loved at night, just like you did. But you couldn't cope with that, as if it infringed upon your manhood."

"I didn't object to your career. I just didn't want you working with random athletes."

"Why?" She stepped closer.

"You know how those guys are. Chasing skirts. Going after anything pretty that moves."

"Exactly." Kendra's self-satisfied expression said it all. He'd justified her reasons for walking away.

His cheeks flushed with heat. "C'mon, Kendra, you know what I meant. Not every guy is like that. I'm not."

"Okay." She shrugged. "Let's look at the most essential point. You didn't trust me."

"Now you're turning this on me? You're the one who walked away because you didn't trust me."

"And you sabotaged my career because you didn't trust that I could deal with your colleagues without ending up in their beds."

They were both silent, stewing over the unhealed wounds they'd inflicted on each other.

Nate inhaled deeply, then released his breath slowly. He shook his head. "For the record, I did trust you. Just didn't want you to put yourself in a bad situation. Besides, I couldn't be sure of what I'd do if one of those guys ever laid a hand on you. Figured it'd be safer if we never had to find out. I didn't realize how important it was to you until it was too late."

"You should've talked to me instead of trying to lay down the law like you were the sheriff in a one-horse town." The corners of her eyes were damp. "Like what I wanted didn't matter."

Nate studied her face. "I was wrong, and I'm sorry. I wish I could take it back and do it all over again."

"Me, too." Kendra swiped a finger beneath her eye; her voice quavered. "The choice I made...it was a mistake. One we all ended up paying for."

Nate had waited a long time to hear those words. For confirmation that what they'd shared was real.

"I shouldn't have brought it up." His fists were balled at his sides as he resisted the urge to take her in his arms.

She sniffled, raising her eyes, wet with tears, to his. "And I shouldn't have made such a big deal about not being able to tuck Kai in tonight. That's what upset you, isn't it? I was complaining about one night without him while you..." She sighed heavily. "While you're away from him most nights."

Nate shrugged, watching a line of dark clouds rolling in and lightning in the distance.

"Every day I regret the pain my choice has caused both you and Kai." Kendra touched his arm. She leaned into him when he didn't respond. "I know it's a lot to ask, but I hope that one day you can forgive me. Both you and Kai."

His chest ached from the pain and regret he saw in her brown eyes. "What do you mean you hope Kai will forgive you?"

Kendra's eyebrows gathered and a deep line creased her forehead, hardening her soft features. She pressed her lips together tightly, as if she were trying to hold back a sob.

"He's been asking for you a lot more since Liam came into our lives. He sees Liam with the girls and he doesn't understand why his dad isn't in his life every day." Her voice grew faint; the tears etched a salty path down her face faster than she could erase them. "He's only six now, but eventually he'll be hurt and angry... he'll hate me for taking him away from his dad." Kendra covered her mouth and turned away.

Nate wrapped his arms around her, pulling her wet cheek to his bare chest. He kissed her forehead. "Kai adores you. He could never stay angry with you. He's too much of a mama's boy."

Kendra laughed against his chest, then pulled away enough to meet his gaze. "Like his dad?"

He held her at arm's length. "Whoa? Me? A mama's boy?"

She raised an eyebrow and punched him in the gut playfully. "Uh...yeah."

Nate peeked through his thumb and forefinger. "Maybe just a tad. Nothing wrong with that."

"No, there isn't." Kendra smiled wistfully. "There's a little mama's boy in every good man."

He pulled her to him again, his body reacting to the exquisite sensation of her curves pressed against him. "You saying I'm a good man?"

"I wouldn't be here now if I didn't believe you are. That's why this campaign is so important. I want people to see the kind, brilliant man I've always known. That's my mission. Once we accomplish that, everything else will come. The contract, the endorsements."

"Didn't think you believed in me anymore." He paused, his next words catching in his throat. "That's what hurt most when you left."

Kendra dropped her stare, but Nate cupped her chin, raising her eyes to meet his again.

"I know that you don't want to talk about this and that what's done is done. But in all these years, it's never felt over to me. There's always been a tiny piece of me that—despite the anger and hurt feelings—still wanted you to be there for me like you are right now."

She tried to pull away, but he held on tight, his gaze not leaving hers.

"I need to know, is there still a chance we can be a family?"

Yes.

That single word hung at the back of her throat, unable to make its way past her lips. She shook her head, trying to clear the warm thoughts that were fogging her brain and spreading throughout her body. Making her want things she had no right to. "Nate, I—"

He leaned down and kissed her open mouth, mid-sentence. His strong arms encircling her waist, he pulled their lower bodies together.

Kendra gasped at the sensation of his lips pressed to hers. She savored the taste and warmth of his mouth as she melted into his strong embrace. The memories of what they'd once been filled her body with heat and caused a delicious ache in her nipples and between her thighs.

Kissing Nate went against every rule she'd established when she agreed to take him on as a client. Rules she put in place to safeguard their working relationship and protect her heart.

Despite the blissful contentment she felt, surrendering to the magnetic pull between them, she needed to put a stop to it and regain control. Kendra pressed the heels of her hands into his chest, but Nate pulled her closer. Kissed her more fervently.

The logical objections her brain posed gave way to the temptation and desire that made her skin tingle. She relaxed into him and pressed her fingers to the warm skin of his muscular back.

She missed the strength of his hands, the tenderness of his kiss. The way his touch filled her belly with fire and made her knees weak.

Her senses were overloaded with the heat emanating from his skin, the scent of his freshly scrubbed skin, mingled with a hint of sweat and the salty taste of him.

Maybe she was overly cautious. They'd done this before—had one night together and then sensibly walked away.

Would it be so wrong if we did it again?

But that wasn't what Nate had proposed. He'd asked whether they could be a family.

That, she couldn't promise.

Kendra pulled away, her eyes searching his. "Nate, please, we agreed to keep this strictly business."

Nate sighed heavily, frowning. He cupped her cheek with his rough palm. "*We* didn't agree to anything. You insisted on it."

"I know, but you promised to keep your hands to yourself." She poked a finger in his chest, attempting to lighten the suddenly heavy mood. The tension between them was finally abating. She couldn't afford for things to go back to the way they were.

"We both made promises." He dropped his gaze, his voice gruff. "Things change."

He didn't need to elaborate. Kendra knew exactly what he meant. The night they'd gotten tossed from the prom, they spent the night on Pleasure Cove Beach, watching the waves crash on the shore. He'd made love to her on the beach under an incredible full moon and a sky full of stars that had never shone brighter.

That night, Nate promised to always love her. She'd promised the same.

They were just kids. Neither of them had a clue what life had in store or how they'd change.

Kendra clenched her fists at her side and sank her teeth into her lower lip as she searched for the right words.

Head cocked to the side, Nate's dark eyes studied hers. His words were a husky whisper that sent electricity up her spine. "There's obviously still something between us."

"We have a lot of history and an amazing little boy. It's hard not to get caught up in those feelings."

"Then maybe we should explore them." He trailed the back of his hand down the side of her face. "See where this thing takes us."

Kendra fought off the overwhelming desire to let Nate take her back to his bed and make love to her. His mouth exploring hers, his hands roaming her skin as she lay in his arms.

Sex and business don't mix. Stay strong.

"Wanting each other isn't enough, Nate." She stepped back, giving herself room to breathe in air that wasn't permeated with his fresh, woodsy scent. "And what we want isn't necessarily what's best for us. No matter how badly we want it."

Nate caught her hand as she turned to walk away, tugging her toward him again. "I don't believe our being together isn't what's best for us or Kai. Neither do you."

"One kiss and you're talking about being a family? I can't promise you that."

Nate groaned, releasing her hand. "We're not kids on a first date, Kendra. We know each other. Most important, we love our son and want what's best for him."

Kendra wanted Nate. Loved him. But did he love her? Or was this just about finally making them a family?

Nate grew up in a big, close family that had earned the moniker "the black Waltons." His parents had been married for four decades. Nate wanted Kai to be raised by both his parents—just as he'd been.

She wanted that, too, but not at the expense of a one-sided marriage where they were just in it for the kids. Relationships like that didn't last.

Her parents were proof of that.

"We both want what's best for Kai. That's why we need to focus on the mission at hand. There's a lot on the line here, Nate. Your career, your future income, the work you've been able to do with the foundation—"

"Your career." His mouth tugged down in a frown. "It's serious, I get it, but *this*—" he gestured between them "—is important, too."

She lifted her chin and met his condemning gaze. "This isn't the time to explore the past. Not with so much at stake for both of us."

"Fine." He gathered his plate, turning to leave.

Kendra grabbed his elbow. "That doesn't mean we can't sit down and have a meal together."

"You want to keep this thing strictly business? Well, I don't usually have shirtless midnight business meetings." He narrowed his gaze, his tone icy.

"You give interviews in the locker room when you're half-dressed. How is this any different?"

"You know why it's different." Nate put the plate down again. "What is it that you want from me, Kendra?"

She stood stunned, her mouth slack, unable to reply.

"I ask you to marry me and you walk away. Just when I think I'm finally over it, you find some way to mess with my head again. I just wanted to have a quiet late-night snack in my room. *Alone.* But you couldn't let it be." His words came in quick, angry bursts. "I kiss you. Tell you I want to be with you and Kai. You say I'm pushing too hard. But, oh, by the way, why don't we sit down for a nice, civil business meal in our pajamas?"

Her stomach clenched and her hands shook. He was right. She was being selfish—trying to hold on to him while maintaining her distance. "I'm sorry. I don't know exactly how to do this. I want us to be friends again. Not just because we're working together or even because of Kai. We were friends long before we dated. I miss that."

Nate shook his head. "After everything we've been through, I can't just be friends. Maybe someday, but not tonight."

Kendra bit her lower lip, concentrating on the superficial physical pain rather than the deep ache in her heart as he walked away.

Chapter 10

Nate dropped his luggage by the front door and stumbled to the couch. They'd landed in Memphis later than expected.

Good to finally be home again.

He dropped Kendra off at a nearby hotel and headed to his place.

He had plenty of room to put her up for the night. But after the night they'd shared at Wade and Greer's guesthouse, they both agreed it would be better if she stayed at a hotel.

Nate just wanted a cold beer and a hot bath before what would surely be a grueling day.

First, there was the meeting with the team. Then he would meet with a couple of his teammates. After he made his personal amends to everyone on the list—except Tyree and Dade, who were still dodging his calls—

he'd take to the podium in a press conference at the team facilities.

Nate made his way to the fridge. He tossed out a couple of suspect take-out containers, then pulled out a bottle of imported beer. He settled on the couch again when the doorbell rang.

His neighbor collected his mail when he was away, and was always a little too eager to bring over his mail and newspapers. Nate opened the door.

"Hello, Nate. Miss me?"

Stephanie Weiss—the devil herself and the cause of this entire fiasco—lifted her head, her face previously shielded by her large-brimmed hat. Her mouth curved in a sly grin.

"What the hell are you doing here?" He gritted out the words between clenched teeth.

"Got a proposal for you." She smiled sweetly, glancing over his shoulder. "May I come in?"

"Not if your ass was on fire and I had the only bucket of water for thirty miles," he seethed. "You've got five seconds before I call security to haul you out of here."

She seemed slightly irritated by his rebuff, but mostly amused. "Fine. Then I'll save my questions for the press conference tomorrow. Just thought you'd welcome the opportunity to sit down and explain your side of things."

"Sit down with the devil who caused this whole shit storm? No thanks." He crossed his arms. "Yeah, I know it was you who sent those girls to ambush me."

She smirked. "Now that's just unsubstantiated speculation." Stephanie echoed the words he'd used in the press conference he had three years ago, when he'd distanced himself from her after the scandal broke.

"Is that what this is about?" He placed a hand high on the doorjamb as he leaned against the frame. "You're still pissed because I wouldn't help you ruin my friend's career?"

"You didn't have any qualms about ruining mine." She narrowed her eyes, the irises the color of muddy water, and pressed her thin lips into a tight line. "This time, I had indisputable proof, and it's you who came out looking like the fool."

Nate clenched his fist and gritted his teeth. Swallowed back all the things he wanted to say to this woman. Things his mama would whup his behind for if she heard him utter them in mixed company. "Get off my property. Now. Believe me, I'd enjoy watching the cops drag you out of here."

Stephanie shrugged, then flipped her shoulder-length dark hair. "Fine, but I came here to offer a truce. Give me an exclusive interview before your press conference tomorrow, and I'll back off. Let this thing die down."

Nate laughed bitterly. "Be a clown in the circus you created? No thanks."

"What are you worried about? You'll come out smelling like a rose. You always do."

"I'll take option two." His patience was gone. "Now, get the fuck off my property."

"War it is then." Stephanie grinned, tying the belt of her red wool coat. She turned and walked away, calling over her shoulder, "Don't say I didn't give you a chance to end this thing peacefully."

Nate slammed the door and pressed his back to it, running his fingers through his hair. He'd screwed himself over big-time when he'd messed around with her.

Aside from letting Kendra walk away, getting with Stephanie Weiss was his biggest regret.

His friends had warned him that breaking a big story would always be her first priority, putting all of them in jeopardy. He hadn't listened. Now he was paying the price.

Stephanie had lost her career and her credibility as a sideline reporter for a major network when things had gone sideways three years before. Seemed she'd spent those years plotting her payback.

Nate picked up his beer and drained the bottle, then headed to the kitchen for another. The doorbell rang again.

He turned, his jaw clenched and his fist balled at his side.

All bets were off. Stephanie Weiss was about to get a piece of his mind—unfiltered. He'd just have to apologize to his mother later.

Kendra shifted her bag on her shoulder, her luggage at her side and her heart racing.

Nate wouldn't be happy to see her. Not when he'd dropped her at the hotel like she was a sack of flaming potatoes and pulled off, barely muttering two words.

When the door swung open, he looked angrier than she'd ever seen him. Like he was prepared for a fight. His shoulders drooped, a look of confusion on his face as he glanced around. "Kendra, what are you doing here?"

Nice to see you, too.

Kendra pulled her wrap around her to combat the chill in the air and the one rolling off her ex. "They were booked, except for a presidential suite. Same story with every other hotel I called. There are a couple of trade conventions in town this week."

"Forgot about that," he muttered, still blocking the doorway. He glanced over her shoulder again.

"If you're looking for your friend who just left, I passed her in the driveway."

"She isn't my friend. That was Stephanie Weiss."

"Your ex?" Kendra asked, then shifted under Nate's withering stare. "I mean, the reporter who started all of this?"

"Seems there are a lot of my exes showing up at my door tonight." He raised an eyebrow, then sighed. He grabbed her bags off the doorstep, opening the door wide enough for her to enter. "Come in."

Kendra stepped inside tentatively, glancing around the house. Despite the tension between them, she couldn't help smiling. She had so many great memories in this house. She remembered when Nate first bought the place. The weeks of house hunting before they'd finally settled on it. The times they'd shared there.

She glanced toward the den, where they'd last made love one weekend when she'd brought Kai to visit his father. They'd been in the middle of a heated argument about where Kai would spend Christmas. Then he'd kissed her, and they'd ended up making love on the sofa while their son slept blissfully unaware upstairs.

They'd almost made the same mistake in Montana.

Kendra stood taller. This time she'd be smarter. Stronger. Use better judgment. Then everything would be fine. "The place looks great."

"Thanks." Nate set her bags near the bottom of the stairs. "I'll take your bags up in a few minutes, but I was just about to get a beer. I could use one right now. Can I get you something?"

"Glass of wine?"

"Red or white?" he asked, then quickly answered his own question, echoing her response. "Rosé, of course."

She smiled. "If you have it. If not, a glass of white wine would be fine."

"Think I've got something in the cooler."

She followed him into the kitchen. "So, what was public enemy number one doing here?"

Nate's delts tensed visibly and he paused for a moment before reaching into the wine cooler. He dug through the bottles silently, then pulled out her favorite bottle of rosé. He opened the bottle. "Proposing a truce of sorts."

"So she acknowledges this is a vendetta against you?" Kendra sat at the kitchen table.

"Stephanie wanted me to know she was the one who took me down." He poured a glass of wine and handed it to Kendra. "She knows I can't do anything with the information."

Kendra thanked Nate for the rosé and took a sip. "Unfortunately, she's right. It would do more harm than good. You'll come off as a whiny athlete blaming someone else for your screwup."

Nate twisted the cap off his beer and sat at the table. He took a swig. "She's probably banking on me using that excuse at the press conference tomorrow. Bet she's already got a segment taped, just waiting for sound bites from the conference."

"Cunning, vindictive and determined. She's a real winner," Kendra muttered, then sipped her wine.

"Yeah, I can really pick 'em." He cut his gaze at her, then drank more of his beer.

Touché.

Kendra straightened her shoulders. "So this truce she offered, what was it?"

"She wanted me to give her an exclusive interview before the press conference. Said if I did, she wouldn't press the issue further."

"Indicating that if you don't, she'll keep fanning the flames." Kendra's stomach flipped. That meant she'd be doing more than just cleaning up the mess that was already made, she'd be putting out fires intentionally set by Stephanie. "Do you think she'd keep her word if you gave her the interview?"

"Not as far as I could throw her conniving ass."

Kendra nodded. "I suspected as much. If you don't mind my asking—"

"What did I see in her in the first place?" He finished her question. When she nodded, he continued, "I was out with an injury, feeling down on myself when I ran into Steph at the grocery store. I was struggling with my leg in a cast. She offered to help me shop and to make dinner for me that night. We were on friendly terms. Figured, what the hell? It could be fun."

"I'm sure it didn't hurt that she's very pretty. Wasn't she a beauty contestant or something?"

"Miss Connecticut. Third runner-up for Miss America that year." He didn't meet her gaze.

"Not judging." Kendra held her hands up. "But she obviously isn't as pretty on the inside."

Nate grunted. "Got that right."

"Okay, so taking the deal isn't an option. We'll have to be prepared for whatever she slings our way." Kendra paused before asking the thing she needed to know, but didn't want to ask. "She doesn't have anything on you, does she? No secretly recorded audio, no sex tapes?"

"No," he said emphatically, sitting up straight as a rod, then dropping his gaze. "I mean, not that I'm aware of."

Fair enough. Anyone could set up a secret camera in their bedroom.

"Anything you might have told her about a teammate or your family that she might use?"

"Not that I recall." His response wasn't as convincing. "Like I said, we were only together a few months. The time we did spend together...we spent very little of it talking."

Kendra ignored the twisting in her gut. "Then we'll just stay alert. Be sure not to give her any new ammunition."

Nate stood suddenly. "Got a long day tomorrow. I'll take your bags to your room."

He was gone before she could thank him.

Kendra poured herself another glass of wine. This time she'd be ready for Stephanie Weiss.

Chapter 11

Nate took his place behind the lectern and straightened his tie. He adjusted the microphone and thanked everyone for coming, then explained that he would play the full video.

Stephanie pressed her lips into an angry slash and folded her arms. Her ire confirmed that playing the entire video was the right move.

Score one more for Kendra.

He stepped aside while the five-minute video played in its entirety. Nate glanced over at Marcus and Kendra standing in the corner.

His brother nodded reassuringly. Kendra's confident smile filled his chest with warmth and eased the tension in his shoulders. He wouldn't admit it to Marcus, but he was glad Kendra was there. Especially since his twin sister—off on one of the solo island vacations she took a few times a year—couldn't be.

When the video ended, the lights came on again. Nate launched into a prepared script, giving a brief overview of what happened that night and why he was so frustrated with himself and his teammates. He made it clear he'd offered his sincere apologies in person to everyone who was available. Nate apologized again for his lack of thoughtfulness and the impact it had on his teammates and the Marauders organization.

He ended by stating emphatically that he intended to suit up for the Marauders for the remainder of his career.

"Our team has come so close to going to the big dance. During the off-season, we'll work hard as individuals and as an organization to ensure we're giving our all every single time we take the field. It's what every man on the team wants. Most important, it's what the loyal fans of this city deserve. Thank you for coming."

Nate stepped away from the microphone, relieved the press conference was finally over. He was especially grateful Kendra insisted they not take questions.

Score two for Kendra.

"Is it true you just returned from Montana where you pressured Wade Willis to retire before next season?" Stephanie shot to her feet, to the surprise of everyone in the room.

"Of course not." The words came out of his mouth before he could stop them. Kendra had already warned him someone was bound to push for questions. He was supposed to say, "No further comment."

So much for that.

"Wade is still one of the elite quarterbacks in this league. This past year wasn't his best year, but it wasn't mine, either. We'll both be stronger next year."

"So you admit you're a big part of the reason the team has stalled in the play-offs three years in a row?" Stephanie could barely hold back her smirk.

Nate's shoulders knotted. He pressed his lips into a harsh line and breathed out slowly. "As I stated that night on the video, I need to be better. We all do. No further questions."

He stepped away from the microphone and made a beeline behind the curtains and away from the hungry pack of jackals clamoring to ask the next question. Nate pressed his back against the wall, angry with himself for not sticking to the script. He'd let Stephanie rile him. She knew he wouldn't let that accusation hang in the air, unanswered.

And how the hell did she know he'd just returned from Montana, anyway?

He looked up at the *click* of Kendra's heels coming down the hallway. She wasn't happy. Neither was Marcus, who was hard on her heels.

"Why didn't you stick to the script?" Marcus gestured wildly. "Were we not clear about not taking questions?"

"I know I should've ignored her question, but I couldn't leave the fans thinking I'm trying to push Wade out."

"There are going to be a lot of accusations hurled at you in the next few weeks, man. You can't respond to every one. We've got a plan. If you stick with it, everything will be fine." Marcus stormed away, likely in search of a strong cup of coffee.

Nate turned his attention to Kendra. "Go ahead. Let me have it."

Kendra's expression softened, and she let out a quiet

sigh as she squeezed his arm. "I know how much Wade means to you and to the fans. It's probably good you combated that accusation right away and that you spoke so highly of him. You handled the situation well."

"Really?"

"Really. Just don't do it again. If we say no questions, then don't address questions. Not even from Stephanie Weiss. Got it?"

"Got it." He looked down at his watch. "We better head out. Marcus and I have a late lunch meeting over at the foundation. We'll drop you off at the house on the way."

"Aren't we flying back to Pleasure Cove tonight?" Her shoulders tensed and there was a hint of panic in the slight elevation of her tone.

"Change of plans. I finally connected with Dade. We're meeting tomorrow for lunch, so we'll have to stay one more night. Hope that's cool."

"It's important that you sit down with Dade and iron things out." Kendra waved a hand. "I'll try again with the hotels."

"No need." Nate shoved his hands in his pockets. "There's plenty of room for both of us."

"If you're sure."

"I am. Feel free to work from my office. I'll even make dinner tonight. To thank you for everything," he added quickly.

She cocked an eyebrow, her adorable nose crinkling. "You cook now?"

"Okay, so maybe I'm just heating it up. Same difference."

Kendra laughed, then looked thoughtful, the gears

turning in that brilliant head of hers. She nodded reluctantly. "Sure."

He gave her a quick nod, then they headed toward the exit, his heart dancing with a growing sense of hope.

Kendra paced in front of the fireplace in the den, her body filled with nervous energy, prompted by the memories of when she was last there.

She halted, catching her breath as she fought back the vivid sensation of Nate planting soft kisses along her collarbone and shoulders. Kisses that led to a wild and passionate night together.

Kendra swallowed hard, then resumed her pacing. Finally, she plopped on the sofa and pulled out her phone. She called her mother, but there was no answer. Next, she called her sister.

"How's the trip?"

Kendra released a slow breath, fortified by the lilt in Maya's voice. "Professionally? Things are going well. Personally? I'm losing it."

"Why, what's going on between you and Nate?"

"I'm sitting on the infamous sofa, trying my hardest to keep my head together, but all I keep thinking about is the last time I was here, when I couldn't keep my legs together."

Maya chuckled. "What are you doing at Nate's anyway? Thought you were staying at a hotel."

"So did I, but we ended up staying overnight in Montana sharing Wade and Greer's guesthouse."

Maya cleared her throat. "The more important question is, did you two share a bed?"

"No," Kendra said quickly. The silence seemed to extend forever. Her sister was the master of the well-used pause to get her to spill her guts. She groaned. "But he kissed me."

"Did you kiss him back?" The lilt returned to Maya's voice. She was on the verge of a giggle.

"Until I regained my clarity."

"Clarity, huh? Sounds more like delusion, if you're still pretending Nate doesn't mean anything to you."

"Of course he does. He's Kai's dad. He was my best friend. My first." She said the words wistfully, recalling that weekend her mother had taken her brother to Raleigh on a college tour. "I'll always care for him. That doesn't mean we're meant to be together."

"And what does Nate think?" Maya's tone was subdued.

Kendra swung her legs beneath her and exhaled. "He wants us to be a family."

"Oh my gosh, Kendra. That's great news." Maya paused when Kendra didn't respond. "Isn't it?"

"Seems like it's more about Nate wanting to be with Kai." A dull ache filled her chest. "He didn't say he wanted to be with me. He just keeps going on about how great it would be to finally be a family."

"Nate loves his son. Why is that bad?"

"Because it can't be the only reason we're together, like it was for Dad when he married my mom."

There was an uneasy silence between them. As much as Kendra loved Maya now, it hadn't always been that way. Kendra had resented Maya and her younger brother.

She couldn't shake the hurt of knowing she was the reason her father left. Curtis Williams abandoned their family less than a year after her birth.

Though he'd left them behind, he chose to stay with

Maya's mother just a year later. They'd gotten married and raised two kids. He'd attended every school function and proudly filmed everything from Maya's and Cole's first steps to their college graduations.

Even now, she sometimes lay awake at night wondering why her father hadn't loved her enough to stay with them. Why he hadn't doted on her and Dash and embraced being their dad as much as he enjoyed being a father to Maya and Cole.

"I don't think it's as simple as that." Maya adored Curtis Williams. She was a daddy's girl. He'd been there for her all her life. Why shouldn't she adore him? "He loved your mom."

Kendra snorted. "He had a damn funny way of showing it. Love like that, I don't need."

"Nate isn't our dad," Maya said quietly. "And for the record, Dad was young and he made his mistakes. He regrets how poorly he handled things."

"Agree to disagree." It was Kendra's signal for Maya to end the discussion of Curtis Williams's virtues.

"Okay." The word came out of Maya's mouth in an odd singsong. "But you're not being fair to Nate. Just because being a family is important to him doesn't mean you aren't."

Kendra understood the sense of indebtedness Maya felt toward Nate. She and Dash had wanted nothing to do with their father or their half siblings. Still, Maya had been persistent, following Kendra to college. Nate and his parents encouraged her to get to know Maya.

"She's family," Nate's mom, Ms. Naomi, had said. "Doesn't matter how she became family. She just is. And you don't turn your back on family."

Kendra had resented Nate's interference at first, but

she and Dash had grown apart as they'd gotten older and she yearned for the deep connection Nate had with his siblings.

Getting to know and accept her younger sister was one of the best decisions she'd ever made. She and Maya owed a huge debt of gratitude to the Johnstons. But she wouldn't be with Nate out of a sense of obligation.

"We're not the same people we were seven years ago." Kendra stood by the fireplace, allowing its warmth to soothe the chill creeping down her spine.

"So get to know each other again. Most important, tell him how you feel," Maya urged.

Kendra's temples throbbed. "I can't."

"Why not?"

"He'll say it just because I need to hear it." Kendra paced in front of the fireplace. Her slippers scuffed against the carpet.

"Nate always says what he feels. That's why he's in the spot he's in now." Maya sighed in response to the cluck of Kendra's tongue. "If he says it, it's because he means it."

"Then why didn't he say it the other night? Why didn't he say he misses me? That he wants to be with me? That he can't stop thinking of me the way I can't stop thinking of him?" Kendra hadn't meant to say the last part, but her mouth was moving faster than her brain.

Maya hesitated before she responded. "The last time Nate confessed his feelings for you, you rejected him and walked away. Can you blame him for being gun-shy?"

Kendra's stomach twisted in knots as the truth of

Maya's words hit her squarely in the chest. She didn't respond.

"Maybe Nate's reluctant to share his feelings because he isn't sure he can trust you with them." An apologetic tone filtered her sister's brutally honest words.

"Maybe. Still, I won't get back with Nate for the wrong reasons. As much as I know Kai wants his dad and me to be together, it would be worse if things blew up a few years down the road. I won't set him up for the disappointment and resentment I experienced at his age."

"You mean, the resentment you feel now." Maya's voice wavered.

"I don't mean to make you feel bad. That's why I try not to talk about Dad. It's never a conversation that will go well between us."

"Even when we don't discuss him, that ugly little truth is hidden in the words we don't say." Maya cleared her throat. "Do you have any idea how much it hurts to know that deep down my sister wishes I were never born?"

"That isn't true."

"I wish it were as easy for me to believe that as it is for you." Maya sighed. "If it were the other way around, maybe I'd feel the same."

"No, you wouldn't. You're the sweetest, most loving person I know. I know it doesn't always seem like it, but I'm grateful to have you in my life. I'm thrilled you found someone who loves you as much as I do. You deserve a great guy like Liam. He's about as close as a guy can get to being worthy of you."

"Thanks, sis." The smile returned to Maya's voice.

"Speaking of that handsome man of yours, when

are you two going to finally set a date?" Kendra settled onto the couch.

"I was thinking we'd wait until next summer to get married."

"Why so long? Is it a family thing for him?" The Westbrooks owned a huge international resort firm based in London, and they were well connected back in the UK.

"It's nothing like that, it's just… I keep hoping that if I wait long enough, you and Dad will work things out."

"I promised I'd be on my best behavior on your wedding day," Kendra reminded her sister.

"I appreciate the sentiment, but the reality is that the tension between you two makes everyone uncomfortable."

"I won't let that happen on your wedding day, Maya. I promise."

"The minute you see him, you'll pick a fight. Happens every time." Maya's voice rose to a crescendo. Suddenly it became sad. "You're not just punishing Dad. It hurts that I can't sit down with two of my favorite people on my wedding day."

Kendra's heart ached. Whatever her issues were with their father, Maya wasn't to blame. "I'm sorry. I had no idea."

"I know, but we can talk about that another day. Right now, let's talk about the real reason you called. You're still in love with Nate, and it terrifies you."

Kendra didn't deny the accusation. "I won't break his heart again. He couldn't take that. Neither could I. Besides, his evil twin would probably strangle me with her bare hands."

"Or at least hire someone to off you." Maya laughed, the tension between them easing.

"No, she'd definitely do it herself." Kendra was only half kidding. Vi would probably relish the feel of her warm blood on her hands. Nate's twin could be your best friend or your worst enemy. Once the former, Kendra was now the latter.

"The solution is simple," Maya said. "Don't break his heart this time."

That was Maya. Making a complicated relationship like the one she and Nate shared seem so simple. Apparently, she'd forgotten what a convoluted relationship she and Liam had just a few months prior. When she was still terrified of bringing someone new into her daughters' lives, afraid Liam would disappoint them.

Thankfully, she'd been wrong. Liam was an amazing man who'd left behind his playboy ways once he found the woman of his dreams—her little sister.

"I didn't set out to break his heart before. I panicked. How can I be sure it won't happen again?"

"You can't, but you can be honest with Nate and yourself about what freaked you out then." Maya's voice was soothing. "And any lingering fears holding you back now."

"I won't put my career aside for Nate again," Kendra suddenly interjected. The declaration took her by surprise.

"Then talk to him," Maya said simply. "No more excuses."

She was gone before Kendra could object.

"They're not excuses," she said to the empty room as she tossed her phone on the sofa. "It's the truth."

"What's the truth?"

Kendra startled, nearly jumping out of her skin. "Nate, I didn't hear you come in."

He grinned. "Obviously. You hungry?"

Kendra nodded. Until he'd mentioned it, she hadn't realized how hungry she was. She'd checked the fridge earlier, but there was very little edible food left. "I could eat."

A slow grin stretched his mouth. "Good, because I thought we could cook together like the old days."

Damn. Now she couldn't look at the kitchen counter without reminiscing about exactly how those times nearly always ended.

Who knew kitchen sex could be so good?

Kendra shrugged. "Okay."

She would help Nate cook because she was hungry. Starving, in fact. But no matter what, they most definitely would not go there. No matter how good he looked in that slim gray suit.

Chapter 12

One of the many things Nate missed about Kendra was their shared love of food. She'd never subsisted on lettuce or gone from one crazy fad diet to the next.

Kendra appreciated a gourmet meal. Savored every bite. Watching her enjoy a perfectly cooked steak or authentic pasta dish was practically foreplay.

Tonight, he would begin his slow seduction by making her favorite meal. He'd nixed his plans to purchase a premade lasagna prepared by a local gourmet chef. Kendra's crack about his not being able to cook forced him to step up his game.

He purchased the meal plan that came with the ingredients and the recipe so they could prepare the meal together, like they did when they first started out.

Nate's pulse quickened as he reminisced over those steamy nights together. There was something almost erotic about the act of cooking together. Filling one basic need led to satisfying another.

He set the bags on the counter and took off his jacket, folding it across the chair. "Can I get you a drink?"

Her hesitant nod, a brief glimpse at the vulnerability she loathed revealing, somehow made her even sexier. "Half a glass of wine would be great."

Nate dragged his gaze up her body, admiring her toned curves. She wore an oversize white T-shirt with a deep vee over a pair of black leggings that hugged her ample hips and thighs. He cleared his throat, raising his eyes to hers again as he pulled a chilled bottle of her favorite rosé from the bag. He poured her a half glass and watched her sensual mouth as she took a generous sip, her hand unsteady.

"Everything okay?" Nate removed one cuff link, then the other.

"Fine." Her voice vibrated with false bravado.

He excused himself to change. When he returned in jeans and a T-shirt, Kendra had removed the lasagna ingredients from the bag and lined them up on the counter. A pot of water was boiling on the stove.

"I think you've forgotten how this whole 'cooking together' thing works."

Kendra snorted. "All I did was unpack the bag. There's plenty left to do."

He washed and dried his hands, then opened the package of pasta noodles, adding them to the salted water. He set the timer, then took out a large skillet and placed it on the burner.

Kendra peeled and sliced an onion while Nate added Italian sausage and ground beef to the pan.

They worked together in comfortable silence. Nate

had missed this. He hadn't realized what a luxury it was to be with someone he was so in tune with that he felt the comfort of her presence without either of them uttering a single word.

Kendra was the only woman with whom he'd felt that kind of warmth and security.

"There." Kendra added the onions and garlic to the skillet as he browned its contents.

"Thank you." He forced the words past the thickness in his throat. It was something he wanted to say since that moment at Wade's when she'd placed her hand on his, calming him when it felt like his world was spinning out of control.

"For helping to make my dinner?" Kendra rummaged through the drawers and retrieved the can opener. He'd upgraded the utensil, but kept it in the same place she'd designated for it when they were together. In fact, the entire kitchen was essentially just as she'd arranged it. Like it was stuck in time. "It's the least I can do."

Nate reduced the flame, then turned to face her, taking her soft, warm hand in his. He pulled her closer and she leaned in to him, her eyes meeting his.

"For taking me on as a client, even though I didn't want to work with you initially. For coming with me on this trip. For being the voice of reason when I needed it most."

She didn't speak. Instead she leaned in closer, meeting him halfway as he captured her warm mouth in a kiss. He slipped his fingers in her hair, his tongue tangling with hers.

Kendra wrapped her arms around him and lifted onto her toes, as if trying to capture more of his mouth. One hand trailed down her back and over her backside.

He missed the feel of her body, pressed against his, and the taste of her sweet mouth. The way her body fit perfectly against his. The elevation of his temperature and the rapid beat of his heart whenever she was in his arms.

How could she not miss this?

Nate gripped her bottom, pulling her tightly against him, enjoying the feel of their bodies pressed together.

He swallowed the soft gasp that escaped her throat in response. She dropped the can opener. The sound of it crashing against the hard tile floor startled them both.

Kendra pulled away. She retrieved the utensil and returned to the work of opening the cans, her eyes focused on her task. "Thank you for saying that, but hold your gratitude until I get the results you're looking for. Because I will."

"I don't doubt that." Nate sighed and went back to stirring the contents of the skillet. Bits of garlic and onion had burned. "But regardless of what happens, I want you to know I'm grateful for what you've done. I appreciate you. I didn't say that enough when we were together. It's a mistake I won't repeat."

"Thank you for giving me this shot." Kendra's eyes met his. "Most exes wouldn't be so gracious."

Nate's heart sank in his chest. He resented the fact that their romantic relationship was firmly in the past. A harsh reality that made his chest ache. Kendra seemed content with it. Able to turn her feelings on and off at will.

The hunger that consumed him wasn't reflected in Kendra's eyes. There was desire, but not the abject need that arose whenever he thought of her. Certainly not with the ferocity with which he felt it. If she'd felt that strongly about him, she would've jumped at his proposal to try again.

Despite the bulletproof force field she projected, Nate was sure her true feelings were buried below the surface, where she could keep them safe.

Even if she refused to acknowledge her feelings, Nate knew Kendra still loved him. It was evidenced by a thousand little things. The affectionate tone of her voice, the dreamy gaze when their eyes met and the soothing touch of her hand. It was couched in all the words she couldn't say.

This time, though, he needed to be sure before he poured out his heart to her.

He loved Kendra, but he wouldn't make a fool of himself again. He couldn't endure the pain and humiliation of another rejection. The feeling of his heart being pierced by jagged, broken glass.

This time, he needed to hear her say the words first. That she loved him and needed him in her life. That she wanted to be with him.

"You're not just an ex." He loosened bits of browned sausage and garlic stuck to the bottom of the pan. "We have a son together, and we were best friends for most of our lives."

A sad smile barely lifted the corner of her mouth as she scraped tomato paste from a can with a small rubber spatula. "That's why we're such good co-parents. Maybe we aren't exactly friends now, but we have that foundation to rely on."

Now it was his turn to snort.

"What did I say wrong?" She set down the empty can, then started to empty the next into the skillet.

"*Co-parents.* That term is a joke. It implies both parties are equal parents, but that's not really possible, is it? One person is always left on the outside, looking in. Wishing they were there in those photos. In the moments that matter. The ones you'll never get back."

Kendra looked thoughtful as she opened one can of tomato sauce, then the other. She poured both into the pan, then carried all of the empty cans over to the sink and rinsed them before tossing them into the recycle bin.

"This isn't how I envisioned my life, either, but it's the best option we have." Her tone was faint, apologetic. She wiped her hands on a towel. "Things could be a lot worse. Every day, I'm thankful Kai has you in his life."

"And every night I go to bed regretting that I can't be in his life every day, the way my dad has always been in mine." Hurt and anger rose in his chest. When he met her gaze, her eyes were filled with tears. "Kendra, I'm sorry. I didn't mean to—"

"I can't do this and still do my job, Nate." She cut him off, shaking her head. "Right now, doing my job is more important." She turned to leave.

When would he learn to keep his big mouth shut?

"I didn't mean to upset you." Nate sighed, catching her elbow. "Would I be making you a home-cooked meal right now if I intended to say something stupid and ruin our night?"

"What you said wasn't stupid. You're right. I made a bad decision, but you're the one who's had to suffer most. It isn't fair. So I promise, after this is all over, we'll work out a more fair arrangement so you get to spend more time with Kai."

"You'd do that?" Nate was stunned. Kai meant everything to her. "You'd be willing to sacrifice some of your time with him?"

She nodded, her lips pursed and her eyes glossy.

"That means a lot to me." He cleared his throat. "But being together as a family would mean even more."

"As much as we love Kai, we can't be together just for his sake. Neither of us would be happy. I want more than that for myself and for you."

"Shouldn't I get to decide what's best for me?"

"I'm sorry." Kendra pulled free from him, her cheeks suddenly wet with tears. "Excuse me."

She rushed from the room and up the stairs.

Dammit.

He'd blown it again.

Nate finished up the lasagna sauce by adding the supplied herbs and seasonings. Then he let it simmer while he drained the noodles. A half hour had passed and Kendra hadn't returned.

His pride hadn't allowed him to go after her following the proposal debacle seven years ago. He wouldn't make that mistake again. If she wasn't back by the time the sauce finished simmering, he'd go and find her.

Kendra cupped her hands under the cold running water in Nate's guest bathroom and splashed it on her face. Her eyes were red, her cheeks were stained with tears and her mascara was a runny mess. Better to strip it all off than to attempt to fix it.

She removed her makeup, cleansed her skin, then patted her face dry with a towel.

Standing there, her face stripped of all makeup, she felt nearly as vulnerable as she had when Nate told her what he thought of her co-parenting.

She'd been lying to herself. Pretending things were good for all of them, when the truth was they were all miserable.

Kai missed being with his dad. Nate was hurting without his son. She lived with the guilt of being the coward who broke up their family because she couldn't deal with her daddy issues.

"Thanks, Dad," she groaned. "You produced one damaged little girl."

There was a tap at the bathroom door. "Kendra, are you okay?"

She opened the door partially. "I didn't expect to take so long. I'll be down in a sec."

"You've been crying." Nate reached his long arm through the door and cradled her cheek in his large palm. "I didn't intend to upset you."

Loosening her grip on the door handle, Kendra leaned into his palm, her eyes drifting shut. She savored his touch—strong, yet delicate—and the warmth of his rough palm against her cool cheek. Heat radiated into her neck and down her spine. A soothing lightness seeped into her bones, and a sense of calm settled over her.

Her eyes fluttered open. Something in Nate's brown eyes was so tender and sweet it melted her heart. Yet the heat in his penetrating gaze and feather-soft touch took her breath away.

She inhaled, dropping her gaze to his stubbled chin. "Nate, I'm sorry I—"

Nate pressed his open mouth to hers, cradling the back of her neck.

Kendra didn't object to his kiss or the way he slung

an arm low around her waist, pulling their bodies together, his firm erection pressed to her belly.

A soft gasp escaped her mouth as his tongue moved against hers. Her fingertips glided up the soft cotton of his shirt. She pressed them to his back through the fabric, aching to touch his heated skin.

Each soft kiss Nate planted along her jawline and down her throat ignited flames along her skin.

"I want you, Dray. Here. Now. Tell me you want me, too," he murmured between kisses.

Her hot, liquid center melted a little more at hearing him use his pet name for her. He hadn't done that since the day she walked out of his life. Not even those nights in Memphis.

"I do." No point in denying the obvious. Her beaded nipples pressed into his chest and her breath came in shallow pants. "But if we do this, you have to understand—"

The muscles of his back stiffened as his eyes met hers. "That it doesn't mean anything?"

She stroked his cheek. "Being with you could never not mean anything to me. But it isn't a promise or a commitment. It's just sex."

He frowned, lines spanning his forehead.

"I want this, I do." She placed a soft hand on his stern jaw, and his eyes met hers again. "But you mean so much to me. My relationship with you is more important than this."

He didn't respond right away. For a moment, Kendra expected him to release her and walk away. Instead, he pressed his mouth to hers and kissed her again. His tongue tangled with hers as he gripped her bottom, pulling her hard against him.

Kendra moaned against his lips, giving in to the prickle of electricity dancing along her spine, igniting low in her belly.

Nate surprised her, scooping her into his arms and carrying her down the hall toward his large master bedroom. He nudged open the double doors with his foot, then laid her on his bed.

Kendra looked around the room. The kitchen had been essentially the same, but this room looked completely different. He'd made a concerted effort to erase any trace of her.

She had no right to be hurt. Yet she was. The walls were a dove gray now, instead of the cocoa beige they'd selected together when he bought the place.

The bed and all the other furniture were different, too. Large, sleek ebony wood pieces. Dark and masculine. All hard lines. None of the soft, organic curves she preferred.

Nate brought her back from her disquieting thoughts with a kiss. His hand trailed down her side, gripping her thigh as he settled between her legs. She whimpered at the sensation of his length pressed to the juncture of her thighs. Her breath became shallow as the heat and electricity building there spread throughout her body. Made her feel like she was floating in a pool of warm water, the steam so intense she could barely breathe.

Nate pulled his mouth from hers, their eyes meeting as he took her in. Something in that dark gaze made her feel as if there were nothing in the world he wanted more than her. And damn if that stare didn't multiply his raw sex appeal by a factor of ten.

Nate planted feverish kisses on her throat that trailed down the vee of her shirt. She inhaled the coconut scent wafting from his dark curls and tried to get out of her own head and enjoy it.

Breathe. Just breathe.

"Stop trying to talk yourself out of this." Nate's husky whisper brought her attention back to him, away from the battle raging between her body and her mind. "There's nothing wrong with two people who care for each other as much as we do being together. Even if one of them believes it's just sex."

"Nate, you promised—"

"Relax, Dray. I know where we stand." There was a hint of strain in his voice and in the tension between his brows. "We're cool, no matter what happens tonight."

She breathed a little easier. "Then what are you still doing in that shirt?"

Nate traced her mouth with his thumb, then kissed her again. "Good question. I could ask you the same."

She gripped the hem of his shirt and tugged it up. He adjusted, allowing her to remove the garment. Next, she shed hers. Kendra pressed her fingers to his back as she pulled him to her again. "Much better."

"A little better." He glided his large palm down her hip and thigh, his eyes locked on hers. "You naked would be a hell of a lot better."

"I can make that happen." She lifted her hips, allowing him to slide off her panties and leggings. Her bra and his jeans soon followed.

"Hey." Kendra snapped the waistband of his underwear. "You're not completely undressed."

"Gotta keep my focus, babe," Nate responded between nibbles and kisses that trailed between her breasts. "Make this last."

Can't argue with that philosophy.

"Fine for now, but—" She inhaled sharply when Nate caressed a stiff peak with his firm tongue. The sensation traveled straight to her sex. "Not fair."

Nate chuckled, the sound vibrating in her chest. He kissed his way across the valley between her breasts and swirled his tongue around her other nipple, causing a rush of dampness at her core. "Who said anything about this being fair?" He trailed kisses down her belly. Each one caused her breath to come quicker as he approached the space between her thighs. "I plan to use every trick in the book to make you reconsider."

A shiver ran down her spine as he lapped at her hardened nub. She gripped the bedding and dug her heels into the mattress. "Nate, that feels incredible."

She'd nearly forgotten how deft Nate Johnston was with that tongue. He hadn't gone there the last two times they were together. Those incidents involved quick, hot, angry sex. This was slow and deliberate.

He wrapped his arms around her thighs, pinning her in place as his tongue grazed her clit and the swollen, engorged flesh surrounding it.

The higher she sailed, the quicker his movements. She was trembling, cursing. Almost there. Suddenly he slowed things down with deliberate laps of his tongue, heightening the sensation.

Kendra's breathing slowed, though her heart still beat a mile a minute. She tangled her fingers in his hair as he worshipped her sex, bringing her to the edge again.

A jolt of desire ran through her veins as Nate plunged his tongue inside her, then slowly withdrew it. She moaned softly, her tense muscles quivering in response to the delicious rhythm. Kendra whimpered, calling his name and begging him not to stop, as she dug her heels into the mattress and clutched the back of his head.

His sly grin indicated he had no intention of stopping until he'd brought her over the edge.

And he did.

The orgasm hit her, hard and sudden. Her legs trembled and her belly contracted. She shut her eyes, allowing the intense feeling of satisfaction to wash over her like warm, soothing water.

Nate trailed kisses over her mound, up her stomach and between her breasts. He gently bit and sucked her neck, as if marking his territory like he did when they were in high school.

He pressed his lips to her ear. "This body will always be mine. No matter where you go or what you do."

His claim was even more arousing than what he'd just done to her body. She wanted to contradict him. Make it clear that her body belonged to her and no one else. But she understood what he meant. *No one will ever make you feel this way. Have you crawling out of your skin, calling his name.*

If the past seven years were any indication, he was right. She'd been with a handful of guys in the time they'd been apart. She could sum up the collective experience with one word.

Disappointing.

Nate never disappointed her. He sent her soaring, shaking, calling his name. Their bodies fit together as if they were designed for each other.

As she stared into his handsome face, hovering over hers, she couldn't deny his claim.

Her body did belong to Nate Johnston, as did her heart.

Chapter 13

Nate kissed the side of Kendra's face, glistening with sweat. It was the middle of winter, but suddenly his sprawling bedroom felt intimate, the space sultry.

Kendra's chest rose and fell as she tried to catch her breath. She hadn't responded to his declaration that her body belonged to him, but had she disagreed, she would've told him so in no uncertain terms. Kendra's silence indicated her reluctant concession to the truth of his words.

We belong together.

They would be again soon, if it was up to him.

"I love watching you come apart like that. It's still the sexiest thing I've ever seen." He kissed her neck and trailed a finger down the center of her chest. "You will always be the most beautiful woman in the world to me."

Kendra's eyes twinkled as she swiped a finger beneath them. A wide smile spread across her face.

Nate kissed her again, then crawled off the bed and dug into his bedside table and sheathed himself. He joined Kendra beneath the covers and kissed her neck, her shoulders.

He'd tried hating her for breaking his heart. He'd tried to replace her with women who were beautiful or famous. None of them made him feel the way he did when he was with her.

It was Kendra he wanted in his bed and in his life. The woman who owned his heart and bore his son. The woman he wanted to retire to Pleasure Cove with and have more children.

The words he wanted to say stuck at the back of his throat. *I love you. I need you. Please, come back.* Instead, he kissed her fervently, conveying everything he felt through his kiss, his touch.

He glided his hands along her warm, slick skin. Caressed her back. Squeezed her hips and the swell of her breasts. Laved her tight, beaded tips with his hungry tongue. He coaxed her back to the edge of the precipice, her body responding to every touch, every kiss.

"Nate, I need you." Kendra's breathy plea nearly broke him down. She gripped his ass, bringing him closer. Increasing the friction of his sheathed length grazing her slick bud. "Please."

His plans to continue teasing her, making her want him more, flew out the window the moment he gazed into those seductive brown eyes. They drained every ounce of his willpower. If she asked right now, he'd give her anything.

He pumped his thick shaft, his body already aching with desire for her. She whimpered quietly as he slid inside her, taking his time. He savored the slow, painstaking reintroduction to every damn inch of her.

He groaned, pressed his lips together as his eyes drifted closed at the sensation of being surrounded by her warm, slick flesh. Nate tried to hold it together as he slowly moved his hips, delighting in every hiss, every whimper coming from her sweet lips.

Nate cursed, his brow damp with sweat. She felt so damn good. Better than he remembered. Her delicate scent mingled with the smell of sweat and sex.

He wanted her in his bed. Every. Single. Night. He would remind her how good they'd been together. How good they could be again.

Nate leaned his weight forward, grinding against her as he entered her. He increased the friction against her hardened nub. Watched the parting of her lips until finally she cried out, writhing and calling his name.

His shoulders relaxed even as he continued his movement, heightening her pleasure until he reached his release. Muscles tense and heart racing, Nate dropped onto the mattress beside her. He tugged the covers over them as he caught his breath.

"I know we shouldn't have done that," she said, finally, one hand pressed to his chest, "but it was incredible."

"Who says we shouldn't?" He chafed at the implication that what they'd done was wrong. "We don't have to answer to anyone."

Kendra frowned, raising her head. "Was that the doorbell?"

Nate strained to listen, but didn't hear anything. "I don't think so."

The bell rang again. This time he heard it.

"See. There it goes again." Panic rose on Kendra's face as she pulled the covers up higher.

"Whoever it is, they'll go away." Nate wrapped an arm around her. As long as it had taken him to get her to bed, he had no plans of letting anything interrupt the moment.

Kendra settled against his chest. She was silent. Pensive.

Nate massaged her back, trying to relax Kendra and return to the blissful afterglow they enjoyed a moment before. A space where it was only the two of them and nothing else mattered. That's where they needed to be if he was going to convince her to stop running from her feelings for him.

He picked up the remote and turned on a streaming audio service, hoping the soft vocals of Luther Vandross and Anita Baker would soothe her.

She propped her chin on his chest. "What if it's important?"

"They'll come back." He kissed her forehead. "Besides, if it were that important, they would've called first."

"I did call first, lover boy, but you left your phone downstairs."

Kendra scrambled to pull the covers up to her chin, and Nate held the sheet firmly in place so she wouldn't uncover all his business to his nosy-ass twin sister.

"For real, Vi? I did not give you the key to my place so you could stroll up in here whenever you please. It's for emergencies."

"Seems like an emergency to me." Vi folded her arms and leaned against the doorjamb. "'Cause I'm pretty sure you've lost your natural mind. I go on vacation for two weeks and all hell breaks loose. Your face is all over the news and now she's all up in your business and in your bed."

Nate clenched his teeth. "Look, Vi, I know you're just trying to look out for me, but you are completely out of line. Now that you're back we can talk about your concerns, but at a more appropriate time. Like tomorrow morning."

Vi gave Kendra her evil stare before returning her attention to Nate. "We need to talk now. Before things get worse."

"I messed up with that video, but I do not need you to babysit me."

"So you don't trust me to look after you, but you and Marcus think it's a good idea to trust her?" Vi pointed at Kendra accusingly.

"That's my choice. Just like it was my choice to have you run the foundation, even though half our family didn't think you were levelheaded enough to handle a responsibility like that."

"So now you're going to throw me under the bus because I'm pointing out the obvious. Ms. Thing here doesn't have your back. She never did."

"That's enough!" Nate blared, his chest heaving and heat crawling up his neck. "I get that you're angry, but don't take it out on Kendra. I made the choice to work with her. Beyond that, she's my son's mother. So you will never, *ever* talk to her like that again. Got it?"

Vi rolled her eyes, then shrugged.

"I mean it." He pointed a finger at his sister.

"Fine. Okay. Sorry." She threw her hands up. "But we do need to talk. Now. Meet you downstairs in ten." Navia left, slamming the bedroom door behind her.

Nate pressed his palms to his eye sockets and shook his head. "Sorry about that. Vi's been out of the country, so we haven't had a chance to talk about this. She'll be fine. I just need to make it clear that this isn't her choice."

"She hates me." Kendra tucked a few curls behind her ear. "You guys are incredibly close. She feels your pain, maybe more intensely."

"Is that why you didn't say a word when she was in here clowning?" When she shrugged, Nate cupped her chin. "That isn't the fierce warrior I know. If we're going to work together, you'll have to deal with Vi. Don't let her run you over. You never did before. You know Vi, if you give her an inch she'll take the length of two football fields before you can blink. I'll set her straight, but promise me you won't take any shit from her."

"We'll work it out." Kendra's tone was less than convincing, but he let it go.

Nate slipped his fingers into her hair, pulling her closer. He kissed her. "Don't move. I'll be back with dinner." He winked.

Kendra slapped a hand over her mouth. "Dinner! God, I hope it isn't ruined."

"It isn't. It's fine." Nate got out of bed, retrieved his clothing from the floor and dressed. "Sit tight. I'll be back as soon as I get rid of Vi." He leaned in and kissed her forehead. "Promise."

"Don't be so hard on her, Nate. She's just trying to protect you. It's been her job since you two were conceived." She smiled, but then her expression and tone grew serious. "I won't come between you two. I'd rather walk away."

"I know you would." He gripped the door handle. "Fortunately, it won't come to that. Working with you is exactly what I need right now. We've already made progress. Bottom line? If she really wants what's best for me, she'll get on board. She'll complain about how rough the ride is, but she'll come aboard just the same."

Nate closed the bedroom door, then padded down the stairs in his bare feet to straighten out his nosy, over-protective, older-by-five-minutes twin sister.

His sister had the worst timing. He'd finally made headway with Kendra, and Vi decided to return from her vacation two days early. He stepped into the kitchen, where his sister paced the floor.

"What the hell is she doing here?" That was Vi. She didn't waste a moment, just got right into it.

Nate gritted his teeth and counted to ten as he rummaged in the freezer for one of the beers Kendra put on ice. "You're not my wife or my mother. So why do you care?"

Vi snorted in the unladylike manner that signaled a smart-ass comment was on the horizon. With one hand on her hip, she shoved a finger in his direction. "If you stopped thinking with the head below your belt and started using the one above your shoulders, I wouldn't need to act like your mama."

Maybe she has me there.

He'd never admit that to her. Vi already thought she knew better than everyone in their family when it came to their careers, love lives and how they raised their kids. Never mind that she had zero expertise with any of the above. He took a long swig of his beer, then set it down.

"Don't oversimplify this. It isn't just about sex. I

care for Kendra. I always will. More importantly, this is a chance for Kai to finally have his parents living together under one roof. Just like we did."

Vi's expression softened and her shoulders relaxed. "Nate, don't get your hopes up. Kendra's only going to disappoint you again."

Nate cringed at the pity in his twin sister's eyes. "Don't look at me like that, Vi."

"Like what? Like I'm your sister who loves you? It's always been my job to look out for you."

"I don't need you to protect me from Kendra or anyone else, and I certainly don't need your pity. You can pack up all that attitude and take it back with you to wherever you came from." He thrust his thumb over his shoulder and gave her his I-ain't-got-time-for-the-bullshit face.

"First, you know exactly where I came from—Barbados. Second, it was Marcus, Mitchell and Drew's job to protect you from other people. My job is to protect you from yourself. We both know you can be your own worst enemy." She raised an eyebrow and twisted her mouth in a smug smirk when he didn't respond. "Like when you run your big mouth on video at a club in the middle of the night and screw up your contract negotiations."

Nate gritted his teeth. If his own family was going at him this hard, he could only imagine what his first TV appearance—scheduled for later that week—would be like. "It was stupid, shortsighted. I know that, but I can't change what happened. Kendra has a thoughtful strategy laid out, which we're executing now."

"'Executing strategy,' huh?" She used air quotes. "Is

that some cute new euphemism for screwing your client?" Vi grabbed a beer out of the freezer.

Nate swiped the beer from Vi's hand before she could open it. "You won't be needing this. You were just about to leave."

"But I smell lasagna, and I'm starving."

"Got it at Maxine's Kitchen." He reached into his wallet and held out a twenty. "Stop and pick yourself up one on the way home. My treat."

"You're kicking me out for her? Really?"

Nate glowered silently, extending the bill.

"I don't need your money." She pointed a finger at him, then sighed, snatching the bill from between his fingers. "But I'll take it anyway. And you should take my unsolicited advice. If you must work with her, keep it professional, before you do something else you'll regret."

Nate grabbed his beer and drained it, hoping his opinionated twin sister wasn't right.

Ms. Thing here doesn't have your back. She never did.

A cavalcade of emotions rolled through her chest as Vi's words replayed in Kendra's head. Anger at Vi's insistence she couldn't be trusted. Gratitude for Nate's staunch defense of her.

Ending up in Nate's bed, in the midst of dealing with the biggest crisis of his career, certainly didn't make her case for being a professional who could be trusted with the fate of his future.

Kendra got up and quickly got dressed. What hurt the most was Vi's implication that she'd hurt Nate before, and she'd hurt him again.

She couldn't do that to him, and she wouldn't give him false hope.

Once Kendra heard Vi's car leave, she made her way down to the kitchen where Nate was preparing their plates. "Smells delicious."

Nate looked up, disappointed. "I hoped to find you in the same state I left you." He winked, giving her a sly smile.

"I know, but Vi has a point. You're my client, and I don't… I mean… I've never gotten involved with a client before. It's unprofessional and completely unacceptable. I violated our agreement, and I'm sorry. If you want to fire me, I'll understand. Just stick to the plan and execute it. You'll be fine."

Nate waited patiently, his arms folded, until she was finished. "Why would I want to fire you?"

Her heart raced as she forced her eyes to meet his. "Because this can't happen again. That may make things awkward between us, and I don't blame you for not—"

"Look, I'm sorry about Vi busting in here like that. Whether or not we work together…sleep together…it's none of Vi's business or anyone else's."

Kendra ran her fingers through her hair. "You know she's going to tell Marcus and probably your parents. God, your entire family will know by morning."

Nate shrugged. "What difference does that make? Doesn't change how I feel. I'm not sorry about what happened between us. Neither are you." He cupped her cheek.

For a moment, she settled into his palm before logic kicked in.

This is how the whole thing started.

She shook her head and took a step back. "We can't. I'm sorry."

Nate sighed. "Fine, but I'm not firing you. Awkward or not, I expect you to fulfill your end of the contract."

Kendra stood straight and cleared her throat. "Of course."

"And I don't see any reason we can't sit down like two rational adults and have dinner together."

Kendra held her breath, the muscles in her back and shoulders tense. Sitting down to a meal and pretending everything was okay, when what she really wanted was to let Nate take her back to his bed, would be torturous. But he'd gone through all the trouble of making her favorite meal.

"On one condition."

Nate raised a brow as he put salad greens into two bowls. "And that is?"

"We can talk about the campaign, your career, Kai, the weather…anything but us or what happened here tonight. It was a lapse in judgment. I just want to get past it."

Nate shrugged. "Fine."

His tone said anything but *fine*. Still, he'd agreed to her terms.

Kendra released a breath and nodded. They could get through this. Get things back on track. She would deliver the results she promised, then things would go back to the way they were.

She'd be miserable, missing him and regretting the day she walked out of his life.

Chapter 14

Nate straightened his tie and inhaled. They'd be live on the air for his first television appearance since the video went viral in five…four…three…two…one…

He pressed his lips into a smile as he gave his attention to the host of the show. He'd always considered John Chase to be a blowhard who knew incredibly little about the sports he reported on.

Being a guest on the John Chase show wouldn't have been his first choice. But as Kendra pointed out, it was one of the most-watched daytime shows on the major sports network. The ratings were through the roof. Most important, Kendra felt John was fair and that he'd keep his word and not discuss the video.

That remained to be seen. There was something in the guy's eyes that Nate didn't trust.

Then again, when did he trust any reporter?

John welcomed Nate to the panel, then began the discussion. Nate followed the rhythm of the panel's conversation about the stellar numbers the Ontario Badgers wide receiver Dean Carson was putting up in the playoffs after his recovery from an ACL injury nearly a year earlier. The same injury he'd sustained three years ago.

John seemed to sense his hesitance. He asked Nate a pointed question. Within a few minutes, Nate was so engrossed in the conversation, he stopped thinking incessantly about the camera, the millions of viewers in the audience and whether John Chase would ask about the video. Instead, he recounted his own comeback from an ACL tear and praised Dean Carson for his play-off performance.

He settled into easy banter with John and the other two members of the panel—both retired pro football players he admired and respected. Once he relaxed and focused on the topic, his eight minutes on the segment went by quickly.

John wrapped up the discussion with a promo for next week's show. "Join me next week when we discuss the impact of the social media age on pro athletes. Something my man Nate here knows more than a little about. If you've got the time, Nate, I'd love to have you back to get your view on the topic."

Shit.

The son of a bitch offered him an open invitation to talk about his social media disaster in great detail on his very next show.

He opened his mouth to tell John Chase exactly what he thought of his lame move when Kendra caught his eye.

She shook her head almost imperceptibly, then gave

him an encouraging smile. He inhaled, then forced a chuckle. "It's a topic I've learned quite a bit about in the past couple of weeks. Unfortunately, my schedule won't permit."

John grinned, tapping the desk. "Fair enough. Just know, you've got an open invitation to come on the show and share more of your analysis of what the Marauders must do to become an elite team in this league." He added, "For the record, I thought everything you said was on the money, and I think it's despicable to secretly film someone and then use the footage to get your fifteen minutes of fame."

John Chase signed off, wishing the audience a good weekend, and then the cameras faded to black.

Nate snatched off the microphone clipped to the lapel of his suit jacket, but before he could stand, Kendra pinned him in place with her gaze. Her eyes pleaded with him to be cool.

He sighed, acknowledging her plea with the slight nod of his head.

"Nate, thanks again for coming on the show." John was standing in front of him, his hand extended. "And thanks for being such a good sport. My viewers would've slaughtered me if I hadn't addressed the issue at all. Tried to do it in a way that would cause minimal discomfort…for both of us."

Nate reluctantly shook the man's hand. "Appreciate that, John. Thank you for having me on the show."

"My pleasure." He turned to talk to one of the other panelists, but then quickly turned back. "By the way, I'm serious about having you back to talk more about what happened that night or your thoughts on the Marauders. Good luck with your contract negotiations."

Maybe John Chase isn't so bad after all.

"Excellent segment." Kendra fell in line beside him as he made his way back to the green room to retrieve his things. "That didn't kill you, now did it?"

It didn't, but he wasn't ready to concede so quickly. "Thought he wasn't supposed to address the video?"

"We agreed he wouldn't make it a topic of discussion in this segment. Clearly, he found a way to skirt the agreement. Thankfully, he did it in a way that was sympathetic and hopefully made viewers sympathize with you, too. Good job on sticking to the script with your response." She followed him into the green room. "And thank you for the way you handled the conversation afterward. John is someone we want as an ally."

"Sure. Anything else?" He lifted his leather satchel onto his shoulder.

She shook her head. "Not until the afternoon taping of that top ten segment for the late-night show. It should be super quick. In and out. Here's the script. It's like three lines." She handed a printed email to him.

Nate reviewed it quickly, then stuffed it in the inside pocket of his suit jacket. "Great. I'll meet you at the studio."

She looked stunned. "Okay, see you then, I guess."

Nate headed out of the studio and into the sunshine on a lovely winter morning in LA.

Nate made his way up the walkway. Jason Hernandez—the Marauders' best tight end and one of his closest friends—was an uncomplicated guy. His place in Cerritos reflected that. The decor was simple and casual, yet attractive. The place was warm and cozy. Someplace you could hang out and drink beer without worrying about staining the furniture or breaking an expensive vase.

Jase had invited Nate over for an early lunch between studio appearances. Before Nate could ring the doorbell, Jase opened the front door, his goofy trademark grin plastered across his face. He was more tanned than usual. "I can't leave you alone for five damn minutes without you stirring up shit."

Nate gave Jase a one-armed hug. "Thought you abandoned me. Tried calling you several times."

"Sorry about that, man." Jase's cheeks and forehead reddened. He retrieved a couple of beers from the fridge. He handed one to Nate. "Went camping and shut off my phone. After that loss, I needed to be alone for a while."

"That place with the luxury tree houses in Oregon?" Nate tilted his head, assessing his friend's quick nod as his gaze raked the floor. There was something Jase wasn't telling him. "Not exactly roughing it."

Jase shrugged. "Wasn't that loss punishment enough?"

"Can't disagree with that." Nate screwed the top off his icy beer. "Still, you and Vi picked a hell of a time to go AWOL."

"Vi's missing?" Jase rearranged the plastic fruit in the bowl on his kitchen counter.

"I wish. After being out of touch for two weeks, she shows up at my place at the worst possible time." Nate took a swig of his beer.

Jase smirked and sipped his beer, too. He sat on a bar stool. "Does that mean what I think it means?"

Nate ran a hand over his head. "Yep."

Jase chuckled, shaking his head. "That twin sister of yours is a little *loca*." They both laughed. "But she loves you and she always has your best interest at heart."

"Maybe she doesn't know what's in my best interest." Nate frowned, returning his beer to the counter. "Maybe she should back off. Let me decide what's best for me."

Jase cocked his head, his dark eyes assessing him. "In the end, it's your choice. You know that. Not like you listen to Vi anyway, unless you agreed with her to begin with."

Nate raised a brow, narrowing his gaze at his friend. "You sound just like her."

Jase cleared his throat and turned to face the bar. He took another sip of his beer. "Maybe that's because it's the truth."

"Hey, if I wanted to hear more of Vi's point of view, I'd be talking to her right now, instead of you." Nate shoved his friend's shoulder.

"So what do you want to hear?" Jase swigged his beer.

Nate shrugged. "Maybe I want you to tell me I'm not *loco* for trying to get back with my ex."

"Hmm…" Jase nodded sagely. "So it was you and Kendra Vi walked in on the other day?"

"How'd you know—"

"I haven't had that many concussions." Jase tapped his right temple twice with two fingers. "Besides, I saw Kendra in the press conference footage. She's handling your PR?"

Nate nodded. "Marcus's idea. I was against it at first, but it was a good call. Kendra's the right person for the job."

"Speaking of which, how's the apology tour going?"

Nate groaned. "According to Kendra, it's going well. Still, this whole thing has been a shit storm."

"Of your own making." Jase pointed the neck of his beer bottle in Nate's direction. "How many times I gotta tell you, man, you don't have to say everything that pops in your head."

"I don't pull punches. You know that."

"This time, you should have. What were you thinking? Especially in a contract year?"

"I know, I know." Nate stood in front of the window overlooking the pool in the backyard. "I screwed up. Big-time."

"Not the first time. Doubt it'll be the last." A half smirk lit Jase's eyes.

"You're having way too much fun with this." Nate pointed a finger at his friend. "And thanks for the vote of confidence."

Jase chuckled. "You're usually the one riding us out there on the field. Not a chance in hell I'd pass on the opportunity for a little payback."

Nate raised his hands, his palms facing his friend. "Point taken. Now, stop avoiding the question. Am I crazy to want Kendra back?"

"Of course not. She's Kai's mother, and it's obvious you still care for her."

"But…?"

"But, the fact that you care what I think tells me Kendra isn't as sure about this as you are. I'm hoping for the best, but I can't help worrying that you'll be disappointed." Jase shrugged.

Nate surveyed the landscape in the backyard. It was a valid concern. One he shared.

Even if he could get Kendra to give them another try, could he trust that she wouldn't walk away from him again?

He closed his eyes, a shudder moving down his spine. *God, I hope so.*

Chapter 15

Kendra paced in the green room of the late-night show. Nate was scheduled for taping in less than half an hour and he wasn't answering her calls.

A wave of sadness rolled over her. The way he'd taken off after the panel this morning...had he gone to see someone else? Was he with her now?

She shook her head to clear it. Who Nate Johnston was with was none of her business, as long as he wasn't doing anything that would further tarnish his brand.

There was a giggle in the hallway, followed by a deep chuckle. Kendra recognized both laughs. The giggle was that of an intern who'd been hovering, hoping to meet Nate. The chuckle indicated she'd finally found him.

Kendra opened the door, and they both looked at her abruptly. "I was beginning to think you'd forgotten how to answer your phone."

There was a gleam in Nate's eye. He smiled and signed the back of the T-shirt the intern was wearing before slipping past Kendra into the green room.

She inhaled, taking a moment to calm herself. "You were supposed to be here half an hour ago."

"You know how traffic is in LA. Besides, I called the studio on my way here. A quick touch-up in the makeup chair and I'm good."

He'd called the studio, rather than calling her? She gritted her teeth, placing a fist on her hip. "And you've been drinking."

He adjusted his tie. "Relax. I had a couple of beers over lunch. Besides, you're my media consultant, not my mother."

Heat crawled up her neck and exploded in her cheeks. She folded her arms and exhaled, straining to keep her voice even. "But it is my job to dig you out of the PR hole you created for yourself and to make sure you don't dig it any deeper."

Nate narrowed his gaze at her. "Your concern is noted, but everything is fine. So just take a deep breath. Your dog and pony show will go on as scheduled."

Despite her blood boiling, she didn't acknowledge the dig.

Nate was trying to get a rise out of her. He was obviously hurt and angry about her decision to pull away.

Kendra silently counted to ten, her fists clenched. She bit back the angry words she wanted to say, her tone neutral. "Our plane leaves in a few hours. I thought maybe we could grab a bite while I catch you up on the appearances scheduled for the next few weeks."

"Actually, I may have other plans after the show." His gaze held hers.

"Oh, well, maybe on the plane—"

"I was hoping to catch a few winks on the plane. It's been an exhausting few days." He folded his arms tightly against his broad chest. His head tilted as he assessed her. Nate was being a world-class ass, but there was something in his warm brown eyes that still melted her heart. Made her want to kiss him.

"Kara will email the updated itinerary to you along with my notes."

"Great." Nate shifted his gaze toward the door. A wide smile spread across his face when the intern peeked her head in to let them know that makeup was ready for him. He indicated he'd be there shortly, then turned back to Kendra. "Anything else?"

She shook her head, overwhelmed with a growing sense of envy. Wishing he'd look at her the way he looked at that intern just now. Her stomach dropped to her knees. "Have a good show."

Something in his demeanor softened. He headed across the room, turning back to look at her over his shoulder. Sadness lurked behind his dark eyes as he opened his mouth to speak, but then he turned and left instead.

Kendra fought back the tears that prickled her eyes, her heart thumping against her chest.

Nate closed the green room door behind him and exhaled.

What an ass.

He'd only meant to be distant. Maybe make her jealous by appearing to eat up the attention of the far-too-young-and-shallow intern. Instead he'd come off as bitter and angry, and he'd been a total jerk.

She maintained her cool, and he was left feeling worse than ever. That's what he deserved for playing childish games.

He wanted to be with her and Kai. Couldn't she see that he was sincere?

Nate tried to shake off the melancholy that settled over him when he saw the pain in Kendra's eyes, despite her forced smile.

He forced a smile of his own as he made his way through a quick turn in the makeup chair, then a brief meeting with the producer and the host of the show.

He fought his way through filming, sporting the broadest smile he could muster. It took a few takes, but finally everyone was satisfied with his performance and he was on his way back to the green room.

"How'd it go?" Kendra greeted him warmly, as if he hadn't been a complete jerk less than an hour ago.

"Pretty well." He grabbed a bottle of water off the table and opened it, ignoring the urge to apologize and admit that he had no interest at all in the intern. "Should get a laugh."

"Great." Her smile rose no higher than the edges of her mouth. Not even close to her genuine smile. The one that rounded the apples of her cheeks, lit her brown eyes and went straight to his heart. "Guess I'll grab a bite, then meet you on the plane."

"Wait, Kendra, I was thinking about your suggestion that we get something to eat and go over things…"

"Yeah?"

"How about we grab dinner, but leave the shop talk at the door. I think we both deserve a break from it, don't you?"

One side of her mouth curved, her eyes dancing. "Are you asking me out to dinner, Nate Johnston?"

"Yeah, I guess I am."

A genuine smile lit her face. "Thought you'd never ask."

"That was incredible." Kendra finished the last bites of her London broil and creamed spinach and then put her fork down.

Nate, who had already finished his culotte steak and lobster tail, leaned back against the booth and grinned. "Told you you'd love this place."

"I had my doubts." The iconic Koreatown steak house looked like a throwback to the 1950s. Dark wood paneling on the walls; comfy, lived-in red leather booths; and crisp white tablecloths lent to the feeling of being transported to the set of an old Rat Pack movie. "But you were right. Thank you for dinner."

"Hate to rush you away after such an amazing meal." Nate stuffed some bills inside the vinyl guest check holder and thanked their server. He helped Kendra into her coat. "But we've got a plane waiting for us."

"No, it's fine." Kendra smiled. "But this was really nice. Much better than the sandwich I had at the commissary."

"About that…" Nate extended his elbow and Kendra slipped her arm through his. "I was a jerk earlier. It won't happen again."

"It's forgotten." She gave him a small smile. After they were both settled in the car, she added, "Hope you had a nice lunch date."

"I did." Nate held back a grin. She was fishing for information about who he'd spent those missing hours with. "Jase Hernandez invited me out to his place for lunch."

"Oh, well, that sounds nice." She sounded relieved. "And on the subject of invitations… I have one for you. Maya and I are taking the kids to the Pleasure Cove roller-skating rink tomorrow."

"Are you kidding me? Is that old place still out on the edge of town?"

"Yeah, and I'm pretty sure there is still gum stuck underneath the benches from when we were kids."

"Don't look at me, it was Q who had the fascination with sticking his gum everywhere," Nate chuckled, referring to his youngest brother, Quincy.

"So?" She looked at him expectantly, her eyes beaming. "What do you say? I know you can't get out there and skate, especially while you're in the middle of contract negotiations, but you can keep me company while I cheer Kai on from the sidelines. That'll give me an excuse to stay off the skates."

"Well, when you put it that way, how can I possibly refuse?" He grinned. "Just tell me the time and I'll meet you there."

"Great. And I know it's my weekend with Kai, but after skating, he can spend the rest of the weekend with you, if you'd like."

"I would, thank you." A sense of warmth and gratitude filled his chest. "He's been dying to show off his new swimming skills."

"Perfect." She opened her portfolio.

"Hey, if you don't have any plans this weekend, you're welcome to stay, too. We could make it kind of a family thing."

"I don't know." Head tilted, she assessed him, then

exhaled. "I don't think it's a good idea for me to spend the night, but I wouldn't mind coming over after the skating rink. I'll even cook. After all, I owe you dinner."

"Sounds nice." It wasn't what he'd hoped for, but at least it wasn't a flat refusal. "But I've got one more request."

"Okay." She regarded him warily.

"This temporary moratorium on discussing business…let's maintain it until Monday morning." He turned toward her. "I'd like to relax, enjoy our time with Kai and forget about the rest of the world. Just for the weekend."

"I know this has been a lot to deal with." Her smile radiated warmth and understanding. "So barring any crisis, you've got yourself a deal."

It was a small victory, but one he savored. The first step to winning Kendra back.

Chapter 16

"Look at me, Dad!" Kai called out gleefully, zipping past Nate and Kendra as he circled the roller-skating rink ahead of his Aunt Maya and cousins Sofie and Ella.

"You're doing great, son!" Nate cheered Kai on, wishing he could join him. The smell of rental skates, stale popcorn, burnt hotdogs and frozen pizza made him nostalgic for the old days.

"Watch where you're going, honey!" Kendra called after him, leaning over the carpeted half wall that separated them from the rink.

"Relax, Dray. He'll be fine." Nate massaged the tension in her shoulders. "Remember how much fun we had out there as kids?"

"It was the place to be on Saturday nights. Every teen in town was here. Oh, and remember the all-night skates?"

"We were dead on our feet by the end of the night." Nate grinned.

The DJ played "Bounce, Rock, Skate, Roll" by Vaughan Mason & Crew and they both cheered, dancing with their hands in the air.

"This song is older than we are." Kendra laughed.

"And it's still the reigning champ of roller-skating songs." Maybe he couldn't put on skates and get out on the wooden floor, but he could dance to his heart's content with his feet on solid ground.

"Every time I hear this song, it's like I'm fifteen all over again." She moved her hips and rocked her head.

"You're showing out now, girl. I need to step up my game." He threw in some popping and locking and added a spin for good measure. "Get it, Dray!"

"Oh, it's on." She pursed her lips, going old school.

"You did not just go TLC on me with the Bart Simpson. Okay, I got one for you."

"Old-school running man!" She laughed. "All right now. How about this?"

They challenged each other with every old-school dance move they could remember: the Humpty dance, the Roger Rabbit, the Cabbage Patch.

"Okay, time to bring it home." He launched into the Kid 'n Play and she joined him until the song finally ended and they collapsed on one of the carpeted benches, both laughing.

"That was so much fun." She panted, catching her breath. "But now I need a rubdown, a soft pretzel and a nap, in that order."

"I can help with all three." He wriggled his eyebrows and laughed.

Watching Kendra grind her hips to the music sped

up his pulse far more than the physical exertion had. He surveyed the space. The walls had been repainted in a cobalt blue and new carpeting covered the floor and walls, but the place was essentially the same.

"We had so many great times in this building, but what I remember most is the first time I kissed you right over there." He pointed to a dim corner of the rink. "Remember that?"

"How could I forget my first kiss?" Her gaze was soft as her eyes met his.

Nate smiled and leaned in closer, whispering in her ear. "Hopefully, I'm a much better kisser now than I was back then."

"I don't know, you were a pretty good kisser back then, too." She grinned. "Aside from that incident when you nearly chipped my tooth."

"My bad." He grinned, his gaze on her sensuous lips as he leaned toward her. "Is it too late to ask for a do-over?"

"Hey, Dad, I'm hungry. Can we get pizza?" Kai skated toward them on the carpeted surface.

"Absolutely, champ." Nate did his best not to sound as disappointed as he felt, but Kendra seemed relieved not to have to answer his question.

Kendra exhaled, thankful Kai had interrupted them before she got caught up in the nostalgia of strolling down memory lane with Nate.

It was the first time they'd both let down their guard, been themselves and simply enjoyed each other's company.

She'd missed that. The laughter, the silliness, the fun and the love.

She wanted that again, but it wasn't that simple. His career and her family's past made it complicated. And she wouldn't hurt him again.

Between working together and her promise to allow Nate to be more involved in Kai's life, she'd have to learn to keep it together. Starting now.

Needing to talk to Maya, Kendra stood and turned to head to the other side of the rink, but she crashed into a woman.

"I'm so sorry, I didn't mean to—"

"No worries. It's Kendra, isn't it?"

She took in the tall brunette, whose dark eyes carefully assessed her. Stephanie Weiss, the reporter who orchestrated the video.

What the hell is she doing in Pleasure Cove?

"You know exactly who I am, Stephanie." Kendra folded her arms. "Here to dig under rocks for more dirt?"

"Guess Nate didn't give you the best impression of me." She almost sounded hurt, but her sarcastic expression indicated otherwise. "That's not my intention. I'm only here to get the real story behind Nate's comments that night. Something beyond that canned speech he served up the other day."

"So why approach me?"

"You're his media consultant. Your client wouldn't consider my offer to give him a chance to explain himself, so I thought I'd make my pitch to you. Perhaps you can make him understand why doing so is in his best interest."

"I'm aware of your offer, and I don't believe it is in his best interest. So if you'd excuse me…"

"It was a peace offering." Stephanie's tone grew

sharper. She pressed her lips into a hollow smile. "One I'm extending again to you."

"No, thank you, and I'd appreciate it if you'd stay away from me and my client. Neither of us has anything else to say to you."

"Suit yourself." Stephanie laughed bitterly, then turned to walk away. She paused, then turned back, a devious grin lighting her eyes. "Did Nate tell you he and I dated?"

"Of course." Every muscle in Kendra's body tensed. "I also know how the relationship ended and that it killed your career."

Stephanie's expression grew bitter for a moment, but then she smiled. "I'm sure that's what he told you, but the truth is, we've known each other intimately since his rookie year with the Marauders." She looked beyond Kendra, to where Nate stood, holding a tray of food. Kai stood beside him. "But I'm sure you've told her all about that. Right, Nate?"

"Stephanie, what the—" Nate started, then looked down at Kai watching him with wide eyes. He cleared his throat, seething. "I told you to stay away from me. I didn't think I needed to tell you that includes my family. Do I need to take legal action for you to get the point?"

A grin spread across the woman's face, her gaze shifting from Nate to Kendra. "Sounds like a man with something to hide."

Kendra's blood grew cold. Her fists clenched and her nails dug painfully into her palms as Stephanie flipped her dark brown extensions over her shoulder and sashayed away in red-bottomed heels.

"Who was that lady, Mommy?" Kai asked, clenching his huge plastic cup of frozen lemonade.

"No one you need to worry about, little man," Nate said quickly. "Mommy and I need to talk, so let's get you set up at the table with Auntie Maya and the girls. Mommy and I will be over when we're done."

Nate escorted Kai to where Maya sat, looking worried. She'd obviously witnessed the exchange between them and Stephanie Weiss.

He quickly returned to her side. "Babe, I'm sorry about that. You shouldn't have to deal with her."

"Don't call me *babe*." Kendra's hands shook and her pulse raced.

Nate frowned. "You don't actually believe that bull, do you?"

Kendra met his gaze, but didn't respond.

"She's a notorious liar. You said so yourself."

"I never said she was a liar." Kendra spoke slowly, her voice soft. "I said she was untrustworthy. She'll use any means necessary to find out the darkest, ugliest truths about people. Anything that will advance her career, no matter how devastating it is to the person. Like what she reported about your friend. It wasn't untrue, it was just something private that he preferred the rest of the world not know."

"It's more than that. If a story isn't salacious enough, she'll put a spin on it, like she's doing right now."

"So there is some truth to what she's saying about you and her during your rookie year."

She shouldn't care. They weren't together anymore. So why did it feel like her heart was about to explode?

"Why don't you just go ahead and ask me what you really want to know?" Nate narrowed his gaze, his voice tight.

"Because I might not like the answer, that's why."

Kendra's voice faltered. She exhaled. "Besides, I can't afford the distraction from the question I *need* to have answered."

"Which is?" Nate's incredulous expression indicated that he couldn't believe there was anything more pressing than the issue at hand.

"What the hell is she doing here?"

Nate sighed, realization in his eyes. He knew enough of Stephanie Weiss to recognize that she hadn't come all this way without something sinister in mind.

"What do you think she's planning?"

"I don't know." Kendra shrugged. "But that's where our focus must lie. Not on what happened between you two eight years ago."

"I thought you said you needed to know everything, so we don't get blindsided?" He shoved his hands in his pockets.

"So you didn't tell me the whole truth about you two?" Her mouth felt dry and tears pricked her eyes.

Nate exhaled and sat on a bench, pulling her down beside him. He turned his body to face her, his eyes barely meeting hers.

"Midway through that first season, I'd become this breakout star. Stephanie interviewed me for her sports magazine over dinner. We had a few drinks. I walked her back to her hotel and…she kissed me."

Kendra screwed her eyes shut against the pain in her chest. She blinked back tears. "So did you—"

"Nothing happened, I swear." He held his hands up, his palms facing her. "I told her I don't get down like that. That I was with someone I loved and was going to marry."

"Then why didn't you tell me?"

"I was ashamed of myself for letting it happen."

"You know about my dad, about what he did to our family." She pointed a finger at him.

"*That's* why I was so afraid to tell you the truth." A vein was visible in his temple as he lowered his gaze. "With your history with your father, I was afraid you'd never trust me again. I wasn't willing to take that chance."

"Guess my concerns about what happens out there on the road aren't so unfounded after all." Kendra stood, angrily wiping away the wetness at the corners of her eyes. "Don't worry, this won't change anything between us. I'm still your media consultant, and I will honor my promise to let you spend more time with Kai, because it's the right thing to do. But I don't think it's a good idea for me to come over after all."

"Kendra, please." He grabbed her hand, but she snatched it from his grip. "It was a mistake, and I know I should've told you, but *nothing* happened. I swear to you. You have to believe me."

"No, I don't. My job is to make everyone else believe you." She bit her lower lip and willed her limbs to stop trembling. "Excuse me, but suddenly, I'm not feeling very well." Kendra grabbed her things and made her way to her car.

She'd been right. Like her father, Nate Johnston couldn't be trusted.

Chapter 17

Nate checked his watch again. The last few days had been stressful. His relationship with Kendra was strained and formal, and Vi was still angry with him, so talking to her wasn't an option.

He felt badly for keeping the truth from Kendra. Maybe he hadn't slept with Stephanie that night, or done anything to overtly encourage the kiss, but he'd lapped up the adoration she'd been pouring on all night. And he hadn't discouraged her flirting. Worst of all, he'd kept it from Kendra.

Nate had convinced himself that not telling Kendra was in *her* best interest. The truth was he should've handled the situation differently. Most important, he couldn't bear for her to look at him and judge him as being no better than her father. By hiding it from her, he'd proven just that.

"Sorry to keep you waiting." Bud Flynn placed a firm hand on his shoulder as he took his seat at the table. The older man adjusted his large glasses and smiled through a sigh. "So, how've you been, son?"

"Well, thanks." Nate would've found it demeaning had anyone else referred to him that way. But Bud Flynn had been as good to him as his own father. He'd given him a shot in the league when no one else would. He mentored him through injuries, slumps and tough times—like his breakup with Kendra. "Look, Bud, I want to begin by saying again how sorry I am about this entire mess. I never intended any of this."

"Yet here we are, dealing with it just the same." Once a staple on the sidelines during games and practice, Bud hadn't been as active with the team as he once had due to health issues. It was the first time Nate had ever looked at the old man and seen his eighty-plus years in his blue eyes and bearing down on his shoulders. "You've always been straightforward and outspoken, and I appreciate that. Reminds me a lot of myself."

"Thank you, sir." Nate squirmed in his seat, the shadow of the other shoe Bud was about to lower loomed over him.

"However, there comes a time when you have to learn to control those impulses. Know when to be open and when to season your words up a bit."

"I just got so caught up in my anger with the guys, with myself. It was a mistake to talk about it outside our walls. I'm clear on that now."

A server came, left glasses of water and then took their orders before taking off again.

"It's good you understand that." Bud took a sip from

his water glass. "However, I'm gonna need you to apply that behind closed doors, too."

"Sir?"

"When I was a boy, we didn't have much. My mother made do with what we had. She often bought liver because she could get it cheap and it's good for you. A super food. But if you don't prepare it just right, it's one of the most god-awful things you'll ever eat."

"Okay." Nate assessed the old man, wondering if he was beginning to lose it.

Bud leaned forward, his elbows on the table. "Consider your words the same way, son. What you're saying is a hard truth your coaches and teammates need to hear. But if you don't season those words up just right and make them palatable, they won't do anybody a bit of good. They'll block out every word and use your poor delivery as reason to discount your advice. They'll be so focused on how you told them that they won't pay attention to the wisdom you're offering."

"Point taken." Nate nodded, tapping his thumb on the table. "Kendra told me pretty much the same thing."

Bud smiled. "Caught a glimpse of her at the press conference. She was good for you. Glad to see you two have worked things out, for your sakes and the sake of your son."

Nate lowered his gaze and drew circles in the condensation of his glass. "I've hired her as my media consultant. As for our personal relationship...we're still working on that. She's a little gun-shy."

"Why?" The old man shoved his glasses up the bridge of his crooked nose.

Nate sighed. "She believes every man out there will

disappoint her like her father did. He left them when Kendra was a baby."

"Does she have a good relationship with her father now?"

"She can barely tolerate being in the same room with him."

"Then start there," Bud said matter-of-factly, then thanked the server for the whiskey smash she handed him.

"What do you mean?" Nate took a sip of his imported beer.

"Help her repair her relationship with her father. Seems like that's the only way she'll let go of that fear and anger and move forward."

He'd met Curtis Williams—Kendra's father—once or twice while they were growing up. It was apparent neither of them liked the other. Nate resented Mr. Williams for abandoning Kendra, Dash and Ms. Anna. Mr. Williams clearly didn't trust his daughter's male best friend. He hadn't seen or talked to the man in years. "Thanks, Bud. I'll consider it."

"Good. Now, there's something else I need you to consider, so take a deep breath. Really think about this request before you reject it out of hand."

Nate's spine stiffened. "I get the feeling I should have ordered something a little stronger." He hailed the server and asked her to bring him a Cuba libre, then turned back to his mentor. "Let's hear it."

Bud twisted his mouth, spreading his hands on the table in front of Nate. "We need to think of the future of the team here. You're a critical piece of the team right now, as you have been for the past eight years. But we both know you're nearing the end of the ride."

Nate sighed. Bud's words—though true—were like a punch to his gut. They were already looking past him. On to the next big thing. "Does that mean there's no longer a place for me on the Marauders roster?"

Bud waved his hand. "Of course there is. In fact, I want you to take on an even bigger role in the years ahead. We need your skill and talent on the field. However, it's even more important that you help us begin shaping the next generation of wide receivers. Build a team that can win now and into the future."

Nate clenched his jaw, then took a few gulps of his beer. Bud's hands were wrinkled and covered with age spots, yet Nate felt like the relic. "So, I assume you plan to draft a star wide receiver."

"I do." Bud's tone was unwavering and unapologetic. "Doesn't mean I don't respect your talent and understand what a critical role you play on our team. It means I have great reverence for your smarts and ability. So much so, I want to ensure that our future generation of wide receivers has been mentored by the greatest wide receiver we've ever had."

Nate finished his beer and handed his glass off to the server when she set his Cuba libre on the table. He took a gulp of it, letting the chilled cola, dark rum and lime juice slide down his throat. He closed his eyes for a moment, wishing he were on the sandy beach where he first discovered this drink, rather than sitting across from the team's owner essentially telling him he was washed up and more valuable as a mentor than as a player.

"Well?" Bud took a sip of his whiskey smash.

Nate shrugged. "Don't have much of a choice, do I?"

Bud's voice was somber, fraught with disappointment. "We always have choices, son. I just hope you'll take some time and think about my offer and make the best decision. One beneficial to you and the team."

Nate nodded, meeting the old man's gaze. "I'll give your request serious consideration. I promise. I'd like to talk your proposal over with my team first before I commit."

"Of course." Bud nodded, steepling his fingers. "There is one other matter we need to discuss."

Nate's stomach roiled. He gripped his glass. "Okay."

"I need your assurance that you've learned from this experience. That we won't find ourselves in the same position six months down the road. Because if we do, I need you to understand that this conversation will go very differently." Bud raised one of his furry eyebrows, punctuated by unruly gray hairs that pointed in opposite directions.

Nate nodded. "I have, sir. I can assure you it won't happen again."

"Good." A warm smile spread across Bud's face. He looked around. "Now, where is that prime rib? I'm starving."

Nate chuckled, his head swirling. As shaken as he'd been by Bud's proposal about his changing role on the team, his thoughts kept returning to Kendra.

Suddenly, Bud's suggestion didn't seem so bad. Kendra would be angry if he interfered in her relationship with her father, but if Bud was right, it would be worth enduring her temporary ire.

After dinner with Bud, Nate drove back to his place in Memphis. Then he booked a flight to Jacksonville, Florida.

Chapter 18

Kendra sat on the set of another midday sports show as Nate took part in a discussion panel. This time they were in Atlanta.

It was down to two teams that would play for the championship. The absence of football action didn't stem the tide of talking heads analyzing every facet of each remaining team and predicting how the contest would end.

Nate was a natural—funny and charming. His words insightful and his opinions thought-provoking. Initially, he'd been against doing the sports shows. Now he was in his element, loving every minute.

His smile was broad and genuine and his deep chuckle was contagious. Not to mention, the man was finer than he'd ever been.

Kendra massaged the knot in her shoulder and breathed through the heat building in her chest.

It was no use.

Flames marched down her spine, fanning the heat at her core as she tried to clear the memories of the night they'd spent in his bed.

You're the one who rejected him. Twice.

Her anger and distrust aside, she still loved and wanted Nate. But how could she trust him again? And what about her career? He hadn't been supportive of it then, why would things be any different now?

Nate made a funny observation that had the entire panel in stitches.

Kendra smiled. She'd missed hearing his genuine laugh. He'd spent the previous few days in Memphis while she'd been back in Pleasure Cove. They met in New York, where he did a few shows before they'd flown to Atlanta for this one. After another appearance scheduled later in the day, they'd head back to Pleasure Cove.

"How'd I do?" Nate approached her, a sheepish smile turning up the corners of his mouth.

Her eyes traveled the length of his body, draped in an expensive blue suit that enhanced his athletic build. She lifted her gaze to meet his. "You're a natural. You'll have a long career ahead of you as a sports analyst, if that's what you want."

"Think so?" He relieved her of her leather briefcase and lifted it onto his shoulder as they headed toward the door.

"Absolutely. The producers loved you. They asked if you'd like to come back and do a few shows during the off-season."

Nate nodded thoughtfully. "That's great, but let's

hope all of this will pay off at the negotiations table. Marcus is meeting with the team later today."

"If they had no intention of paying you, Bud wouldn't have asked you to mentor James Eastland."

"I guess." Nate's shoulders tensed. He was obviously still unhappy about being asked to mentor a younger player. A sure sign his days with the team were numbered. "How much time until the next show?"

"A few hours. Plenty of time for you to grab a bite or go back to the hotel and get a little rest. I can meet you at the next studio, if you'd like."

"No." He lightly gripped her arm. "Let me take you to lunch, if you don't have any plans."

Kendra's heart beat faster. Her mouth felt dry as she stared into his warm eyes. "Why? Did you want to go over the appearances scheduled for next week?"

"No, we need to talk about us. I'm sorry for my bad judgment then and for not telling you when it happened."

She pulled away. "Nate—"

"I know you'd rather not talk about this." He countered her objection before she could make it. "But that's always been our problem. We've avoided the tough conversations. Maybe that's because we got together so young. Maybe we weren't mature enough to deal with all of this then. But we need to talk about it now."

Nate cupped her face in his strong hand, lifting Kendra's chin so her eyes met his.

Kendra backed up until she was pressed against the wall. Her heart beat so quickly she was sure he could hear it. She stared at him, unable to speak. Her chest was heavy with all the things she wanted to say;

her head spun, reminding her of all the reasons she shouldn't say them.

He captured her mouth in a kiss. Slow and sweet. Filled with warmth, affection and desire. Her hands slipped beneath his jacket, pressing into his back. Her body softened against his.

She was kissing Nate Johnston in a secluded hallway at a major sports network. She'd lost her mind. Yet she had no desire to stop him. Nor would she pretend that she didn't want more.

Kendra pulled away. She bit her lower lip as their eyes met. There was so much they needed to say, but she didn't want to talk. "I know exactly what I'd like for lunch."

A slow smile spread across his face as he traced her collarbone. "What?"

"You." Kendra's heart raced, hardly able to believe what she'd said.

From the widening of Nate's eyes, he could hardly believe it, either. Nate nodded his head toward the door. His voice was a hoarse whisper. "Let's get out of here. Now."

They took the waiting car service back to their hotel, Nate gripping her hand for the short ride.

A quiet, nervous energy buzzed between them as they rode in silence in the back of the black SUV.

Kendra wasn't prepared to think about where they stood or Stephanie's accusation. She simply wanted the comfort and solace she'd only ever felt when she was in Nate's arms.

Nate had planned to apologize to Kendra again and outline all the reasons they belonged together over lunch. But he'd kissed her and then Kendra proposed the very thing he wanted so desperately: to spend the next few hours making love to her.

The temptation too great, he couldn't say no.

When they arrived at the hotel, Nate escorted Kendra to his suite, nearly holding his breath, afraid she'd reconsider.

Once inside, he kissed her. Gripped those heart-stopping curves, hauling them against the hard planes of his body.

Nate sizzled with heat everywhere his skin met Kendra's. He yanked her blouse from the waistband of her skirt, desperate to touch her heated flesh. His hands glided down her back, over the firm curve of her soft behind. He hiked the tight navy skirt as high as he could, giving him better access to the soft, smooth flesh at the back of her thighs. He squeezed one leg, lifting it higher.

"God, I want you." He barely managed to get the words out as he planted kisses down her throat. "I haven't stopped thinking of you since you left my bed."

Nate's long fingers glided over the damp satin material shielding her sex. His need for her spiraled with each sensual murmur escaping her throat. He swallowed her soft moans as she arched her back and tugged his shirt from his pants.

His gaze locked with hers as his chest reverberated from his erratic heartbeat. His breathing ragged, a rush of emotions flooded over him.

Love, admiration and raw desire inflamed by the abject need he saw in her eyes.

Beads of sweat trickled down Nate's back as he stripped Kendra of her suit jacket, letting it fall to the floor. He trailed kisses down her neck, along her collarbones and across her shoulders. Nate inhaled her jasmine and gardenia scent. It was an expensive perfume he'd splurged on before he'd signed his first contract. She'd made it her signature scent. Still wore it after all these years.

Would she still be wearing such a personal gift if she didn't still love him the way he loved her?

Nate dug his fingers into her soft ebony curls and sucked her lower lip between his before exploring her warm mouth—sweet and minty—with his eager tongue. Heat and electricity flowed through his spine, into his fingertips and toes.

No one had ever come close to making him feel the way he did when he was with her. Like he could conquer the world, if only she were by his side.

No one ever would.

Kendra was enticing, but her real beauty lay in the depths beneath her surface. Confident in her abilities, she could go toe-to-toe with anyone. She could be gentle and kind or determined and fierce. And the woman just got sexier with each passing year.

He wanted her body. Admired her mind. Most important, he needed her and Kai in his life.

He loved her. Wanted her so much that the thought of losing her again made his chest ache.

What if he confessed everything in his heart and still she rejected him?

Sweat formed over his brow. His heart, pounding in his chest, was too raw to handle another rejection. His ego couldn't sustain another blow like that.

Kendra seemed to notice his distraction. She stepped just beyond his reach and kicked off her heels. Unfastening the button at her waist, she made a show of slowly tugging down the zipper of her skirt. She kicked aside the material pooled around her ankles.

Standing there in a blue camisole and a silky pair of panties that provided limited coverage for her firm, round bottom, she was breathtaking.

Nate pushed aside the dark thoughts that tormented him and focused on the moment. A moment he'd fantasized about since he'd last had Kendra in his bed. He licked his lips. His pulse raced as Kendra stripped off the camisole.

He reached for his tie, but she tugged him closer by the narrow strip of fabric, loosened it and slid it from his neck. Kendra slipped his jacket from his shoulders, then painstakingly unbuttoned each button of his dress shirt, relieving him of it and the undershirt he wore beneath it.

The corner of her mouth curled in a sexy smirk that hit him below the belt, tightening his length. He restrained the desire to rip off what little remained of her clothing and take her hard and deep. To remind her how perfectly their bodies fit together, and how good he could make her feel.

She'd taken control, and he'd gladly let her have it... for now.

Kendra pressed her warm mouth to his bare chest, laying gentle kisses on his heated flesh. He inhaled at the sensation of her cool tongue grazing his nipple, then swirling around it. She slid her hands down his back and gripped his ass.

He groaned at the glorious sensation of his taut rod pressed between them. She unbuckled his belt, then unzipped his pants.

Kendra tugged her lower lip between her teeth as she scanned the ridge beneath his underwear. She slipped her hand underneath the waistband and curled her warm fingers around his shaft. Pumping it, she elicited involuntary groans of pleasure. Her gaze locked with his as she worked him with her hand until he could barely remember his own damn name.

Conversation was out of the question.

The muscles of his legs and back tensed, pressure building as she brought him closer to release. Nate gently gripped her throat, pressing his open mouth to hers in an effort to wrest back control and slow his ascent to climax.

Kendra released her grip on his painfully hard shaft. Digging her fingers into his back, she sighed softly. Her hands trailed down his back as she gave in to his fervent kisses. Impatient, she shoved his pants and underwear down his hips, freeing his rigid length.

So much for a slow seduction.

He'd planned to take his time. Convey his deepest feelings through each kiss and touch as he made love to her.

His plan dissolved in the rush of adrenaline in his veins.

She'd brought him so close to the edge. He ached for the intense relief he could only find being buried inside her slick walls, his name on her lips.

Nate fumbled to retrieve a condom from his wallet before clumsily shedding his pants and briefs and kicking off his shoes. He sheathed himself, then stripped Kendra of the bra and panties that were the last barrier to the uninhibited glory of her captivating curves.

He lifted her, his arms bracing her legs and her back pressed against the wall as he drove deep inside her wet heat.

Nate's gaze met hers as he lifted her slowly, then eased her back down until he was fully seated inside her, creating a rhythm. The exquisite sensation was intensified by the call-and-response of Kendra's hushed moans and his soft curses as they accelerated toward bliss.

Her arms around his neck, Kendra pulled his mouth to hers in frantic, hungry kisses that catapulted his spiral out of control.

Muscles tense, he strained with the effort of maintaining his focus as he lifted her higher, then plunged deeper. His movements swifter, more powerful. The sound of her naked skin slapping against his filled the space.

Kendra tensed, her nails scraping his back as she called out his name. Her slick walls spasmed, milking his throbbing flesh as he soared to his own release.

Their hearts still racing, he pressed his damp forehead to hers and held her as they caught their breath.

"That was incredible." He kissed her, then reluctantly released her to the floor, his breathing still ragged. "Can I get you anything?"

She pressed a kiss to his chest. "More of you."

"Can a brother have a sec to recharge?"

Her mouth twisted in a sensuous smirk that tested his will. "Fine, but we're leaving in time for your next show...round two or not."

"Yes, ma'am." He winked, swatting her bottom playfully before heading to the bathroom.

When he returned, Kendra was seated on the bed, the sheet strategically positioned across her body. One foot dangled off the edge of the bed; the other was folded beneath her.

Hair tousled, her cheeks and chest flushed, she was a vision of loveliness. One he wanted in his bed every night, not just in his dreams.

"You're beautiful, you know that?"

She smiled sheepishly, straightening the leg beneath her. "You're pretty handsome yourself."

Nate pulled Kendra to the edge of the bed and knelt between her knees. He trailed a finger down her chest. "You're an amazing woman, Kendra. I'm lucky to have you in my corner."

"And I'm proud of you, Nate. Of the man you've become."

Her sincere expression filled him with warmth. It meant more to him than she could possibly know.

He kissed her. Made love to her. Allowed himself to imagine the joy of never having to let her go again.

Kendra's body hummed with energy and her cheeks were filled with heat. The friction of her taut nipples grazing the fabric of her clothing made it difficult to concentrate.

She fanned herself with a brochure, hoping the producers didn't shush her for making too much noise on the set.

Could everyone else see the glow she felt after leaving Nate's bed less than two hours ago?

Kendra surveyed the crew on the set of the sports talk show. Preoccupied with running the program, they paid her little attention.

Kendra squirmed in the director's-style chair, crossing her legs tightly. Her foot bounced involuntarily.

When she looked up, Nate caught her eye. A mischievous grin animated his handsome face before he returned his attention to the panel's discussion about whether the all-star game should be played before or after the championship game.

Desperate for a distraction, Kendra looked down at her phone. The ringer and alarms had to be silenced when they were on set. She'd missed several calls. She scanned them. It was her sister.

A chill ran down her spine and her fingers suddenly felt cold. Maya wasn't a serial caller. She left a message and waited for her to call back, especially when she knew they'd be on set.

At the next commercial break, Kendra left the set to call her sister.

Maya answered right away. "Kendra, I'm sorry to call you like this. Everything will be fine, but there's been an accident."

She held her breath. "Who?"

"It's Kai, sweetie. He fractured his left arm."

A fleeting sensation of intense pain ran up Kendra's left arm. She could only imagine how Kai must feel. "How did this happen?"

"Liam took the kids to the playground." Maya said after a brief pause. "Kai jumped off the jungle gym. We're so sorry this happened. Liam insists on paying for the surgery."

"Surgery?" Kendra kneaded the back of her neck. A fresh wave of panic swept over her. "Can't they just put on a cast?"

"He fractured the bone between his elbow and wrist in two places. They have to put in pins."

The room seemed to tilt, and her knees nearly gave way. Kendra sank onto the sofa, her hands shaking. "When are they performing the surgery?"

"They want to do it right away. Liam is trying to delay it until you and Nate arrive. I know he's on air right now, but can you get here as soon as possible? I don't know how much longer it's safe to wait."

"We'll be there as soon as we can. Hold them off as long as possible. I need to see him before he goes into surgery." Kendra wiped her cheeks. She hadn't even realized she was crying. "Kiss Kai and tell him Mommy and Daddy love him and we'll be there as soon as we can."

Chapter 19

Kendra rushed off the elevator on the surgical floor with Nate hard on her heels.

"My name is Kendra Williams. I'm looking for my son, Kai Johnston. He's scheduled for surgery on a broken arm."

The woman tilted her head, her dark eyes narrowing. "I remember you. You were in here with him a few months ago. He knocked out his front teeth."

"Yes." Heat filled Kendra's cheeks. There was something accusatory about the woman's tone. "Can you please tell me where my...our son is?"

"Nate Johnston." The nurse's eyes lit up with recognition. "I saw you on the *Donnie Jones Sports Hour* earlier today."

"That's right." Nate's tone was measured. "Could you please just tell us where we can find our son? We're hoping to see him before he goes to surgery."

The woman seemed miffed at Nate's rebuff. She pointed down the hall. "Check in at the next nurses' station. They can help you there."

Before they made it to the nurses' station, Liam approached them. His tall frame seemed shorter and there were deep furrows across his forehead.

"Kendra, I'm so sorry. We tried to hold them off as long as we could, but the surgeon couldn't wait any longer." Liam's British accent was more pronounced, his voice heavy with distress.

Kendra's heart fell. Kai had gone into surgery without her there to assure him everything would be okay. "Thank you for getting him here so quickly, and for doing what you could. We appreciate it."

She turned back to look at Nate, who was scowling at Liam as if he was considering pounding him into the floor.

She placed a gentle hand on Nate's arm, hoping he received her silent plea. "Nate, this is Maya's fiancé, Liam Westbrook. Liam, this is Kai's dad, Nate Johnston."

Nate didn't extend his hand and Liam didn't force the issue. He simply nodded and repeated his apology to Nate.

"Why was he with you?" Nate folded his arms.

"Kendra's mum had a doctor's appointment, Maya had a big meeting at work today and our nanny has come down with a bug of some sort. I took the day off to care for the children. We went to see an animated film, then they wanted to stop at the playground before we returned to our flat."

Nate grunted. "And exactly how did this happen?"

"Kai climbed atop the climbing frame while the girls played on the slide. Ella came down the slide too fast and hit the ground. I was tending to her when Kai called out to me, 'Uncle Liam, look what I can do.' He was airborne before I could tell him not to jump. I only turned my head for a minute. It happened so fast. I've gone over it in my head again and again, wondering what I could have done differently."

"Don't." Kendra squeezed Liam's arm. "Boys do crazy things. We ended up here just a few months ago when he fell down the stairs at my mom's house. These things happen."

Liam didn't look convinced.

"And you won't believe the crazy things this one and his brothers did when we were kids." Kendra jerked a thumb over her shoulder in Nate's direction, hoping to loosen up his sour face and genie stance. "He's got quite a collection of scars and broken bones to prove it."

Liam hugged Kendra and sighed. "I still feel absolutely dreadful about it, but I appreciate your kindness. Please, allow me to take care of the medical bills. Kai was in my care at the time—I should be the one to handle it."

"We can take care of our own kid." Nate's words had a sharp edge. "So thanks, but no thanks. We're good."

"Of course." Liam nodded solemnly. "Didn't mean to cause any offense."

"You didn't." Kendra narrowed her gaze at Nate before turning back to Liam and forcing a smile. "We appreciate the offer. Now, can you tell us what the doctor said?"

Kendra slipped her arm through Nate's. He softened his stance, allowing his hand to fall to his side as Liam explained that Kai had Monteggia fractures of the left radius and ulna. Pins would be inserted to hold the bones in place. However, the growth plates weren't affected and he should recover fully after wearing a cast for several weeks.

Nate seemed to breathe easier. He threaded his fingers through hers, and the rapid beat of her heart slowed. She nodded as Nate asked questions, glad to let him handle it.

Once Liam briefed them, he led them to the small private waiting room where their families were gathered.

"You're a great uncle, Liam," Kendra reassured him. "Thank you again for taking care of our son. It could've happened with any of us."

Kendra didn't miss Nate's subtle sneer when she referred to Liam as Kai's uncle.

"Liam, would you tell everyone we'll be there in just a minute? Nate and I need to ask the nurse a question."

Nate raised an eyebrow and frowned. He clearly suspected why she wanted to talk to him.

Nate trudged through the open waiting area and dropped into one of the chairs. He dragged a hand down his face. "What did I do now?"

Kendra stood in front of him with an expression that scolded him like a child. She folded her arms, bringing attention to her chest. He dropped his gaze. Right now he needed to stay focused on their son, not reminisce about what they'd done earlier in the day.

"Why are you being such an ass? Liam loves Kai. He'd do anything for him."

"I don't need him to do anything for my son. Maybe he's a big shot in merry old England—" Nate feigned a terrible British accent "—but I don't need his charity."

"He didn't mean anything by it. He feels guilty. He only wants to help. That doesn't make him a bad guy."

"It makes him a condescending one."

"If you knew anything about Liam, you'd know he's not like that at all."

"Well, I don't, and I don't appreciate him acting like I can't take care of my own kid. No one asked for his help."

"He's Kai's uncle and your son adores him."

Hearing how much his son adored some other man felt like a punch square in the jaw. He pressed a stream of air through his nose and shook his head. "Maybe if I got to spend as much time with my own kid as he apparently does, Kai would feel that way about me instead of that guy."

Kendra's eyes widened for a moment, then her expression softened, her eyes filled with what he was sure was pity. She released an audible breath, then sat beside him.

She placed a warm hand over his. "I know it's hard not seeing Kai as often as you'd like, but he loves you, Nate. You'll always be his hero."

Nate grunted, his gaze still on the gray hospital floor tiles. "You don't see the glow in his eyes when he talks about Liam the Great."

Kendra shook her head and laughed. "You're being funny, but the truth *is* Liam is pretty great. He's great for my sister. Great for the town of Pleasure Cove. And he's great with the kids—our son included. We should be thankful Kai has a big family of people who love him."

Nate gritted his teeth. The muscles in his jaw tensed. "Shacking up with your sister doesn't make him family."

Lips pursed, Kendra narrowed her gaze. "So you're going to go all 1950s on me? Fine. They're engaged, so he will be soon. But in my book, he couldn't be a better uncle, even if he were blood."

"From what I hear, he hasn't always been so good to his blood brother, either." He huffed, hating that he'd revealed his hand.

Now she'd know he'd talked to his brother Mitchell, who worked as Liam's next in command at Pleasure Cove Luxury Resort—one of the many resort properties owned by Liam's family.

What he hadn't gleaned from Mitchell—or his brother hadn't been willing to reveal—he'd learned by searching the web. Liam had sustained a feud with his brother Hunter for years over a woman Liam had dated and his brother eventually married.

Kendra stood, glowering down at him, her expression filled with disappointment. "People make mistakes, Nate. Hopefully we learn from them and eventually grow up. You should try it."

Nate caught hold of her hand as she turned to walk away. "I'm not trying to be difficult. It's just hard seeing Kai so excited when he talks about this guy. It feels like Liam is trying to take my place in Kai's life."

Kendra's eyes glistened. She cupped his cheek. Her sweet, familiar scent soothed his anxiety, warming his chest.

"Our son is growing up, Nate. New people will constantly come into his life. No matter how much he admires or cares for them, it doesn't mean he doesn't love us, too." She smiled. "You'll always be his number one. Always."

Nate grasped the hand on his cheek and kissed her palm. He slipped his arms around her waist and pulled her closer, pressing his ear to the thumping of her heartbeat.

"Marcus was right. You've always been able to talk me down off the ledge."

She leaned down and kissed his head. "That's why they pay me the big bucks."

Laughter rumbled in her chest, immediately followed by a sharp intake of air. Nate glanced up at her face. The corners of her eyes were wet with tears. He pulled her onto his lap. "What's wrong, babe?"

She shook her head and wiped her eyes with the back of her hand. "Nothing, because Kai is going to be fine, right?"

"Of course he is." He swiped her wet cheek with his thumb. "He's a Johnston. Takes more than a couple of broken bones to take us out."

She nodded, a nervous laugh bubbling from her pursed lips. "He's a warrior. Like his dad."

"There you are." Liam stood in the doorway, his expression a mixture of guilt and relief. "Kai's out of surgery. Everything went brilliantly. The doctor wants to see you now."

Kendra hugged Nate, thanked Liam and headed off in search of the doctor.

Liam shifted his attention to Nate. He cleared his throat. "Again, I can't tell you how sorry I am."

"I know. And about earlier…" Nate sighed deeply. "I'm sorry. I'm not usually that much of an ass. I was just really worried about our son." He extended his hand and shook Liam's firmly. "Thank you for taking care of Kai today."

If he couldn't always be there for his son, it was good to know someone else who cared about him would.

Chapter 20

Kendra's eyes fluttered open in response to the harsh sunlight filtering through Kai's hospital room window. She repositioned herself in one of the comfy recliners and pulled the plush throw up around her neck.

It wasn't her own bed, but the setup was remarkably comfortable. Despite her insistence that it wasn't necessary, she was glad Liam upgraded Kai's room to a family suite so she and Nate could both spend the night there in comfort.

She looked around. Kai was resting peacefully, unbroken limbs akimbo, in his blue-and-white-patterned hospital gown. She moved beside him and leaned down to kiss his forehead.

The door opened and Nate stepped inside carrying a pastry box and a carafe of coffee. From the delicious scent of both, there was no way either item came from the hospital cafeteria.

"That coffee smells delicious, and are those dough-nuts?"

Nate popped the lid open, revealing her favor-ite doughnuts in the world. Maple bacon, from Lila's Cafe. They'd met there for coffee a few times during the weeks they'd been working together.

"Thank you." She reached into the box and grabbed one. She took a generous bite of sweet, salty perfec-tion. The doughnut was soft and fresh. It melted in her mouth. An involuntarily murmur conveyed her satis-faction.

Nate's eyes widened in response. He cleared his throat. "Got your favorite coffee, too."

"A mint chocolate mocha from Lila's?"

"You know it."

Kendra stood on her toes and kissed his cheek. Cedar and citrus filled her nostrils as she inhaled his fresh-out-of-the-shower scent.

"Is that a maple bacon doughnut?"

Nate and Kendra both turned toward the small, groggy voice coming from their son, his eyes barely open.

Kendra dropped the remainder of the doughnut back in the box and rushed over to him. "Kai, sweetie, you're awake. Don't you ever scare Mommy like that again."

"Hey, champ." His dad sat on the opposite side of the bed and mussed his son's hair. "Didn't we tell you that time you fell down the steps at Nana's that you can't fly?"

Kai swallowed hard and nodded. "This time I wasn't trying to fly. I just wanted to show Uncle Liam how far I could jump down after I climbed up the mountain, just like he did."

"Honey, your uncle is an experienced mountain climber. And he didn't just jump off the mountain. He had special equipment and training." Kendra squeezed Kai's hand, ignoring Nate's frown. "So promise Mommy you won't ever try anything like that again."

"I promise."

"Good." She kissed his forehead. "How do you feel?"

"Tired and thirsty and hungry. Can I have some water and a doughnut?"

"Yes and yes." Nate poured a small glass of water. "You want to sit up, li'l man?"

When Kai nodded, Nate picked up the remote and adjusted the bed.

"Cool. Can I play with it?"

Nate and Kendra laughed.

"It's not a toy, honey. It's the remote to the bed," Kendra explained. "Tell you what, you can have your doughnut, but only after you eat a real breakfast. How about some eggs and bacon?"

Kai agreed reluctantly and she called in his breakfast order while Nate found a children's program for him to watch on television, then showed Kai how to work the remote. When she hung up the telephone, Nate was there, frowning at her.

"You want to tell me again how Kai's accident wasn't Captain Awesome's fault? He was probably bragging about his mountain climbing, BASE jumping adventures. No wonder Kai got the crazy idea to jump off the jungle gym."

"Mommy, Daddy..."

"Just a minute, sweetie," Kendra called over her shoulder, then turned back to Nate. "You're being ridiculous. He's a little boy with a vivid imagination.

Just like you and your brothers were. Stop trying to make this Liam's fault. I thought we'd squashed this yesterday."

"But Mommy…"

"Just a sec, champ," Nate said. He lowered his voice and turned back to her. "All I'm saying is maybe this guy is as great as everyone seems to think he is, but that doesn't mean he knows the first thing about taking care of a kid."

"Who does when they first have children? Liam's never had kids before, but he's really good with them." Kendra pointed a finger at Nate for emphasis. "What happened with him is no different than when he fell at my mom's or yours. Not to mention the time he got that knot on his forehead when he was with you in Memphis."

"You're on TV, Daddy."

"I know, champ. That was from yesterday," Nate said.

"Look, there's Mommy, too."

Nate and Kendra both looked toward the screen. There was a picture of her and Kai at the skating rink, then another of her at the press conference.

"Sweetie, turn up the volume, please." Kendra tried to keep her voice calm, despite the fact that her heart was beating like a jackhammer and her legs suddenly felt like jelly.

The news story raised suspicions about Kai's injuries, painting a picture of her as either an abusive mother or a very neglectful one.

"What the hell…?"

"Don't say bad words, Daddy."

"Sorry." Nate rubbed the back of his neck. "Do me a favor and turn back to the cartoons, okay?"

Kai happily complied.

Nate turned to Kendra. "Don't panic, babe. Everything is going to be fine."

"They're making me look like an unfit mother." She clenched her fists as she paced the floor, tears spilling down her cheeks. "Your ex-girlfriend did this."

She couldn't help her accusatory tone. Kendra knew it wasn't fair. Nate didn't ask for any of this.

"She must've had someone at the skating rink taking photos."

"I knew she had it out for me, but I had no idea she'd stoop low enough to involve you." He gripped her shoulders and held her gaze. "Listen to me, Kendra, I promise I'll do whatever it takes to fix this. Everything is going to be fine. All right?"

He hugged her to his chest. Kendra pressed her face to Nate's sweater and melted into him, hoping she could trust him, and that everything would be okay.

Nate paced the floor of his beach house, clutching his cell phone. He'd promised Kendra he would do whatever it took to make this right, and he meant it. Even if it meant dancing with the devil herself.

He forced out a slow breath, then dialed the phone.

There was a smirk in her voice when Stephanie answered. "I wondered how long it would take for you to reconsider my offer."

Nate clenched his teeth and breathed, saying the vile things he thought of Stephanie Weiss in his head, rather than aloud.

"Look, Stephanie, I'm sorry about how things worked

out between us and about what happened with your career. I discredited your story, not because I wanted to hurt you, but because you put me in a position where I had to protect my friend. But what you're doing in retaliation is ruthless and unethical. The Stephanie Weiss I knew was ambitious, but a generally decent human being. What happened to you?"

"I got blackballed from legitimate sports networks, thanks to you." Her tone was icy. "You made me look like a fool in front of the entire world. Don't like it so much when the shoe is on the other foot, do you?"

"I don't care what you say about me, but bringing my family into it… That's low, even for you." Nate tried to keep his voice level.

She clucked her tongue three times. "Not a smart way to talk to the person whose help I assume you're about to request."

He clenched his fist and willed himself to calm down. "Actually, I'm calling to help you. You want people to view you as a legitimate reporter? Start by reporting honestly. Stop creeping around taking pictures of my kid and his mother. She's a genuinely good person and a hell of a mom. She doesn't deserve this."

"And I did?" Stephanie's voice reached a high pitch. "I was sleeping in your bed three nights a week, but you chose your teammate's reputation over mine. Now I'm supposed to feel bad for some baby mama of yours?"

He cringed at the term *baby mama*. "She's my son's mother, and yes, I expect you to behave as if you have a shred of decency." Nate massaged his temple. "Maybe I'm not entitled to privacy, but my kid and his mom, they are."

"You know how this works. Anyone associated with

a public personality is fair game. Now, are you calling just for old times' sake, or have you reconsidered my offer?"

Nate was silent. Appealing to her sense of decency had been a bust—though he'd put little faith in that possibility. Now he scrolled through his remaining options. Give in to her demands or beat her at her own game.

He chose the latter.

"Actually, I'm calling to make you an offer."

"Oh?"

"Lay off me and my family or I swear to you, one day soon, you'll be lucky to get a job at the daily gazette in Bumfuck Nowhere."

She laughed incredulously. "You of all people, Nate, should know I don't respond well to threats."

"You of all people, Stephanie, should know I'm willing to protect my family by any means necessary."

"Then I guess there's nothing more for us to say." Despite Stephanie's bravado, her voice was tentative. "One day you'll look back and wish you'd taken me up on my offer."

"I won't," he said, "but I assure you that you'll wish you'd taken me up on mine." Nate ended the call, then dialed another number.

"This is Edge. What can I do for you, Nate?" Edgerton Mathis, a private investigator often employed by members of the Marauders, always sounded laid-back, like he was drinking a beer and smoking a blunt.

"Remember that dossier I asked you to put together on that reporter a while back?"

"The one you told me to burn because you were afraid of causing irreparable damage to her career?"

Nate swallowed. "Yeah, that's the one. Any chance you can re-create that?"

"Maybe," Edge said. "This have anything to do with that piece running today, implying your ex is a bad mom?"

Nate didn't acknowledge the question. "How long will it take you to put it together?"

"Two hours."

Nate had always suspected that a guy like Edge held on to files like this. He didn't comment on exactly what he thought of that. "Good. You think it's enough to discredit her?"

Edge chuckled. "What I showed you three years ago? That ain't even the half. Been keeping tabs on this one just for the hell of it. With the way she operates, it was only a matter of time until she ended up on someone's shit list again."

"Good. Same as we agreed on last time?"

"Double the content, double the price."

Nate gritted his teeth. Hell, he'd be willing to pay four times what they'd agreed on previously if it would expose Stephanie for the snake she was and help clear the rumors about Kendra. "Fine. There's a generous bonus in it if you use your pipeline to put this info out to the media, rather than having it come from my camp."

"Done." There was a smile in Edge's gritty voice. "I'll send you a text with my account number in the Caymans. Wire half now, the rest after the news hits the airwaves. Then ding dong, the wicked witch's career is dead."

"I'll wire the money as soon as I get the info."

"One more thing," Edge said. "My gut is telling me Weiss isn't in this alone. If I tug on that thread, it may unravel something you aren't prepared to deal with."

"What do you mean?"

"The person she's colluding with may be a team-mate." There was the clink of ice in a glass in the background. "Maybe even someone you consider a friend."

"I don't believe it." Nate paced the floor. Could one of his teammates have enough malice toward him to jeopardize his career and his family? "But if it's true..."

"It'll be included in the story."

Nate ended the call with Edge and poured himself a shot of whiskey. When the truth came out about Steph-anie's "reporting" methods, she'd be done. She'd be a pariah with whom no reputable news outlet would want ties.

He hadn't resorted to this option three years ago, because despite what Stephanie had done, he'd once cared for her. He hadn't wanted to destroy her career.

But now she'd left him no choice.

His family meant everything to him. He'd do what-ever it took to protect them. Even if it meant Steph-anie Weiss and her co-conspirator getting what they deserved.

Chapter 21

"Have you seen the news?" There was a lilt in Kendra's voice that he hadn't heard since the reports questioning her parenting abilities hit the airwaves.

"Been preparing for a trip." Nate threw a couple days' worth of socks and underwear in his luggage. "Why, what's up?"

"Stephanie is all over the news. It looks like the Marauders' personnel manager, Lee Davis, conspired with her to compromise your image, so the team wouldn't offer you a new contract."

"Marcus mentioned it," he said nonchalantly. "He suspects that's the reason the Marauders were so quick to offer me such a generous final contract."

"She's been tapping people's phone lines and using a bunch of shady tactics. Plus, it looks like she's been known to falsify sources. It's been going on for years."

"Hmm…" He put the phone on speaker and tossed it on the bed while he rummaged through his nightstand for a few pictures of Kai and Kendra he kept there. "Guess we won't have to worry about her anymore."

Kendra was silent for a moment. "Nate, you didn't have anything to do with this, did you?"

He scratched the back of his neck. "You really want to know?"

"Did you do anything illegal or unethical to make this happen?"

"I did not." He couldn't vouch for Edge, but that was the beauty of working with a guy like him: plausible deniability.

"Then I don't need to know anything else." She paused momentarily. "I didn't realize you were going out of town. You have another segment on the Donnie Jones show in a few days."

"I'll only be gone a day or so. I'll be back in plenty of time."

"Good, because Stephanie might be out of commission, but we're still on mop-up duty. I'm negotiating a one-on-one with John Chase to clear the air about the video and the rumors about me. Unless you've changed your mind. You've got your new contract and your two major sponsors have offered you new deals, so skipping the interview won't hurt you financially."

"This is what we need to do to finally put this all to bed, right?" When she sighed heavily, but didn't respond, he continued. "Then that's what we're going to do."

Nate valued his privacy, but he valued his family more. Whether she believed it or not, Dray was family. He'd do whatever he needed to do to prove that to her.

* * *

Nate exited Jacksonville International Airport, picked up his rental car and drove to the home of Curtis Williams—Kendra's father.

He didn't expect to fix a decades-long problem in a single visit. But if Kendra took even the smallest step toward working things out with her father, maybe it'd go a long way toward helping him regain her trust, too.

Or maybe this was a horrible idea that would destroy everything they'd rebuilt in the past weeks.

Nate scrubbed a hand across his forehead. It was a risky move, but the payoff would be worth it.

He entered the pretty little gated community near Dutton Island and parked in the drive of the idyllic home with its covered porches spanning the width of the house on the first and second floor.

Nate rang the bell and held his breath as a shadow approached through the glass door with a colorful, geometric design.

The door opened, and the aromatic scent of spicy beef cooking wafted out to greet him. "Mr. Williams, I don't know if you remember me, but—"

"You were my daughter's *best friend*." The older man emphasized the phrase. "And the father of my grandson. Of course I know who you are." Curtis Williams folded his arms and held his gaze. "How's he coming along after his surgery?"

"Kai's doing well, sir. He loved the musical greeting card and arrangement of cookies you and your wife sent." There was an awkward pause. "May I come in?"

The man stepped aside and let him in, leading him to the living room of the spacious first floor. He invited him to have a seat.

A wave of sadness passed over the man's face. His gaze raked the floor before returning to Nate's. "Saw that nonsense on the news about her. Kendra loves Kai more than anything in the world. She ought to sue their asses for implying otherwise."

"The past week or so has been tough for her." Guilt tugged at Nate's chest. He hated that Kendra had gotten caught up in the crosshairs of the plot aimed squarely at him. "I know she'd love to hear from you."

"It's not as simple as that. Kendra is as stubborn as her mother." The old man scowled and rubbed the back of his neck. "I left her a couple of voice mails, but she hasn't returned them. I only got to speak to my grandson because Maya put him on the phone when she and the girls were visiting Kai." He eyed Nate. "Did Kendra send you?"

Nate shook his head.

"Didn't think so." He heaved a sigh, then leveled his stare at Nate again. "Then what brings you here? You asking for her hand? If so, I don't think my blessing would make much of an impression on her."

Nate scooted to the edge of his seat. "I'm here to ask you to make the effort to fix your relationship with your daughter."

Curtis raised an eyebrow. "Why do you care? You two aren't together anymore."

"I believe that your estranged relationship with Kendra is a primary reason things didn't work out with us." Nate held the man's gaze.

"You sure I'm the reason?" He poked a thumb in his chest. "I remember the report about that groupie in your room. Wasn't too long after that she left you."

"I didn't invite her to my room." Nate frowned. "And nothing happened. Not that night or any other night while we were together."

"Still don't see what that has to do with the relationship between me and my daughter."

"Frankly, sir, you don't have a relationship. You're simply related."

"If you came here to tell me things I already know—"

"I didn't." Nate held up a hand. "I came to tell you that Kendra might act like she doesn't need you, but she does. She needs her father as much now as she did when she was a little girl."

Lines spanned the older man's forehead. His expression was weary with years of hurt and rejection. Something they had in common.

"She hated me even when she was a girl. Not at first, but between her mother and brother...she became so resentful. I wanted to set the record straight, but she was a kid. I couldn't get into all the reasons things didn't work out between her mother and me. The way she saw it, I chose my new family over her and her brother."

"Didn't you?" Nate worked to keep the accusation out of his tone, but the words dripped with it.

Curtis groaned. "No, I didn't leave Anna for Alita. Didn't even know her then. I left because I was unhappy. We both were. I wouldn't spend my life that way, like my old man did."

"I respect that, sir, but I'm sure you understand how it made your children feel. Especially Kendra. From her perspective, *she's* the reason you up and left."

"That's ridiculous." He rubbed his chin. Deep lines spanned his forehead.

"Have you told her that?"

"I've tried to show her and her brother how much I care for them. When they were younger, they'd come down and spend summers and holidays with us. As they got older, they resented being made to visit. It only made them hate me more." A pained expression accompanied the man's memories. "When they were old enough to choose, they both stopped coming. I tried giving them space, but they became more and more distant."

"I don't doubt you've tried in the past, Mr. Williams. All I'm saying is, it's worth trying again. Because if you don't, I don't know if she'll ever learn to trust any man. She'll always be afraid that the next guy is going to cheat on her or leave her."

"So you do want her back."

"I never wanted to lose her. I love her, asked her to marry me. As angry as I've been with her all these years, the truth is, I haven't met anyone I'd rather be with. I know she feels the same, but she's afraid."

"You tell her that?"

"Not in those exact words."

"Hmm..." The old man leaned forward, his hands between his knees. "Guess Kendra's not the only one who's afraid."

Nate's nostrils flared. "If I were afraid, I wouldn't be here."

"Maybe it was easier to come and talk to me than to lay it all out on the line and risk her walking away again."

Nate's gaze dropped to his hands. What the old man said was true. He hadn't been very romantic or heartfelt with Kendra. Instead, he'd pointed out that getting back together was in Kai's best interest. That line of thinking relegated Kendra to a nice bonus accessory. Something a woman like her would never stand for.

No wonder she'd turned him down. In an effort to protect his heart, he'd handled the situation poorly.

Curtis nodded knowingly, pain in his voice. "Been there. A man can only take so much, I suppose."

"You're right, Mr. Williams. My approach to Kendra was all wrong." Nate tapped the table with his forefinger. "But I'm right, too. I know she hasn't made it easy for you, but she has the right to be angry about you leaving her and Dash. She handled it badly. Maybe we're all guilty of that. But Kendra is an amazing woman. She deserves the best from both of us. It's time we both man up and give her that."

Curtis frowned at the censure, then sighed. "I convinced myself it was best just to give Kendra and Dash space and hope they came around. I guess that was just what was easiest."

"I'm having a little party this weekend to celebrate my new contract with the Marauders. I'd appreciate it if you and your wife would come. If you're willing, I'll have my assistant book your flights and hotel. Just say the word."

"I want to be the father my daughter deserves." The older man nodded. "We'll come to your party, but you don't need to pay for anything. This is something I need to do."

Nate's heart beat against his rib cage. *Mission accomplished.* Mr. Williams would make another effort to work things out with his daughter.

He'd call Kendra's mother to let her know her ex-husband would be at the party. He owed her that. On the other hand, it would be best not to tell Kendra in advance about her father's visit.

A sense of dread suddenly crept over him like kudzu vines climbing a pole.

What if Kendra resented his interference?

He heaved a sigh, releasing the tension knotting the muscles in his neck and shoulders.

Only one way to find out.

Chapter 22

Kendra dusted her face with a little powder, then applied a matte lipstick.

They'd actually pulled it off. Nate had inked his new two-year contract with the Memphis Marauders and generous deals with both his previous sponsors—a soft drink company and a rapidly growing athletic wear company poised to overtake the market within a few years. Two other sponsorships were in the works—a Memphis car dealership and a home builder based in the Carolinas.

Once Nate was ready to hang up his cleats, the sports network had already expressed interest in adding him to their parade of former players turned sports analysts.

Several months remained on her contract with Nate, but Marcus had already requested that she work with two of his other clients. The only thing that wasn't settled was her relationship with Nate.

Kendra slipped in diamond studs Nate had bought for her birthday the year he signed his first pro contract. She put on her high heel boots and a light coat, thankful the unusually cold weather had finally abated. Kai was already at Nate's, where he'd spent the night. She got in her car and swung by to pick up her mother.

Anna Williams looked lovely in a black pantsuit, her salt-and-pepper hair in pin curls, fresh from the salon. She greeted Kendra as she placed the tray of heart-shaped cookies she made for the holidays in the back-seat, then got inside the car.

"Everything okay, Mama?" Kendra pulled out of her mother's small drive and headed toward the opulent beach community where Nate lived. "You're awfully quiet."

There was sadness in her mother's eyes. "You know I would never do anything to purposely hurt you or Dash?"

"Of course." A knot formed in Kendra's gut. "Why would you even have to ask?"

"Because I didn't do right by you two when it comes to your father."

"Dad made his choice when he walked away from us." Kendra's heart beat faster.

"He walked away from *me*. He loved you two. Wanted to be in your life as much as he could. It was me who made it hard for him. I was so angry. I shouldn't have talked about him the way I did in front of you kids. It made you resentful and ruined any chance of either of you having a good relationship with him."

Kendra released a long, agonizing breath. She couldn't disagree with her mother there. It was the primary reason she'd been careful to never say anything disparaging about Nate in front of their son. She didn't want him thinking ill of his dad the way she did of hers. Of course, it was easier for her. Nate hadn't been the one to walk away.

"We all make mistakes, Mama. That was a long time ago. Dash and I are adults. How we deal, or don't deal, with Dad is our choice now."

"You don't think things would've been different between you and your father if I hadn't filled your heads with the bitterness I felt toward him?" Anna's voice broke.

Kendra grimaced, her chest heavy with regret.

"I don't know. But I understand why you were so angry with him." It felt as if a weight was on her chest, compressing her lungs. "It's the same reason Nate resents me."

Her mother put a hand on her shoulder. "He was angry before, but isn't it clear how much he loves you?"

"Does he, or does he just want to keep the Johnston family tradition going?"

"Family is important to Nate, sure. But you can't honestly believe he doesn't love you. It's in his eyes when he looks at you, when he talks about you." A wistful smile broke across her mother's face. "Been there since he was a little boy. It's a special thing to have someone love you like that."

"I love him." Kendra sniffed, refusing to let the tears fall. "But I don't think things will ever be the same between us."

"I should hope not. You're both older and wiser now. Been through the fire and come out on the other side. You'll build something stronger."

"Some part of him will always resent me, and some

part of me will always be anticipating the moment he falls for a newer, shinier model." The words felt like sandpaper in her throat. "How do we get past that?"

"Forgive yourself and believe in him. It's as simple and as complicated as that." Anna's voice was firm but sympathetic. "Is giving in to your fear over what you might lose worth losing what you could have?"

Kendra pulled into the long driveway that led to Nate's beach house, not answering her mother's question. "You go ahead to the front. I'll take the tray around to the back."

Anna opened the car door and stepped out reluctantly. "Just think about what I said."

Kendra flipped down the visor mirror and gave herself a long, hard look. If only it were as simple as her mother made it sound.

She grabbed the tray and went around toward the back entrance. A light suddenly came on in a second-floor guest room. Through the sheer, gauzy curtain she could make out two figures in an embrace—Nate's twin sister Vi and Jase Hernandez.

Suddenly Vi's solo island vacation and Jase's supposed camping trip made sense. Something was going on between those two.

When Kendra looked up again, Vi was in the window staring down at her.

They were both busted.

Kendra made her way to the back door. She practically floated inside astride a warm cloud of air carrying the aroma of a variety of Southern comfort foods. Naomi's shrimp and grits, Marcus's wife Alison's chicken and dumplings, and the batch of crispy chicken Nate's youngest sister, Sydney, was frying. There was a tray of

Maya's famous Cuban pork and another of her yummy empanadas,

Alison and Sydney greeted her.

Naomi, smelling of bacon and shrimp, hugged Kendra tight, then kissed her cheek. "Thank you for helping Nate through this crisis."

"It was my pleasure." Kendra smiled.

"Things didn't work out too badly for her, either," Vi interjected. "I hear Marcus has got you lined up with two more athlete clients."

"Don't start, missy." Naomi pointed a finger at her oldest daughter. "Be nice."

Vi turned to Kendra, taking the tray of cookies from her hand. "Why don't I help you put that away?"

Kendra followed Vi to a small table overflowing with desserts, including banana pudding with a perfect meringue topping and Vi's famous bourbon–brown butter pecan pie.

Vi made room for the tray of cookies, then folded her arms. She leaned closer to Kendra and lowered her voice. "Why didn't you out me in front of everyone just now?"

Kendra shrugged, removing her coat. "Figured if you wanted everyone to know you wouldn't have been sneaking around in the guest room upstairs or pretending you went to Barbados all alone."

Vi's cheeks turned crimson. She took Kendra's coat. "Walk with me while I hang this up?"

Kendra followed her to the back hall.

"Thank you." The words seemed to cause Vi physical pain. "Nate would go ballistic if he knew."

"I know, but I also know you're a grown woman and it isn't your brother's business who you're spend-

ing your vacation with…or kissing in his guest room."
Kendra couldn't help the smile that tightened one side
of her mouth.

Vi gave her a look that indicated she didn't appreciate her humor, which only made Kendra break out
into laughter.

"This isn't funny." Vi hung her coat in the closet,
then ran a hand through her box braids.

"Oh…it's serious." Kendra watched Vi's entire face
flush. "Are you in love with him?"

"Don't be ridiculous." Vi folded her arms. "We're
just… I don't know exactly what we're doing, but whatever it is, Nate doesn't need to know about it."

"Fine." Kendra turned to walk away.

Vi grabbed her arm. "Look, I appreciate you not rat-
ting me out in front of my family, but this doesn't mean
we're best friends."

Kendra shrugged. "Of course."

"And whether you decide to tell my brother about
me and Jase or not, there's something I need to say."

Kendra folded her arms, prepared to stand her
ground. "What is it?"

"Nate isn't as tough as he thinks he is. He was dev-
astated when you walked away. I know because I was
there to pick up the pieces. I won't watch my brother go
through that again." There was anguish in Vi's voice.

Kendra relaxed her stance, her arms at her sides.
"I didn't intend to hurt him. At the time, I thought I'd
made the best decision for everyone. I was wrong. I regret that, but I can't change the past. Because of Kai,
Nate and I will always be a part of each other's lives,
whether you like it or not. I'd rather we be friends or at
least not enemies."

Vi sighed. "I promise to take it easy on you, but you have to promise me you'll either love my brother or let him go."

"There you are." Kendra's mother came around the corner. "Just making sure you got in all right." Her gaze shifted between the two of them, then followed Vi as she returned to the kitchen. She lowered her voice. "Everything all right?"

"Nothing to worry about." She kissed her mother on the cheek.

"Good. Then I'll go and give Naomi and the girls a hand in the kitchen."

Kendra made her way into the great room. The place was overflowing with the Johnston family: Naomi and Levi; Mitchell, his wife, Monique, and their adorable infant daughter, Stella; Marcus, Alison and their two boys; Vi, Sydney and their oldest brother, Drew. The only Johnston not present was their youngest brother, Quincy, a freelance photographer on a shoot in Qatar.

Liam and Maya were caught up in an animated conversation with Monique and Mitchell—Liam's second-in-command at Pleasure Cove Luxury Resort.

Kendra sank onto the couch beside Drew and slipped her arm through his. "Thank you again for agreeing to do those interviews for the foundation. I know that went a long way in helping fix Nate's career and increasing funding."

"Glad I could help Nate for a change."

Drew's slow, crooked smile made her heart melt. He was handsome and easily the smartest of the bunch. After an attack on his unit in Fallujah, he struggled with PTSD and had been forced to retire from the military. He often opted to stay at home or called it an early night, fearful he'd have an episode.

"You've done so much for the family, and for our country. Don't you dare think otherwise."

Drew patted her hand. "Thanks, Dray. But we should be thanking you. Without you, not sure we'd be celebrating Nate's return to the Marauders."

"My thoughts exactly, big brother." Nate stood in front of them, looking handsome enough to eat in a light blue sweater and a pair of charcoal-gray pants. He clinked a fork gently against his glass to get everyone's attention, then asked them to fill their glasses.

Nate raised his glass and turned to her with a wide smile that made her heart dance.

"To Kendra Williams, the smartest, most beautiful and most talented woman I've ever known. You've given me a chance to finish out my career with the team I love and another shot at winning it all. Most important, you've given me the best gift I could ever ask for—our son, Kai. To Kendra."

They clinked glasses and drank champagne, her heart overflowing with the love in the room and the love in Nate's eyes.

After the toast, Nate grabbed her hand and led her to his office.

"Maybe you should have a seat."

"Why, is something wrong?" She sat down, a sinking feeling in her stomach.

"Nothing's wrong." He sat beside her. "But I've invited someone here to see you."

"Who?"

Nate pushed the intercom button and asked someone to come to his office.

"Nate, what's going on? You're making me really nervous now." She studied his face, but he turned his attention to the footsteps coming down the hall and the door that slowly creaked open.

"Hello, Kendra."

"Dad? What are you doing here?" She turned to Nate, her voice lowered. "You invited him? Why?"

"Hear him out," Nate pleaded.

Kendra folded her arms. "My mother knew he was coming, didn't she?"

"I wanted to make sure she and your sister were okay with this." Nate placed a reassuring hand on hers. "We all want you to be happy, and you might not think so right now, but the state of your relationship with your father has caused a lot of pain."

She pulled her hand away. "That's my problem, Nate, not yours."

"You don't think it was my problem when you walked out because you were afraid you couldn't trust me? That it isn't Maya's problem when she won't set a date for her own wedding because of your dysfunctional relationship with your father?"

Kendra's face was hot. Each stinging accusation felt like a jab with a hot cattle prod.

"I know what I'm asking isn't easy, but it's important. To all of us." He whispered in her ear. "If something happened to your father tonight, would you be okay with how you two have left things?"

"No." The answer came without thought.

"Then talk to him. You can do this." Nate kissed her cheek. "And if you need me, I'm just down the hall."

Nate patted her father's shoulder briefly as he exited the room, closing the door behind him.

Kendra inhaled, remembering her mother's words. *He loved you...wanted to be in your life as much as he could.*

It was the very opposite of what she'd believed her entire life, no matter how hard he'd tried to convince her otherwise.

Kendra looked ahead, her eyes not meeting her father's. "So how've you been, Dad?"

Curtis Williams seemed to release a long-held breath as he sat beside her. "Physically, not too much to complain about. Mentally? It kills me that you and Dash aren't part of my life. That I hardly get to see my grandson."

Her father's voice vibrated with raw emotion. For the first time, she felt his pain. Understood that he'd been hurting, too.

She placed her warm hand on his noticeably cooler one. He clutched it as if he'd been thrown a lifeline.

It was the first time she'd let him hold her hand since she'd been old enough to cross the street alone.

"I never meant to hurt you and Dash, but I couldn't spend the rest of my life in a marriage that made your mother and me miserable. I know you don't understand—"

"As an adult, I get that, but as a kid...it was devastating." Tears rolled down her cheeks and she wiped at them angrily. "It was hard enough knowing that you'd left us. But what hurt most is I couldn't understand why you didn't love me and Dash enough to stay, but you chose to stay with Maya and Cole and their mom."

"Don't ever think I didn't love you and your brother." He squeezed her hand. "Walking away from my little boy and my baby girl was one of the hardest things I've ever done."

"Then why'd you do it?"

Her father sighed. "Because I didn't want you to grow up the way I did. With parents who resented the hell out of each other. In a house filled with anger and tension and constant arguing. I lived through that, and I didn't want it for you and Dash."

"Why didn't you ever tell us that? All this time, I kept thinking that there must've been something about me that drove you away."

"Kendra, I'm sorry I made you feel that way. I never meant to hurt you and Dash. I only wanted to protect you. Instead, I lost you both."

"It was hard watching you be the perfect father to Maya and Cole. All I could think about was all the times you weren't there for me. It hurt too much to be there and pretend everything was okay. It was easier to hold onto the resentment. So I did. And when I pulled away from you, you didn't put up a fight. That only made me angrier."

Her father shook his head. "I kept telling myself that you and your brother just needed a little space and then you'd come around. The truth is, I was hurt by your rejection, and it was easier not to deal with it. For that, I'm truly sorry. But know this…not a single day has gone by that I haven't thought of you and your brother, hoping we could one day be a family again."

"I believe you, Dad." She accepted the handkerchief her father offered and wiped the tears from her cheeks. "I'm sorry I pushed you away."

He held her in his arms. "Sorry I put you and Dash in a position where you felt you had to choose between your mother and me. I should've handled it better."

"Me, too," Kendra mumbled against her dad's chest. She missed the smell of his cologne.

He squeezed her shoulder. "I can't make up for how I've hurt you in the past, but I'd like to build a relationship with you now. We've already lost so much time."

Kendra found comfort in her father's embrace. One conversation wouldn't instantly heal the deep wounds they'd inflicted on each other. But it was a start, and she had Nate to thank for it.

Chapter 23

Everyone had gone home and Kai was asleep in his bed. They'd had a wonderful night, celebrating with family and a handful of his teammates. But now it was nice to have the house all to themselves.

"Thank you, Nate, for what you did today for me and my dad." Kendra sat beside him on the sofa in the den. "We had a really good talk today, and we're both determined to work on building our relationship."

"That's great, Dray." He squeezed her hand, genuinely happy for them both.

"My dad said something tonight before he and Alita left. He said he was sorry that he was the reason I had trouble trusting people, and that he hoped I'd learn to trust the people in my life who love me. He was talking about you, wasn't he? That's why you arranged this."

"Yes." Nate threaded his fingers through hers, his throat suddenly dry. He turned his body toward hers.

"Kendra, I care about you…no…" He released a deep sigh and raised his eyes to hers, his pulse racing. "I love you, and I need you in my life."

She stared at him, wide-eyed. His declaration had taken her by surprise. "We've been through so much these past few weeks, Nate. Experiences like that can make you extremely emotional."

"I know." His breathing was slow and measured. "And despite the crazy ups and downs, I haven't been this happy in a long time. I want you and Kai in my life every day. That's what makes me happy."

"I care about you, Nate. I want us to be a family, too. But you need to be sure about your feelings. That you truly want to be with me, and not just because I'm Kai's mom."

"The way I feel about you… It isn't just because we have a son together. It's because you're still that girl I fell in love with at the roller-skating rink all those years ago. The best friend I shared my feelings with when they were too raw to share with anyone else."

He pressed a hand to her cheek and smiled. "You are the *only* woman I've ever truly loved. The woman I want to wake up to every morning. The one I want to cook dinners with. The person I want to dance to old-school jams with until I'm eighty."

She laughed as she blinked back tears.

Nate smiled. "Being with you these past few weeks, I've come to realize how incomplete my life is without you. I miss my best friend, the woman I have so much history with. The woman I want to build my future with."

"I love you, too, Nate, and I want to be with you, but I also want my career. I shouldn't have to choose."

"No, you shouldn't. I was wrong to ask you to do

that before. I was so busy trying to give you the life I thought you deserved that I didn't stop to listen to what you actually wanted. I won't make that mistake again. I promise you, I'm going to support your career, just like you've always supported mine."

Kendra grinned, leaning into him. She pressed her mouth to his and gave him a slow, lingering kiss that made heat rise in his chest and his pulse race.

"One last thing." She locked her gaze with his. "Now that we've laid all our cards on the table, we wipe the slate clean. No more apologies, no more guilt. I love you and I trust you to be the man that Kai and I need. One day, I hope you'll be able to trust me, too. That I won't walk away from you or hurt you."

He cupped her cheek and kissed her softly on the lips. "I do trust you. I trust that if an issue ever rises again, that you'll come and talk to me so we can work it out together."

"I promise." She nodded, kissing him again.

Nate held her tight, his heart overflowing with joy and contentment.

His life was good.

He had his family, a generous new contract and lucrative endorsement deals that would allow him to continue supporting the people and causes he cared about.

Still, there was one prize that eluded Nate. He'd do everything in his power to help the Marauders win the big one and walk away champions.

But nothing—not even a championship ring—could make him happier than he was right now.

* * * * *

COMING NEXT MONTH FROM

HARLEQUIN *Desire*

Available August 6, 2019

#2677 BIG SHOT
by Katy Evans
Dealing with her insufferable hotshot boss has India Crowley at the breaking point. But when he faces a stand-in daddy dilemma, India can't deny him a helping hand. Sharing close quarters, though, may mean facing her true feelings about the man...

#2678 OFF LIMITS LOVERS
Texas Cattleman's Club: Houston • by Reese Ryan
When attorney Roarke Perry encounters the daughter of his father's arch enemy, he's dumbstruck. Annabel Currin is irresistible—and she desperately needs his help. Yet keeping this gorgeous client at arms' length may prove impossible once forbidden feelings take over!

#2679 REDEEMED BY PASSION
Dynasties: Secrets of the A-List • by Joss Wood
Event planner Teresa St. Clair is organizing the wedding of the year so she can help her brother out of a dangerous debt. She doesn't need meddling—or saving—from her ex, gorgeous billionaire Liam Christopher. But she can't seem to stay away...

#2680 MONTANA SEDUCTION
Two Brothers • by Jules Bennett
Dane Michaels will stop at nothing to get the Montana resort that rightfully belongs to him and his brother. Even if it means getting close to his rival's daughter. As long as he doesn't fall for the very woman he's seducing...

#2681 HIS MARRIAGE DEMAND
The Stewart Heirs • by Yahrah St. John
With her family business going under, CEO Fallon Stewart needs a miracle. But Gage Campbell, the newly wealthy man she betrayed as a teen, has a bailout plan...if Fallon will pose as his wife! Can she keep focused as passion takes over their mock marriage?

#2682 FROM RICHES TO REDEMPTION
Switched! • by Andrea Laurence
Ten years ago, River Atkinson and Morgan Steele eloped, but the heiress's father tore them apart. Now, just as Morgan's very identity is called in question, River is back in town. Will secrets sidetrack their second chance, or are they on the road to redemption?

**YOU CAN FIND MORE INFORMATION ON UPCOMING HARLEQUIN® TITLES,
FREE EXCERPTS AND MORE AT WWW.HARLEQUIN.COM.**

HDCNM0719

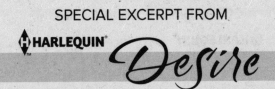
I hate my boss

My demanding, stone-hearted, arrogant bastard boss.

You know those people in an elevator who click the close
button repeatedly when they see someone coming just to
avoid human contact? You know what?

That's my boss. But worse.

As I settle in, I notice that my boss, William, isn't around.

He's the kind of person who turns up early to work for
no good reason. It's probably because he has no social life—
he's a lone wolf, according to my mother, but to me, that
translates as he's a jerk with no friends. Despite the lackeys
who follow him around everywhere, I know he doesn't have
any real friends. After all, I control his calendar for personal
appointments, and in truth, there aren't many.

But where is he today? Not being early is like being late
for him. Until he arrives, there's little I can do, so I meander
to the coffee machine and make a cup for myself. As the

machine is churning up coffee beans, the elevator dings and William appears.

I'll admit, something about his presence always knocks the breath from me. He stalks forward, with three people following in his wake. His hair is perfectly slicked, his stubble trimmed close to his sharp jaw. His eyes are a shocking blue. I can picture him now on the front cover of *Business Insider*, his piercing eyes radiating confidence from the page. But today his eyes are clouded by anger.

He spots me waiting. The whole office is watching as he stalks toward me with a bunch of papers in his arms. His colleagues struggle to keep up, and I discard my coffee, suddenly fearful of his glare. Did I do something wrong?

"Good morning, Mr. Walker—"

"Good morning, India," he growls.

He shoves the papers into my arms and I almost topple over in surprise. "I need you to sort out this paperwork mess and I don't want to hear another word from you until it's done." When he stalks away without so much as a smile, I notice I've been holding my breath.

And this is why, despite his beauty, despite his money, despite his drive, I can't stand the man.

Will she feel the same way when
they're in close quarters? Find out in
BIG SHOT
by New York Times *bestselling author Katy Evans.*

Available August 2019 wherever
Harlequin® Desire books and ebooks are sold.

www.Harlequin.com

SPECIAL EXCERPT FROM

HQN™

Gabe Dalton knows he should ignore his attraction to Jamie Dodge...but her tough-talking attitude masks an innocence that tempts him past breaking point...

Read on for a sneak preview of
Cowboy to the Core
by New York Times *and* USA TODAY
bestselling author Maisey Yates.

"You sure like coming up to me guns blazing, Jamie Dodge. Just saying whatever it is that's on your mind. No concern for the fallout of it. Well, all things considered, I'm pretty sick of keeping myself on a leash."

He cupped her face, and in the dim light he could see that she was staring up at him, her eyes wide. And then, without letting another breath go by, he dipped his head and his lips crushed up against Jamie Dodge's.

They were soft.

Good God, she was soft.

He didn't know what he had expected.

Prickles, maybe.

But no, her lips were the softest, sweetest thing he'd felt in a long time. It was like a flash of light had gone off and erased everything in his brain, like all his thoughts had been printed on an old-school film roll.

There was nothing.

Nothing beyond the sensation of her skin beneath his fingertips, the feel of her mouth under his. She was frozen beneath his touch, and he shifted, tilting his head to the side and darting his tongue out, flicking it against the seam of her lips.

She gasped, and he took advantage of that, getting entry into that pretty mouth so he could taste her, deep and long, and exactly how he'd been fantasizing about.

Oh, those fantasies hadn't been a fully realized scroll of images. No. It had been a feeling.

An invisible band of tension that had stretched between them in small spaces of time. In the leap of panic in his heart when he'd seen her fall from the horse earlier today.

It had been embedded in all of those things and he hadn't realized exactly what it meant he wanted until the right moment. And then suddenly it was like her shock transformed into something else entirely.

She arched toward him, her breasts pressing against his chest, her hands coming up to his face. She thrust her chin upward, making the kiss harder, deeper. He drove his tongue deep, sliding it against hers, and she made a small sound like a whimpering kitten. The smallest sound he'd ever heard Jamie Dodge make.

He pulled away from her, nipped her lower lip and then pressed his mouth to hers one more time before releasing his hold.

She looked dazed. He felt about how she looked.

"I thought about it," he said. "And I realized I couldn't let this one go. I let you criticize my riding, question my authority, but I wasn't about to let you get away with cock-blocking me, telling me you're jealous and then telling me you don't know if you want me. So I figured maybe I'd give you something to think about."

Don't miss
Cowboy to the Core *by Maisey Yates,*
available July 2019 wherever
Harlequin® books and ebooks are sold.

www.Harlequin.com

PHMYEXP0719